One Night, Two Lives

Also by Ann Victoria Roberts

Louisa Elliott
Liam's Story
Dagger Lane
Moon Rising
The Master's Tale

ONE NIGHT,

CAN THE PAST BE FORGIVEN?

TWO LIVES

Ann Victoria Roberts

Matador
9 Priory Business Park,
Wistow Road, Kibworth Beauchamp,
Leicestershire. LE8 0RX
Tel: 0116 279 2299
Email: books@troubador.co.uk
Web: www.troubador.co.uk/matador
Twitter: @matadorbooks

ISBN 978 1838590 123

British Library Cataloguing in Publication Data.
A catalogue record for this book is available from the British Library.

Typeset in 11pt Sabon BT by Troubador Publishing Ltd, Leicester, UK

Matador is an imprint of Troubador Publishing Ltd

To the women who provided the inspiration.

Author's Note

The subject of unplanned motherhood and its effects is one I explored in my first novel, set in 1890s York. *Louisa Elliott* was inspired by an intriguing family history, in which two generations of independent and remarkable women became mothers without the protection of marriage.

In recent times, the TV series, *Long Lost Family* – in which people separated by adoption try to make contact with their birth families – set me thinking about modern times. After watching a couple of episodes, I wanted to know more. What was it like for single mothers, pre-Women's Lib, who were coerced into giving up their children?

Nowadays, it seems incredible that the subject of sex without marriage was once talked about in whispers, and to be pregnant and unmarried was regarded as shameful. But in Great Britain, before 1967, single women did not have access to the contraceptive pill, and abortion was illegal. Thanks to pressure from women's groups, the law was changed, both became available, and society's attitudes gradually began to soften.

Another change in the law occurred in 2005, allowing birth mothers to search for their adopted children. In *One Night, Two Lives*, these proposed changes prompt James Fielding to contact his former girlfriend, Suzie Wallis.

Suzie and James, like all the characters in this book, are entirely fictional, although what happened to them was harsh reality for untold thousands of people. I was assisted in my research by stories from friends, but most particularly by accounts recorded by Rose Bell for her MA in Public History in 2013, and published online.

http://www.motherandbabyhomes.com/

While writing this book, various sexual abuse scandals have come to light, but one story, published by Scribe in 2017, was significant. *South of Forgiveness*, by Thordis Elva and Tom Stranger, is a real-life confession by both parties, concerning rape and its aftermath. Their story reinforced my belief that no man escapes his actions entirely.

2004

One

At a turn in the road, they crested the rise. Below, in all its Victorian vanity, the town of Iredale was there before them, hugging the valley to either side.

Approaching the venue, one of several hotels overlooking the town, Suzie felt a stab of apprehension. Even at midday, it looked like an advert for Hammer House of Horror. Somehow familiar as they drove up the hill, but how could it not be? She must have seen it dozens of times. But then they were turning again, into a drive flanked by formal gardens, following the signs for the car park.

As her friend locked the car, for a second the two women gazed at each other before breaking into nervous giggles. Suddenly, it was like being kids again, about to embark on a new adventure.

'You look lovely,' Cathy said, giving her a hug. 'Get in there and knock 'em dead!'

Doors open, a mass of people in the foyer, and thankfully no creepy manservant in sight. Instead, a sharp-suited lad – looked about twelve – took Suzie's name and directed them towards a stand where her books were on display. The poster, with its golden Spanish landscape – *To the Ends of the Earth, by Suzie Wallis* – looked good. Until she spotted the addition, bottom left. Oh no, not *that* photo: Judy Dench crop, a tan that showed every wrinkle, and an inadvisable grin. Taken by those lovely people she'd met at – where was it? Some sun-kissed village along the Camino. By then she'd quite forgotten that missing eye-tooth, the crown lost to a crusty bread-roll on Day 3 of her walk. Could have been worse, though – could have been centre front.

Daughters Jo and Sara had laughed, of course, while the publishers beamed and said it was real, a perfect illustration of what one had to endure whilst away from civilisation.

Losing a crown? It was nothing compared to what she had endured during those weeks on the road.

The publisher's rep greeted her, and that nice girl from Waterstones, both of them keen to remind Suzie of the other photo on the back cover – the one with groomed hair, make-up, and every tooth in situ.

A few minutes later they were moving on, along to the 'green room', where the other authors were gathering for Iredale's annual Literary Lunch. One was a well-known novelist with half a dozen books to her credit; another, an aging guitarist, solitary survivor of a punk-rock group from the 1970s. Making a beeline for the two older women, he introduced himself as Mick, and – in contrast to his gaunt features and spiked black hair – turned out to be surprisingly kind and witty. Laughing with Cathy, Suzie forgot her nerves. The novelist, she thought, looked like a teacher viewing an unruly class.

They were waiting for a biographer from Oxford. She arrived at last, with her famous actor husband, full of apology for having been held up on the motorway. Suzie wondered aloud how she fitted in, and why they'd each been chosen.

The guitarist leaned towards her. 'Well, lass, we're all from God's Own Country.' But as the other two women gravitated towards each other, he gave Suzie a wry grin. 'Not that you'd know it…'

Escorted along a carpeted corridor, Suzie caught her breath as they reached a vast room packed with tables. By her side, Cathy gasped as a wave of applause greeted them. They mounted the steps to take their places at a long table on the stage.

She'd imagined she wouldn't eat a thing, but with the chief organizer to her left, and the guitarist and Cathy to her right, conversation distracted her from nerves. It wasn't until the novelist stood up to speak that Suzie began to look around. And that was when her mind focused on the place itself. In the last few weeks, so much had been happening – trips to London to the publishers, followed by local TV and newspaper interviews – she hadn't had chance to think about today. Other than preparing a speech, of course.

The hotel's name, for instance, and its oddly familiar aspect. The last time she'd frequented this part of Iredale was during her student days, over forty years ago. Then, she and her art-school friends had longed for cutting-edge design or even something genuinely decrepit to inspire them. To their eyes, the Victorian spa town, with its mock-Gothic hotels and manicured gardens, was simply too boring for words, never mind for what passed as art.

Applause and another introduction, another speech. Half-listening, Suzie studied the room, trying to imagine it at night, without the chairs and tables. Could this be the hotel where they held the Arts Ball that year – and this the ballroom where the jazz band was playing?

More applause. *Oh, ye gods, it was her turn to speak.*

Swallowing hard, Suzie grabbed her notes, found a smile and rose to her feet. She got through it, although a mention of why she'd started walking – in the wake of her husband Freddie's death – sounded alarmingly wobbly to her own ears. Even her tale of walking the pilgrim route to Santiago – with mountain climbs, mud-slides, crowded hostels and terrifying farmyard dogs – seemed but a pale reflection of reality. Speaking of kindness – and there was much kindness and humour along the road – she gathered confidence at last. Even made the audience laugh, describing Santiago's golden angels as something out of Hollywood: supersized Marilyn Monroe lookalikes without the boobs.

She closed by saying the most gratifying part of the walk was reaching the *Ends of the Earth* – Cape Finisterre – where, like a medieval pilgrim, she'd cast off her clothes and plunged naked into the Atlantic's rolling breakers. An ending which prompted hearty applause, not least from the ex-rocker.

'That was cool,' he said, which made her laugh.

'Certainly was!'

Weak with relief, Suzie relaxed to listen to the star of the show. At first she thought he was going to be terrible, shuffling his notes and clearing his throat. But it was part of the act. Playing up the ex-druggie image, he told his tale in disjointed but hilarious fashion, referring to her reminiscences of the Pilgrim Way to highlight his own stumbling efforts along the punk-rock road to hell.

'Well, I'm delighted you found your way back,' she confided later as they left the stage.

'You too, Suzie.'

'Oh, it was easy – I just had to find an airport. I think your road must have been pretty tough.'

Mick gave his death's-head grin and kissed her cheek. 'Like you, Suzie, I just kept looking ahead…'

Cathy, petite and pretty, was gazing in something like awe, so he kissed her cheek too. 'Gotta love and leave ya, ladies – fans waiting!'

And off he went along the corridor.

Following, Suzie paused by a grand staircase, caught by a sinking feeling, a physical reaction more powerful than logic. Yes, it was here. Here we gathered, laughing and talking...

She remembered feeling a failure, not wanting to go to that end-of-year celebration, and Liz saying, *Oh, let's – my Dad will pick us up afterwards – it'll be a laugh...* And then worrying about Liz not fitting in with her art-school friends. As it turned out, with her striking looks and clothes, Liz was welcomed by the crowd from Dress Design. In fact, they were all getting on so well, she was the one feeling out of it.

'Goodness,' Cathy said, grabbing her arm, dragging her back to the present, 'have you seen them, chasing after Mick? And they look so *respectable!*'

Suzie found a smile. 'Ah well, better fight our way through...'

They reached the foyer with its tables and posters and piles of books, already bustling with people.

'I don't know who's got the most fans,' Cathy said, 'himself or that novelist woman.'

'Betty Biographer's not doing so bad, either.'

'Oh, it's the husband *they* want to meet! Mind you, he is a bit tasty...'

With a wry grin, Suzie cast her eye over the half-dozen waiting for her. 'Ah well, every book's a plus.' Clutching her favourite pen, she made her way through, trying not to wince at the poster. Cathy, still viewing the guests coming in from the ballroom, joined her.

'I don't know who that was, Suzie, but he's been looking hard at you.'

'Where?'

Cathy stood on tip-toe, trying to find him again. 'Tall, white hair... Oh, damn, I can't see him now.'

Some time and more than a dozen books later, Suzie was bidding farewell to her latest fan, an elderly lady in a wheelchair. 'I still love to travel,' she said with a wistful smile, 'even if it's only in my mind...'

As the lady and her carer moved away, a sudden well of gratitude brought a lump to Suzie's throat. Thinking they were the last ones, she stood up and turned to Cathy. But Cathy was gazing bright-eyed at someone else. A tall man in a grey suit, making his way towards them.

Thick white hair, and a gaze behind the glasses that caused her heart to falter. For a moment she couldn't move, couldn't breathe, couldn't *believe*...

He placed his book on the desk. She looked at it as though she'd never seen it before. Some detached corner of her mind noticed his hands were trembling.

'Hello, Suzie.'

She blinked and swallowed hard. 'James?' It was barely a whisper.

'I'm sorry to startle you like this – not really the time or place, I know... But I just want to say how much I enjoyed your book – and your speech. I found it very moving...' Clearing his throat, handing her his card, he said, 'I'm staying here until tomorrow. I wonder if you'd give me a call, later?'

He paused, clearly waiting for a reply. 'I really do need to speak to you.'

Stiff as marble, she watched him move away. She felt Cathy's hand on her arm, heard concern in her voice, and blinked hard. 'I'm fine. Can't explain. Must say goodbye.'

Forcing thanks and a smile for the organizers, Suzie thought her face would crack. Somehow, she made it to the door. Outside, the gardens were bright with spring flowers, but it might have been midwinter. By the time they reached the car, she was shaking.

Fumbling with the seat-belt, that scene, his voice, replayed itself over and over.

'My God, Cathy,' she got out at last, I'd just been *thinking* about him. Back there, by the stairs, it all came back. That's where I first saw him, first spoke to him…' Gabbling, repeating herself, it seemed she couldn't stop. 'I can't get over him appearing like that – just there, that place, after all these years!'

'What? Look, love, you've had a shock. Let's go back in and get you a cup of tea…'

'No, no – start the car – let's get away from here.'

'Café, pub or home?'

'Home.'

'Okay.'

Not until they cleared the outskirts of town did Suzie speak. 'It's changed so much, I didn't recognize it at first…' But she could see the hotel how it was, a run-down, white elephant of a place, so desperate for business they'd even agreed to hold an art-school hop.

'My final year – the night of the Arts Ball. What a farce! Lord knows who thought of it – the whole thing was a disaster. Just now – where we had lunch, on the stage – a jazz band was playing. That room – all those tables – it was the ballroom. Sprung dance-floor, the lot. Not that anybody was dancing…'

Tempted by the music, she and another Dress student had tried to draw people in, but it didn't take long for the springy floor to defeat them. Helpless with laughter, they'd abandoned the idea and returned to the crowd in the foyer.

'Remember Liz?'

'The name, yes – we never met.'

'Well, we went together. I thought she wouldn't know anyone, but she did – some lads from grammar school. They'd come with the girls from Moorcliffe. Anyway, when I joined them – right there, at the foot of the stairs – Liz was chatting away, having a great time. Suddenly I was on the outside, looking in – and so was he…'

'Who? The chap who turned up just now?'

'Yes. James Bloody Fielding. And I felt sorry for him – you know, on his own, looking like a spare part…' Glancing at his card again, Suzie shook her head. 'How in hell's name did he get to be a vicar?'

'*A vicar?* He wasn't wearing a dog-collar.'

'Well, that's what it says. *Reverend James Fielding, St George's Church, Norton Parva* – wherever that is. Looks like an Oxford postcode.'

'And is he the one…?'

'Yes.' For a moment she was silent, remembering; and then, 'Did I really say I'd call him? Was I *really* sweet and polite and smiling?'

With a rueful chuckle, Cathy changed gear for a sharp corner. 'Well, more a rictus grin than a smile – but yes, you were most polite.'

'God above – how *dare* he just turn up like that? What I should have said was, *Piss off – you're forty years too late!*'

'Well, you could always phone him,' Cathy laughed. 'Although I'm not sure you should say that to a vicar.'

'Well, he wasn't a vicar when I knew him.'

They were still weighing the pros and cons of the situation as the outskirts of Heatherley came in sight. Cathy said, 'What do you want to do? Come back to my place, or would you like me to come to yours?'

In the end, they had tea at Cathy's before continuing to Suzie's with two bottles of Côtes du Rhone and a packet of cigarettes.

'But you stopped smoking years ago,' Cathy exclaimed.

'And I'll stop again, but right now nothing else will do.'

– o –

Safe in the knowledge that Cathy's husband would pick her up later, the two women settled down in Suzie's sitting room. With glasses and an ashtray between them, they resumed their discussion. As Cathy said, it was a question of what would give most satisfaction: telling this man to get lost and never bother Suzie again, or, appear reasonable and attempt to get answers to questions that had bugged her for years.

Bolstered by a couple of glasses of wine, Suzie went through to her office to call the mobile number on his card.

A few minutes later she returned, shaken to the core.

'What did he say?' Cathy asked as she slipped a wrap around her friend's shoulders.

'He's staying in Iredale. I'm meeting him tomorrow afternoon.'

'But what does he want?'

'To find our son.'

Two

Betty's, she thought, walking through sunny Iredale; why did I suggest *Betty's*? Was there anywhere more dainty and respectable than *Betty's Café*? Tea and crumpets, frilly caps and aprons, it was like something out of Agatha Christie. She certainly couldn't scream and shout in there. Not that she felt like it today. After the session with Cathy, she'd slept badly, drifting in and out of dreams so vivid they were more like nightmares. She'd even dreamed of Freddie – he was young, they were at some exhibition. The pictures were all abstracts, and she was upset, didn't understand them; and Freddie was saying – as he'd said so often in life – *Give it time, love, give it time…*

God, she wished he were here now.

Time: shrinking, expanding. It seemed incredible that so much could have happened in the summer she was eighteen. Now, June to September was nothing, weeks flew by, summer gone before spring's gardening jobs were complete. Then, it felt like forever. And as for the following year – best not think about that right now.

Anger surfaced again, mostly at his effrontery in just turning up yesterday. Did he not think that it was her moment, a rare chance to speak in public? She'd been nervous enough beforehand – a wonder she hadn't collapsed on recognizing him.

Deliberately late, Suzie spotted him by the window, looking out for her – looking nervous. Despite her deep breaths, she was shaking. Thin-lipped, trying to hold herself together, she told the waitress she was expected, and made her way to his table.

With old-fashioned courtesy, he stood and pulled out a chair for her. She wanted to snatch it from his hands.

'Thank you for agreeing to see me,' he said as she sat down.

'Did I have a choice? Ever?'

Removing his glasses, he set them carefully on the table. Deep brown eyes gazed at her. 'Suzie, I doubt you could blame me more than I've blamed myself over the years.'

His tone was soft, but a nerve in his cheek was twitching.

'Really? And is that the man of God speaking, or the James Fielding I knew forty years ago?'

'Both,' he sighed. 'You've every right to be angry – I behaved appallingly. I knew it then and I know it now.'

'That's something, I suppose.' Only slightly mollified, she reminded herself to keep a check on her temper. 'All I can say is, you're lucky I was with my oldest friend yesterday. Anyone else and I could have been in big trouble – again!'

He looked stricken under Suzie's glare. Surprised by the waitress, she drew breath and ordered tea. James simply nodded.

Suzie took the opportunity to study him. Older, yes, but so were they all. His white hair, once a rich chestnut, was less curly now, while the long, well-structured face had aged. But still, she'd known him. Despite self-righteous anger, she could feel the adrenaline beginning to subside. In that well-tailored grey suit, James Fielding looked what he was, a clergyman in mufti. Had his calling changed him? Could she believe *anything* he said?

Her mother had not disliked him. *Oh, go away, Mum, I really don't need to know that at this point in the proceedings.* But yes, the inescapable truth was that after spending an hour in James's company, Connie Wallis – shrewd assessor of her daughter's friends – had judged him a decent lad. She'd even tried to give him some advice. But he'd rejected it.

'Did you ever tell your parents?'

He winced. 'No. Too much the coward, I'm afraid. Or should I say, too cowardly ever to tell my father. Only plucked up courage to tell him I was going into the Church, shortly before he died.'

'And your mother?'

'Eventually, yes – the year I got married. She said it explained a lot, God bless her. I was thirty-six,' he added. 'Took me a long time to grow up.'

With a tight smile, Suzie agreed. 'Unlike me. I had to grow up pretty damn quick.' After a moment, she added, 'They were away, weren't they?'

'Yes, they were. Came back from Germany just as I was starting my second year at Durham. I must say, not living at home made things easier. Lying, particularly.'

Suzie nodded. She knew all about lying. 'But surely you told *someone* what was going on?'

'My tutor. Had to, my work was suffering.'

'Oh – your *work* was suffering? What about my life,' she snapped, 'didn't you think of that?'

Briefly, he looked away, his mouth working. 'It was precisely that. Thinking of you, Suzie, what was happening to you – made it hard to focus on anything else...'

He paused as the waitress arrived. Tea pot, hot water, milk, sugar and cups were set neatly on the table.

'I was referred to the Chaplain – counselling, we'd call it nowadays. As you can imagine, he'd come across the situation before – from both sides. It helped to talk about it. Didn't cure the guilt, I'm afraid, but it stopped me from messing things up completely.'

Taking a moment to digest that, Suzie nudged the milk jug in his direction. 'Well, bully for you.'

Compressing his lips, James looked away. 'It wasn't easy,' he said at last.

Leaning across the table, in a furious whisper she said, 'Probably not, but it was a damn sight worse for me! You could have offered to marry me, James – then we could have brought up our child together!'

– o –

James knew she'd been planning to go on to a London college, but it hadn't happened. He wondered what she'd done afterwards, which paths she'd followed to become the Suzie Wallis she was today. This woman with the short, fashionably streaked hair, looked well-tailored and professional. Only her eyes were unchanged, green with flecks of gold that shone whenever she was happy or excited. Now they were glinting with suppressed fury.

Her expression might have silenced him, but he'd read her book, knew there was more to this woman than a smart outfit and justifiable anger. Nor was it purely anger; he sensed other emotions bubbling beneath. Clearly, after one cup of tea and barely half an hour of *Betty's* genteel atmosphere, she was as keen to escape as he was.

Glancing sideways as they left the café, he tried to match this older woman with the free-spirited girl he'd once known. Skinny as a racehorse, all eyes and legs and long brown hair, she'd worn eye-catching clothes she made for herself. *But that's what we do*, she'd said at the time. *From design to finished article – two days a week in the Dress Department. The other days we mostly draw and paint, and mess about with clay...*

She'd seemed so confident, even then.

With her barbed comments still at the forefront of his mind, he said, 'But you know, Suzie, it's all very well to say I should have done the decent thing all those years ago. I remember, when I said I couldn't marry you, you said, *I wouldn't have you if you came free with a packet of tea!*'

'Oh, yes,' she gave a tight smile. 'So I did. I'm glad it stuck in your mind.'

'It stuck all right. Cramped my style for years,' he admitted with forced lightness. *That and something else she'd said...*

'Really?'

'Yes.' They walked on, down the hill and into a park by the river.

'But you succumbed to marriage eventually?'

'Eventually.' A picture of Maggie came into his mind, her eyes and smile. Tall, fair and statuesque, she was nothing like Suzie in looks; although perhaps he'd been attracted by a similar sense of fun. Not that fun was in evidence today.

As a teenager, Suzie had seemed a bit wild, a bit scary; but then, just a year out of an all-male public school, most girls terrified him. His parents imagined staying with relatives would do him good. Working on one of his uncle's building sites for the summer, earning some money, getting out and about with his cousin's friends. Yes, he could see the logic, but they didn't know cousin Alex the way James did.

The sun was warm, the gardens dotted with spring flowers. As his companion headed for a seat under the lilacs, he joined her, keeping a foot or so between them. She fumbled in her bag and moments later was trying to light a cigarette.

'Here, let me...' He flicked the lighter and cupped the flame, resisting the urge to comment as she puffed away.

'Haven't done this in years,' she said; adding, with a touch of defiance, 'but last night, Cathy and me smoked a whole packet between us.'

'That bad?'

She nodded. 'Be thankful. I got a whole load of grief out of my system.' Holding up the cigarette, she said, 'Of course, I'll have to hide it from the girls – they'd kill me if they saw me smoking again.'

'Tell me about them.'

'Have you got kids?'

He'd been expecting that, but still it was painful. 'No – no children. We would have liked them, but…'

She turned to him then, green eyes wide in mock surprise. 'Oh, I see,' she said, her voice heavy with sarcasm. 'So *that's* what this is all about. I did wonder.'

Furious with her – her ability to cut deep with a look or a phrase – James glanced away. Breathing deeply, he told himself she had every right to be angry, every right to strike back in whatever way she chose. It was her first opportunity – and what's more, he'd invited it.

But how do I explain? He thought of his life with Maggie, full of music and laughter to begin with, and so much sadness towards the end.

'When Margaret and I married, we were both in our thirties,' he said, 'which was perhaps not the ideal age. I was at theological college, and she was teaching – we were both looking forward to starting a family…'

'But it didn't happen?'

He shook his head. 'I'd told her about you – how we met, what happened – before we married. Later, I wished I hadn't. She blamed herself, you see.' Remembering the tests, the dashed hopes, the misery, he shook his head. With an effort he straightened and stood up. 'Shall we walk? I don't know about you, but I could stand a drink.'

They walked back to a bar Suzie remembered from her student days. She said it had changed, although after the sun's glare it was cool and dark inside and somehow comforting. James ordered whisky, Suzie shook her head.

'I'll pretend – tonic with ice and lemon, no gin.'

Drinks in hand, they chose a booth where they could talk without being overheard.

Her tone still brittle, she said, 'Did you never think of adopting?'

Reverting to his pet name for her, James said, 'Maggie refused. If she couldn't have my children, she said, she'd prefer to carry on teaching. After that, it was never discussed. Until – well, not until she became ill. Cancer,' he explained, 'and pretty far advanced by the time it was diagnosed. It's almost two years since she passed away.'

'I'm sorry,' she said. 'As you'll have gathered, Freddie's end was rather more sudden – a car crash.'

She'd said something about that in her speech; from her book, he understood it had been traumatic. 'It must have been a terrible shock. I admire you tremendously for the way you dealt with it.'

'Thanks, but it's five years now,' she said with a shrug. 'Lots of water under the bridge since then.'

Contemplating death, they both fell silent. At last he said, 'I wouldn't have thought of any of this – contacting you, bringing up the past – except Maggie wanted me to find my son before it was too late.'

Sensing her tension, he ploughed on regardless. 'I didn't think it would be possible – I had nothing to go on, bar your name. You could have been anywhere in the world – and if you'd married, how would I find you?'

'Exactly.'

'But the book – your maiden name – leapt out at me one morning from the Yorkshire Post. Pure chance, really –

someone had left it behind. Anyway, as I said before, I could have written, but – well, I wanted to be sure.'

He didn't say that after months of struggling with his promise, that moment had seemed like fate; a sign he was meant to follow. The name, the photo, it had to be her. He'd ordered the book, and somehow, as he started reading, it was as though Suzie Wallis was speaking directly to him. He'd been stirred by the account of her journey; not simply the one from grief and anger to acceptance, but her observations of life along the road, the humour as well as the deprivations; the people, the places, the beauty and the pain.

Above all, the purity of the pilgrimage. He envied her the experience of the Camino; it was something he'd thought about after Margaret's passing, but the time required was impossible then.

Suzie claimed not to be religious; or rather, not to have chosen the journey for religious reasons. And yet, whether she realized it or not, something akin to spirituality ran through every page, especially towards the end. He was drawn to that aspect of her psyche, one he had not been aware of forty years ago; but then, forty years ago, what had he known about her? Not much. Strangely, after reading her book he felt he knew her intimately; but yesterday, seeing her, hearing her speak, he was unsure. She was different; not quite the woman of the book, and certainly not the girl he'd known forty years ago.

'Did you remember the hotel?' she asked.

Thrown by a question at odds with his thoughts, for a moment James struggled to reply. 'Not at first,' he admitted. 'Not until I saw you standing by the stairs, looking a bit lost – that was when I knew, when I recognized the place...' He shook his head, not really sure whether he'd imagined that odd sensation – as though he'd stepped back in time.

– o –

He'd come along at the invitation of his cousin Alex's art-student friends, Babs and Avril; and after spending half the evening in a pub, then the hotel bar, they'd wandered along to listen to the band. Not that jazz was his thing, but through the open doorway he'd seen Suzie and another girl trying to dance in the empty ballroom. Their antics made him smile, but as they approached he turned away, not wanting to be caught staring.

To his surprise, the girls joined the group he was with. Alex, typically, was at the heart of it, but he'd sighted a challenge. This time, the girl in the red dress – Suzie's best friend, as it turned out. She was exactly his cousin's type – striking, quick-witted, fielding the chat-up lines with ease. She'd have rendered James speechless in seconds.

He kept glancing at the pretty girl who'd been laughing on the dance-floor. Looking sad now, and clinging to the newel post as though to a lifeline. She seemed as out of things as he was.

He caught her eye, she gave a rueful smile and, to his surprise, came to join him. It was as though she'd read his mind and felt the need to commiserate. Suddenly, he was no longer feeling awkward – *extra to requirements*, as his father would have said – they were talking about his subject, history, and she was admiring, enthusiastic, even confessing she'd once wanted to be an archaeologist. He could barely believe it: most people thought history dull. He'd also discovered that she'd failed the end-of-course exams, would not now be going on to art college in London; at least not until she'd done this second year again, and managed to succeed at painting.

'But I thought you and – Avril, is it? – were on the same dressmaking course?'

'Dress *Design*,' she'd corrected. 'Yes, but we have to pass the other subjects too. Fail one, fail the lot. Got to do it all again.'

He'd sympathized, she cheered up, and just as the evening was turning out to be the best he could remember, Suzie's friend was pointing to her watch and saying they had to go.

Hard to say who was the more disappointed, himself or Alex.

– o –

'So, you thought it was a perfect opportunity,' Suzie said, 'spotting my name on a book.'

'Well...' he began, but she wasn't interested in reasons, only the effect. The shock he'd given her, in such a public place, when she should have been enjoying the occasion.

'Yes, I'm sorry, I...'

'You can forget it, James, it's out of the question. Forty years ago, I gave up my son – do you think that was easy?' Heartbroken at the time, waves of anger choked her now. 'Two months later, I signed the final adoption papers.

'They said I could change my mind,' she went on in a furious whisper. 'But those people who took him – whoever they were – had been caring for my son, thinking of him as theirs, for all that time. They'd had him longer than me. I couldn't just *change my bloody mind!*'

'Of course not.'

'It wasn't right – how could I take him back? I couldn't – I just *couldn't*.' Angry with him, angry with the tears, Suzie found a fresh tissue and wiped her nose. 'So I signed. I had to swear on oath not to go looking for him – not to attempt to make contact in any way. I swore it before some legal person, with my hand on the *Holy Bible*. You, of all people, should understand that?'

'Yes – yes, of course.'

'So don't ask me to break my oath now.' She leaned across the table. 'If *my* son wants to find me, he can – and I continue to hope that one day, he will. Until then – sorry, no.'

With grim acknowledgement, James nodded and stood up. Watching him go in the direction of the gents, she took the respite to light a cigarette and pull herself together.

He returned via the bar, setting fresh drinks on the table. His hands – with a wedding ring on his third finger – were trembling.

'Look,' he said tersely, 'I know this is distressing for you. I'm sorry – believe me, I am truly sorry to have upset you like this. I should have written first, I see that now.'

Before she could reply, he said, 'I understand where you're coming from regarding that oath, but things have changed – are changing. You may not be aware of this, but a law is going through Parliament at the moment, making it legal for birth parents to look for their adopted children...'

'So I've heard.'

'The point is,' he went on, pleading now, 'if you give me the information, *I* may be able to trace him. I signed no oath, and you needn't break yours.'

Stunned for a moment, she didn't reply, but as though he could sense a flutter of hope, he held her gaze.

'Hard for you, I know – and you'll need time to think things over. You've got my address and phone number – won't you give me yours, so we can keep in touch?'

In spite of what she'd just said, Suzie knew it wasn't over. It would never be over; and now the wall had been breached, she could feel the past surging in like a tidal wave. Too much, too soon. Now, she needed to get home.

He offered to walk with her back to the car. Curtly, she refused. But as she rose and picked up her bag, suddenly, the important question was on her lips.

'Tell me something. Why did you just dump me, afterwards?'

He looked confused. 'Dump you? When? What did I say?'

'*Nothing!*' she hissed. 'That's the point – you couldn't even apologize!'

Three

At some point on the way home to the little village of Felton, Suzie's anger dissipated, fading away to a familiar kind of sadness, one not felt for a long time. Pulling into the drive, she slowed and braked to look at the house. In the westering sun its weathered stones looked warm and welcoming, and gradually, she came to herself. Fumbling with keys, she made her way to the kitchen door, and went inside. Dropping her bag, she filled the kettle and turned her gaze to the family photos on the dresser.

Parents, daughters, grandchildren, all smiling at her as she tried to picture the one who was missing. When her girls were young, such sad, wondering moments would catch her without warning; especially at holiday times and birthdays or preparing for Christmas. She'd wonder how it was for her little boy, the absent child, living a different life in a different family. As he grew older, such thoughts became less; past eighteen, she guessed he'd be more in control of his own destiny; she hoped – always hoped – that life was being kind to him, throwing no more than governable challenges his way. On his thirtieth birthday, she wondered if there was someone special in his life; did he have a wife, and children of his own?

Now, in his fortieth year, she'd begun to think that soon, perhaps, he would begin to look back at what he'd achieved, rather than focusing on the future. Like most people in their middle years, she imagined he'd need to assess his life and progress, see what decisions were still to be made. She wondered if he ever thought of her, his birth mother; if he was as curious about her as she was about him. She hoped and prayed that there was love in his life; most of all she prayed that he hadn't felt rejected.

Catching her mother's gaze, she sighed. 'Oh, Mum,' she said wearily, 'you've no idea…'

But as Freddie smiled from another photo, for a moment he seemed so close she could almost hear his voice: *Take it easy, sweetheart, don't be so hard on yourself…*

Tears sprang to her eyes. Despite the heartaches, she missed him, his pragmatism and common sense.

Dad had approved of him. 'One of us,' he'd said when they married. 'Lad knows what's important – he'll see you right.'

Whether he'd have said that if he'd known about Freddie's later infidelities was unlikely. He certainly wouldn't have said it about any of the other arty-farty types, as he called them. The thing was, Dad had worked with Freddie's father for years. *Working class, came up the hard way, knows what's what –* and all the other truisms Dad was fond of repeating when he'd been down to the local and had a few.

In a way, he was right. They shared common ground, and ultimately that was what drew them together. When they met, however, she was just sixteen while Freddie was a stranger and three years older. Even so he came to the house to introduce himself, and that first day accompanied her to college in Iredale. How they'd laughed about it years later – it was almost Victorian, they said, being introduced by their papas. The fact that they were a couple of art students made it even funnier; but as Freddie remarked, it proved how much Joe Wallis cared about his daughter.

Suzie remembered her first impression of Freddie: blue eyes, bright with good humour, a ready smile and a thatch of dark hair that proved untameable throughout his life. A kind face, not handsome, but in paint-stained jeans and faded sweater he was tall and well-shaped. He looked capable, like a workman, which was how he often described himself.

– o –

They'd chatted easily enough on the bus journey to Iredale. He'd given her the run-down on who was who amongst the staff, who was likely to be her tutor, and what to expect in the first few weeks. She'd warmed to him at once. What she hadn't realized was that Freddie was a bit of a star in college; walking in with him that first day, had raised more than a few eyebrows.

'Do you know *Freddie?*' was uttered in awed tones. It surprised Suzie, intensified her awareness. Yes, she could say she knew him, and yes, he would often stop for a word in passing, but that was more or less it. She'd had a crush on him, but to him she was just a kid out of school; and besides, he lodged in Iredale during term-time, so that first journey was never repeated. A few years later, however, they'd met by chance in London, and by then she was no longer a kid.

She was just thinking how different he was from James Fielding, when the phone rang. Her younger daughter's voice, sounding crackly over the miles from Majorca, rattled off several questions before Suzie could answer.

'Sara, love, I was about to phone you – only just got in… Yes, it was great… My mobile? Oh, I'd switched it off for the talk… I would have called you,' she said as Sara paused for breath, 'but I met – an old friend – which kind of took my mind off things... No, it's long story – I'll tell you when you get back. Anyway,' she rushed on, 'Cathy came home with me, and we had a few drinks...'

Thank God she'd been with Cathy, was the thought flitting through Suzie's mind. If either of her daughters had been able to make it to the lunch, she dreaded to think what might have happened.

Changing the subject, Suzie asked about the holiday, said they must catch up when Sara got back. Later, checking her messages, she listened to one from her elder daughter. Jo, the TV researcher, was chasing a story in Paris, but would be back to go sailing with Marianne at the weekend. Wishing her mother all the best, and break a leg, Jo signed off with her usual throaty chuckle.

Sighing, Suzie felt a wave of relief. At least she wouldn't have to explain things to Jo right now. But what to do? What to say and when? Ideally, she would have liked to get the girls together, to do the explaining just once, to both of them. Whatever happened after that – and this was a rolling story, to use Jo's phrase – they could confer to their hearts' content. Then neither of them would feel left out. But with Sara's crammed everyday life, managing both business and family in York, and Jo in London with demanding job and self-centred girlfriend, that looked well-nigh impossible for the moment. Suzie could see herself having to time things so she could tell each of them within at least a day or two.

– o –

'How did it happen?' her daughters had asked when she first told them. Jo was about to go to university, and Sarah was just starting her A Levels. Suzie had thought it advisable to share a morality tale before history had chance to repeat itself.

'In short, I went to party, got drunk, and was pounced on.' To her relief, the girls hadn't asked for details. *Sex & parents? All too much.*

It wasn't simply a morality tale. Her deepest fear was that one day, one of them might meet a young male, all unknowing, and fall in love – and that young male might turn out to be their half-brother. She thought it best not to put that particular thought into their minds, although she'd become quite good at subtle questioning where boyfriends were concerned.

Not that Jo had many boyfriends. Friends, yes, but not of the romantic variety. And as for Sara, well, despite the cautionary tale, she had gone off the rails for a while at college. Not quite the same circumstances, but close enough. Pregnant and distraught, the poor girl had come home and confessed all. She'd been a fool, he no longer wanted to know her, and suddenly, her work was more important than anything else…

It was so depressingly familiar, Suzie had first wept, then raged, then wept again. Freddie, laid-back Freddie who rarely let anything get to him, was all for beating the living daylights out of this prat. And then they both calmed down and set about the practicalities.

In effect, it was much as Suzie's parents had done in the 1960s. Connie had said something similar, but she was looking back to wartime, the mid 1940s, when she'd fallen for Suzie's father. He'd married her – she said – because she was pregnant. A sad comment on the state of their marriage, although they had been going through a rough patch at the time.

'Don't make the mistake I made,' she'd begged when Suzie had finally confessed. 'You don't have to marry him – you can have the baby adopted…'

'Don't worry,' Suzie had said to her daughter, years later, 'you don't have to have the baby – you can have a termination…'

Simple answers to a timeless problem. Answers that took no account of the aftermath: neither the surface pain, nor the deep psychological wounds.

Meanwhile, other couples – like James and his wife – were longing to have children, nowadays going through all kinds of tests and treatments to produce what nature denied them.

Looking back to the '60s, with IVF still in the future, adoption was the only answer. Meanwhile, girls like Suzie were quietly and shamefully providing the babies these people longed for.

Shame, that was what it was all about. Shame at having been caught out, shown up before all the other clean-living, law-abiding citizens of a Christian country. A country where sex was acceptable only within marriage. Where to be unmarried and pregnant was to be labelled a tart. Or was that just in the provinces? Where Victorian values clung on, where sex was still unmentionable, and middle-class women did not work after marriage. Where even working-class mothers stayed home for a few years and brought up their own children. Legitimate ones, of course.

'It's history,' Cathy had said last night when they were talking it over. 'We've got to accept it, Suze – we're part of history...'

Yes, Suzie thought, they were part of history; and she and Cathy had a history all their own. They went back to the middle of the last century, to a street of wartime bungalows known as prefabs, on the wrong side of Denshaw. It was impossible to say whether they'd become friends because of their parents, or the parents had become friends because of their little girls. Whichever way, it had lasted. They'd played together amongst a crowd of other kids along the street, but Cathy, with her sense of fun and bright, enquiring mind, had always been a special friend. If her irrepressible curiosity often got them into trouble, Suzie was a ready accomplice. A pair of mischief-makers, was how one teacher described them, but what she'd loved about Cathy – then as now – was that what you saw was what you got. There was nothing underhand about her; whatever she had to say would be straight to your face, never behind your back. And she was loyal.

When the prefabs were demolished, they moved to new houses up the hill and just a hundred yards apart. For a couple of years all was as it had been, except they had different areas to explore, different games to play. It was a hard day when Cathy's parents bought their own house in a village a few miles distant. Not insurmountable, but after that, going on to different senior schools, for several years the girls kept up only sporadically, and mainly through their mothers.

At Heatherley Grammar, Suzie became one of a group which banded together at break and lunchtimes; but she and Liz had become special friends when it transpired they both fancied the same boy. The fact that he showed no signs of fancying either of them in return drew them together in wistfulness, and finally made them laugh.

Suzie went on to art school and Liz did a secretarial course in Leeds, while Cathy left home to begin her training as a nurse. They were the practical ones. Suzie, the starry-eyed innocent, was gazing ahead to where dress design and *haute couture* were shimmering like pretty bubbles.

Not that she'd planned to do that. No, her original aims were far more down-to-earth. On leaving school she'd wanted to be a window-dresser in a big store. The idea of creating an impression of a room within a window, with furniture, artwork and ornaments – and mannequins in the latest fashions to people it – was an exciting prospect. When she consulted the art master at grammar school, he hadn't sneered, but pointed her in the direction of an arts foundation course. He was delighted for her when she was accepted.

– o –

The first day had started so well, Suzie was ready to embrace everything and everyone with open arms. Some twenty new students were gathered in the main hall, bags, folders and drawing boards piled around them. She smiled at everyone who met her eye, noting different ages and styles of dress, from one girl in gypsy scarves and beads, to a lad wearing a formal shirt with drainpipe pants and winkle-picker shoes. Most, she was pleased to note, were clad in jeans and sweaters not unlike her own.

Anticipation tingled, but when their new tutor walked in, Suzie was so astonished she gasped. 'He taught at my old school,' she whispered to the girl beside her. Not recently, and only for a year, but he was unforgettable. One of her friends had fancied him to bits. Suzie hadn't, even though he was relatively young and good-looking, No, she remembered Mr Winter for different reasons. During his reign, her art marks had plummeted.

With his introduction, he managed to startle them all.

'Call me Rod,' he said boldly, 'I don't want to hear *Sir*, from any of you...' Having thus gained their attention, he asked his new students what they saw themselves doing in life. Most answered vaguely, or said they didn't know – answers to earn disapproval at Suzie's old school. At Heatherley Grammar, pupils were encouraged to be positive. When his gaze fell on Suzie, she said clearly, 'I'd like to be a window-dresser.'

There was a long moment of silence. 'I'm afraid,' he replied loftily, 'we don't run *window-dressing* classes here, young lady. I suggest you think again...'

Feeling silly, wishing she'd shoved *positive* into a corner, Suzie tried to melt into the background. Clearly, he did not recall her face or name, so to hear him say, sardonically, that his new students no doubt thought themselves, *good at art*, because they'd all been *top of the class at school*, she wanted to say, 'Actually, no – because when you were teaching, I was *bottom!*'

Cheek like that would have earned a school detention, so she kept quiet. Besides, she'd been quashed once and had no desire to be flattened again. Rod Winter may have looked like Jesus from a Victorian illustration – even down to the sandals – but that was where the resemblance ended. With all the subtlety of a sledge-hammer, his aim – apparently – was to guide his students towards a suitable craft.

With an image of mannequins still in her mind, plus the practical advantages of learning to sew, Suzie opted for Dress Design, which no doubt marked her as frivolous in Rod Winter's book. She didn't care. Dress, she discovered, was not only a practical craft, it was fun. With one boy and half a dozen other girls, two days a week she studied in a different building under a female tutor who was as kind as she was talented.

The atmosphere was light; they gossiped and giggled while poring over *Vogue* and *Harper's Bazaar*, commenting on style, trends and colours; they adapted Paris fashions to their own designs, and they learned about fabrics. From block patterns cut to their own measurements, tutor Elaine explained how to adapt them to different styles; and from set-in sleeves to invisible hems, showed them how to sew. Suzie still recalled the thrill of the first dress she'd made, and the Chanel-style suit she could never bear to throw away.

Fashion drawing, she discovered, was all about suggestion. With tons of practice, a light pencil line could describe elegance from the top of the head to the tip of the toe; conversely, in the Life Class, Rod Winter was encouraging them to be bold; extolling the virtues of charcoal and shadows to express their model's Rubens-like curves.

It was two years of contrasts. Clear teaching on neatness and accuracy on the one hand, and a loose kind of encouragement to 'explore' on the other. Like being a child again, Suzie often thought, messing about with paint and clay; a lot of fun, but somehow, when it came to painting, she never quite rose to the mark. Taught the basics of mixing colour and handling oil paint, like her classmates she used brushes, palette knives, and even fingers to explore the effects. As time went on she got all the stuff about perspective and balance – but she wanted the painting of a railway station to look like what it was supposed to be.

One of the part-time tutors was always encouraging. 'Yes, I can see what you're after. And this bit's great,' he'd say, focusing on one small area. 'See if you can expand on that…'

Despite his kindness, Suzie was hidebound by her own ideas. Failing in her own eyes, her work failed even more when viewed and judged by Rod Winter. The trouble was, having pored over her grandfather's art books for years, her heroes were Vermeer and the Dutch Masters. At sixteen, not even the Impressionists had made much of an impression.

'Representational,' was the word her tutor used. And that, it seemed, was a curse. *Abstract* was the buzz. But great blocks of colour, like Rothko's canvasses – and the self-indulgent splashes of Jackson Pollock – struck her as nothing more than a waste of paint.

For almost two years she suffered the dismissive comments, and not until her final term – when her tutor was giving Suzie and a couple of others a lift back from some far-flung sketching expedition – did she pluck up courage to mention his time at Heatherley Grammar. At first, he seemed not to recall; but, when pressed, admitted that, yes, he had taught there for a while, implying that he'd been doing the school a favour.

'You know it's funny, Rod,' she said lightly, 'but you didn't appreciate my work then, any more than you do now…' She even managed to laugh while saying it, as though she hadn't been devastated and no longer gave a damn. 'I was bottom of the class while you were there.'

He laughed. He actually laughed. 'Nothing personal,' he said. 'All I did was stick a pin in the names.'

'What?' From the back seat, she leaned forward. 'Stick a pin in the names? You're joking!'

'You can't tell with children's work,' he declared airily. 'None of them have the first idea – so what's the point in giving marks?'

Swerving to avoid a cyclist, he ignored her after that, directing his next comments to the boy in the front seat.

Lost for words, Suzie sank back. Hard to believe any teacher could mean that; and if he didn't, that he could be so crass as to claim it. She glanced at the girl beside her, who raised her eyebrows and shrugged.

Half to herself, Suzie said, 'So the fact that my name was Wallis, meant I was bottom of the list anyway...'

Four

Despite her crushing failure at the end of year two, Suzie had been determined to carry on and prove her tutor wrong. She signed up for another year at Iredale, and, as soon as the summer term was over, started waitressing during the holidays

In many ways the big store café in Leeds was not unlike *Betty's*, with morning coffees, light lunches and afternoon teas; white china, silver cutlery, and magpie waitresses with frilly caps. Needing a black dress – she'd never worn black in her life – Suzie bought a remnant on Leeds Market and ran one up on her sewing machine. The slim line made her look skinnier than ever, but at least the shirt-waist style with turn-back cuffs was classy. Connie admired it, said she could wear it anywhere – minus the apron, of course.

The store was distinctly up-market, the clientele in similar bracket, mostly ladies of a certain age. Occasionally, Liz dropped in during her lunch-hour, as did some of the store assistants. To Suzie's astonishment, a couple of Saturdays after the end-of-year hop in Iredale, Alex Thornton and his cousin James turned up. In jeans and rugby shirts they looked like scrum-halfs at a vicarage tea-party. She hardly knew whether to go and serve them or hide in the kitchen.

Clearly out of their depth, they were both trying to keep straight faces as Suzie, cheeks burning, took their order.

'We're all meeting at the Blacksmith's Arms in Moorcliffe,' Alex said, studying the menu. 'Next Saturday – party at Avril's later. We thought you and Liz might like to come along?'

Suzie glanced at James. As soft brown eyes looked up in appeal, her heart melted. Minus the specs, he was really good-looking. She hadn't expected to see him again, despite Liz saying she'd scored a hit that night of the hop.

'I'll ask Liz,' she said, scribbling an order for tea. 'How can I let you know?'

James fished a piece of paper from his pocket. 'I'm staying with Alex – this is their phone number.'

'Right – thanks. I'll ring you when I've seen Liz.'

A few minutes later, as she served them tea and cakes, Alex said, 'Dig the uniform, by the way…'

Liz laughed when Suzie told her. 'Alex Thornton – he would say that, wouldn't he? Honestly, I can't believe what he's like. At school, I thought he was just a kid.'

'Until you met him at the hop!'

'Mm, yes,' Liz agreed, laughing again.

'So what do you think? Do you want to go?'

'Do you?'

'Yeah, let's – it'll be a laugh. Anyway, Avril's friends are a bit older, you won't feel like a baby-snatcher with them.'

'Who says I'm a baby-snatcher?'

'You did – after the hop!'

– o –

Moorcliffe was about three miles from where Suzie lived at Denshaw, and, like the third point of a triangle, Liz

Bradley's home in Heatherley was a few miles from both. Their homes were semi-detached council houses on quiet streets, and since neither girl had siblings, friends had always been encouraged to come back for tea or stay the night. Now they were older, if they were out together on a Saturday, it was accepted that Suzie would stay over with Liz, or Liz with Suzie.

It amused both girls that Connie Wallis envied Mrs Bradley because Mr Bradley was a tradesman and something of a DIY enthusiast, while Mrs Bradley envied Connie because Mr Wallis was always smartly dressed after work and took his wife out at the weekend. Since both sets of parents were given to occasional blazing rows – and in Suzie's case, rather more than occasional – the two girls felt they had much in common.

The invitation to a party at Moorcliffe, however, presented something of a problem. Only one bus an hour went via the village, otherwise it was a mile from the main road. The last bus to Heatherley was half past ten, so again Liz enlisted her father as chauffeur. And midnight was his limit.

In Denshaw, as Suzie was getting ready for the evening, her father looked up from his newspaper. 'Where did you say you were going – Moorcliffe? Bit posh up there, isn't it? Who's giving the party?'

'Avril – a girl from college.' She focused on her image in the mirror, coiling her back-combed hair into a neat French pleat.

'Hmm, must have some money to live up there. What does her father do?'

'Don't know,' she muttered, holding several hairgrips between her teeth.

Joe Wallis put his paper down. 'Well, I hope her parents are going to be there?'

'Of course,' she said, although she doubted it.

'And you're staying with Liz?'

Suzie turned. '*Dad* – I told you. Mr Bradley's picking us up at *midnight* – and yes, I'm staying with Liz. I'll be back for dinner tomorrow – all right?'

'Oh, get on with you.' He glanced at his watch. 'And if you're catching that bus to Moorcliffe, you'd better get your skates on.'

Sighing, Suzie reached for the can of hair lacquer.

'And don't spray that stuff in here – you'll set the place on fire!'

– o –

She was wearing a sleeveless shift dress she'd made last weekend, a chocolate and lime-green jungle print with the hem just above the knee. No tan this year, thanks to working indoors, and no money for a new summer coat. Her old cream mac would have to do. Anyway, she thought, once inside she could discard it; and at least her new stilettoes looked good.

The old single-decker came gasping up the hill and sighed to halt. Suzie stepped on and found a seat, fished in her handbag and paid the conductor. Leaving the council estate and trundling down through old Denshaw, they stopped at every bus stop. Once past the mill they were climbing again, passing cottages and a chapel, and increasingly bigger houses with cars in the drive, where the bus didn't need to halt. As Denshaw gave way to open fields, eventually they reached the main road; she could see Liz on the far side, waiting at the bus stop.

Spotting Suzie as she climbed aboard, Liz paid her fare and sat down beside her. 'Lord,' she exclaimed, 'it's windy up here – I've been waiting ages!'

As Liz slipped off a protective scarf, Suzie admired her friend's beehive hairstyle. 'You look brilliant – love your hair – and, oh, the dress! Where did you get that?

'C&A last week – they had a sale on. Do you like it? I wasn't sure about the colour...'

Pale blue was unusual for Liz, but with her dark hair she could wear anything. 'Matches your eyes,' Suzie said. 'Looks great!'

'And that's a new dress too – did you make it? Wish I was as clever as you...'

Suzie peered out of the window. Fields, an outlying farmhouse, and, just beyond, the dark mass of the old village. 'Hey, we're nearly there – must be our stop.'

'Moorcliffe,' the conductor sang out, adding, 'Have a nice evening, girls!' as they stepped off the bus.

By the sign for the Blacksmith's Arms, they paused to take their bearings. The old inn was set back from the street, its parking area almost full.

'Crumbs,' Liz said, taking in the gleaming array of expensive cars. 'Have you been here before?'

'No. Been through the village a few times, but not to the pub.'

'Well, you know what your Mum says – stand straight and keep your chin up...'

'And try to look as though we're used to better things!'

Giggling, they linked arms, weaving their way through parked cars to the door. Inside, the place was heaving, the noise of laughter and voices almost deafening.

'Hell's bells,' Suzie groaned, removing her scarf, 'how are we supposed to find them in this lot?' Standing on tip-toe, she tried to see over the throng of heads and bodies; men pushing to and from the bar, women waving, drinks teetering; and somewhere to the left a great fireplace appearing and disappearing as the crowd moved and swelled like a wave.

Liz was looking to the right. 'There's another room through there – beyond the bar. Shall we try it?'

Just as she pushed her way forward, above the crowd Suzie caught sight of familiar profile, topped by a mop of thick chestnut hair. James turned and saw them; with a broad grin he elbowed a few people aside so they could get through.

'I was just trying to get some drinks. What will you have?'

Suzie, used to penniless students, ordered a half pint of beer; but Liz said she'd have gin and bitter lemon. As James pushed his way to the bar, Suzie frowned at her friend. 'Naughty.'

'So? They've more money than sense.'

'Yes, but what will you have when *we* buy a round? We can't not.'

'Bitter lemon,' Liz replied, and headed for the other room.

Avril and Babs were at a table with Alex and a couple of lads Suzie knew from school, plus a few students from Iredale. Faces lit up in welcome as Suzie and Liz arrived, and they were absorbed into the group at once. For an hour or more they were laughing and talking; drinks were bought, crisps consumed and cigarettes smoked in the low-ceilinged room. By ten o'clock the atmosphere was stifling. Gradually, they migrated to the beer garden outside.

The crowd had dissolved into twos and fours by the time Suzie and James joined them. They'd been talking about their holiday jobs, James complaining that he'd never worked so hard, carrying bricks, climbing ladders, digging trenches; while Suzie claimed her feet had never walked so far in a day.

In the darkness beyond lay an open expanse of fields and hills. In the distance, sparkling like diamonds, myriads of tiny lights lit up the valley. This view, which she'd never seen at night, was breath-taking.

'Is that the Aire Valley?' she whispered.

'Yes – that's Bradford down there. Fabulous, isn't it? From Alex's place, the view's even better – not so pretty during the day, though.'

'Where does he live?'

James waved a hand to the right. 'It's an old farmhouse near the crags. Uncle Harry's done an amazing job on the place – you should see it.'

'If only,' she laughed. 'Sounds like a great place to do some painting...'

After a moment, he said, 'Well, you never know. Maybe I can arrange it?'

'Oh, don't tease. I've got to get some work done this summer, but lord knows when – I only get Sunday and Monday off. I need to do a series of sketches – and then a painting.'

'You could maybe come up on Sundays – I'm off then, and I'm sure my aunt and uncle wouldn't mind.'

She turned to meet his gaze. 'Are you serious?'

'Yes, I am...'

As he bent towards her, Suzie thought he was about to kiss her; but then Alex's voice broke in.

'Hey, come on you two – we've got a party to go to!'

Five

Avril's home was a few minutes' walk away, one of a group of substantial detached houses in a kind of enclave set apart from the village. Looking up at the mock-Tudor façades, Suzie was awed at first by their confident style. A moment later she was suppressing a grin, remembering art school parties she'd been to in Iredale: freezing cold student flats with vast ceilings, crumbling cornices and ancient bathrooms. Colourful artwork though, and always some great discussions going on. Following James and Alex up the drive, she wondered what this house, this party, would be like.

The short driveway led to an imposing front door. Stepping inside with Liz, a spacious hall with an oak staircase met their eyes, and, through an open door, a large sitting room. But Avril was leading the way to the kitchen, indicating bottles of beer and soft drinks on the table. Reaching into a fridge, she pulled out plates of sandwiches, cheese on sticks and sausage rolls.

'Tuck in,' Avril said, 'or dear Mother will be mortified…'

Suzie caught Liz's eye and they exchanged a look; Suzie smiled and pretended this was normal. Taking a sandwich and a serviette, she said, 'Are your parents out?'

'Dinner with friends – they won't be back till late.' Avril swept out again and headed down the hall. 'Now, let's get some music on – this is supposed to be a party!'

Moments later a dancing beat filled the house. Feet were tapping in the kitchen, and in the sitting room Avril had pushed back the furniture. When Suzie and James went through, the record player was stacked with 45s and Alex and Liz were *Twistin' the Night Away* to Sam Cook, the others laughing and clapping.

Suzie was astonished. Turning to Babs, she said, 'I didn't expect Avril to be into pop music – I thought she was another jazz fan?'

'Most of the records are mine!' Babs laughed, and went to join the fun.

Next, it was one from Gerry and the Pacemakers, followed by the Beatles' *From Me to You*. So infectious, everyone seemed to be dancing, out in the hall and even in the kitchen. Clutching his glass like a lifebelt, James laughingly shook his head, so Suzie simply joined Babs and danced with the others. It was only when a plaintive Ray Charles number came on that she stopped to catch her breath.

She sank down beside him on the stairs. 'The music's great,' she said, 'why won't you dance?'

'Never learned how.'

'Oh, don't be an idiot – there's nothing to learn, you just move to the music.'

'All right for you to say,' he grinned. 'I prefer to listen.'

'Well, it's not like learning to waltz or quick-step – I never learned that either.'

He gave her a glance. 'You're good to watch,' he said gruffly, and cleared his throat.

Even as she smiled, Suzie warmed with pleasure. No one had ever said that before, and she didn't know how to respond. 'Thank you,' she managed at last, because it was a compliment, and maybe...

James drew her close. Again, he was looking at her as though he wanted to kiss her; and she was wishing he would. Somewhere in the background, Buddy Holly was singing, *Brown-eyed Handsome Man*, and she was thinking, *yes, you are*. Smiling, she touched her lips to his, and just as hesitantly, he responded; but at the sound of feet on the stairs behind them, he broke away. Taking her hand, he led her through the house and out into the garden.

His embrace was gentle, unsure, but it felt good. She liked the clean smell of him, the smoothness of his cheek against hers; liked the way he didn't grab at her or assume she was his for the taking. Not like some of the boys she'd met at college parties, unwashed, unshaven, assuming you were there to be groped, and then not wanting to know when you pushed them away.

Clearly, he liked talking to her, listening to what she had to say. Not that he was talking now. His breath was warm against her neck, lips tender against her cheek, seeking her mouth in a lingering kiss. His hands caressed her waist and hips, drawing her ever closer. They broke apart, kissed again; she wanted it to go on forever.

At last, needing air, she drew back, surprise and delight bubbling into soft laughter as his lips traced the curve of her cheek and ear. She stroked his neck and shoulders, ran her hands down his back and could feel him trembling; as she pressed closer, he held her tight, sighing as he gradually released her.

There was a seat on the terrace. As one, they went for it, collapsing like puppets, laughing as he rescued his specs and a squashed packet of Embassy from his breast pocket. For a while they smoked in silence, listening to the breeze; high above the rooftops, clouds were scudding across a pale half-moon.

'I know you're staying at your friend's,' he said at last, drawing her closer, 'so you're probably busy tomorrow. But would you like to come over next Sunday? There are some great walks across the moor, and you could bring your sketch book?'

'That's an idea,' Suzie agreed. 'Mind you, there's only one bus an hour, so I'd have to time it right. And Mum always does dinner at half-past one, so it could be three by the time I get here.'

'That's okay, I could meet you off the bus closest to three. How does that sound?'

With another lingering kiss, they sealed the arrangement. But as they broke apart, repeating their promise, Suzie remembered Liz's Dad and the fact that he was picking them up at midnight. 'Oh, damn, what time is it? I can't see my watch.'

Under light from the kitchen window, she saw it was twenty to twelve. 'Sorry, James – got to find Liz. And we've got to get back to the pub to meet her Dad…'

'It'll be closed.'

'I know – we hadn't got Avril's address, so he's meeting us there.'

James followed as she went inside. Bodies were sprawled in twos over chairs and sofas, something quiet playing from the record-deck. It was dark in the sitting room, and by light from the hall she couldn't see Liz or Alex.

'Probably upstairs,' James murmured.

'Oh, damn. Where's Avril?'

He shrugged, opened another door, but that was only the dining room. 'Nothing for it – we'll have to go up.'

At the top of the stairs, they met Avril, coming out of the bathroom. She tried the first bedroom door, stepping back as one of the third-year students appeared, tucking a half-buttoned shirt into his jeans. James tried the next, calling Alex's name into the darkness. A muffled reply told them he'd found his cousin.

Suzie poked her head into the room. 'Liz, are you here as well? We've got to go – it's nearly midnight.'

'Yeah – okay – I'm coming…'

'Not yet she isn't!' Alex called back, his laughter broken by a sudden yelp.

Wanting to thump him herself, Suzie pinned on a smile as Avril checked her watch.

'You're not going already?'

'Got to – Liz's Dad is picking us up.'

'Oh, I see. Shame you can't stay.' She turned to James. 'But you're not going, are you? Nobody's picking *you* up. Unless, of course, it's Suzie, here,' she added with an arch little smile.

Lost for a reply, Suzie gritted her teeth, but James slipped an arm around her shoulders and gave her a squeeze. 'Suzie can pick me up anytime,' he said cheerfully, and she could have kissed him.

It was several minutes before Liz joined them in the hall, mouth looking bruised and still tucking her hair back into place.

'For goodness' sake, put some lipstick on,' Suzie hissed, nudging her towards the hall mirror. With a rueful smile she turned to James. 'Sorry we've got to rush off like this – but I'll see you next week, okay?'

'Let me get Alex – we'll walk along with you.'

'No, honestly – we'll be better on our own.'

He squeezed her hand. 'Okay then – next Sunday it is.'

Once outside, she and Liz hurried along, high heels clicking on the pavement, Liz checking her watch at every street lamp. 'We're late – Dad'll be furious.'

'Well, it's your own fault – good job I was keeping an eye on the time. What were you up to in that bedroom, anyway?'

Suzie knew fine well that some heavy petting was going on and was curious to know what Liz would say. Had they been taking it to the brink, or what? When Liz mumbled something about Alex being a fast worker, Suzie said, 'I can imagine.' Again, no reply. Wondering was it serious or just a party fling, she said, 'So are you going out with him now?'

'Bit difficult – I'm seeing somebody at work.'

Astonished, Suzie turned to her friend. 'Are you? You never said…'

But by then they were in sight of the Blacksmith's Arms and Mr Bradley's works' van, parked in the forecourt. And Liz never did explain the chap at work.

– o –

Getting ready for her Sunday date with James, Suzie worried about her freshly-washed hair. Should she pin it up or leave it loose? Eventually she brushed it back and tied it in a simple pony-tail. And finally, having tried several different tops to go with her one good pair of jeans, she was ready. Stuffing a rolled-up plastic mac into her canvas shoulder bag, together with sketch book and pencils, she bolted her lunch and made it to the bus stop with barely a minute to spare.

James was waiting at Moorcliffe, to her relief looking casual in an old green parka. He seemed to be frowning as she stepped off the bus. But then he smiled and said, 'You look different today…'

As she started to explain, he coloured with confusion. 'No – sorry – different but nice. I like your hair like that.'

Suzie squeezed his hand. 'Thanks. This is the other me – not exactly *Midnight in Moscow*, more midweek in Iredale!'

As he laughed, she touched the camera slung around his neck. 'This looks serious, though.'

'I thought some photos might be useful.'

'Certainly would,' she agreed, thrilled that he'd been thinking about her work. 'Mine's just an old Brownie – fine for people, rubbish for distance.'

'This one's German – used to be my Dad's. It's not bad.'

A stile in the drystone wall led to a track running behind the pub and out towards the moor. It was a cool and blustery afternoon, grey clouds scudding high over distant rocks, sheep grazing in fields close by. Taking deep breaths, Suzie suddenly felt light and free.

With a grin, James glanced at her hair, strands already dancing around her face. As he smoothed it back, she said, 'We used to come up here for walks sometimes when I was young. Sunday afternoons, usually. Dad loved it, but Mum hated the wind destroying her hairstyle!'

'It's always blowing a gale up here – *Wuthering Heights*, my mother calls it.'

Agreeing, laughing, Suzie asked when his parents would be back from Germany. He said mid-September, when they'd be returning to Aldershot. 'For a while, anyway. Dad will be retiring in a year or two – after that, I don't know. But they've always been on the move – that's why I went to boarding school.'

'What does he do?'

With a wry smile, James said, 'He's a major in the Paras.'

'Goodness! Aren't they supposed to be a tough lot?'

'You can say that again,' he grinned. And he's always trying to toughen me up – that's why I'm working for Uncle Harry.'

Suzie slipped her arm through his. 'Well, you look tough enough to me!'

'Thanks.' After a while, he said, 'Trouble is, Dad thinks studying history is namby-pamby. Can't see the future in it – pardon the joke. Didn't like it when I quoted someone – Santayana, I think – who said, *Those who cannot remember the past are condemned to repeat it…*'

'Oh, I like that!'

'Anyway, don't let's talk about him. What about your father? What does he do?'

'Oh, nothing so grand. He's an engineer. Another one who thinks the future is everything – and the past's just a waste of time.'

They reached the outcrop of rocks, climbing to a point where they could shelter from the wind. At once, Suzie was eyeing her surroundings with a view to making a picture. In the foreground, dark-walled pastures and bright green fields flecked with sheep; in the distant valley a swathe of greys, rising to blue where the next Pennine ridge met the sky.

At night, a week ago, Bradford had been a sparkling mass of lights; now it was a misty haze, impossible to define. Industrial, yes, but far from classifiable as *Industrial Landscape*, one of Rod Winter's favourite themes; even as a traditional landscape, it was hardly inspiring.

'If you were trying to do an abstract painting,' she said, indicating the view, 'how would you do it?'

He pulled a face. 'Don't ask me. Most of the paintings I see are historical.'

'Mm, they're the ones I like.' Sighing, after a moment or two, she said, 'Well, I suppose green triangles, black lines and bands of grey would do it. Thrillsville.'

'Does it have to be abstract?'

'In theory, no. But if I want to impress my tutor, yes.'

Turning, she looked up at the outcrop of millstone grit, weathered over millennia into shapes and shades of grey. 'I know – let's go back down and have another look at these rocks...'

From fifty or sixty paces away, the outcrop was massive against the sky; she'd been too busy looking at James to take it in before. Moving further away, Suzie made a square with her hands and looked again. Yes, it made a pleasing shape against the sky.

Suddenly excited, she said, 'I think I've got it…'

While James moved back and forth taking photographs, Suzie found a good position from which to draw. Using a dry-stone wall as a leaning post, within half an hour she had outline and shadows sketched in, giving a rough idea of what she wanted. Mass of rocks upper right quarter, land falling away to the left… More detailed sketches to give form and shape to the rocks; but yes, today's afternoon light was coming from the right direction… Blow Rod Winter and his empty abstract notions; a threatening sunset was already taking shape in her head.

With her sketches literally in the bag, it seemed right to relax afterwards against the wall, sealing satisfaction with blood-warming kisses. Although a searching wind soon cooled their ardour, Suzie called a halt before James could think he was entitled to more.

As they gathered their belongings, he suggested going back to the house for a coffee. Shivering, unsure, she hesitated for a moment; but then he said his aunt and uncle were at home, and no doubt Alex too.

They made their way back to the field path, and from there along another track edged by stunted hawthorns, leaning all one way. To Suzie's eyes, the old farmhouse at the far end seemed to be crouching for protection into a fold of land. To one side she could see outbuildings and a bright yellow JCB, and, as they drew closer, a Land Rover and a mud-splattered but expensive-looking car in the yard.

'Oh-oh, Alex hasn't cleaned the car,' James muttered as he opened the gate. 'He'll be in trouble – he was supposed to do that this afternoon.'

'You too?'

'No, I get different jobs. This weekend, mine was sweeping the yard – but I did it yesterday.'

'So your Uncle's tough as well as your Dad?'

James laughed. 'Oh, I don't know – he's pretty fair.'

He led her round to the kitchen door, calling out as they went inside. A woman's voice answered from another room, and then she appeared, smiling a welcome as she saw Suzie. Tall, with coppery hair, there was enough family resemblance for Suzie to see that this was James's blood relative. Dark-haired Alex, she thought, must take after his father.

Suzie said hello, and thanks, yes, she would love a hot drink. Mrs Thornton set the kettle to boil, offering a seat and asking if her sketching expedition had been successful.

'Do show your drawings,' James urged, 'they're really good...' At which Suzie was suddenly bashful, feeling sure they'd disappoint someone who knew the place well.

'Well, these are just a first attempt. I should really come back another day and do more...'

But Mrs Thornton seemed genuinely impressed. 'They're lovely,' she insisted. 'I can't draw so much as a straight line.'

'But that's really difficult,' Suzie smiled. At Mrs Thornton's confusion, she added, 'Drawing a straight line...'

Amidst the laughter, Mr Thornton joined them. He was a big, bluff-looking man with thick grey hair and a Bradford accent. No sign of Alex, but it seemed he was out. 'Little bugger, I told him to clean the car.'

Only when James's aunt asked if she'd like something to eat, did Suzie realize the time. 'No, honestly, thanks, but I must get going – Mum's expecting me back.'

'Can I give you a lift, love?' Mr Thornton asked, but Suzie refused, said she'd walk down for the bus. She could just imagine her Dad's reaction if she arrived home in a posh car.

Six

On his return from Iredale, James picked up letters and newspapers and took them through to the lounge. Ignoring the post, he glanced at his wife's photo and shook his head. 'This,' he said dourly, 'was supposed to be a good idea...'

In search of calm, he pushed a CD into the stereo and lay down on the sofa, gradually relaxing as sublime voices sang Allegri's *Miserere*.

Agnus Dei, qui tollis peccata mundi, miserere nobis...

Lamb of God, who takes away the sins of the world, have mercy on us...

As the voices faded away, he stirred reluctantly. Chilled, in need of warmth and sleep, he tried to recall his last meal – breakfast in the hotel, and very little since. Shivering in the kitchen, he poured a tot of whisky before making some supper to take up to bed.

After two years, James had grown used to sleeping alone, but nowadays, the room he'd shared with Maggie was as tidy as a monk's cell; even its fitted furniture looked like a blank wall. The bed, the chair, the chest of drawers, said what it was, the sleeping place of a single man. As for the watercolour of the Cotswolds, where he and his wife had often walked, all it suggested was emptiness.

Expecting another broken night, for once he slept heavily, rising late and thankful it was Saturday. In the wake of Lent, and after the intensity of Holy Week, the post-Easter break was never long enough, and after the trip to Yorkshire he was wrung-out.

How many times, James asked himself, had he been consulted about dying wishes and ill-conceived promises; how many times had he tried to relieve the petitioner of guilt? And yet, in trying to console his dying wife, he'd fallen into the same mire. And as for his notion about the piece in the Yorkshire Post – that it was some kind of sign he was meant to follow – it seemed worse than deluded.

In his work, he was supposed to empathise with people, find out what drove them. And yet it seemed he didn't even understand himself. He hadn't anticipated that seeing Suzie in the flesh – being with her, talking to her – would rouse such conflicting emotions. Even being in that part of Yorkshire had affected him more than he could have believed possible.

What a waste of effort and emotion. How could he have been led so far astray, not anticipating the levels of shock and bitterness? Imagining that Suzie, the girl he'd loved but abandoned, would agree to his request, was nothing short of folly. Yes, she'd been the gentlest, kindest girl he'd ever met, but that was then, before the nightmare.

The first thing he saw when he went downstairs was her book, cast face-down on the kitchen table. Mocking him from the back cover, the author's portrait with its faint half-smile seemed to be saying, *Ha! Thought you knew me, did you? Well think again!*

Suzie Wallis was not a collection of words on a page. She was a living, breathing, human being, a mature woman with a history he could barely imagine. Granted, he'd made deductions from her writing, but were they the right deductions? This woman was not the girl he'd known. Once, a long time ago, he had inflicted unforgettable pain – why should she accede to his request? The biggest mystery of all was why she'd agreed to speak to him.

He thought he'd dispensed with guilt years ago, but Suzie's question – *why had he just dumped her?* – was still burning. He hadn't *dumped* her, as she put it, he simply hadn't had words to explain. Not then. Yesterday, given chance, he might have answered with just one word – *shame*. But that would have opened a new set of questions.

As it was, she was gone before he could recover himself.

Typical woman, he thought, to exit left on a parting shot. He couldn't recall if he'd apologized or not, but either way, he did not expect to hear from her again.

– o –

Having spoken to his curate, Amy, and later shopped for essentials, that evening James heated a ready meal from M&S, and took it through to the sitting room. Turning on the TV, his one desire was to blank out the doubt and self-disgust still raging through his mind.

The day's news, announced in the ringing tones of Big Ben, was not the best distraction. War in Iraq, conflict in Israel, threats of an Islamic terror attack on London – no wonder religion had become a dirty word. As the presenter moved on to an interview with the Prime Minister, James switched channels. The last thing he needed was Tony Blair pontificating on the UK's position in any of this.

Hoping for a good detective drama to distract him, he searched the TV listings. As a film, *The Great Escape*, caught his eye, his heart lurched. Was everything set to remind him of the past? Of all the films he must have seen around that time, this was the one he remembered. Of course, he'd seen it first with Suzie, at the cinema in Heatherley...

– o –

Alex had missed the first showing in Leeds and was keen to go. 'Steve McQueen's in it, and James Garner – you know, him from *Maverick*. Should be good. Anyway,' he added, 'we'll ask the girls.'

'Will they want to see a war film?'

Alex mimed despair. 'What's wrong with you? *Of course* they'll want to see it – they'll be with *us!* Anyway, we'll be able to give them a lift home – that'll be good, won't it?'

'If your Dad lets you borrow the Land Rover...'

Alex had recently passed his test, and was hoping for – nay, expecting – a car for his 18th birthday in two weeks' time. Naturally, he was not allowed to drive Uncle Harry's pride and joy, the Rover saloon, but he was allowed to borrow the ex-army vehicle. Occasionally, that is, and not if booze was involved. Anyway, by the time the film ended, the pubs would be shutting.

Uncle Harry said yes, they could take it – but he wanted James and Alex back home by half-eleven at the latest.

They met the girls outside the cinema. Such was the quality of the film, all four were riveted by the action and the tension and McQueen's great motorcycle sequence. But afterwards, instead of taking them straight home, Alex decided to do a detour via some wooded country lanes. While Liz shrieked with laughter in the front, James and Suzie were sliding along bench seats in the back, begging Alex to slow down. Without warning, he pulled into a lay-by under some trees, and proceeded to make a grab for Liz. In the darkness, her protests were soon silenced, while in the back, Suzie was gasping, trying to find her bag, and generally consigning Alex to perdition.

Untangling his legs from hers, James reached for her, drawing her across to his side, holding her until fright subsided and desire took over. After that it was a while before someone – probably Suzie – came up for air and said it was time they went home, the parents would be worried. No doubt Alex would have ignored her had it not been for James being firm for once. Adopting his 'suitably reprimanded' act, Alex was persuaded to drive them back towards Heatherley at acceptable speed.

Dropping Liz outside her home on the outskirts, they took Suzie back to Denshaw. James watched as she hurried along the pavement, high heels clicking down the path leading to small modern semi with a tiny garden. Not until she'd turned and waved them goodnight did Alex comment.

'I thought they were better than this,' he said, indicating another bleak street with unforgiving lighting. 'No wonder they're not on the bloody phone.'

James stared at him, hurt for Suzie, but in a way, shamed too; so angry he couldn't speak. What he wanted to say, was, *Don't be such a bloody snob, Alex – your Dad was brought up in a back-to-back in Bradford!* But confrontation was never his strong point; and besides, he had to live with Alex for the rest of the summer.

Once, on the way back from a job, Uncle Harry had taken them through a run-down part of the city. James could see the place still: a huge, soot-blackened mill, storeys high; and endless rows of houses climbing steep cobbled streets. He couldn't believe it when his uncle said he'd lived there as boy.

'Back-to-backs,' Uncle Harry had said. 'You know what that means, lads? One backs onto t'next. No gap between 'em. Maximum use o' land. Three adjoining walls and three poky rooms, one above t'other.' He'd turned the Land Rover into one of the streets, changing gear as they climbed uphill past rows of dark little houses. 'This is my old street. Rabbit-hutches,' he said with contempt. 'About time they were all pulled down. Cold water, no bathrooms, just a row of stinking closets down the alley. And that, lads, is why I became a builder – to make decent homes for working families…'

Clearly, he'd been making a point: one that certainly impressed James. He'd always liked his Uncle Harry, but after that his admiration soared. Alex, however, had heard it all before.

With snobbery on his mind, to James' surprise, when he asked who Alex was inviting to the party, it seemed Liz was still on the list.

'I thought she wasn't good enough for you?'

'Oh, she'll do for the time being,' he said airily. 'Anyway, you're making progress, aren't you? Can't invite one without the other…'

– o –

At this distance in time, James was appalled, not just by Alex's attitude to women, but his own acceptance of it. Yes, they were teenagers, and yes, James had lived in an almost exclusively male environment from the age of eight; but when he considered where it led, he could have wept.

Perhaps if he'd lived at home, spent more time with his mother, he might have been better equipped to differentiate between lust and love.

Seven

Almost two hundred miles away, Suzie noticed the film title with a similar sense of *déjà vu*. *The Great Escape*: the night she'd come in late, Dad's fury erupting as she walked in. He didn't need to resort to violence – his voice alone could reduce her to tears. His anger, fuelled by concern, was understandable now. At the time though, it felt cruel as well as unreasonable, especially when he said she'd be kept in as punishment.

That upset her even more. The Thorntons were going on holiday; and if she didn't go to Alex's party on Saturday night, she wouldn't see James again for three whole weeks.

Three weeks: at the time it seemed an eternity of Tuesdays to Saturdays at the café in Leeds, while at home Mum and Dad had only to meet to have a blazing row. Arguments were nothing new, but the major topic of money – who spent it and how – had changed since they'd become friendly with a local couple. Dad didn't drive, but the husband had a car and would give them a lift home on Saturday nights; they'd even had the odd day out together.

That Dad fancied the wife was something even Suzie had noticed; but whether he was having an affair was doubtful. Even then she'd wondered when and how he would have managed it. But Connie was convinced he was playing away, and she'd been giving him hell for more than a year. She wouldn't let it drop, and Dad wouldn't admit to something he said he hadn't done. What's more, he refused to change his routine, kept on seeing his cronies at the usual watering holes in Crossgate – frequented of course, by *that woman* – and the more Connie attacked, the more Joe retreated in that direction. Which meant yet another row when he came in.

Dad was a foreman at the engineering works and he worked hard, from eight in the morning until six at night. Mum worked too – part-time as a dinner lady at the local school. She shopped and cooked and kept house, while Dad sat down with the evening paper and the telly and left everything else to her. Even so, when he came home, Mum would have his dinner ready – she did that every day, no matter how angry she was. Remembering, Suzie felt her stomach tense, a reflex from the old days. In fact, she'd become so used to eating under tension, she'd eaten her way solidly through some of the worst times of her life. If she hadn't burned it off in anxiety, she'd have been like Bessie Bunter.

In her mind, it was a black period, one crisis followed by another; conflict at home echoed by world news paraded every night on TV. As Khrushchev and Kennedy bandied words like some terrifying double act, the world held its breath and waited for the mushroom clouds. Ducking behind the parapets, she checked out novels every week from the library, indulging her taste for 19th century classics, the bigger the better. A desire to understand something more of Russia than Khruschev's USSR, led to the suitably titled *War and Peace*.

Even skipping most of the war scenes, it gave her hours of reading when she couldn't sleep; but it was Tolstoy's later novel, *Anna Karenina*, which lingered in the mind. It said so much about love and betrayal, indifference and cruelty; describing and explaining situations that were new to her but as old as time. When she thought about her parents, Tolstoy's words were not exactly reassuring, but at least they made sense, made her feel less alone, less unique in her private misery.

Those emotions were mostly a wisp of memory, but at times – like now – triggers to memory were everywhere. Looking back at her own personal crisis, she was surprised by how angry she felt.

She couldn't recall feeling like that at the time. Cheated, yes; let down, definitely. What had lingered over the years was the feeling of betrayal; less clear but still present, like viewing a distant island from the safety of the shore. But anger and hatred, no. Maybe there'd been no room for it. Perhaps anger had simply been overwhelmed by panic; by the terrifying reality of being eighteen years old, pregnant and alone.

She'd never forgotten James: how could she? From time to time his face would be conjured by some vague similarity to an actor or presenter on TV. Since Thursday afternoon, however, the older face had taken precedence, his words constantly at the forefront of her mind. He might be looking to the future, but she couldn't face it. And why should she? She was still furious at the way he'd walked back into her life – and at such a time! – expecting smiles and forgiveness and information. If she gave it, if James started searching, what would he find? Envisaging resentment, disaster – even death – she shrank in fear. How would she deal with the guilt?

No, there was enough of that in the past. Thinking about it now was unbearable.

Although Cathy knew the basics, unlike Liz, she hadn't been around when it was happening. The long gap in their relationship, while living at different ends of the country, meant Suzie had never gone into detail before. But after coming face to face with James, she'd had to let it out.

Thank God she'd been with Cathy that day. How she'd have dealt with it had Jo or Sara been there, she dreaded to think. But Cathy, after years of nursing and marriage to a GP, believed in the healing power of talking – and listening. The trouble was, having suppressed the agony for years, Suzie was now recalling more and more of what led up to it; but like jigsaw pieces tipped out on a tray, she wasn't even sure where and how they fitted together.

– o –

Cathy's home on the far side of Heatherley was the kind Suzie thought of as a typical doctor's house, stone-built, with bay windows, tall hedges, and a small parking area. Once, the surgery had been part of the house, but now, with a joint practice and purpose-built medical centre in town, Cathy and Ian had the place to themselves. She said it was too big and they should move; but then she'd smile and shake her head. Suzie knew why. It had an air of privacy, a beautiful rear garden, and there was ample space for her children and grandchildren to visit.

Cathy's husband came out as Suzie locked the car, greeting her with a hug before casting a professional glance over her. 'How are you? I gather you're having a tough time at the moment.'

'Oh, I'm okay, Ian, just not sleeping so well.'

'Well, don't suffer – get yourself down to the surgery. Things can get out of proportion when you're tired.'

She smiled and kissed his cheek. 'Thanks, Ian – I will.'

'Anyway, come on in – I've got the wine open, and the roast's just about ready…'

The aromas of Sunday lunch greeted her as she walked into the kitchen, reminding Suzie that she hadn't cooked a meal like this since Freddie's death. For all his avant-garde ideas, Freddie had enjoyed what he called, 'a proper Sunday dinner', especially when the girls were at home. For a moment, memories brought a catch to her throat: how she wished he could be with her now.

Cathy, bubbly as ever, hugged her, and Ian presented her with a glass of shiraz, the heartening, full-bodied flavour setting the world back to rights. Exchanging family news and local gossip, they chatted easily over the roast beef and perfect Yorkshire puddings, the two women laughing as Cathy admitted she'd not made them herself.

'Frozen Yorkshire puddings – imagine – Mother would have a fit if she knew!'

'No she wouldn't,' Suzie said. 'She'd be delighted. Remember beating the batter by hand?'

'Well, it got rid of a lot of frustration.'

'Certainly did!'

As they finished the meal, Ian said he'd clear away, and waved the women into the conservatory. Armed with a tray of tea and biscuits, Suzie and Cathy seated themselves in a sunny corner. Even as Suzie dug out cigarettes, she was telling her friend about the coincidence of last night's film on TV, and how it reminded her of a night out with James.

'As soon as I saw the title, it all came back. I was there in that bloody Land Rover, thinking we'd never get home…'

She'd been grounded for a week, and it had taken all her mother's persuasion to make Dad relent about the party. Eventually, he'd agreed she could go, but only on certain conditions. She and Liz had to get a taxi back to Denshaw – which Dad would book and pay for – and he wanted the Thorntons' phone number as well as their address.

'So, like Cinderella, I did get to go to the ball. A pity, really…'

'Was that when it happened?'

'Not that night, no – but we did get pretty close.'

Events, she said, had followed a similar pattern to the previous party, except they left the pub earlier, and Alex ferried them to the farm in his new car. No parents around, but beer and food were laid on, music belting out from the record player for the first hour or so. After a while the dancers began to thin out, and then James, still the non-dancer, asked her up to his room.

'To see his etchings?' Cathy asked dryly.

'Not exactly,' Suzie laughed. 'I remember it was a book on the Pre-Raphaelites – something pretty well guaranteed to spark my interest.'

'Clever lad!'

'Anyway, as you can imagine, we didn't just look at a few pretty pictures...'

She had a fleeting memory of lying on the bed in James's arms, half-undressed and enjoying the feel of his skin next to hers. Intensely pleasurable to be so close, kissing and stroking yet not being pushed to go any further. She remembered pulling back to look at him in the lamplight: the angle of head and arm, shoulder and chest muscles, smooth lines tapering to waist and thighs. Whilst he smiled and studied her in return, she was thinking how beautiful he was...

'I remember looking at him,' Suzie said wistfully, 'and wishing I could draw him...'

'What? You were almost having it off, and you wanted to *draw* him?'

With a wry grin, Suzie nodded. 'Oh, I know it sounds weird. But why do you think there are so many intimate drawings by famous artists? They're always taking a mental step back, examining the picture as well as their reaction to it. I should know, I lived with Freddie...

'Anyway, we won't go there. Look at it this way. Compared to the saggy male model we had in college, James was like a Greek god. And the thing was, he didn't know it – which made him even more attractive.'

'Ah, I see,' Cathy said, rolling her eyes. 'No wonder you fell for him.'

'Yes, no wonder... I don't know how long we were up there – an hour, maybe – but suddenly, Alex was banging on the door, saying, *Get dressed, the taxi's here*. Liz was waiting in the hall by the time I came down, and clever sod Alex was standing with the door open, bowing us out to the cab.

'After that we didn't see them for a couple of weeks,' Suzie went on, 'because they were on holiday. But there was another party just after they came back...'

Reflecting on it, she said, 'You remember me mentioning Babs and Avril? Well, they lived in the posh houses at Moorcliffe. Anyway, Babs had hooked up with somebody and was keen to get it together before the holidays were over. The last weekend in August, her parents were going away and Avril was keeping her company. So they invited everybody round for an all-nighter.'

'Bloody hell, they were real party animals up there in Moorcliffe, weren't they? Can you imagine the folks we knew in Denshaw getting up to all that?'

'What, on the council estate? Lord, no – far too respectable!'

'Too worried about what the neighbours would say!'

'Exactly,' Suzie agreed.

'But you were saying about this party. Was that the fateful evening?'

'Certainly was.' Suzie sipped at a cooling cup of tea. 'The music was great – I remember that clearly. Between them, the girls had all the latest hits – do you remember the Beatles' *Twist and Shout*?'

'Oh, that brings back memories!'

'They played it over and over. I remember trying to drag James into the crowd, and feeling cross because he wouldn't even try. No confidence, of course – unlike Alex, who had more balls than a bloody cricket team.'

As Cathy laughed, Suzie raked her memory for the next sequence of events, but all she could see was a hallway with people milling about.

'And that's where I've got a blank. I know I'd been dancing and I was thirsty. James handed me a beer and I gulped at it. Anyway, I remember feeling a bit dizzy soon after that, and thinking I'd had one too many...'

Eight

Suzie had tried many times to clarify what led up to that moment, but she could never be certain. Afterwards, Liz confirmed that they'd arrived at the pub just before nine, and everyone started moving on to Babs's house about ten, so there couldn't have been time for more than two drinks. At the party she may have had a couple more; enough to make her happy, but not exactly drunk.

But maybe she was wrong; maybe she had lost count. She remembered mumbling something to James, and looking around for Liz before staggering upstairs to find the lavatory. Relief as she sat down, but standing up was a challenge. Dizzy again, she fumbled with the lock, got the door open and almost fell into James's arms.

He'd said something, no doubt asking was she okay. The next thing she knew, she was in his arms, the world was spinning and she was sprawled across a bed and he was kissing her. Suddenly feeling sick, afraid of throwing up all over him, Suzie tried to protest, tried to push him off. But he wasn't listening. Next thing, his hand was under her skirt. Moments later he was on top of her.

One stinging thrust – and then it was over.

As he rolled away, Suzie lay there, shocked, dizzy, trying to fathom what he'd done. *Had he…?* Yes, he had; between her legs, she felt wet. When she could find her voice she said scathingly, 'I hope you're proud of yourself.'

Without speaking, he got up, straightened his clothes and left.

As the full impact dawned, shame forced her to find her knickers, pull them on. She collapsed back onto the bed, unable to reason, unable to think beyond the act itself. *How could he?* She hadn't wanted this, but he'd carried on. With no forewarning, no sweet words, no gentle persuasion.

Why? And what if…?

Weak tears were pouring into her hair when the door opened again.

'Suzie? What's wrong?'

With an effort she pulled herself upright. And then comforting arms were around her, and she was sobbing into Liz's shoulder. 'Oh, no,' Liz said, 'not *you…*'

'Yes, he – he just… Oh, my God, Liz – what if…?'

'Oh, don't be daft – you won't – not the first time…'

Liz wanted to know how it had happened; incredulous when Suzie said she'd drunk too much and felt sick. Liz said, 'But you were all right half an hour ago. What were you drinking?'

But Suzie couldn't recall. Crushed by James's betrayal, all she wanted to do was go home. Ironically, she and Liz had planned it so they did not have to rush off at midnight, either for a taxi or Mr Bradley's works' van. They were staying with Babs. Not that either set of parents knew that. Liz had said she was staying with Suzie, and Suzie said she was staying with Liz. And with no telephone communication between the two, who was to know?

That lie formed a kernel of guilt around everything that came afterwards. It was as though she could hear her mother's voice saying, *Well, that's what you get for telling lies…*

A little later, reassured by Liz, Suzie was composed enough to go downstairs. She half expected people to stare at her, but it was as though nothing had happened. The party was still in full swing; people were snacking on pork pies and drinking beer. In the kitchen, Alex and James were talking with a group of lads, Babs was snogging in a corner and Avril stabbing cocktail sticks into bits of cheese. It was all so normal, Suzie was half convinced she'd imagined the scene upstairs.

Backing out, she left Liz and retreated into the darkened sitting room. Spotting an empty chair, she slumped into it and let the music wash over her.

She came round to urgent voices, but it was just the Everleys singing, *Wake up, little Susie, wake up!* The first time she'd heard it with James, they'd both laughed. She expected to see him now, but it was Babs who was laughing and shaking her shoulder.

Trying to focus, she looked at her watch. 'Four o'clock? Where's James?'

'Oh, he and Alex went ages ago. Liz is upstairs, getting ready for bed – you're sharing, I hope you don't mind? First room on the left.'

When she went up, Suzie saw that it was the room she'd been in with James.

– o –

Depressed and hungover, she arrived home about midday, thankful that her mother was too busy preparing dinner to notice how ill she looked. Dad came back from his usual Sunday lunchtime visit to the pub – not late for once – and their meal was eaten in an atmosphere of armed truce.

It was a fine day, but she declined Connie's invitation to go out for a walk, saying there was a film she wanted to watch on TV. She stared blankly at the screen while her father fell asleep behind his Sunday paper. As the day passed, numbness gave way to confusion. Aware that she was different in some indefinable way, Suzie didn't know whether she was upset because of what James had done, or more hurt by the circumstances. She didn't understand. If it had followed on from their previous time together, she could hardly have blamed him. But to pounce on her like that – why? What was it all about?

And then she blamed herself, reflecting on how she'd behaved that night in his room. On his bed, half dressed, his for the taking. That's how he must have seen it.

Well, there was no changing the facts. It had happened. She was no longer a virgin. It was hardly a world-shattering event. Pragmatism said she was probably lucky not to have had it happen earlier. Parties, drink, fumbling in the dark. But everybody did it, didn't they? *No excuse*, her conscience repeated; *you'd have been happy to go on fumbling until the cows came home. Boys are different, you know that. This, my girl, is what you get for lying...*

But still, she couldn't see how or why James had changed so radically, from tender boyfriend to rampant male. It just didn't fit. Or was she simply a poor judge of character? A gullible fool? What really hurt though, was that she'd loved being with him. He was different; she'd liked him, trusted him. *And he'd betrayed that trust...*

Yet despite what he'd done, she couldn't imagine this was the end. If she could only understand why, she might be able to forgive him – maybe even go on seeing him...

The argument battled back and forth: hurt crying out against logic; logic sneering at emotion. But as the week wore on, hurt turned to anger. She half expected a letter from him; a note at least, to say he was sorry, carried away, never happen again, etc, etc. But there was nothing. By Friday, she couldn't rest. Come what may, she had to see him.

Liz hadn't been into the café all week, so she rang her at the office, asking her to call in before going home.

When Suzie put her plan into words, her friend pulled a face. 'Are you sure? It might not be such a good idea.'

'Why not?' she whispered. 'I want to know why he acted like that – why he did what he did. If I don't understand, how can I forgive him?'

'*Forgive him?* God, Suze! What planet are you on? Maybe he doesn't want to be forgiven? Maybe he's just a creep like his cousin?'

'Okay, I'm an idiot, but... Hang on, what did you just say? Have you finished with Alex?'

'Yes.'

'Why? Was it at the party?' As Liz nodded, Suzie said, 'Why didn't you say?'

Raising an eyebrow, Liz said, 'It was hardly the time, was it? Anyway, he's a pig and I don't want to talk about it.'

She would say no more. Catching a look from the manageress, Suzie returned to serving. But their brief exchange left her in even greater confusion.

– o –

Even if Liz thought she was mad, she had to see James. Just to look in his eyes and ask him why he'd taken advantage when she was drunk and incapable of stopping him. Incapable of responding, for heaven's sake. Before that night, her thoughts had veered along romantic avenues in which losing her virginity had been a mutual thing; even enjoyable. Well, it was supposed to be enjoyable, otherwise why would people do it? Feeling cheated as well as abused, Suzie wanted James to know just how hurt and angry she was. Maybe then, having talked it out, they could get back to where they were before it happened.

But she was not brave enough to march into the Blacksmith's Arms alone. Needing a reason for being there, after work she rang Babs from a call box and asked if she'd be in the pub the following evening. She said she would, so they agreed to meet up; meanwhile Suzie fudged the Liz question and claimed she'd got another date.

Saturdays in the café were always busy, so there was no chance to stand around worrying. Once home, she had to rush to catch the bus to Moorcliffe. Only as they left Denshaw behind did her nerve begin to wobble. A light shower of rain was turning into a downpour, and her spirits sank with it. For a moment, waiting for the bus to stop, Suzie was tempted to do the round tour and go home. Only fear of looking an idiot made her step off as planned.

Feeling scared and alone, her heart was pounding as she made her way through the car park and into the pub. Thank heavens, the girls were there in the back room, Babs with her new boyfriend, welcoming as ever, while Avril looked surprised to see her. Focusing on the girls, trying desperately to seem as though she was her usual happy self, she didn't see James. Or his cousin Alex. Only as she sat down did she realize she'd passed them at the bar.

'Oh, be a love, James,' Babs said as he set drinks on the table, 'get another half for Suzie, will you?'

She glanced up; their eyes met for a startled second before he looked away. 'Sure.'

It seemed an age before he returned. She caught a glance from Alex, at which he raised his glass with an ironic, 'Cheers,' and promptly turned away.

Suzie, it seemed, had taken James's seat. He stood behind her, leaning against the wall, listening to the chat but not joining in beyond the occasional comment. Unable to see him, Suzie felt as though every nerve was stretched to breaking point. Yet still she smiled and chatted, willing him

70

to move, say something, just give her reason to look round and speak.

At last her opportunity came. Babs, on the subject of college and the new term ahead, asked if Suzie had managed to do any painting. 'Oh, yes – thanks to James here...' She turned and looked up. 'You took some great photos, didn't you, James? Really helped my sketches along. The painting is almost finished...'

'Is it?'

'You should come and see it.'

Nodding like a donkey, he said lamely, 'Yeah, that'd be great...'

She wanted to kick him. Conversation stopped, she could feel everyone looking.

Babs laughed and said, 'You are good, Suzie. I haven't done a thing – I'll be rushing at the last minute, as usual. How about you, Avril?'

And then everyone was talking about getting stuff ready for the new term. Suzie stood up, feeling better now that she and James were almost face to face. 'I need to talk to you,' she hissed, but he refused to meet her gaze.

'What is there to say?'

'You could start with *sorry*.'

He coloured up, shrugged. 'Okay, I'm sorry.'

'Is that it?'

For the briefest moment, he looked lost, haunted. 'What else can I say?' he managed at last. He returned to studying his pint.

She turned, saw Alex staring at them, and suddenly felt stupid, the victim of some kind of conspiracy. Wanting to hide, to cry, she couldn't wait to get away.

Swallowing hard, she turned and picked up her bag. 'Sorry, Babs – got to go – bus to catch. See you later, okay?'

She was almost at the door when Babs came hurrying after her. 'Hey, Suzie, you forgot your brolly!' Handing it over, she saw her friend's face. 'Are you okay? What's wrong?'

'Nothing – it's fine – I'm fine. Honest – got to go.'

Babs squeezed her arm. 'See you in college, okay?'

'Yes, sure.' And with that she walked out into the rain.

Nine

There wasn't a bus for another half hour. She started walking, but despite the umbrella she was soon soaked. '*Stupid, stupid,*' she muttered between sobs, wondering how and why she'd ever thought she could change anything. Humiliated didn't even come close. James hadn't expected her to turn up tonight, and how she wished she hadn't. *Living on another planet?* Liz was right. James didn't want *her* – just the experience. He'd got what he wanted and that was that. Finito. Over. On to the next one.

There was a bus shelter on the main road, but the wind and rain felt like January, and her teeth were chattering by the time a bus came along.

Apart from the hall light, the house was in darkness when she reached home. She fumbled for her key, groaned when she saw her reflection in the hall mirror, and hurried upstairs to get ready for bed before her parents came home.

'You're back early,' Connie called as they came in a little while later. 'Are you all right up there?'

'Fine – I'm only just in.'

By the time her mother came up with a cup of tea, Suzie had combed out her hair, washed her face, and was in bed with a book.

'Your coat was wet – did you get caught in the rain?'

'I'd just missed a bus – had to walk to the junction.'

'You never walked down that dark lane on your own? That was a daft thing to do. Couldn't you have gone back inside – waited for the next one?'

'Didn't want to.'

'Why not?' Connie waited, but when her daughter didn't answer, she said, 'It was throwing it down at closing time, so we hung on for it to stop...' Bending closer, she whispered, 'Your Dad wanted to go to the Swan, but I said to him, *over my dead body* – I'm not going in there while *that woman* frequents the place...'

Suzie turned a page of her book.

'... so we went to the Liberal Club instead.'

'The *Liberal Club*? Since when was Dad a Liberal?'

'It's not about politics. Nicer people go in there.'

'Oh, good.' Suzie returned to her reading.

Connie stood for a moment, looking down at her daughter. 'You sure you're all right?'

'I'm *fine*, Mum, honestly – don't fuss.'

– o –

Next day, Suzie found herself answering similar questions from Liz. But when she'd given her a blow-by-blow account of the night before, all Liz said was, 'I told you so.' Pressed to explain why she'd given Alex the push, she said he was a stuck-up little snob, and that went for his cousin too. A couple of spoiled little rich boys, convinced they could have it all, including whichever girl they fancied.

'We've been used,' Liz said, 'and the sooner you get that through your head, Suzie, the sooner you'll get over it.'

'But James didn't seem that sort…'

'They never do to start with. But once they've got what they want – well, you've seen for yourself. Forget it – forget him – he's not bloody worth it.'

Her logic was all too clear. Aware of her home, her parents and the council estate, Suzie felt angry and humiliated all over again. Was it true they saw her and Liz as lesser beings, just because of where they lived? No wonder Liz was so bitter. But after they'd parted, with only a vague agreement to meet sometime soon, Suzie wondered at the depth of her friend's experience.

– o –

Liz, of course, was still working, while Suzie's job had ended. She had two weeks' break to get things ready for the new term, and to finish her painting.

While her mother was out, she unlocked the garden shed and turned the board to the light. At first, she could hardly bear to look at it. Then, on a deep breath, she forced herself to be objective. The picture was already the best thing she'd ever done, but it was not quite finished. A little more impasto to the foreground, and, to centre right, maybe the suggestion of an old stone house overshadowed by those towering rocks. It would make the rocks seem bigger, more threatening; and if she added a glimmer of light to the windows, it would add balance to the glowing mass of clouds on the left…

Representational – dirty word – but it was certainly dramatic. The thing was, she hated what it represented to her: weeks of work when she'd been happy, confident even. James approving her ideas, even helping with the photos; Suzie believing they were on the same wavelength. Trusting him, starting to believe she was important; while he was setting her up. Turning on her heel, she slammed the door shut.

Upstairs, she grabbed her sketch book, found a drawing she'd done of him, and scribbled charcoal all over it. The stick crumbled, but she kept on scratching until the paper was torn through. Ripping out the page she threw it at the bin.

What she really wanted to do was chuck the painting after it, but she'd have to break it first.

Only the thought of Rod Winter's sneer if she failed to show something, drove her back a couple of days later. Every dab of the brush felt like poking at a raw wound, made worse by the need for self-control. Touching her pallet knife to bottom left, Suzie gave way to a sudden stab of fury. As the knife broke on impact, again she rushed out cursing; thankful later that it was not a canvas.

– o –

Finding it hard to sleep at night, and even harder to wake in the mornings, once the painting was finished she languished in bed, reading novels until early afternoon. After her mother came home from her job, Suzie spent at least an hour listening to a litany of her father's sins. It wasn't that she was unsympathetic – Dad would try the patience of a saint – but Connie was like a hamster on a wheel, going over and over the same old ground. What he'd said, what she'd said, what that awful woman had done. But what had she done? So much of it was surmise and speculation. To say it was wearying didn't come close.

One evening, after Dad had slammed out of the house, Suzie could bear her mother's tirades no longer. 'Oh, for heaven's sake, Mum – why don't you leave him? Get a divorce – give us all some peace!'

Connie looked so shocked, it seemed she'd never considered it. Maybe she had, though, because after an anguished look, she said, 'And how would I manage for money?'

She said she couldn't afford to leave on the pittance she earned, and Suzie's Dad would never go – he was too well looked-after.

'Well then – don't look after him!'

'Don't be ridiculous – I can't feed you and not him! That's what the housekeeping's for!'

Defeated by such logic, Suzie shook her head. But her mother calmed down for a while after that.

On odd occasions over the next few days, she asked about Suzie's plans for the weekend. Would she be seeing Liz? When, for the third time, Suzie said she didn't know, Connie pressed a bit further.

'Has she got a new boyfriend?'

'Dunno – probably.'

'Oh, Liz – she's never reliable, is she? All over you one minute, and then you don't see her for ages. Anyway, what about that Moorcliffe boy you were keen on? You're not seeing him on Saturday night?'

'That's off,' she muttered.

'Oh, I see. I wondered why you were so down in the dumps.' A longish pause while Connie poured more tea. 'So what have you been doing? Did you get your painting finished?'

'Yes.'

A heavy sigh. 'Well then, aren't you going to show it?'

Like a martyr going to the stake, Suzie dragged herself out to the shed, and turned the hardboard round for her mother to see.

'Oh! Suzie, love, that's – well, it's just *marvellous!* Did you really do that?' Connie beamed with delight. 'I just love sunsets – and those colours…'

When she'd dabbed her eyes and enthused some more, Connie insisted on bringing it into the house for Suzie's Dad to see. But when Joe Wallis came home, clearly tensed for another full-frontal attack, he seemed bemused when he walked into the lounge and saw Suzie's picture propped on the sideboard.

'What's that? Did you do it?'

'Of course, Dad – who else?'

For what seemed an age, he just gazed at it. 'Those rocks up at Moorcliffe?'

'Yes.'

'You've made them bigger.' It sounded like an accusation. Maths was his thing, artistic licence a foreign concept. A pause while he studied some more, and then his final judgement. 'A bit grim, isn't it?'

Suzie could have kicked him. 'Yes, Dad,' she ground out, 'it's a bit grim. As we say in college, I've been exploring the darker side. And you know what? It says exactly what I feel about you and Mum!'

With that, she stomped off upstairs, grabbed her bag and went out.

– o –

'I can see you've put some feeling into this,' Rod Winter said when he saw it. 'Dark, brooding, a sense of threat, somehow...' He shot her a penetrating look. 'Keep this up, Suzie, and we might make a painter of you yet!'

She was so ridiculously pleased she had a lump in her throat. Praise from Rod Winter – it almost made up for the anguish she'd felt, finishing the damn thing.

Slipping back into routine with the new term, she threw herself into work. Easier, somehow, because most of her old friends from Dress had moved on, while others of her year were focusing on Graphic Design, Sculpture, Pottery or even Painting. Babs, who'd been in the year below, had now moved up and was taking the same classes as Suzie.

For the first day or so she felt like the troublesome kid

kept behind in school, but it wore off, especially when she realized that despite the somewhat chaotic fun of the previous two years, she'd learned a few things. One step ahead of her bemused classmates, it gave her some satisfaction to reduce Rod Winter's pretentious twaddle to simple terms.

All was going well; she was feeling better and had almost, but not quite, put James Fielding out of her mind when he was back with a vengeance. A couple of weeks into the new term, Suzie realized she should have had her period a week ago. At first, she was simply concerned; she'd never been like clockwork, and sometimes it was well over a month between shows. Getting down on her knees every night, she prayed for a gush of blood. *Painful as you like, Lord, I don't mind, it'll serve me right for being such an idiot…*

But then another week went by, and by the fourth week of term she was trying not to think the obvious and praying for a miracle. And then, *what if I'm really pregnant,* became, *what am I going to do?*

She dropped a note to Liz, saying she needed to see her, but not at home; could they meet in Heatherley? She guessed Liz would be free on Saturday lunchtime, and also that she could read between the lines. They'd discussed the possibility already, Liz doing her best to reassure Suzie with words like *shock* and *anxiety,* and – quite frankly – refusing to believe her friend could be pregnant after one quick poke.

'You could try gin and a hot bath,' she suggested. This while sipping at gin and bitter lemon in the Old White Rose. Suzie had a glass of orange; the smell of beer as they entered the pub had been revolting.

'You're joking?'

'No, it's supposed to work.'

They went to the off-licence and between them scraped enough together to purchase a small bottle of the cheapest gin on the shelf. Giving Suzie a hug, Liz wished her the best of luck.

That evening, while her parents were out, Suzie consumed several large gins, easing them down with orange cordial before running a scalding hot bath. Within seconds she felt like a boiled lobster, nerves screaming, head spinning; but there was no way she could bear it. Letting the cold tap run, she lay down and considered drowning herself. God, no, not that. What else did people do? Perhaps she could cut her wrists and bleed to death?

She sat up and reached for Dad's razor, extracted the blade and laid it against her wrist. But even the faintest scratch repulsed her. The idea of doing herself harm, she realized, was even worse than admitting she was pregnant. Perhaps she wasn't. She didn't *feel* pregnant. Not that she knew what it was supposed to feel like. Perhaps she was suffering from some unnamed illness. Something incurable. Perhaps she would die. Well, it'd serve her right if she did.

Nothing happened after the hot bath, except next morning she felt sick and had a headache from the gin.

Sometime later – around the time her next period was due – she began to notice that her jeans and skirts felt tight. She measured her waistline, saw it was over an inch bigger than normal and thanked providence for sloppy sweaters and the old shirts she wore as painting smocks.

In bed at night she tossed and turned, wondering how she was going to tell her parents. They'd done so much for her, supported her crazy ambitions, found the money to buy her a sewing machine, paid up for all the fabrics and paints and stuff, which they couldn't really afford; when other kids her age were out earning a living. They wanted her to make something of opportunities they'd never had – not blow everything on a sordid little grope in the dark.

She couldn't bear for them to know what she'd done. That she'd lied, got drunk, and let some stupid idiot take advantage of her.

Not that she thought they'd throw her out, not seriously; but the *anger*, the *blame* she knew was coming her way was terrifying. At thought of her Dad's voice, shouting, accusing, she felt sicker than ever.

Ten

Misery was compounded by constant sniping at home, distracted only briefly by the worldwide shock of President Kennedy's death. Glued to the TV news, to repeats of that drive through Dallas, even her parents' petty war was forgotten.

As November became December, the tragedy in America paled beside more urgent concerns. With the Christmas holidays looming, all hope fled. Suzie didn't need Liz's prompts, she knew she had to tell her mother. She'd been screwing herself up for days, but in the end, dropping the bombshell was easy.

Saturday afternoon, a fine day, and Dad was out at a rugby match while Mum was cleaning windows in the lounge. Suzie came downstairs, made a pot of tea and took it through. Quaking, wondering how she was going to begin the conversation, she sat down. With a heavy sigh, she poured the tea. Connie left what she was doing, turned to look at her, and asked what was wrong. Suzie shook her head, tried to speak, and was suddenly choked by tears.

Her mother stared as though she was seeing her daughter for the first time. 'What's wrong, love? Can't you tell me?'

As Suzie shook her head again, Connie said, 'You're not expecting, are you?'

Suzie nodded. Like a rag doll, her mother collapsed into a chair. 'No,' she gasped, as though all the air had been punched from her body. 'Oh, no, Suzie – not *you!*'

'I'm sorry, Mum – I'm *sorry*...'

'But... But you've always been so *sensible*,' Connie whispered at last. 'How? When did it happen? Who? Not that boy you were seeing – him up at Moorcliffe?'

Suzie nodded. When she dared to look up, she wished she hadn't. Her mother's face was grey, her body slack against the chair.

'But that's *ages* ago... Good God,' Connie said suddenly, pulling herself upright, 'how far on are you?'

'About three months. Maybe a bit more...'

'Oh, Suzie!' she wailed. 'Why didn't you say so *before?* And I never noticed – oh, dear God, forgive me! So tied up with my own problems...' Tears were streaming now. 'And you've been worrying about it all this time? Why on earth didn't you tell me sooner?'

'I've been so *scared*, Mum...' And with that she was in her mother's arms and they were both weeping. 'I've been so stupid – after all you've done for me – I've let you and Dad down...'

'What? Don't be silly – you're our daughter. Nothing changes that.' Sniffing, searching for a handkerchief, Connie wiped her eyes and reached for her cigarettes. With a trembling hand she flicked her lighter and handed the packet to Suzie. 'Go on – have one. I know you smoke – known for ages.'

Despite the tears, after a few deep drags, Suzie felt better; light-headed, even, but that was the relief. Not because she'd admitted it, but that Connie wasn't berating her, simply wanting to know the how and why of it. Haltingly, she described the night of the party, and most of what she could recall up to that awful moment in the bedroom.

'So, you were drunk. And what about him – was he drunk too?'

Suzie said he must have been – it was the only explanation.

'Could he have put something in your drink?'

Until Connie asked the question, Suzie hadn't even considered it. 'I don't know…'

'No, I don't suppose you would. But it sounds like that to me. The stupid fool could have slipped a vodka into your glass and you wouldn't have tasted it.'

'I don't know, Mum. He might have done – but as I said before, he just didn't seem the type. Mind you, I didn't imagine he would… you know…'

'Take advantage? Well, clearly he did. And clearly,' she added, 'he needs to know about this!'

Connie's fighting spirit was back, and that in itself was a relief. Mum was taking charge, Mum would sort it out. Briefly, she voiced the idea of abortion; then dismissed it as being too late and too risky, and illegal besides. The marriage question was soon disposed of: in Connie's opinion, forcing a man to 'do the right thing' by a girl was always a mistake.

How did Suzie feel about it?

'Why would I want to? He didn't want to know me afterwards.'

Only when Connie asked if she was able to contact this youth, did they see the problem. James would be back in Durham, Suzie said, and no doubt going to his parents for the Christmas holidays – Aldershot, rather than Moorcliffe. Suzie had no contact address.

'Well, his aunt and uncle will know where he is. Ask them.'

Suzie quailed at the thought, wondering what reason to give for wanting to get in touch with James. Not the truth, that was for sure.

'As for telling your Dad,' Connie said, dragging Suzie back to more immediate things, 'you'd better leave it to me. Did you say you were going to Liz's tonight? Well, get yourself off now, and don't come back till tomorrow afternoon.'

'But what will Dad say?'

'He'll swear and curse, you can be sure of that. But if you're not here, it'll give him chance to calm down.' With that, she hugged Suzie and kissed her. 'I know your Dad's hard, but just remember he loves you…'

Did he? Suzie wasn't so sure. Dad never said so, never showed affection. All he seemed to do was criticize. Well, he'd got plenty to criticize this time.

Although she dreaded facing him, the situation was now out of her hands. Somehow, as Connie had promised, it would be dealt with.

– o –

Relieved and tearful, Suzie packed a toothbrush and set off for Heatherley. When Liz heard the news, she hugged her friend. 'Oh, thank God – you've no idea how worried I've been…'

It seemed Mrs Bradley knew already, although she didn't let on until Suzie told her, when she had plenty to say about thoughtless men and empty promises. Even if there'd been no promises, Suzie thought, it was comforting to talk and not be judged.

Only next day, when she was on the bus going home, did her spirits sink back to zero. Thinking about her Dad, she envisaged tirades against feckless students, not to mention the folly of art school and all that tosh about 'exploration'. Well, he couldn't say she wasn't exploring real life now, could he? Being pregnant and unmarried was about as real as you could get.

Sunday afternoon, the sky was grey and the streets deserted. The few paces from the bus stop felt like crossing the Atacama Desert. Sweating, her mouth dry, Suzie crept into the house, standing like a stranger in the hall, not knowing whether to head for the kitchen or bolt upstairs to her room.

In the end, she croaked a greeting and went to the kitchen. She'd just put the kettle to boil when her Dad came through from the lounge.

Head down, shoulders bowed, she didn't turn.

'Come on, Suzie, love – this is your Dad...' With that he reached out, turning her to face him. And then his arms were around her, he was giving her a gentle hug and she was crying her eyes out. 'It'll be all right, love,' he said, kissing her forehead. 'It's not the end of the world...'

All she could think afterwards was that it was the first time he'd hugged her since she was a little girl.

– o –

Whatever Connie and Joe's personal problems were, this crisis swept them aside. As Connie told her later, Joe's initial reaction had been one of fury – less at his daughter, more at the idiot youth for using her and ruining her life. But once he'd calmed down, they'd talked things over and reached some kind of agreement.

'Let's just be clear about this,' Dad said when they were all settled in the lounge. 'Your mother says you don't want to marry him?'

'No, I don't.'

'What about the baby?'

Baby? It was hard to grasp the idea. Yes, babies were cute and cuddly, but beyond that, she'd never given them much thought. Babies belonged in other families; she'd never been close to one – at least, not in an emotional sense. She could only think that this – this *situation* – had been forced on her. It wasn't what she wanted. She'd had a future in view; she wasn't ready to think of marriage and children. Certainly not marriage to James Fielding; and after what he'd done, she didn't want responsibility for his offspring, either.

But all the anger in the world couldn't stop her throat from closing at the question, and her eyes filling with tears. Sniffing, she dashed them away. 'Mum says it can be adopted, so yes, that's what I want.'

'Right. So long as you're sure.' Joe Wallis cleared his throat. 'In that case, there's no point everybody knowing about it. You'll finish college, and maybe go to Aunt Dolly's up in Richmond...'

Aunt Dolly was Dad's widowed sister. Uncle Bert had been killed in the war, and Dolly had brought up her family single-handed. She was a kind woman, one of Suzie's favourite relatives; if anyone would understand, Dolly would. Suzie breathed a sigh of relief.

'Your Mum'll write to her, and we'll settle any costs, so don't worry about that. Anyway, you'll be seeing the Doc tomorrow, so we'll take the rest of it from there...'

– o –

Sitting in the silent waiting room with her mother, Suzie felt as though her condition was obvious. Not only did the receptionist give her a look, it seemed as though other folk waiting were also taking an interest. *A girl in here with her mother – oh, aye, what's that about?* Then a young woman came in with a snuffling baby, and all eyes turned in their direction. When the baby began to cry, smiles turned to frowns and half a dozen pairs of eyes returned to studying the floor.

Suzie picked up a magazine – an ancient copy of *Woman's Weekly* – and flicked through, looking for a short story. Oh, God, knitting patterns – for babies. Feeling sick, she returned it to the pile and tried to ignore the frazzled mother and squalling infant.

Her name was called: she went through with Connie, and, as Dr Illingworth looked up, it seemed to her his expression changed at once from enquiring smile to one of weary resignation. He'd known her since she was a toddler, had seen her through the usual childhood ailments; and now he was about to pronounce news that was hardly news at all.

He listened, asked questions and examined her. With genuine sadness, he announced his verdict. 'Yes, I'm afraid so. About twelve to fourteen weeks, I'd say. Does that fit?' When Suzie said it did, and gave him the date, he turned and looked at her. 'You're certain?'

'Absolutely. It was just the one time.'

'And you were a virgin until then?'

'Yes!'

Her mother started to explain, but Dr Illingworth wanted it from Suzie. His frown deepened as she gave a short explanation. By the time she'd finished, his mouth was a tight line. 'Well, my dear, I'm grieved to hear it. Deeply grieved. All I can say at the moment is that we'll do our best to help. I'll refer you to some people in Bradford – they'll contact you for an interview. If you're set on adoption, they'll take it from there.

'But in the meantime,' he added grimly, 'this young man must be made to face up to his responsibilities. Even if his assistance is purely financial. Get in touch with him – find out his address – and try to see him. He needs to know!'

– o –

That afternoon, Suzie walked down to the phone box; shaking so much she had to walk past and come back before she could trust her voice not to give her away. Forcing brightness into her tone, when Mrs Thornton answered, she said squeakily, 'Oh, hello – I don't know if you remember me? I'm James's friend, Suzie – you know, the art student? I'm sorry to bother you, but I want to return some photos to him – and I'm not sure if he's still in Durham?'

Mrs T said yes, she did remember Suzie, and how was she? How was the painting coming along? Suzie was forced to chat on, feigning enthusiasm for the picture and James's help. Eventually she got what she wanted – and more. An address for his parents in Aldershot; but a short pause was followed by an apology and the news that James wouldn't be there yet, he'd still be in Durham.

'I don't have the address, but I've got a phone number for the house he shares...'

'Oh, that's great,' Suzie said, scribbling the number down. She thanked her profusely and brought the conversation to a close. Replacing the phone, leaning against the box, she felt as though she'd run a marathon.

What to do? Go home and think about it, or phone him now? It was mid-afternoon, he could be in a lecture, or maybe even in his room, studying. It was worth a try; maybe someone would answer and she'd get the address. But not just at the moment. Needing to calm herself, Suzie walked on to the local shop and bought some cigarettes.

Twenty minutes later, she was back, praying for success and sufficiently primed to give James Bloody Fielding the shock of his life. The phone rang out for more than a minute; she was about to give up when a male voice answered. It sounded like James but she needed to be sure.

Pressing coins into the box, she said, 'I want to speak to James Fielding...' and relief swept over her as he replied.

'James – this is Suzie. Remember me?'

He said yes, of course; and, after the briefest pause, asked how she'd got the phone number.

'Never mind that, I've got something more important to say…' After a shaky breath, her words came out in a rush. 'Actually, I'm just back from the doctor's. He says I'm pregnant – I thought you ought to know.'

There was no exclamation of shock, just a long silence. At last, as she was ticking off the seconds of this long-distance call, she heard him say faintly that he was sorry, but he couldn't marry her.

'*What?*' It took a second to take in what he'd just said. And then she was furious. 'Don't flatter yourself! I wouldn't have *you*,' she snapped, 'if you came free with a packet of tea!'

There was no reply, but she could hear him breathing. As the pips went, she pushed more money into the box.

'I haven't told anybody else – yet. But I need to see you,' she said urgently, 'I know it's not exactly *convenient*, but it's got to be soon. Give me your address so we can make arrangements…' Into the silence, she said, 'Look, I've got your Aldershot address, so you'd better co-operate – otherwise, I'll be writing to your parents…'

Eleven

It was difficult, he wrote in answer to her letter, but he'd be leaving Durham on the Thursday before Christmas. He could catch an early train, break his journey at York and travel on to Leeds, if she'd be willing to meet him there. He gave her some train times and asked which would be most suitable. He suggested meeting in the station buffet.

What Suzie hadn't told him, was that her mother would be there. Not only did she need a witness to whatever was agreed, Connie had insisted on meeting him.

'Just so long as you don't lose your temper, Mum.'

'Oh, Suzie, give me some credit – I'm not a complete fool, you know!'

Term at Iredale was also drawing to a close. Prompted by her father, Suzie knew she had to speak to Rod Winter. Had her tutor been anyone else she might have told the truth, but he hardly deserved it. 'Call me Rod', hadn't changed, he still had little of any worth to say, still preserved his god-like distance.

When she finally got her few minutes alone with him – 'I hope this won't take long, I've got a meeting in five minutes' –

Suzie's practised words came out in a rush. She thanked him for taking her back this term, said she was sorry if she'd denied someone else a place in college, but she'd decided to leave.

That brought him up short. All at once he was focused on her, not his meeting. 'Why?'

'Well, a combination of reasons, really.' She looked down, studying her bitten nails and paint-stained hands. 'You see, I'm not happy at home – and I don't feel I'm making much progress here… So, I'm heading for London.'

'Oh.' He frowned. 'London's a big place. Have you got somewhere to go? A job?'

'Well, I'll be staying with my aunt for a while. But yes, I have got a job lined up.'

'Doing what?'

Suzie lifted her chin, took a deep breath for the fiction. 'Selfridges. Window-dressing…'

Stick that in your pipe and smoke it, she thought, striding back to the Life Class.

That evening, she packed up what was important of her college work, said cheerio to the friends who were still around, and went home. She didn't tell anyone that she wouldn't be back. Rod Winter she could lie to; her friends, never.

– o –

The prospect of meeting James again made her feel vulnerable, and that made her angry. Searching her wardrobe for something smart that would fit, made her angrier still.

Faced with a slew of clothes across the bed, Suzie knew she would have to spend the next few weeks making herself some maternity wear; and, in the next minute, realized that all the clothes she loved would be out of fashion by the time she could fit into them again. In a foul humour she slipped elastic around a skirt button, pulled on a loose jumper, donned her winter coat and went downstairs. Connie said she looked nice, but that didn't help.

The bus journey to Leeds seemed to take forever. At last they came to City Square, grim under a grey sky. As a child she'd always wanted to stop and look at the Black Prince statue, but today the naked nymphs caught her attention. Suzie found herself wondering what they had to do with anything, apart from advertising Victorian taste for sexy statues in public places, and prudery in private.

'We've got twenty minutes yet,' Connie said. 'Do you want to go in and wait or have a walk first?'

'Oh, let's look at a few shops.'

Ignoring the station entrance, they headed towards the nearest shopping street. Usually, Suzie was intent on studying line and style in dress shop windows, but today her thoughts were elsewhere. Having checked her watch for the umpteenth time, she finally agreed it was time to head for the station buffet.

Against a wash of nondescript colour, she spotted James at once. Waiting at a table facing the door, he stood as Suzie approached, darting a look of alarm as she introduced her mother.

'Hello James,' Connie said. 'Don't worry, I'm not here to cause a scene.'

His glance flickered between the two of them. Clearing his throat, he said, 'Can I – can I get you a cup of tea or something? Or – or would you prefer to go somewhere else?'

Connie glanced around. The place was crowded. 'How about the bar? I don't know about you, James, but I could stand something stronger than tea...'

A few minutes later they were seated in a quiet corner, Connie and Suzie sipping at sherry, while James gulped at a pint of bitter. Connie opened the proceedings by saying she wasn't there to point the finger of blame, although she was naturally upset that her daughter should be in this situation.

'I think Suzie's made it clear she doesn't want to marry you. But,' she added, giving James a hard look, 'what I want to know is that you accept responsibility.'

He looked scared. 'Yes – yes, of course.'

'Good.' Connie relaxed visibly, while Suzie continued to glare, watching him fumble with a packet of cigarettes, hands shaking.

Nudged by her mother, she said quietly, 'You'll be relieved to know I've decided to have the baby adopted – but that's a long way off yet. Arrangements have still to be made.'

Acknowledging that, he offered her a cigarette. Abruptly, Suzie shook her head. 'I've finished college – obviously, I can't carry on in this state. And what I was hoping to do is out of the question now.'

Nodding, clearing his throat, James said, 'So when – when's the baby due?'

God above – could he not work it out?

'Last week in May,' she said between gritted teeth. She knew James's birthday was the 28th, because once, in the days of innocence, she'd read about star signs and wanted to know if his sign was compatible with hers. *Gemini* and *Aquarius* were supposed to be good together – which only went to show how wrong such nonsense could be.

Swallowing hard, he said, 'So what happens with regard to – to the adoption?'

'Not sure. My interview's next week.' She paused, biting her lip. 'I'll let you know.'

'Yes – yes, of course.' Nervously, he paused, then said quickly, 'Only please don't send anything to Aldershot. If you have to give my address, make sure it's Durham – I'll get it next term.'

Studying him, Connie said, 'What about your parents – will you tell them?'

Startled, he looked up. 'Oh, no – they'd never understand.'

'I think you'd be surprised,' Connie said gently. 'They are your parents, after all.'

At that, James stubbed out his cigarette with what seemed unnecessary force. 'You don't know my father.'

'No, I don't, but what about your mother? I'm sure she'd want to know.' As he continued to shake his head, she added, 'Look, this has been a shock for you, I can see that. But when you've had chance to take it in, you'll need someone to talk to…' When he did not respond, she said, 'If I were your mother, I'd want to know.'

'No – sorry – couldn't possibly.'

Suzie could see determination in the set of his mouth, and desperation in his eyes. Before she could stop herself, she said, 'It made *me* feel better, talking to Mum…'

Connie smiled and squeezed her hand; but James would not be persuaded. At last, he looked up at Suzie, holding her glance for a long moment. 'I'm sorry – so sorry. I never meant for this to happen. It was…'

But whatever it was, he didn't say. Head bowed, after a moment, he looked at his watch and said he really should be going. As he gathered up his belongings, they stood, the table between them. Seeing emotion in his eyes as he said goodbye, Suzie's own sight blurred. Turning away, searching for hate, she found only sorrow.

'He's not what I imagined,' Connie said after he'd gone. 'I'm not surprised you trusted him.'

Twelve

After talking things over with Cathy, Suzie was restless. Age gave a different perspective, but with so many emotions raised from the dead, and so many questions left hanging, her mind was darting around like a flea. From James Fielding to her mother, and from Connie to the girls, wondering what she should say to Jo and Sara.

Thinking about Sara reminded her of business matters set aside due to the book's publication, but even though the local media fuss had died down, she still had commitments to fulfil: a book signing in York, a talk for the WI in Heatherley and yet another for a local Ramblers' group. She couldn't keep dwelling on James or his request, it was too distracting.

As she'd already discovered, public speaking was nerve-racking, different from challenges faced on the Camino, and different again from struggling as a writer. But as her publisher said, it took the book out of bookshops and into the wider world.

She could see its importance – basically, it was advertising the product – and during her interviews she'd usually managed to include a mention of her other 'product', the shop in York.

Its name, *The Wallis Collection*, was her little joke, a play on words referring to the famous collection of art in London – one of the reasons she'd chosen to use her maiden name for the business. Of course, the pictures she displayed were not Old Masters – far from it – although amongst the prints she did feature original paintings by local artists, and back in the day, many of them were by her late husband, Freddie Lawrence.

For several years, the shop had given Suzie an opportunity to use her skills as an interior designer. Updating old furniture, restoring small items, making *objets d'art* out of battered boxes and broken jewellery, was not only satisfying, it made a reasonable income. Nowadays, Sara was in charge, and of necessity the contents were less antique and more the kind of quirky items to attract modern customers. Suzie still did much of the buying and restoring – work that had been interrupted by her trip to Spain and writing the book.

She longed to get back to it – focusing on the shop's requirements might just push James Fielding back where he belonged.

– o –

Sara didn't open on Mondays, but Suzie knew she'd be busy catching up with paperwork after her holiday. Tuesday was better, when she was likely to be in the shop and working alone. It wasn't the place for long conversations, but that was the point – Suzie didn't want to say more than necessary about her meeting with James.

And really, she reflected on her way to York, if she hadn't already mentioned him, she might have kept it to herself.

Parking outside the walls, she walked into the heart of town by Monk Bar, her spirits uplifted by the fine day. Catching a view of the Minster, she smiled in its direction as she crossed Deangate and carried on to her own little bit of York. Well, not strictly her own, not anymore, but still she was proud of it. Like a child, she thought, growing from small beginnings, changing its face over time, but still there.

The window looked good. An artist's easel displayed a modern painting she hadn't seen before, a storage chest was draped with colourful fabrics echoing the Clarice Cliff pottery on the updated dresser. As Sara spotted her and grinned, Suzie went inside, complimenting her on the window display.

'Anyway, how was the holiday?' she asked as they hugged and greeted each other.

'Great,' Sara countered, laughing. 'How was the literary lunch?'

'Oh, make me some coffee and I'll tell you...'

But first, she insisted on hearing Sara's news. Thanks to the business, family holidays had been out of the question for several years, and Suzie wanted to know how young George and Grace had enjoyed themselves. And on the shop front, how Millie, their assistant, had coped while both Sara and Suzie were absent.

The answer seemed to be enjoyment all round. 'So you're happy to leave Millie in charge?'

'Absolutely – she was fine. But tell me about the lunch – how did it go?'

After describing the other authors – and delighting Sara with the story of Mick the punk rocker – they were interrupted by first one customer and then another. Suzie was wondering if she could slip away without having to mention James Fielding, when Sara shook her head.

'No, don't rush off,' she murmured, 'I want to hear about the old friend who turned up...'

Reaching for a duster, Suzie glanced at the customer, mimed work and went upstairs to make herself useful. The array of furniture, pictures and knick-knacks would have challenged a Victorian housemaid – and looking around often occupied customers for extraordinary lengths of time. Not always with a sale at the end of it, although she gathered the current one had found what she was looking for. Hearing the door close, Suzie took a deep breath and went back down.

'You know, love,' she said hesitantly, 'about that friend I mentioned – I'm not sure this is a good time. The thing is, I didn't want to talk about it over the phone…'

Sara's smile became concerned. 'Why ever not?'

'Well, you see, the man who turned up after the book-signing was an old flame of mine – from my teenage years…'

Her expression must have said it all, because Sara's jaw dropped. 'Oh no! Not that one – the one you told us about?'

'The very same.'

Struck dumb for a moment, Sara shook her head. 'The total shit – how dare he?'

'Long story…'

But it was surprising, she thought afterwards, how such a traumatic event could be reduced to so few words. A brief outline of who James was, and why he'd come, was all that was necessary for Sara to condemn him out of hand.

'I hope you told him where to go?'

'I did, but…'

'But what? It's none of his bloody business!'

'Yes, but the reason I'm telling you – and I'll have to tell Jo when I get the chance – is that he's made me think. I mean, I never even thought about searching before, but now…'

'You think you might?' Sara whispered. As Suzie nodded she put her arms around her and gave her a long hug. 'It's a big step, Mum – are you sure?'

'I'm not sure of anything, love, and that's the truth.' Clearing her throat, she forced a smile and said, 'Anyway, I can't even think about it for the moment – I've got far too much on. But when I'm ready, I'd like to talk it over with the two of you. When Jo comes up next time, we'll have a chat about it then.'

Sara had asked how and why James had become a priest, and Suzie wondered about that too. For the moment, however, other questions were uppermost. *Why* did James take advantage of her like that? She'd always blamed herself, but recalling things said by Liz, Suzie wondered what else was going on at the time. With more than enough to occupy her, Suzie found she could ignore it during the day; the nights, however, were a different matter. That was when James sprang to mind; when she found herself going over past events as well as their recent meeting. He was even present in her dreams.

Every free day she had, she went out walking – it calmed her mind and helped her sleep, but it was never enough to last. As Cathy's husband had advised, she went to the surgery, saw her own GP, and after a weepy consultation, came away with a prescription for some mild tranquillisers. After that, anxiety dulled and sleep came more easily.

She was coping quite well until the day of her talk to the local Ramblers. It was just a month since the lunch in Iredale, and in a couple of weeks – May 28th – it would be her son's 40th birthday.

And James's 60th…

That cruel twist of fate – bringing her son into the world on James's birthday – had ensured she could never think of one without the other. As the years passed, she'd pray for her son, that he was in a good home, and most of all, that he was loved. Inevitably, she'd also wonder what James was doing, and whether he was thinking along similar lines. James knew the date, of course – Suzie hadn't told him, but Liz had.

— o —

The last of her bookings as a speaker went well – so well, that before she left people were discussing the possibilities of walking the Camino themselves. Having sold out of her small stock of books, Suzie came home happy but shattered, expecting to fall into sleep at once. But despite the book she was reading – and despite the tablets – her mind refused to switch off, going over every aspect of the evening. When that was done, she started worrying the major problem all over again.

After a few hours' sleep, she woke with a vivid a dream of derelict property – and her mother's voice, clear as though she was by her side, insisting she could do something with this place... That they should be together in Denshaw, of all places, was odd; she didn't ever recall dreaming about it before. More unsettling was the location, Crossgate, her father's haunt during the troubled years. The property – neglected on the outside, and worse within – was alarmingly real, but the weirdest part was that Connie, who detested Crossgate, was urging her to buy it.

Crazy. Her mother would never have invested time, effort or money in property older than she was – and certainly not there. Yet in the dream she was insistent, while Suzie, protesting, was pulling away. Wide awake now, Suzie couldn't shake off her mother's voice. *Come on, love, you can do it – you'll soon get it sorted...*

Downstairs, she stood for a while looking at her mother's photo on the dresser. Connie's half-smile seemed particularly knowing, as though she knew far more than she was saying.

With the dream upfront, it seemed to Suzie that a walk over the tops was the order of the day. Maybe it was time to lay a few ghosts.

'All right, Mum, you win...'

– o –

The most direct route was through Heatherley, then a climb towards Denshaw; from there she could return by a different route. Usually, she avoided the village and could not recall the last time she'd driven through the council estate. Fighting reluctance, she told herself it would be interesting to see her childhood home again. Unconvinced, she headed in that direction anyway.

The way to town was fairly level but climbing Heatherside Ridge was a challenge. Despite having used it when she was training for her Spanish walk, she'd almost forgotten how steep it was. Worth it, though; looking back over the valley was such a joy, especially on a clear day. As a child, Suzie had often walked to this point with her parents; but that was from the opposite direction, half a century ago. Would she be able to find those old field paths? Deciding to take a chance, she walked on, spotting a stile and sandy path going in roughly the right direction.

A coppice of stunted trees gave shade for a short stretch, and when she emerged she could see Denshaw in the distance. *Named for the Danes who settled here*, her primary school teacher had said. Under a clear sky it looked bigger than she recalled, nestling in a dip below the next moorland ridge. With no tall chimneys it was almost unrecognisable. The old woollen mills were long gone, replaced by supermarkets, DIY outlets and houses. On this side of town, she could see how they'd mushroomed, reaching out into fields where she and Cathy had played as children. Pausing to view the changes, feeling a well of reluctance bubbling afresh, Suzie wondered why she was doing this. Did she really want to see the old place? Surely memory was enough.

'It wasn't all bad,' she murmured, 'you had fun as a kid. It was only latterly...'

Pressing on, leaving the fields behind, she saw that the newer houses were much like any other modern estate, with neat gardens, a parade of local shops. It was only as she came to what had been the council houses, built in the 1950s, that everything looked smaller, meaner than she remembered. Utilitarian was the word, with no pretence to style. On what had been her street, once-red bricks were now a dull brown. Some well-tended gardens and trees here and there, but their old house looked tired and unloved, the front garden just a square of parched grass.

Grim, her father would have said. Not then perhaps; but looking at it now, it seemed to embody all the unhappiness of that time. Suzie felt desperately sad, for her parents as well as herself. Approaching the bus stop, she found herself remembering journeys to and from school, and later, to Iredale and Leeds. And to Moorcliffe, she thought with a jolt, raising her eyes to where a distant hill met the cloudless sky. Standing there, Suzie relived the pain that view had given her – every clear day for month after month. Eventually, she'd schooled herself not to look.

With a sigh, she turned away, downhill, towards the centre of old Denshaw. Even at a stroll, it took less time than she remembered. Differences kept catching her eye: cars whizzing past but no people; an old barn converted into flats; a new housing development where Crossfield Mill once stood. But that was nothing compared to Crossgate. She'd been expecting soot-blackened stonework, yet everything here was golden, polished, new. No, not new, just sand-blasted into the 21st century, with shiny paintwork and only two of the original four pubs left. Even the market cross had been moved. The Parish Church was still there, though; shadowy as ever, squinting between the trees like an old lady behind net curtains.

Stopped in her tracks, she looked around, trying to reconcile this new picture with the old one. Connie, she thought, would hardly know this place. Crossgate, where Dad liked to hang out with his cronies; where he'd met *that woman*, and the battles had begun in earnest.

It took Suzie a moment to recognise the building on the corner. Now it was pristine, but a derelict version had been part of that vivid dream.

Very strange, but impossible to ignore the significance. A load of old rubbish from the past, that's what the dream suggested. And it all started here, with misery at home and a burning desire to break out, escape, seek life and fun with her friends. It reminded her of how she'd longed to be eighteen, believing she'd be grown-up by then, able to do her own thing, escape to London, carve a future for herself. Not stuck in dreary old Denshaw, with all the rows and the news and *Coronation Street* twice a week.

It was all very well her Dad saying it was good to see northern life portrayed on screen – as far as Suzie was concerned, it was too close to home. But maybe that was what the dream was saying and what her mother meant: it was time to sort things out. Look at the past, battle with it, try to make sense of it. But dear God, she thought, sinking onto an old folks' bench nearby, she was exhausted already, and this was just the beginning.

Whether she liked it or not, James Fielding was back in her life. A different man? Older, yes; wiser, maybe. And here she was in Denshaw, faced by the renovated present while the past flickered like black and white film from a distant era.

She'd considered walking further – maybe as far as Moorcliffe – but now she felt hollow, unfit. Only the thought of home gave her the energy to walk back.

Turning away from Crossgate, Suzie followed a steep country lane which led past farms and smallholdings to the top of Heatherside Ridge. Reaching the rocky crest, she found a place to sit and think. Way below, the sight of the little market town nestling in the valley brought a lump to her throat. Just a few miles from her dull childhood home, Heatherley was colourful, open, different. For Suzie, if not for her old friend Liz, it had always been a place of safety and content.

Perhaps not least, Suzie thought, because she couldn't see Moorcliffe from there. Turning to look back, she could see its shadow clearly now on that distant Pennine rise. Someday soon, she would have to go there and face it. Nothing would settle until she had answers, and James Fielding was the one to ask. She needed to see him, read his reactions, push hard until he told the truth. Although she hated the thought of inviting him into her home, reason said it was the only way.

– o –

Early evening was the best time to call, but still Suzie hesitated before picking up the phone. Heart racing, she keyed in the numbers, counting the seconds until he replied.

Anxiety made her abrupt when he answered. 'I need to see you,' she said. 'I don't know how you're fixed, but it needs to here and it needs to be soon.'

Clearly taken aback, James stumbled over his reply. But a moment later, as he asked what was wrong, suddenly there was a lump in Suzie's throat. All she could do was shake her head.

'I'm sorry,' she managed at last, 'it's been a hellish few weeks. Thanks to you, James, I haven't been able to stop thinking about that night of the party. So many questions, and you're the only one who can answer them…'

For a moment, there was silence on the line, and she was immediately reminded of a call made from a phone box, decades ago. Before stress could erupt into fury, she heard an apology followed by soothing words, and a plea to leave it with him for the moment. He'd get back to her within half an hour; would she be all right until then?

'Yes, I'm fine – really…' Suddenly, she was swamped by emotion, as though that deep voice, loaded with sympathy, was all she needed to make things better. As though he could and would mend the broken bits, when he was the one who'd done the breaking.

When James called back, he apologized, said he had a lecture to give next day, one that couldn't be covered by anyone else. He could drive up the day after – Friday – it was his day off. But he would need to be back in Oxford by Saturday evening. Was there a local B&B where he could stay?

'There must be,' she said. 'I can't think for the moment, but I'll find out and book it for you.' She went on to give him directions to the house. He said he'd be there by lunchtime.

– o –

Friday morning, doubting everything, she could barely think straight. She'd have to give him lunch – but what? Something simple but good – she refused to let herself down. A salad, prepared in advance. Hard boiled eggs and cold new potatoes, with lettuce and – and tuna fish. Yes, a *Salade Niçoise*. Perfect.

Wine? She checked the rack, put two bottles of rosé to chill. With regard to appearance, that was less of a problem. Clean hair, minimum make-up, no fuss. Jeans and a shirt – enough to let him know she didn't need to make an impression.

What she was less sure of, was her temper. She'd had no choice when he took her against her will, no choice when it came to dealing with the consequences, and no choice but to bear his child. His arrogance in asking her to search, took her breath away. Dog collar or not, just who in hell did James Fielding think he was?

No, she must keep control. Not get upset, not lose her temper. She had questions to ask, and home truths to spell out. He wasn't going to get away with it this time.

Thirteen

After the way they'd parted, he hadn't expected to hear from Suzie again. A miserable week or so had been followed by a strict determination to get over it, mostly by focusing on his work and the needs of other people. Keeping busy was a good distraction, but his religious life had taken a serious dip recently and James knew he should see his spiritual adviser. He'd been thinking about it when Suzie phoned.

She'd sounded upset, and once James had mastered his astonishment, he'd switched automatically to calming mode. Asking if he could call her back was more of a holding operation; in truth he needed to gather his wits. She'd said she needed to talk, and even though he dreaded it, James could not refuse.

That morning, rising early, he said the morning office in church, packed a few essentials into an overnight bag, and climbed into his old Ford Fiesta.

Once he cleared Oxford, traffic was flowing, the motorway busy but not ridiculously so. Three hours later, on the outskirts of Heatherley, he followed Suzie's directions to

Felton, reaching the little village a few minutes later. He'd been fighting apprehension all the way, but now he was about to step up to the wire. Spotting the church, he pulled into a layby, taking several deep breaths before getting out of the car.

His glance took in the village green, a group of substantial stone houses, and a row of cottages along the roadside. According to Suzie, her house was just beyond them. Needing a moment to collect his thoughts, James climbed the steps into the churchyard. The building's smooth 19th century stonework ended by the rough blocks of a much earlier tower; but as he'd expected, the church was locked.

Clearing his mind, he prayed for insight, and that Suzie might forgive him for re-opening old wounds. Most of all, he asked for humility to accept whatever lay ahead. Even so, his heart was pounding as he returned to the car. Which Suzie Wallis would be waiting for him today?

With a sigh he pulled out into the road, spotting Suzie's house only as he passed it. He drove on for almost a mile before finding somewhere to turn. On the second approach, he could see the stone-clad roof over a flourishing hedge, slowing in time to make the entrance. Pulling up behind a chunky red VW in the drive, he took a moment to look around. The house itself was detached but modest-looking, with sash windows, an ornate wooden porch, and what he took to be a large detached garage on the left. Beyond the shadows he could see splashes of colour in a sunlit garden.

He stepped out onto gravel, rescuing a small pink and white bouquet from the boot as Suzie appeared from a side door.

'I hoped these would cheer you,' he said tentatively as she came forward to greet him. 'But I've just seen your beautiful garden…'

Although she smiled, her keen gaze seemed to strip both him and the flowers for hidden agendas; but then the flowers were accepted and the smile relaxed.

'Thank you, James, they're lovely.'

Feeling that he'd passed some kind of test, he released his breath and followed her down the shadowy path.

'I use the kitchen door nowadays – do come in...'

There was a small lobby with coats and boots, but as he stepped into the kitchen, he was taken by surprise. No Victorian windows here, but a glass-walled extension with dining table and chairs. The kitchen area was light, somehow managing to be both traditional and modern, with the focus on the garden.

'What a beautiful room!'

'Thank you. Took a while to get to this stage, but yes, I like it.' Putting the flowers in water, she said she'd arrange them later. 'What will you have? Tea, coffee, or something stronger?'

'Coffee, thank you – and instant will be fine.'

'Instant it is – I don't know about you, but I find the real stuff's too much trouble for one.'

'It is,' he agreed, taking in her appearance. Her casual clothes reminded him of a distant afternoon when they'd gone walking up at Moorcliffe, and the photos he'd taken that day. Particularly one of Suzie, sketching, which he'd never been able to throw away.

As she turned, he looked out at a mass of cottage-garden flowers in the borders. 'Do you do all this yourself?'

'The planting's down to me, but I have a chap come in once a week in the summer, just to keep on top of things. Of course, it's at its best at the moment. Do you garden?'

'Half-heartedly. Maggie was the gardener. I just try to keep it tidy.'

Suzie took their coffee outside, to a wrought-iron table in the sun. Garden talk led him to expand a little about his wife, and to ask about her husband, Freddie. At their previous meeting, she'd said he was someone first met at art school, but little more than that. Somehow, he hadn't imagined an artist living in a house like this. Not that he thought all artists existed in garrets or tumbledown cottages; just that he'd pictured a chaotic lifestyle. Evidently, Suzie was more organized.

'Yes, Freddie was a painter, but he was practical too – knew he couldn't support a family on painting alone.' With a look part indulgent, part defensive, she said, 'In fact he started off teaching, doing other stuff on the side. Then he got into set-design – theatre and television. A friend got him his first big break – but,' Suzie added dryly, 'I was the one who pushed him into it.'

'How was that?'

'Well, after all the chaos, I finally got to do what I'd always wanted. Back then, we called it window-dressing – small scale compared to theatrical sets, but I had a few skills. We pooled ideas and got better. It was great for a while but the pressure was phenomenal. And we ended up having so many – shall we say, artistic differences – it was better for me to focus on something else.'

It took a moment for James to absorb these facts of a life beyond his experience. 'Was that the shop you mentioned in York?'

'That's more recent. I've done all sorts over the years,' she said, reaching for her coffee. 'Interior design while we were in London – until we moved north for the children's sake. Had a shop in Leeds for a while – basically, home décor – but the big boys cornered the market. After that, I started the home boutique in York – my daughter Sara runs it now.'

'I'm amazed,' he admitted, smiling and shaking his head. 'I shouldn't be, I know – you always knew your own mind.'

For a moment, he thought he'd said the wrong thing. But with a tight smile she said, 'I've worked hard, James – physically hard at times – and I'm glad to say I married the right man. Life with Freddie wasn't always easy – but we made a good team.'

Wondering about that, James smiled and nodded. As Suzie excused herself to serve the lunch, he breathed a sigh of relief before following her inside. With his offer of help waved away, he took the opportunity to look at what he assumed were family photographs arranged on the dresser. Two laughing teenage girls, arms around each other, had to be Suzie's daughters – pretty girls, he could see Suzie in both of them.

He almost passed over the portrait of a smiling, white-haired woman, but then he looked again – Suzie's mother. He'd never forgotten her kindness – or the advice he'd been too cowardly to follow.

'Ah, you've found my rogues' gallery,' Suzie said as she came to explain who they were. 'This is Jo and Sara – just a snap, taken years ago on holiday, but it always makes me smile.'

'Isn't that the best kind? I have a couple like that of my wife...'

'I love this one...' Putting the girls back, she reached for another, of two angelic-looking children. 'This was taken a couple of years ago, when George was six, and Grace was four...' Amused, she said, 'Don't they look sweet, as though butter wouldn't melt – but they were always fighting! Poor Sara despaired of them – thank heavens they've settled down since.'

James experienced a stab of envy. Two daughters, two grandchildren; a history he knew nothing about. He wondered if his son had children; wondered if he would ever know. He said, 'And your other daughter – does she have children?'

'Oh, goodness, no. Jo's a career woman, like her partner – works in television. I doubt they'll ever be parents. Her partner's a woman, by the way.'

Glancing up at him, Suzie nodded. 'Yes, Jo's a lesbian. Something I kind of suspected from when she was young. And then, as a teenager, well – she had male friends, but nothing romantic. Her heartbreaks were always over girls – falling in love with the wrong ones.'

'That must have been difficult?'

'Not really. Jo was Jo, we just accepted it. Thankfully, people don't point the finger as they did in our day. As long as she's happy – and she seems to be – that's all that matters.'

'Yes, of course.'

James found himself thinking of what he called his wilderness years, when all he had was work, and happiness had been so elusive. And yet happiness shone out of these casual family snaps, speaking of years of close family life; evidence, if he needed it, that Suzie's life had not been irrevocably blighted.

As his glance came to rest on another photo, one of a man caught laughing as he turned to the camera, Suzie said, 'Yes, that's Freddie. Another holiday snap, but it reminds me of the happy times...'

From the way she turned back to serving the lunch, he understood that Freddie was not up for discussion. Looking again, he saw a man with spiky grey hair in a bright blue shirt. The impression was of an open, good humoured character, but James couldn't help wondering.

Later, over a delicious salad, she asked about his work. 'I'm curious about the lectures you mentioned? I'd imagined you were a parish priest?'

'That too,' he said, sipping at a glass of chilled rosé. He explained that he was in a fortunate position, with an excellent curate taking care of most of the parish work. 'Without Amy, I wouldn't have time to do much else...'

'A woman curate?'

'Why not? The Church,' he added lightly, 'has moved into the modern age. Amy's married with a teenage son – and between us, we minister to a group of three small parishes. Sunday services are shared, so it's not too onerous.'

'I see,' she said. 'Sounds rather like our local churches, but without the curate.'

With sympathy for the local priest, he shook his head, 'All too common nowadays – not enough clergy to go round.' After a moment, he said, 'Do you attend church?'

'Not usually, no. But there again, services here aren't held every week, and I tend to forget when they are.'

Recalling her claims not to be religious, he wondered why she went to church at all; but before he could ask, she asked about his lectures. His brief, he said, was the History of the Church; mostly for the Anglican training college just outside Oxford.

'So, what was it that made you change direction?'

Familiar with questions like that, James gave his usual answer, saying it was a long story; that having focused on the later medieval period for his MA, he'd gone on to lecture on the beginnings of the Reformation.

'Which was when Christianity really started to mean something to me,' he added easily. 'You might say Christ was knocking at the door for some time before I finally answered…'

'Were you still at Durham?'

'No, by then I was lecturing at Bristol.' With a short laugh, he said, 'Everyone thought I had a great future ahead of me – especially when I talked of giving it up!'

'You've never regretted it?'

'Not at all.'

After a pause, she looked up and said, 'And what did your wife think?'

The unexpected question threw him a little. 'Oh, we weren't married then. Maggie and I were more – friends, I suppose you'd say – at that stage.' The *interregnum*, as he tended to think of it, not simply between careers, but between falling in love and finally being able to do something about it.

Before Suzie's quizzical glance could turn into another personal question, he said, 'As I think I told you the other day, Maggie shared your enthusiasm for walking – she dragged me out when I was still in a quandary about what to do. Exploring parts of the Cotswolds and the Chilterns, made a big difference. Like your experience in Spain, it helped me to think more clearly, see the way forward.'

'Yes,' she agreed, 'walking does put things in perspective...'

She went on to talk about the Camino, and when he asked what had prompted her to write the book, she said it was largely down to her daughter Jo, the TV researcher. She'd not only bullied Suzie into writing it, she'd used her contacts to find her mother a suitable publisher, and later, organized interviews with the local media.

'None of it would have happened without her,' Suzie said, 'but I must admit it was a hectic few weeks around the time the book came out. Nerve-racking, if I'm honest, all that fuss with journalists and TV people. Unlike Jo, I'm not used to it. And then, just as I thought the pressure was over, suddenly I had a request to speak at the lunch in Iredale. I was really sorry she couldn't be there. Afterwards, of course,' she admitted with a sharp glance, 'I was relieved.'

Seized by fresh regret, James shook his head. 'Yes,' he said, 'it was thoughtless of me, Suzie, and I'm sorry about that, really I am.'

Shaking her head, Suzie started clearing the table.

'I must admit,' he added, 'I didn't expect to hear from you again.' He paused, swallowing apprehension, 'I've been wondering what prompted your phone call. You sounded quite upset?'

Suzie turned to face him. 'Yes, I was – I still am. I've hardly slept for weeks. And the more I remember, the worse it gets. And next week is...'

'His birthday – yes, I know.'

With an abrupt nod, Suzie said, 'Yes, well, before we get started on all that, will you come with me to Moorcliffe?'

'Moorcliffe?' His heart sank.

'I was going to go the other day – but only got as far as Denshaw. That was upsetting enough, but I've not been to Moorcliffe since that night I went to the pub and tried to talk to you. I need to face up to it, James – put all that crap in a box and chuck it out!'

The words hurt. He wanted to say, *it wasn't all crap, just my part in it.* 'Facing up to the demons, is that what you mean?'

Nodding, she bent her head, gripping a chair back so hard her knuckles were white. 'Maybe it's not the same for you…'

'No,' he agreed, 'it can't possibly be, can it?' He cleared his throat, stood up. 'My demons are different.'

– o –

There were more houses, James noticed that at once. Fields which had separated the main road from the village were now an estate of what might be described as 'desirable residences.' Barns had been converted, farmyards built upon, green spaces filled in, although the new developments seemed to have stopped before the heart of the village. Driving slowly as they reached the main street of weathered stone cottages, he was pleased to see they were largely unchanged; but the corner shop where he and Alex used to buy sweets – and later, cigarettes – had gone.

He pressed on, past the Blacksmith's Arms – clearly still in business – speeding up as they approached the mock-Tudor enclave where Alex's friends had once held their parties. Suzie turned as though to speak, but James drove past, not slowing again until fields and open moorland met their eyes.

'Well,' she said, 'at least they haven't built up here…'

'I imagine it's protected land.'

He was thinking of the last time he came along this road. A family gathering for Uncle Harry's funeral. Rounding a bend, he tensed; the farm was still there, although it took more than a moment to recognise it. The barns were gone; the yard, once a parking place for JCBs, was now a pristine square faced by some neat cottages and a gentrified farmhouse.

'I don't believe it,' he murmured.

'Is this the place?'

Unclipping his seatbelt, he looked around. 'Has to be.'

They both stepped out of the car, standing for a while by a new dry-stone wall. Astonished by the farm's transformation, James could only think of the way it was when he was young, how he'd looked forward to coming here, to a warm welcome and holiday freedom.

'I wonder what the old man would say if he could see it now?'

'You never know,' Suzie shrugged. 'He was a builder, wasn't he? He'd probably approve.'

Reluctantly, James nodded. 'Maybe he would,' he said at last. 'Time's moved on, after all…'

Contemplating the past, it was a while before he noticed Suzie gazing towards the skyline. Following her glance, spying the crags, he suspected she was thinking of the Sunday afternoon they'd spent together, him with his camera, Suzie with her sketch-book. At once, the happiness of that day returned like a stab to the heart. If only he'd believed in himself, he thought; trusted his own instincts. How different life could have been.

Suzie turned and looked at him. For a fleeting moment, he was reminded of Maggie and her ability to read his mind. Unnerved, he couldn't look away. All he could do was shake his head and say again that he was sorry.

Slowly, she nodded. 'Me too. I thought we were on the same wavelength, James. How did I get it so wrong?'

'You didn't,' he said. 'It was me – I was the one who got it wrong.'

'Care to explain?'

'I can't – not here.'

Expecting a volley of questions, abruptly he shifted his gaze to the farm. When Suzie spoke again, it was to ask about his aunt and uncle.

'They were very different, weren't they? I mean, she sounded quite posh, but from what you said at the time, your uncle was very much a self-made man?'

James found himself smiling. 'Oh, he was. A charmer, according to my mother. The thing was, Uncle Harry had a sense of humour – a bit off-colour sometimes, but he could always make people laugh. I thought he was great. And he had brains – he wasn't going to work in the mills like the rest of his family. What was it he said to me? *Progress for them was going from sweeper-up to weaver – and weaver to foreman.* Uncle Harry wanted none of that...

'He met Isabel – my mother's sister – during the war. Swept her off her feet, apparently.' Recalling his mother's disapproval of Harry, he chuckled. 'But Isabel believed in him. She ran the business side – he couldn't have done it without her.'

Remembering how everything changed after Alex, he turned back to the car.

Following, Suzie said, 'I imagine they're long gone?'

'Yes. Must be nearly twenty years since Harry died – then Isabel had to sell up. She passed away a few years ago.'

'I'm sorry – I know you were fond of them.' But at the next question there was a harder note. 'And what about your cousin – what did he do?'

He risked a quick glance, wondering how little he could get away with. 'Oh, Alex made a mess of everything. Married and divorced by the time he was thirty. Then he met an American woman – an actress or model, I forget – went to live over there...'

'It doesn't sound as though you kept in touch?'

'We didn't, really,' he said with forced lightness. 'You know how it is at that age – different universities, different friends.

Plus, my parents were home-based at last, so I went to them in the holidays.'

'And of course,' Suzie added lightly, opening the car door, 'there was the small problem of yours truly – and a baby...'

That stung; but she was right.

'I couldn't face them,' he admitted, getting in and starting the car. 'I'm not proud of it, but that's how it was. If they'd asked about you, I'd have given myself away. By the time I saw them again, it was past history.'

'How convenient.'

James didn't respond. The bad memories were crowding in, one after the other, unbearable. His one thought was to get away, back to Heatherley. But as they neared the side-road where Babs and Avril had lived, Suzie asked him to turn in.

'Do we have to? I'd rather not.'

'Yes, we have to.'

Grimly, he obeyed. Gardens had changed, there were extensions and more cars parked in the driveways, but essentially the Tudor-style houses were much the same. It was disorienting, like seeing this place and himself in a nightmare. If only he could have grabbed that boy, shaken him, and socked his cousin on the jaw while he was about it.

In a small voice, Suzie said, 'Which one was it? They all look alike to me.'

All these years later he couldn't be sure. 'It was this side of the road,' he said bleakly, pulling up halfway along. 'I don't remember which one.'

After a while she nodded. 'It hurts, doesn't it?'

He bowed his head to the steering wheel. 'Yes,' he whispered, 'it does. Suzie, if I could go back...'

She pressed further. 'What happened that night, James? I've never been able to understand it. Was Alex involved in some way? Did he dare you to do it, or what?'

Abruptly, he shook his head, drove on to where he could turn. 'Please, Suzie – I don't want to talk about it here.'

– o –

She directed him through Heatherley, past the B&B where she'd booked him a bed for the night. James barely noticed. His mind was back at the farm, the night of Alex's eighteenth birthday.

He'd been happy. With Suzie in his arms, everything had felt so good, he could hardly believe it. He'd always been the awkward outsider, never able to talk to girls – but with her, he'd lost his shyness. That night in his room, so warm and tender as they kissed and caressed, he didn't want to hurt her. Yes, she was beautiful, and yes, he would have liked to go on, but it wasn't right. He knew it wasn't. Despite the boys-only school, he'd been taught to respect girls; and he knew about condoms, just never had the guts to buy them.

But Alex, his good-looking cousin, was not only a year younger, but way more experienced. To hear him talk, he'd made it with every girl he'd ever dated, and to him, Suzie's friend was just another lay. Liz was so easy, he boasted to James, her best friend had to be the same – she was an art student, wasn't she? Looking at naked bodies all day – bound to be up for it!

Which proved – in retrospect – just how little Alex knew about women.

At the time James had believed otherwise, allowing himself to be brain-washed by Alex the great con-merchant. Did he want Suzie to think he was a wimp? No, of course not. He should be a man, take what he wanted. So what if she said no? They all said that to start with. Keep going, Alex said; she'd not only enjoy it, she'd be begging for more!

James hadn't admitted his tender feelings, but listening to his cousin made them seem outdated, even unmanly – and according to Alex, he'd just passed up the perfect opportunity. He could have done it while she was virtually in bed with him – why, Alex wanted to know, hadn't he followed through? Anyway, Babs's party was likely to be the last of the holidays – a final opportunity, Alex said, for James to lose his cherry. It was time for him to act.

Well, James reflected as he drew up outside Suzie's house, Alex might have sold the idea, but he, James, had bought it. Simple as that.

Fourteen

It was barely five o'clock when they reached Felton, but as James followed her into the house, Suzie suggested a drink.

She could understand his need to get away from Moorcliffe, it was a trial for her too, relieved only by the fact that the farm had changed, even if the houses hadn't. Rather like her reaction to Denshaw, it seemed James had stepped back to a place of complex memories. Not just the events of that summer, but the years before and since. If being back there was painful for her, clearly it was as bad for him. Worse, if his white-faced silence was anything to go by.

Get him drunk, she thought now; or at least relaxed. That way she might get to the truth of what happened that night. And why James had just dropped her afterwards.

'There's wine,' she said, taking the rosé out of the fridge, 'or would you prefer something stronger? I could call a taxi, later?'

'Thanks, yes – good idea. I'd like a whisky, if you have it.'

Somewhere at the back of the kitchen cupboard was a bottle of Black Label. Finding it, reaching for glasses, she put them on the table and pulled out a chair. 'Help yourself.'

Watching him pour a generous measure, Suzie waited while he sipped at it, seeing colour return to his face. Repeating her earlier question, she said, 'What was it all about, James? Did Alex dare you to do it?'

Taking off his glasses, James rubbed at the bridge of his nose. 'Oh, please, Suzie, don't make it sound so trivial. Alex didn't force himself on you – *I* did.'

'I know that,' she said sharply. 'What I want to know is *why*. Why it had to be like that.'

'*Never speak ill of the dead* – isn't that what they say? Alex is no longer here to defend himself, so I hope he'll forgive me…'

'Alex, *dead*?'

Abruptly, he nodded. 'Years ago – California. He was still in his thirties. A combination of drink and drugs, after some wild party or other. Typical Alex, always pushing the boundaries – except that time he went too far.'

Shocked, at once she pictured his parents. Alex had been their only child. She couldn't feel sympathy for him, but she did for them. If she lost one of her daughters…

She listened as James described the impact of his cousin's death, the way it reverberated through the family. Uncle Harry struggling to keep going, Isabel seeming to fade while supporting a grieving husband as well as a faltering business. James's mother had spent a lot of time up there, trying to help her sister; meanwhile, James had been devastated in his own way. The death of a close relative – of his own age – had shaken him badly, making him dwell on the bleakness of his own situation.

'What made things worse, I felt guilty. I'd blamed him for years, you see – for everything that happened in the wake of that party. I barely spoke to him afterwards – couldn't wait to get away from Moorcliffe, to a place where no one knew me. Only after he was gone, did I see that the fault was mine in listening to him in the first place.'

Suzie started to protest, but James silenced her with a gesture. 'Did your mother never say to you, *if your friend told you to jump off a cliff, would you do it?* It's as simple as that, Suzie – the decision to do something, no matter how wrong you know it to be.'

'Oh, well, Alex always did have an answer for everything.'

'He did, that's true – and I probably knew him better than most...'

As James went on to talk about his cousin, Suzie could see from his expression that he'd admired Alex the daredevil, even though the younger boy was often in trouble for defying his parents.

'And as we grew older, there he was, playing the field with girls – whereas I rarely met any, except in the holidays. Alex's schoolfriends, daughters of army families, sometimes. To them,' he added with a dry smile, 'I was the ginger-haired geek in glasses...

'Durham was a different world, of course. After boarding school, all that freedom was terrifying. Instead of letting go, having a good time, I spent most of my evenings studying.'

'Hardly the dissolute life of a student...'

'Quite. I hope you can see how it was that summer – how *I* was – when you spoke to me that night in Iredale.' He took another sip at the whisky. 'You made me feel like I was part of the human race at last. You were special, Suzie – and God knows, I didn't deserve you. I certainly didn't intend things to go the way they did.'

Slowly, she nodded, willing him to explain. 'So why did they?'

After a moment, running fingers through his hair, he said, 'You remember the night we were together – in my room at the farm? Alex dragged it out of me, what happened. Or rather, what *didn't* happen... And then he talked me into believing that what you really wanted was to go the whole way...'

For a moment, she couldn't speak. 'The little shit...'

'But I was scared – terrified, if I'm honest.'

'Why?'

'Oh, Suzie, come on – I was nineteen and hadn't a clue.'

'Oh, don't give me that,' she snapped. She stood up, emphasising her words with an accusing finger. 'You didn't have to pounce on me when I was so drunk I was nearly throwing up. Why did you do that? Without so much as a by your leave, you just got on with it!'

Head in hands, his reply came out like a groan. 'I know, I know...'

In full flow now, she couldn't get the questions out fast enough. 'And talking about being *drunk* – did you slip something into my drink that night? *Vodka*, maybe?'

'Of course not! I was the one drinking too much. I wanted you to stay with me, but you were *dancing* – remember? Every time you came back to me – every time you remembered who I was – you grabbed my beer. And when you'd gulped at it, I went and topped it up...'

'It was more than that, James. It was sudden. I was *suddenly* drunk, you know? Tell me honestly, *did* you slip me a vodka, just to be sure?'

'No – don't make it worse!' Angrily, he got to his feet, pacing the kitchen as she watched him battle the fog of memory.

'It wasn't long after we left the pub...'

'It was after midnight,' he protested. 'I know, because Alex pointed to the bloody clock and told me it was time I got moving!'

Insulted by that, she almost spat at him. 'Oh, great! Alex egging you on – so was it him with the vodka? Doing the dirty behind your back?'

'There was no vodka – where did you get that idea? *You* were drinking *my* beer, Suzie – that's all. Think about it – we're talking a couple of hours after leaving the pub. Time to sink far more than either of us can remember!'

Even though he was looking straight at her, hiding nothing, she didn't want to believe him. 'Are you sure?'

'Certain.'

Suzie felt for her chair, needing support as conviction crumbled. 'The only drink I remember is the one *you* gave me. But maybe,' she added faintly, 'they all blurred into one.' Feeling stunned, she said, 'Bloody hell, I can't believe this. All these years I've been telling myself that I wasn't drunk before that final glass...'

'Does it matter?' he asked, gently now.

'*Of course* it matters. If you're right, I've been kidding myself all these years. Didn't want to admit that I was the drunken fool!'

Suddenly, she wanted to cry. Backing away from him, she turned for the door. 'No – stay there – just let me be.'

– o –

James watched as the smoke from a freshly-lit cigarette left a ghost trail behind her. He felt hollow, drained, but it wasn't over. He saw her place both hands against a tree, pushing against it, arms taut, head bent for almost a minute. She moved and he lost sight of her, but as she came back her expression was unreadable. Tensed for a fresh assault, he told himself it was no more than he deserved. He must try to keep calm, not add fuel to the fire.

'Okay, so memory plays tricks,' she declared as she came in. 'If I was as drunk as you say I was, then on that score we're about even. But it still doesn't answer the real question. *Why* did you just pounce on me? How could you even *think* it was okay?'

Shame burned so acutely, he couldn't answer. Couldn't even look at her.

'And afterwards, you just got up and walked off – didn't say a bloody word. Not even *sorry* – oh, I'm wrong there. You did say it – when I came to the pub that night and *prompted you*.' She paused for breath. '*Why?* When I trusted you – when I thought you cared about me. Why did you do it?'

'I don't know.' But that was a childish defence. He did know. He'd had years of searching his conscience for the answer. Yes, he'd wanted to know what it felt like – what teenage boy didn't? But he hadn't imagined the reality. The pathetic, drunken reality.

How to claim he cared for Suzie, when in reality he'd been more afraid of Alex's scorn? How could he blame a dead man, when the act – the volition – had been his?

'You must know! And don't say you were carried away by the heat of the moment,' she snapped, 'because there was no heat of the moment. We were barely together.'

'Okay,' he said, spreading his hands in appeal, 'you're right. But it was on my mind.' *The whole time, watching her, longing for her, wishing she'd stay by his side.* 'I wanted us to be together, like it was before, in my room. But how? We were in someone else's house. Then you went upstairs... And by that time,' he finished lamely, 'I was too drunk to think straight.'

Before she could protest, he said, 'Honestly, Suzie, I was so ashamed afterwards, I thought you'd despise me. God knows, I despised myself. I couldn't face you, that's why I left...'

When she made no reply, he forced himself to look up, but Suzie was staring as though he'd surfaced through slime.

'God – what a coward! You didn't consider how *I* felt, did you? Having you push me down, and – and – stick your *thing* into me, like I was just a piece of meat.'

Wincing, he turned away.

'But we mustn't forget Alex, must we? He was there, that night in the pub. I saw the way he looked at me when I was trying to talk to you – pityingly, like I was last week's news. I knew then – knew he'd had something to do with it.'

Shaking his head, wishing she would stop, James said wearily, 'It wasn't a plot. Alex said you'd expect it, that's all. With your experience, you'd think I was a wimp if I didn't try it on.'

She stopped her pacing. 'With *my* experience? Me? How the hell would he know? You thought...? Don't tell me you thought I did it all the time – is that what Alex said?'

It was too close to the truth for denial.

'Well, let me tell *you* something, James – strictly speaking, I didn't lose my virginity until *after* you'd had your wicked way!'

Completely lost, all he could do was stare as Suzie swigged some wine and glugged more into the glass. As though she couldn't bear to be near him, she stepped away, and with the door at her back, said, 'That home I went to – for unmarried mothers. I had to go for a health check beforehand...' She paused, shaking her head. 'Imagine, there I was, eighteen years old, seven months pregnant and finding myself in a VD clinic...'

'No ...'

'And you know how they test women for VD?' she went on. 'They use a metal instrument like a duck's beak – a speculum, it's called. They stick it in you, open it while it's up there, and take a swab. All pretty straightforward for a pregnant woman, wouldn't you think? A woman who's used to having sex?'

He could barely breathe, let alone speak, but she carried on.

'When they stuck this *speculum* inside me, I nearly went through the roof. Why? Because they'd torn the hymen. *That's* how virginal I was. I saw the nurses look at each other. One even apologized. Don't you see? What you did was a one-off. If I'd been having sex all over the place, there'd have been an easy way in – for you, *and* the VD team.'

It was the first time for her too? Head in hands, trying to take it in, James could find no words. In a shattering moment of clarity, her pain and humiliation connected with his. That night in the bedroom: on the bed, knowing his erection was inadequate but determined to do it anyway. What was the phrase? *Going off half-cocked*: that was it exactly.

Even as he tried to understand, her words went rushing on, so fast he could barely keep up. Something about feeling cheated, wondering what the hell it was all about, and wishing things had been different.

'I made such a fool of myself afterwards – coming to see you that night in the pub. I thought, okay, I'm no longer a virgin, so what's the big deal? Did the world end? No, it didn't. Maybe we could talk about it, get over it, maybe even start again. But you – you didn't want to know!'

– o –

Startled by the slamming of the door, he looked up to see her striding down the garden. In the ensuing silence, he tried to work out what she'd been saying. That she'd been a virgin was almost too big a shock to take in. That he'd hurt her emotionally was another twist in the tale. He'd been so humiliated by failure, at the time it never entered his head that she might be hurt and humiliated by what he'd done.

Words uttered in the aftermath of that drunken fumble came back to him. *I hope you're proud of yourself*, she'd said. He'd never forgotten, but now they took on fresh meaning. A comment on his actions, that's all. While he'd imagined she was judging his performance, mocking him. It wasn't her scorn that had crippled him, but his own vanity.

I thought maybe we could talk about it, start again...

Had she really said that? That she'd believed in him enough to want to forgive? It was almost as shocking as her brutal honesty. If what she was saying was true – and he didn't doubt it – then his shameful rejection was almost as bad as the act itself.

If only he'd known – but he'd misunderstood…

Oh, dear Jesus, he'd taken the wrong view from the start.

He had to explain; had to be honest, no matter how excruciating. He owed her that. Would she sneer at him? Would she use it to twist the knife? He didn't know. For a moment, he quailed; muttering a fervent prayer, he opened the door and went outside.

He found her by the stone wall at the bottom of the garden. She seemed to be watching cows in the field beyond. Tentatively, he placed a hand on her shoulder; as she jerked away, he saw pain and resentment in her eyes.

'Please, Suzie, listen to me. What you've just said – I didn't know…' *Forgive me*, was on his tongue, but he held it back. 'There's no excuse for what I did. It was all wrong – act, intention, all of it.'

She would have moved away, but he took her hands in his, holding hard, trying to convey his sincerity. 'That night – what you said, afterwards – I couldn't forget it.'

She frowned. 'What did I say?'

'*I hope you're proud of yourself.* Do you remember? I thought you were mocking me…'

'Mocking you? I was shocked, for God's sake – couldn't believe what you'd just done.'

'I see that now. But then – do you understand? It was my first time, and I'd made much a hash of it…' Taking a deep breath, he said, 'I felt a fool – inadequate doesn't begin to describe it. You were important to me – and I'd… Well, you know what I did. I was so bitterly ashamed, I couldn't face you.

'When you turned up a week later, my heart sank. I was expecting a verbal lashing. I wanted to say something, but what? And I could see Alex watching us. Honestly Suzie, it was like…' He struggled for words. 'Well, like I was gagged and wearing handcuffs. I couldn't speak, couldn't even *move*. So I let you go…

'Afterwards,' he began, steeling himself to confess the repercussions, but Suzie cut in.

'Yes, *afterwards*, James – what about that? I hear what you're saying, and I appreciate your honesty. But what about when I rang to tell you the awful news? You had your answer off pat – you weren't even *surprised*, for God's sake, when I phoned you in Durham. How did you know?'

With his mind on other, more important things, he frowned. 'I didn't. But I knew what I'd done. I knew what the result could be.'

'You *expected* it?'

James shook his head. 'More like waiting for the axe to fall, and then it does...'

In the silence that followed, he leaned against the wall, looking not at her or the grazing cows, but at the shallow bowl of the valley, at fields and forests and hazy blue moorland beyond. He'd almost forgotten this part of Yorkshire; dark memories of that summer had blotted it out. He wondered if Suzie would ever know how difficult it was, coming here, going back to Moorcliffe. How difficult now, confessing what a miserable apology for a human being he'd been in those days. And was he any better now? He still hadn't told her about the effects of that night...

'But no matter how much you *cared* – allegedly – you weren't going to stand by your sins and do the decent thing.'

'No, you're right,' he sighed, too mentally drained to gloss over the truth. 'After fighting to get to university, I didn't want to give it up. Plus, I knew what the reaction would be if I told my parents. But if I had,' he went on, 'if I'd said, never mind, Suzie, we'll get married – how would I have supported you and a baby?'

'Other people did...'

Something in her tone made him suspect she was just saying that. Risking a smile, he turned to her and said, 'At the time, remember, you said you wouldn't have me if I came free with a packet of tea...'

Suddenly, to his relief, she laughed. 'Fair enough. But it would have soothed my pride to be asked.'

'I'm afraid psychology wasn't my strong suit in those days.'

'And is it now?'

With a wry grin, he said, 'Let's say I've learned a few things in the years between.'

Fifteen

Resisting more wine, Suzie busied herself with kettle, mugs and teapot, determined to sober up while adjusting to a different perspective. Trying to accept that she had indeed been drunk that night was upsetting, but in a sense, she'd always known it. It was just easier to latch onto her mother's idea that someone had doctored her drink. That way, she could pretend it wasn't her fault at all.

The lifelong feeling that she'd invited the assault previously, by going to James's room at the farm, wasn't entirely off-beam, even though her mature self said it shouldn't have led to what happened at Babs's party. Now, though, she could see where James had gone wrong. In telling his cousin, he'd given him the basic sums from which Alex had drawn the wrong conclusions. Thinking about it, perhaps she'd been guilty of something similar? According to Liz, her argument with Alex had led to some scathing comments about class. Her account had coloured Suzie's view, so she'd seen herself as the victim of two spoiled little rich boys, who thought working class girls were there to be used and thrown away.

In the light of James's honesty – in *not* blaming his cousin but taking everything upon himself – Suzie was seeing things differently. It seemed Connie's assessment of James had not been far wrong. He was not a malicious rapist, but a frightened, inexperienced boy, minus parental support and desperately trying to keep up with the pack. The pack, in this case, being his cousin Alex.

When she turned, she saw James was draining his glass. 'Oh, sorry, I didn't ask. Would you rather have whisky?'

'No,' he replied with a sheepish grin, 'but it's a shame to let good Scotch evaporate…'

As she returned what was left of the wine to the fridge, James's next words echoed what she'd been thinking.

'I know life looks clearer with hindsight, but what you've told me gives everything a new perspective. Knowing you weren't mocking me that night – or later, when you turned up to sort things out… Well, it's made me feel lighter. What can I say, except I didn't understand, and sincerely wish that I had?'

'It hurt like hell, James. I felt I'd been used and cast aside – took me a long time to get over that. Must admit I never imagined you suffering pangs of guilt over it.'

'Oh, I did. For years. And when Liz wrote to tell me our son had been born…'

Our son… Hearing those words from his lips was a shock. Baby was hers, always had been. Her responsibility, no one else's. But in the midst of these frank exchanges, she was having to accept that her absent child was James's son too.

'…and that it should be my birthday too…' He shook his head.

'I know,' she said at last. 'I couldn't forget you, either.'

Putting cake and biscuits on the table, she noticed James gazing blindly at the garden. As his gaze returned to her, he said, 'You must have hated me.'

With a little huff of amusement, Suzie shook her head. 'For a while, yes. But I had more important things to think about. Besides, I was too busy hating myself for allowing it to happen.'

'You blamed *yourself*?'

'Of course. Women always blame themselves, didn't you know that?' With a grim smile, she said, 'To be honest, once I'd told my parents – and that took some doing – I tried to put you out of my mind. And once I'd left home, it was like the past really was another country...'

– o –

It was a long way to her aunt's house in Richmond. Leeds to Darlington on the train, and then the bus. A week or so into the New Year, after what had been the quietest Christmas she could recall. No sniping, no bickering, and when Dad went out he came home on time. Meanwhile, except for evening visits to Liz's house, Suzie mostly kept indoors, rarely venturing out despite being assured that 'it' didn't show.

When she was a child, she'd only visited Richmond occasionally, and that was in the summer. Seeing it in the winter, she said to James, was different. Snow crusting the castle like a cake, with a frosty white haze across distant woods; all rather beautiful, except for the feeling of being exiled to a foreign land.

Quiet, that's what she remembered most – peace and quiet – so healing after the stress of living at home. Three months of rest in that small town with its cobbled streets and steep hills, had enabled her to come to terms with herself and her situation.

Apart from her little black terrier, Aunt Dolly lived alone. Her terraced cottage was just a short walk from the castle ramparts, standing in line with others on a steep and neatly kept street. No gardens at the front, but fresh paintwork, lace curtains and whitened steps to every house; so uniformly smart, to Suzie the houses looked like soldiers on parade. Aunt Dolly had chuckled at that, saying that Uncle Bert, if he'd been around to hear it, would have been tickled pink.

She started to explain about Catterick garrison being close to Richmond, but James said he knew it – his father had been stationed there for a while.

'Ah, so you'll understand its advantages where I was concerned. To anyone who asked, Aunt Dolly said my absent husband was a soldier, serving overseas…'

James nodded. 'A tactful way out of a difficult situation.'

'Oddly enough, my cousin Ken really was with the army in Germany.'

Smiling, he said, 'So we've more in common than we realized?'

'Strange, isn't it? And you'd have liked Aunt Dolly – she was a true Christian. Not only did she go to church every week, she lived her beliefs.' Overcome by memories, Suzie shook her head. 'She was one of the kindest women I've ever known…'

'Did you go with her to church?'

'I did. It was good to be there – so calming and uplifting, I managed to stop hating myself. For a while, at least.'

'Perhaps you should have kept it up?' he suggested gently, but Suzie shook her head, unwilling to get into that kind of discussion.

'I couldn't. For a long time, being in church reminded me of that time, and afterwards, well… I just wanted to forget. Anyway,' she went on, 'I was telling you about Aunt Dolly…'

Suzie had offered to help around the house, but her aunt said it was nice to have company, so Suzie must regard herself as a guest and please herself. But if she wanted to take Jim, the little Fell terrier, out for walks, then it would no doubt do them both good…

Instructed not to worry, Suzie had taken the advice literally; apart from a constant awareness of the child growing within, she worried not at all. Richmond was peaceful, the surroundings so beautiful even in the depths of winter, she simply embraced it. With the eager little terrier leading the way, she climbed the hills, explored the castle grounds, and strolled along the River Swale's wooded banks, discovering a ruined abbey just a few miles distant.

'Sometimes I went off alone with my sketch book. What I was seeing – ancient trees, medieval ruins – were the kind of things I'd longed to draw for years. I remember thinking, if only dull, Victorian Iredale had been like this, I might have done better. But after a while I thought, if this was where art led me, what's the point? All the hopes and dreams were gone. So I closed the sketch book for good...'

James's sigh, the lightest touch of his hand, brought her back to the present; he looked so stricken, she could only shake her head.

But then, recalling something else, she smiled. 'I had my nineteenth birthday while I was there, and Aunt Dolly made me a cake, bless her. Nineteen, for heaven's sake, and I was like an old dear in a retirement home!' Chuckling at the image, she said, 'Can you imagine? A good book, the radio on, and a little dog at my feet – unbelievable!'

James nodded as though he knew exactly what she was saying. 'Well,' he said dryly, 'I was twenty, and minus the dog...'

Amused, she shook her head at the irony. When he asked how long she'd stayed in Richmond, she said it was almost three months. 'Of course, I'd met my cousins several times before, but Denise and Pat seemed much older when I was a kid. Meeting them again, I was nervous. Couldn't help seeing myself through their eyes – you know, the spoiled only child whose parents couldn't keep her in line...'

'Did you really see yourself like that?'

'God, yes – I was so ashamed.'

Recalling awkward moments, she said, 'Denise was the youngest, with three little ones. But somehow, she couldn't see my predicament – she talked babies all the time, which was the last subject I wanted to discuss. Pat, on the other hand, had her own dress shop in Middlesbrough – we spoke the same language, so we got on well.

'In fact,' Suzie added, 'it was Pat who took me for that health check I was telling you about. Furious when she realized what the clinic was for! Anyway, when the time came, a week or so later, she volunteered again – this time to drive me to the mother-and-baby home.'

'Was that in Richmond?'

'No – it was out in the country, a little village. Not your Magdalen Sisters sort of place – far from it. A big house – could have been an old rectory, once upon a time. Big, spacious rooms – quite beautiful – with a walled garden...'

But the garden was as far as she and the other girls were allowed to go. After the freedom of Richmond, all the walking she'd done, she'd found the restriction hard to bear. Although Matron and Sister – both midwives – were strict, they'd seemed kind enough in the beginning. Suzie had even been given a room of her own, under the eaves, two floors up. At first, she'd been grateful for the solitude as much as the view over fields and distant woods.

'Later on, I discovered the drawbacks. Anyway,' she went on, 'we girls were probably a dozen in all – a changing group as some came in and others went home...' She recalled a farmer's daughter; a thirty-year-old secretary; a girl from Northern Ireland and another from Newcastle. 'Ordinary girls with different backgrounds – all reduced to wearing the same label... *Unmarried Mothers*...'

Suzie lit a cigarette, pushed her cup aside and reached for the wine. 'But at least I wasn't alone – and it helped to hear their stories. Most of us were intending to give up our babies – we'd been told it was for the best, you see. Our babies deserved a better chance in life – we'd be selfish to even think of keeping them. And I, for one, believed it.'

With a catch in her voice, she said, 'I know I said I didn't want my baby – but that was in the beginning, James, when I wasn't even aware of him. By the time I was six months pregnant it was different. Even though he wasn't born yet, he was moving around inside me. He'd become real, and I wanted the best for him…'

With a muttered exclamation, he pronounced it archaic. 'I know it's only forty years ago, but when you think how things changed after that. It could only have been – what? – four, five years later?'

'I know – the Pill and abortion and Women's Lib. It didn't come soon enough.' With a harsh sigh, Suzie shook her head. 'But in 1964, that was how things were. We were single mothers, and with no husbands to support us, how were we to survive? Get a council house? Get benefits? I don't think so – not then. Basically, we had no choice…'

Looking back at the way she'd changed during the months of her pregnancy, Suzie could see how she'd slipped back from fun-loving teenager into a cowed and anxious child. It was not depression exactly, more a desperate fear of the unknown. If she'd tried to buck the system, she could have been in even worse trouble.

'After all,' she said bitterly, 'it was my fault for getting into this mess, and being locked up was the result.'

'But it wasn't your fault!'

'Okay, I can see that now. But at the time… Standard female guilt-trip, James – and we were all in the same boat. We'd all been ever so busy, *getting ourselves pregnant!*'

Even though she gave a hollow laugh, he winced and shook his head. 'How can you say that?'

'Oh, come on – people said it all the time. They still say it today. And the other one, *she's no better than she should be* – what the hell does that mean? *Got herself pregnant* – it's as though she forced herself on some unsuspecting male…'

'Putting rape on the victim.'

It was the first time either of them had used that word. Even though she'd laughed a moment ago, Suzie felt the jolt of it.

'Is that what it was, James?'

He held her gaze. 'You know it was.'

For a while they were both silent.

In a harsh whisper, he said, 'Can you forgive me, Suzie?'

He looked so haunted, she had to avert her eyes. In truth, she'd come to terms years ago with the act that made her pregnant; what was the point in blaming him now?

Twisting the ring on her wedding finger, she said, 'If it makes you feel better – yes, James, I forgive you.'

He looked relieved, but she knew he'd sensed some qualification. As he poured himself some whisky, she lit a cigarette.

'Which is all very well,' Suzie sighed, 'but the trouble is, I still can't forgive myself. Not for that night, I don't mean that. No, for what came afterwards…'

– o –

Not that the Home seemed a bad place at first; more like a weird kind of boarding school, with Home Economics top of the agenda. Chores in the morning, school dinners at lunchtime, afternoons spent knitting as though for an exam – one devoted to bonnets, bootees, mittens and matinee jackets. And meanwhile the girls gossiped, mostly about themselves, parents, boyfriends, what had landed them in there. None were trouble causers; they were like Suzie, too cowed to say a word out of turn.

But then Stella arrived. She'd been turfed out of the Wrens for getting pregnant. 'But did *he* get thrown out?' she'd demanded at the end of her tale. 'No, he damn well didn't!'

Stella, Suzie observed, was like a Hollywood starlet suddenly finding herself in suburban rep. The others were grey by comparison. Stella couldn't believe the pettiness of the rules; she questioned everything from the start. *Why* couldn't they watch television after 7.30 at night? It was just when the best programmes were starting. And she was right, they couldn't even watch *Top of the Pops*, never mind the raunchier *Ready, Steady, Go*. As for the radio, it was the BBC *Light Programme,* with *Mrs Dale's Diary* – not even their mothers listened to that – and *Music While You Work* grating away as they prepared veg for the midday meal.

On reflection, it was as though some higher authority had deemed pop culture too sexy by half – the cause of all these girls getting into trouble. Not that Suzie had figured that out at the time – it was simply part of the punishment. But how she'd longed to hear the latest hits, what her favourite groups were doing now. Catching occasional snatches on the early evening news – the Beatles conquering America! – she wanted to cheer, hear more, dance and be happy again…

And *why*, Stella demanded, could they not leave the house and grounds? Was Matron afraid they'd run away? Or was it for fear of offending the locals with their bulging, unwed stomachs?

To the others – who daren't say a word out of turn – this was shocking stuff. And Matron was not amused. Those were the rules, she declared chillingly; and if Stella didn't like it, she would soon find herself in some other, less salubrious place for unmarried mothers.

– o –

'And that,' Suzie said to James, 'was when Matron would remind us how lucky we were to be in this *home for decent girls*. At which everyone else bar Stella, said, *Yes, Matron, no Matron, three bags full, Matron,* ducked their heads and got on with their knitting. But as soon as Matron was out of earshot, we'd all crack up at Stella's daring...'

If the others found her shocking, Suzie had rather admired Stella. 'She was a breath of fresh air. Reminded me of some of the characters at art school – frank to the point of embarrassment at times, but she could always make me laugh. And unlike the rest of us, she wasn't ashamed. Okay, so she was pregnant and not married, but so what? That was her attitude. Stella was liberated before anybody thought of the word.'

'She sounds quite a character. How old was she?'

'Not sure – mid-twenties, I think.'

'I wonder what happened to her afterwards? Did you ever find out?'

'No, I left before she did. Anyway, why would any of us want to keep in touch?'

'Support, maybe?'

'You must be joking! We were told to forget it, put it behind us – move on!'

'The wartime mantra,' he sighed. 'Stiff upper lip and all that. Thank God we don't say it now.' Sipping at his whisky, he said, 'But tell me more about this home – it was run by the Church, you say?'

'Yes, it was. That interview I went to – just after we met up in Leeds – was at some sort of church office in Bradford. I was left in no doubt that their homes were for decent girls from good backgrounds.' After a moment's reflection, she said, 'Lord knows where the other unfortunates went.'

'But you say you weren't allowed out? Not even to go to church?'

'Ah, yes – we were allowed to go to church. But I only went the once. It was too humiliating. Having to sit in a pew at the back – everyone looking at us as we went up for communion. Made me feel like a criminal – didn't go again.'

'That's sad.'

'It was horrible.'

Mention of church reminded Suzie that a clergyman had come to interview her at the home – he was kind and quite young – wanting to know her circumstances, and if she was certain about the adoption. She'd said yes, of course. Then, after her son was born, a woman came – probably a social worker – asking much the same questions. But that was later.

It was hard, putting it into words; facts were all she was capable of. Not an easy birth. She'd been in labour for well over twenty-four hours. After a hefty dose of pethidine at the hospital, she'd been unconscious for most of it, coming round only as delivery was imminent. She was so befuddled, the pain so overwhelming, she didn't know where she was or what was happening. So terrifying, she'd refused the drug ever again.

Even when her baby son was laid in her arms, he seemed unreal, nothing to do with the ordeal she'd been through. Only later, when she was back on the ward and presented with Baby and a bottle of milk to feed him with, did she grasp that this tiny scrap of humanity was hers. Overwhelmed by love, by wonder at this miracle, she'd held him close and wept.

– o –

'He was beautiful,' Suzie said huskily, 'and he reminded me of you. Dark grey eyes, and perfect little starfish hands…'

When James asked if she had a photograph, she shook her head. 'Photos were forbidden.'

'What did you call him?'

'Well, I called him Baby...' For a moment she couldn't go on. 'You see, I knew his name was bound to be changed. Anyway, I registered him as Dominic...'

She could see he was moved. 'Was there a reason?'

'Oh, there was a book of names. Dominic – it means, belonging to God. I felt he needed some protection, and since I couldn't give it...'

As she blinked tears away, James reached for her hand. 'I'm sure your prayers were heard...'

'You think so?' she sniffed. 'I hope you're right...' Aware of wanting to hold onto him, Suzie pulled away.

Clearing her throat, she described a week being cared for by bustling midwives. A cheap wedding ring entitled her to be addressed as *Mrs*, rather than *Miss*, but she didn't think that fooled anyone. While the other mothers had visitors, proudly showing off their babies to husbands and relatives, Suzie had none. Ducking her head behind the current paperback, she'd ignored the looks and whispers.

'At least they taught me basic baby-care,' she said with forced brightness. 'Bathing, changing, feeding. Even better, nurses fed the babies during the night, so we mothers got a fair stretch of sleep from eleven till about five.

'Not so back at base,' she added grimly. 'That, I'm afraid, was the cruel awakening.'

– o –

Suzie had to explain a few things. James had no idea how baby care had changed in those forty years. How breast feeding in the old days had switched to a fashion for bottle feeding, before it changed back to breast feeding in modern times. How so-called experts at some time in the 1950s had trained midwives to believe that regular, measured feeds – delivered to the hour – was the way to bring up baby. The way to train baby to a routine.

'Routine? What a load of effing nonsense! Babies don't understand *routine* – they only know when they're hungry or uncomfortable. I tell you, James, my daughters were fed on demand – no matter if it was three hours, two hours, or six between feeds!'

Back at the Home, the mothers were slaves to Matron's rules. Every four hours, no matter what, throughout the day and night. That was it, even if baby was exhausted from crying, falling asleep with the teat in his tiny mouth, only to wake an hour later, screaming with hunger. The bottle was emptied, cleaned, put in the steriliser, ready for the next feed, four hours hence.

Mothers, she said, were not allowed to feed their babies between times. Boiled water, yes, but no milk. They could change a nappy, comfort them for a few minutes – then leave. The hungry baby had to wait. It was enough, she said, to break the hardest of hearts.

'The feeds,' she went on, 'were measured according to baby's weight – just a few ounces of water with a scoop of dried milk. It wasn't much. They weren't allowed more until they gained weight. And Matron's eagle eye was on every bottle. It was not only ridiculous, it was unspeakably cruel. My baby wasn't gaining – he was using all his energy just crying...'

Mostly, Baby managed an ounce before drifting into sleep. After that, she said, nothing could wake him, not even gentle flicks to the soles of his tiny feet.

Almost choking on the words, she forced herself to keep going. 'The babies were kept in the nursery – on the ground floor. My room was two floors up. If I went up to rest during the day, I couldn't hear him. But the mothers-in-waiting could. They were constantly calling me – *Suzie, Suzie, come down, your baby is crying...*'

She could see it still: narrow stairs, then a broad staircase down to the hall; the sitting room with its big bay window;

faces raised in reproach as she hurried across to the nursery. A table in the middle of the room; maybe three cots occupied; one cot shaking; shrieks echoing; tiny fists raging. Day after day, night after night, for endless weeks. Holding Baby, cuddling him, trying to calm the distress. Another wet nappy, adding it to a pile to be washed. A brief respite as he was dressed and cuddled; whimpers followed by more screams as she tucked him into his cot...

'Torture,' she whispered, 'that's what we went through, my baby and me. I'll never forget it. There's a huge change from pregnancy to motherhood, James – I loved him from the start. I had him for six weeks and no matter how I tried to harden my heart, telling myself he couldn't be mine, he was my baby and I *loved him*...'

Trying to control her emotion, she said, 'I'd hold him, try to comfort him, knowing he was hungry from taking so little at the last feed. With hours to go to the next one. The milk was locked away. Water – that's all I could give...'

She was sobbing by then, and James was holding her, trying to comfort her, but she pushed him away. He wasn't there – he didn't know – he didn't suffer.

'I couldn't wait to get him out of there. Surely, I thought, his new mother will have taken lessons, she'll know what he needs. Food – constant care! Comforting when he cries – surely, she'll know this?'

She'd had her mind focused on the day of rescue; but inside, a volcano of love and pain was threatening to erupt.

'God, I was so ignorant! Towards the end,' she confessed, 'I started adding more powdered milk to the water, in a foolish attempt to give him more nourishment. But all it did was give the poor little scrap a sore bottom...'

Gulping, choking, wiping furiously at the tears, she said, 'Then Matron had the nerve – the *nerve* – to say he shouldn't leave until his sore bottom was properly healed.

That was when I lost it. I literally saw red – shouted at the bloody woman – said at least out of this prison, he'd be cared for properly, and not left to starve when he was crying for food!'

Sixteen

The long evening twilight was drawing to a close as she saw James out to the taxi. It was late for the B&B; in fact, they'd almost forgotten his bed for the night when Suzie realized they hadn't eaten and were both on the way to being maudlin drunk.

A snack stabilized them a little; enough for her to make a sober enough call to the landlady. Inventing a family party, she asked what the time limit was for guests checking in. Ten o'clock was the answer. As the taxi left, she hoped he'd be in time.

With no one to notice, she allowed herself to totter unsteadily back into the house. Squinting at the kitchen clock, she saw it was a quarter to ten. When it came to leaving, James hadn't wanted to go, said something about sleeping on the sofa, but she wouldn't hear of it. Dear God, the thought of waking up with a stranger in the house – too much. Except he wasn't a stranger, was he? Not after all they'd discussed, voices croaking by the end. Trouble was, the house felt empty now he'd gone.

On the kitchen table were glasses and a half-empty whisky bottle; but if James had been putting it away, so had she. An empty wine-bottle from lunchtime, another with not much left in it; no wonder she was staggering. The remains of a sliced tomato looked like blood on the floor; feeling slightly sick, she was tempted to turn her back and go to bed.

All at once, it was too much; she gave way to self-pity and wept. 'Oh, for heaven's sake,' she muttered, 'pull yourself together…'

Taking a deep breath, she stacked the dishwasher, wiped tomato off the floor and pushed bottles into the recycling bin. A glass of water, a mug of tea, and that was that. Blow the rest.

Turning, she caught sight of Freddie's photograph on the dresser. 'Oh, don't you start,' she said, 'or I'll stick you back in the drawer! As for you, Mum – I just don't want to hear it…'

– o –

Against all expectation, she fell asleep almost at once, tea virtually untouched, light still on. She woke an hour or so later, sweating, her heart pounding, convinced James was in bed beside her. It took several moments of laboured breathing to recognize reality. Muttering curses, she looked at the time: just after one o'clock. The tea was cold but she drank it anyway. Dreading a hangover, she went down for more water; and for good measure set the kettle to boil as well.

Tea was a mistake but it tasted good. Anyway, nothing could have quelled the thoughts racing around her head. She wondered if James was wide awake too. Dear God, her words had shocked him. Not even his professional cool could disguise that. Pale and drawn – haggard, even, by the time he left. And Suzie had to admit she'd enjoyed shaking his complacency. Perverse, perhaps, because it hurt her too; but after weeks of not enough sleep and a cauldron of bubbling memories, she'd needed to blow the lid and let it out.

To give him his due, he'd taken it like a stoic. He hadn't grabbed his keys and marched out, as Freddie would have done. Latterly, he'd kept quiet, drinking steadily, taking everything in; speaking only when a question arose, or when he needed to understand more of her garbled account of those months in the wilderness.

The trouble was, the relief in letting go was like the blasting of a dam; she felt damaged, empty, weak. Not unlike the day she came home – which after the days preceding it, was hardly surprising.

After that row with Matron, she'd been on a knife-edge of stress, knowing nothing, but carrying on like an automaton. As it was, the adoption had gone ahead as per the time-frame some nameless official had already determined. Two days later, she was told to pack – she'd be leaving next morning.

On the day itself, Cousin Pat picked her up from the Home, with Baby well-fed for once, swaddled in his best blue outfit and shawl. During the hour's drive to the adoption office, he slept most of the way, but as the city came in sight he started to squirm and whimper, no doubt picking up on her fear and anxiety.

The day was sunny and hot, the trees in bright summer leaf. They didn't say much, she and Pat; Suzie had emptied her mind, afraid to dwell on what lay ahead. Except she prayed, and kept on praying, that these people would be kind and loving, that they would feed her baby, care for him, and bring him up to be a child that they – and she – would be proud of. She hoped they were the Christians the society claimed they were – she'd put that on her request form – and she'd written a letter about her baby. She hoped they would get that too. No name, of course – no signature.

And then they were in York, looking at street names, Pat wondering if she was in the right area. Eventually, they found the street, found the office in a terrace of tall houses with steps up to the front door.

As soon as they stopped, Baby stared at her in alarm, then started to cry in earnest as Pat helped them both out of the car. For a moment, gazing up at those steps and the open doorway, Suzie quailed.

What am I doing?

Once in there, that would be it – no going back.

No choice.

Taking a deep breath, she drew Baby closer, hushing him as she kissed his sweet-smelling forehead. And then she straightened her spine, lifted her chin and climbed the steps.

A woman met her, leading the way upstairs to an office. There were forms to be filled in, to be read through and signed. Overwhelmed by this reality, Suzie's self-control was held by a thread. Baby was twisting in her lap, crying again; she couldn't concentrate, tears were blurring her vision. She paused to rock him in her arms, but Baby refused to be pacified and started to yell...

'Why don't you give him to me?' Another woman, appearing from nowhere, smiled and held out her arms. 'It's warm today – he's probably thirsty. If you give me his bottle, I'll give him some water while you finish the forms.'

'Thank you,' Suzie managed, handing him over. He must have quieted almost at once, because she didn't hear him after that.

Sniffling, wiping her nose and eyes, she completed the forms and handed them over. The woman behind the desk gave a sympathetic smile and stood up.

'There we are,' she said gently. 'All done. You can go now.'

'Go?' she gasped. 'What about Baby? I didn't say goodbye...'

'He'll be fine. It's time for you to go,' the woman repeated, firmly this time.

Ushered out, down the stairs and down the steps, she could barely see for tears. Almost falling into the car, unable to speak, she buried her face in her hands.

Pat started the engine and drove them back to Richmond.

– o –

If she'd wept in the telling – hot, bitter tears, welling as much from anger as remembered grief – Suzie wept again as the wreck of the past surfaced afresh.

Finally, as the waves subsided, she switched off the bedside light and tried to sleep; but the memories, having found the light, refused to be pushed back.

So good of Pat, she thought; so brave of her cousin to volunteer for a job like that. Even though the journey to Aunt Dolly's had passed in a blur, she'd been aware of Pat's silent sympathy. Asked what she planned to do now, Suzie said she didn't know. She couldn't see beyond tomorrow.

What Aunt Dolly said or did when they got back, Suzie couldn't recall. There wasn't much anyone could say; the deed was done. All she remembered was dear little Jim, looking up at her, his head cocked to one side, eyes registering sympathy and confusion. She remembered picking him up, hugging him close and letting the tears flow; and for once, Aunt Dolly didn't call him back when he followed her upstairs.

That night, she slept for twelve hours, waking to a glorious day. The sun was peeping through the curtains, telling her she was rested and free, and the beauty of Richmond was hers for the asking. The Home and those three months might have been in another life, another age; she didn't think of it once. Instead, she donned her lightest clothes and planned to go for a walk with the little terrier, over the bridge and along the shady riverside.

Aunt Dolly had said to leave Jim at home as it was market day; but Suzie hadn't really taken it in. Only as she approached the Market Place did colour and movement – and, yes, the *joy* of the scene – make its impact. Amongst the crowd, she felt like a child at a funfair, dazzled, hardly knowing where to look, which direction to take. Awnings surrounded the old church in the centre, beneath them were fruit and vegetables; cheap cotton frocks; sandals, handbags; meat stalls, fishmongers. The stalls went on and on.

'And the *people*,' she'd exclaimed as she described the scene to James, 'laughing, talking. It was so strange – overwhelming – like I'd been let out of prison and into a fairgound...'

After the crippling confines of the Home, the sense of joy – the sense of *relief* at being able to breathe again – was euphoric. She hadn't wept, she hadn't been upset – she was just glad to be free.

Given what she'd done, such joy seemed inappropriate now. Not that she cared whether James understood or not; but he'd said that he did.

'I was like you,' he admitted huskily, 'when Maggie finally gave up the fight. The relief – it was overwhelming.'

She'd glanced up then, and his eyes were brimming.

He said he'd been numb for weeks, but for Suzie the euphoria had evaporated overnight. After that one delirious, dizzying day of freedom, she'd woken next morning longing for her Mum, for home and comfort and a place to cry. Coming home was when reality hit, when she realized what she'd done, when she discovered no one could make it better, least of all her mother.

In her mind, she could see their street as it had been that day, bleak against her memories of Richmond. The house was a shock too, small and cramped after the big, high-ceilinged rooms of the Home. Being back with Mum and Dad was even more disconcerting; in one sense as though she'd never been away, in another, as though those missing months had been part of someone else's life. And yet she had been away; those life-changing events had indeed happened.

Her parents had visited Richmond before the birth; and later, they'd made the journey to meet their grandson. Although glad to see them, for Suzie it had been upsetting. Aware that she was different, no longer their little girl but a mother, it was as though the locked door of home and safety had been forced open, letting in an arctic wind. And yet the ghost of that little girl had wanted to cling as they said their goodbyes, begging them to take her with them, turn back the clock...

−o−

Coming home, as she admitted to James, she was a mother bereaved, yet expected to be the girl who'd gone away. As the sense of loss descended, she'd wanted to let it out; but after trying, inadequately, to express her grief and outrage, Connie had said the words and the weeping must stop. It was no good dwelling on sadness; what was done was done.

'After the first few days, I wasn't allowed to talk about it...'

Putting in a plea for her parents, James said it was how the wartime generation dealt with things. In a sense, he was right; but now, as a grandparent herself, Suzie knew it went deeper than that. How would she and Freddie have felt if their daughter Sara had given away her first child? It was bad enough that she'd terminated her first pregnancy.

No wonder Mum had found it unbearable. Dad never mentioned it.

Seventeen

Grief kept him awake. Grief and anger and regret. He couldn't even pray. What Suzie had gone through was as real to him as though he'd been there. Particularly that final day. The journey to an adoption office in the city; the form-filling; the baby's distress...

He could see it all. And when, inevitably, Suzie reached the point where their son was taken away, James was ahead of her. Of course, they'd be well-versed at preventing a scene. But oh, God, the pain as Suzie described being ushered out, down the steps and onto the street, her cousin waiting in the car.

The return home to that bleak street in Denshaw – he could see that too – and her mother's refusal to let her talk it out. Dear God, he knew what guilt and grief were like, especially when bottled up. No wonder she'd had a breakdown a year later. Under the circumstances, he thought, it was a wonder she'd held out so long.

He'd wanted to stay with her; hold her, comfort her, share the regrets; but she'd pushed him away. It was time he left, she said; and she was right, it was. But how it hurt to leave her.

Stumbling away into the night, almost falling into the taxi, he'd barely held himself together. Drinking for courage: always a mistake. Whisky hadn't numbed the pain; it had sapped his self-control. Somehow, he'd managed to collect himself, finding a note with which to pay the driver – too much, but he was past caring. A few deep breaths later, just before the deadline, he was ringing the bell of a house on Heatherley's main street, controlled enough to greet the owner, receive his key and find his room.

At some point he'd dropped into an uneasy sleep, only to be wakened by the buzzing of his mobile at seven. Dazzled by a shaft of sunlight between heavy drapes, James wondered where he was. It took a moment to remember, and when he did, he groaned. Thick-headed, he was glad to get into the shower. Hot water, followed by a blast of cold, shocked him into life, but red-rimmed eyes bore witness to the night before. A shave made him look less haggard, but there was nothing to cure his body's deep-seated ache.

Yesterday's clothes, crumpled on a chair, were bundled into his overnight bag. Finally, in clean shirt and chinos, he stood by the open window, trying to clear his mind before saying the morning office.

It was difficult. Since Maggie's death, he'd often found it so. His prayer book's printed page blurred before his eyes; phrases he knew by heart – phrases he often struggled to make sincere rather than said by rote – refused to come. Despite his efforts, he could not shake off the memories of the night. In the end, allowing the grief, he knelt; and, in his clumsy way, set it before Almighty God. A god he envisaged, not as a person but as positive energy; building, working, striving against destruction.

All very well, he thought, but it was hard to think in terms of a personal relationship with such an impersonal force. Picturing the human form of Jesus Christ was easier, although sometimes, like now, only the crucified Christ seemed real.

'Take my pain,' he whispered at last. 'Use it. Help me.'

After a while he was calmer. Rising from his knees, he reached for the book.

– o –

Fogged by the shadows of a dream, as Suzie woke, she found herself thinking: *If it weren't for the sainted Margaret and her inability to conceive, would I be going through all this?*

As she dragged herself to the bathroom, a dull headache throbbed behind her eyes. Too much wine last night; too many tears. All too much for a woman her age. Tempted to languish in bed with water and painkillers, Suzie turned her back on that idea. Before long, James would be turning up; she'd have to make herself presentable, swallow some breakfast; kill the hangover, smother the grief.

Toast with lashings of marmalade helped; after coffee and a cigarette, she felt almost human again. Human, but horribly sensitive. Last night, despite her outbursts, James had done his best to listen constructively; it can't have been easy. But one wrong word today...

Maybe she should phone, tell him not to come. If he felt anything like she did, he'd be happy to clear off back to Oxford. On the other hand, if she didn't see him today, he'd want to come back. Or, worse, she'd feel they were only partway through this pseudo-psychotherapy session, and she'd be chasing him. Because that's what it felt like: psychotherapy.

Suzie had been there. Years ago, in the midst of marital troubles with Freddie, she'd sought help as a means of releasing all her pent-up anguish. His casual attitude towards fidelity was driving her crazy; but of course, therapy was never about the *other* person, always about the sufferer's hang-ups, and where they originated. In Suzie's case, fear of becoming her mother, Connie, worrying at something until it turned her from kind, loving woman into a neurotic heap of suspicion and resentment. Nor was that all. In Suzie's experience, casual sex too often ended in grief for someone, usually the innocent party.

Besides, she hadn't yet told James everything. Focusing on the anguish of it all, she'd forgotten some pertinent facts, like there was no way he could do the search himself. He might have admitted responsibility, but they weren't married and his name wouldn't appear on the birth certificate.

– o –

'I must say, you look better than you should,' Suzie said as she handed him a cup of coffee. 'And certainly better than I feel…'

James smiled, weighing an answer. 'You look fine,' he assured her. In truth, she looked more than fine to him, cool and summery in a pale green shirt. Perhaps it was the light, but this morning her eyes were reflecting the colour, reminding him of other times, long ago.

'Well,' he said at last, 'it's amazing what a good breakfast can do.'

'That and a good walk, if you can stand it. Perfect cure for a hangover.'

James nodded in gratitude, thinking how much better it would be than sitting here, going over more painful ground.

'If you like, we could drive up to the Fox and Hounds. It's an easy walk from there to the old castle. Not much left of it, but there's a great view.'

He said little as Suzie drove northwards along narrow, twisting lanes, climbing all the time. Apart from the odd farmhouse, he could see no settlements, and, as they crested another hill, there was the pub, solid and stone-built, isolated at the side of the road. It seemed oddly familiar.

'Used to be an old coaching inn,' Suzie said as they got out of the car.

Looking around at stone-walled pastures and a forested valley below the road, James followed her across to a bridleway leading through the pines. 'An old plantation,' she said. 'Thank heavens they're planting more mixed woodland now – more in keeping.'

'I think I came here once, when I was a boy. Did you say there's a castle?'

'Well, people call it a castle – doesn't look much like one, to be honest.'

The bridleway led down a gentle slope, but as they reached a footpath leading off to the right, Suzie turned and led the way uphill through the trees. A few minutes later, she was chuckling as James paused to catch his breath.

From her backpack, she brought out a bottle of water. 'Thought we might need this...'

A little further and they were beyond the tree line, in sight of an old stone ruin with moorland rising in the distance. Close by were dark patches of heather and golden gorse; somewhere hidden and far below, he was sure there was a river.

'I think this is the place we came with Uncle Harry,' he said, shading his eyes as he looked around. 'I was really into castles when I was a kid – but this place seemed strange, in the middle of nowhere. A bit of a disappointment, to be honest. I was expecting something more like Richmond...'

Suzie laughed. 'It's hardly that! Besides, the windows are all wrong.'

'Later additions, I'd say. Could be medieval,' he conceded, walking around, looking at the foundation course. 'Rebuilt at some point. Probably a hunting lodge...'

Thinking of his childhood, of enthusiasms which led to a career, he turned to her and said, 'I wonder if our son was ever into history – or art, for that matter?'

'Who knows?' she answered tersely, turning away to stare at those empty windows.

'Have you never wondered?'

'Of course I've wondered,' she snapped back. 'What do you take me for?'

'Sorry – that was thoughtless.'

Breath coming hard, she rounded on him. 'Yes it was! For your information, I've *wondered*, as you put it, since before he was born. Most of all about the family he went to. Who were they? What were they like? Were they fit to bring up my son? Would they *love* him?'

James flinched, but Suzie hadn't finished. 'Anything else – what he was interested in, what career he's followed – how would I know? Probably bright enough, but how do we know he didn't drop out, take drugs, end up homeless or in prison? How do we know he's still *alive?*'

Shocked by that, he watched as she strode away, back along the footpath. Following more slowly, he saw her pause to light a cigarette, smoking intensely while staring into the trees.

'Look,' he said as he caught up, 'can't you see it's hard for me too? Wanting to know everything, not knowing if I'm treading on dangerous ground?'

Her eyes glinted gold in the sunlight. 'Yes,' she conceded, 'you're right. I'm sorry.'

Carefully, she stubbed out her cigarette, making sure it was dead before tossing it into the undergrowth. As they starting walking again, she said, 'Let's talk about something else. Why don't you tell me about Margaret? I've been wondering about her – you know, how you met, that sort of thing.'

He tried to say he was supposed to be here for her; but she bit back and said this was supposed to be a two-way thing; it was time for him to give a little. James didn't want to talk about his wife, but if he did, maybe Suzie would calm down.

They'd been introduced, he said, by a mutual friend at a fund-raising concert; Maggie had been one of the soloists and he'd been captivated at once. He'd imagined she'd be very serious, very dedicated – which she was, but only about her music. In every other way, she'd been light-hearted and funny.

'It was when I was still at Bristol – to be honest, I'd become a bit of a hermit. But thanks to various college events – and I suspect a bit of female plotting – we met fairly often after that.' Clearing his throat, he said, 'Anyway, we started going out together – to concerts, the theatre, that sort of thing. Which was fine, but...'

'But what?' Suzie asked as his words tailed away.

He paused, caught afresh by the memory of conflict. He'd meant to tell Suzie yesterday, but the moment, swamped by other questions, had passed. 'Well, it wasn't what you'd call a straightforward courtship. Unfortunately, I was going through my own crisis at the time...'

Looking back, he could see he'd been suffering a form of depression for years, made worse by his cousin Alex's death. Not long afterwards, he'd met Maggie.

'She was like a shaft of sunlight – for a while, I started to enjoy life again. Until I realized I was in love with her, and she with me.' Sighing, he said, 'And as you know, Suzie, love isn't just those dazzling moments when the world seems a better place. Real love means responsibility for someone else's happiness...'

Beside the track a few yards away was a smooth log. As they sat down, he accepted the water she offered. 'I knew I wanted to be with Maggie. But it wasn't a good time...'

'Why on earth not?'

Considering various aspects of the truth, James knew he wasn't up to confessing the heart of it. Eventually, he shrugged and said, 'Well, it was my career as much as anything. I'd been lecturing for ten years, and it had lost its magic. Believe me,

Suzie, I'd met some crabby old academics in my time, and I could see myself turning into another one – obsessed by my own research, hating to be challenged, refusing to consider anything new. And meanwhile, all these bright young students, coming and going – and what was I imparting to them? Late medieval history…'

As he paused for breath, somewhat surprised by his own vehemence, Suzie said tentatively, 'I've been meaning to ask – why that particular period?'

Shaking his head, he laughed, and suddenly the tension was gone. 'Why do you think? I could never resist a castle!'

'Romance, chivalry? *Morte d'Arthur*?' she asked, teasing now.

'I suppose so. Although the reality was somewhat different…'

– o –

It was a different world, Suzie thought as they made their way back to the Fox and Hounds; but in listening to James, she could see why research had led him to specialise in the 14th century. He described that distant, turbulent period as being like the tapestries of the time, with threads leading to battles and betrayals and the all-encompassing power of the Church. As he explained why the Reformation had happened, it seemed no longer dull, but relevant to the modern world. Different players, different weapons, but similar political motives.

'Ultimately, my research into two of the era's leading figures had a profound effect. And it all came to a head around the time I met Maggie…'

Venturing a question, she said, 'Was this to do with you going into the Church?'

'It was,' he agreed as the pub came in sight. 'But I didn't think Maggie would understand – I barely understood it myself…'

James paused as they reached the road. A few minutes later, in the cool and shady bar, they were ordering some refreshing drinks. As they carried their glasses to a table by the window, Suzie repeated her question about his change of direction.

For a moment he seemed far away, but then he said worship had been part of his life since schooldays. 'Less so as an adult, but mostly I'd leave a service with a sense of something gained. Humility, usually, and a determination to count my blessings. But by the time of my breakdown, I was barely functioning. Classic symptoms, I suppose – working too hard, not sleeping, drinking in order to sleep. Meanwhile, what little faith I'd had, was disappearing into the mire...

'Until that day in the lecture hall, when light flashed through the murk and stopped me, almost in mid-sentence. Not quite a Road to Damascus experience,' he added with a smile. 'God didn't speak, but one who'd suffered for his faith was spelling a message I'd been too deaf to hear...'

A little lost, Suzie asked him to explain, but instead he asked her a question. 'Have you heard of John Wycliffe, who started translating the Bible into English?' As Suzie nodded, he said, 'And William of Wykeham, who founded the abbey and college at Winchester?'

'Heard of them – don't know much else.' She couldn't help smiling as James became brisk; she could almost see him with a roomful of students.

'In short, they were both born about 1330, with similar names and not dissimilar backgrounds – what we'd call the middle class. The Yorkshireman, Wycliffe, became an Oxford scholar, while Wykeham in Hampshire had only a basic education. Even so, he rose to become Lord Chancellor – largely thanks to his ability with figures and a talent for designing buildings.

'For a while, these two men – opposites in lifestyle and thinking – mixed in the same court circles. Extraordinary when you think about it. Anyway,' James went on, 'I was in the middle of a lecture about them – a lecture I'd given many times before – when suddenly, I stopped. Couldn't go on. Talk about seeing the light!

'As it flashed through my head, I saw these very different men – metaphors, I suppose, for my own life. On the one hand, Wykeham, embracing worldly success – on the other, Wycliffe, philosopher and theologian, preparing to take on the might of Rome for what he believed to be right and true.

'And what was I, but the worldly figure?' he added with a dry smile. 'Chasing success at the expense of everything else. At the expense of what was important. So I didn't have to address what was wrong with me…'

By the sudden change in his expression, Suzie knew it had to be something profound. After a moment, she said, 'And what *was* wrong with you?'

'Guilt,' he said quietly. 'As simple and as complicated as that.'

He said he didn't want to talk about it where they might be overheard. Drinks in hand, he led the way outside, to a sturdy wooden table in the sun. Silence stretched as he surveyed the landscape; he was so clearly struggling for words, Suzie ventured a prompt. 'You were talking about guilt…'

'I know.' Nipping the bridge of his nose, he said tersely, 'How do I put this? That night with you – I was drunk. To put it crudely, I could barely get it up. And then I came, virtually straight away…'

As he clutched at his pint glass, suddenly, she was seeing the young James. At once, she began to understand; but before she could speak, he said, 'Yesterday, when we were talking about mockery – what you said afterwards…'

'Ah,' she said softly, 'you thought I was mocking your performance?'

'Exactly – and after that, I mocked myself.' He looked up and she could see the torment in his eyes. 'The truth is,

Suzie, I was so afraid of being a failure, for years I could barely perform at all.'

Shocked, for several moments she was beyond speech. *Impotence? Was that what he was talking about?* She might have laughed at the irony, but it wasn't funny.

'Good grief, James – I don't know what to say…'

He grasped her hand. 'No need. I just want you to know that night had repercussions for me, too. Not simply that moment – everything else. For nearly fifteen years, my sex-life was memorable for all the wrong reasons. Falling for Maggie was an agony I could barely cope with. When it came to intimacy, I backed off. Couldn't risk it – she was too important.'

Slowly, Suzie nodded. 'Guilt,' she said quietly. 'It lingers. We both took what we thought was the easy way out…'

'And only later did we discover the cost…'

– o –

Yesterday, he thought, hearing Suzie's story had been torture. Hard to take the pain, hard not to respond with his own crippling memories. Now, having shared the worst, James found it easier to tell her the rest.

'It wasn't just the sexual problem,' he said as they returned to the car, 'although it was a vital factor…'

Meeting Maggie had coincided with more mundane levels of frustration to do with academia. Thanks to his research he'd already felt a call to the church, but he'd been rejecting that in much the same way as he was rejecting the woman he loved.

'Not exactly, *I can't do this*, more a case of, *why is God bothering me now, when I can't even solve the other problem?*'

'And all this on top of Alex's death and bad memories?'

'Exactly. I felt like…' He shook his head, unable to come up with an acceptable word.

'Shit?'

With a rueful laugh, he agreed. 'But oddly enough, it brings me back to that day in the lecture hall. I call it my moment of crisis, but it was, I suppose, a classic breakdown. I had to face up to the fact that things were seriously wrong.'

'So what happened?' Suzie asked as they drove away from the pub

'Well, luckily, after I walked out, almost the first person on the scene was the college chaplain. I can't have been making much sense, but he must have remembered me mentioning Pusey House.

'It's in Oxford,' James explained. 'A religious foundation with a huge library. I'd spent quite a bit of time there, doing research – I was even thinking about writing a book, but that's another story. Anyway, I'd been impressed on several fronts, not least by their music and services – and particularly by the staff. All clerics, all staunch Anglo-Catholics – monks, some of them, from the Community of the Resurrection here in Yorkshire.'

'Anglo-Catholics?'

As they drove back towards Felton, James found himself explaining the Oxford Movement, a reaction to the evangelical trends of the mid-19th century. 'They wanted to focus more on the Eucharist, and the kind of ceremony associated with the Roman church. On the other hand, they've always been hot on social reform. Leading by example, working in deprived areas, that sort of thing – following the example of Christ in everyday life.

'Impressive, particularly for me at the time, surrounded as I was by snobbery and sniping. Anyway, when I cracked up that day, the Chaplain gave me the name of an elderly priest who'd helped him in the past. He urged me to see him, said he would probably sort me out quicker than a whole panel of doctors…'

'But you did see a doctor?'

'Had to – in order to be signed off work. The doc prescribed drugs – which certainly helped. But it was Father Allen at Pusey House who cut through the confusion. He enabled me to see what was really going on…'

'And what was going on?' Suzie asked as they rounded a corner and Felton came in sight.

'A lot,' he replied.

Moments later, tyres were crunching on gravel as Suzie pulled into the drive.

James waited until they were inside before telling her the rest. 'Today, the Doc would probably refer me to a therapist. But when you think about it,' he added with dry smile, 'the Church was onto the notion of psychotherapy long before Freud…

'Father Allen's questions about work and striving for success weren't hard to grasp – all to do with my father… But once he got me talking about why I was so reluctant to get involved with women, I knew where he was going. And strangely, I didn't mind admitting it to him. He asked me to describe my first sexual experience – and when I told him about you, and the baby, he wasn't at all surprised.'

Suzie glanced up. 'Ah, I'm beginning to see what he was getting at – your guilty conscience.'

'Precisely. And once I could see it for myself, the pattern became clear. No matter how strong the desire, something was stopping me at the vital moment. It got so bad, latterly the thought was conscious – along the lines of, *you're going to regret this*… By that stage, I didn't even want to start.'

'Oh, James,' she sighed, 'I felt exactly like that for a long time…'

'Did you?' He was surprised, never thinking she could have been affected too. 'I'm so sorry…' Tentatively, he took her hand in his, and when she didn't immediately pull away, he gave it a gentle squeeze.

'Anyway, carry on,' she said, moving away to fill the kettle, 'I want to know the rest.'

'Well, having got to the source of it, Father Allen asked me a simple question. *Did I believe in God?* I said yes. So, then he asked me another. *Did I believe that God could forgive me?* Again, I said, yes – but his next question really brought me up short. *Did I think I was greater than God, that I couldn't forgive myself?*'

'As simple as that?' Suzie was clearly incredulous.

'A simple question, yes – but it helped to change my thinking. Not an overnight miracle by any means, but making my confession that day was probably the most important moment in my life. It showed me the way forward – a long road, as it turned out, but thank God, I had help.'

Pausing, holding her gaze, he said, 'I started to connect with people – really connect – for what was probably the first time in my life. It made a huge difference.'

'Yes,' she said softly, 'I can see that. But Margaret – Maggie – how on earth did you manage to explain all this to her?'

James shook his head. 'I didn't. Not at first. Although she did keep in touch while I was off sick – we saw each other from time to time…'

Maggie had been his good Samaritan, there but never intrusive, standing by until he was well again. In the beginning, he'd prevaricated, using acceptable reasons for his breakdown, saying he'd come to see that moment of crisis in the lecture hall as an act of God, meant to show him where he was going wrong. Not exactly a lie, but a long way from the truth; something else for him to explain afterwards, when he finally told her the whole story.

'Thankfully, apart from giving sound advice, Father Allen recommended some helpful reading – it showed how priests really were in touch with the world. You know, ministering to all kinds of problems, not just the obvious ones…

'Of course, I didn't know whether the Church would accept me – but at least it was something Maggie and I could talk about – face to face, I mean. To my surprise, she wasn't shocked. It turned out her uncle was a priest – and as a singer, she'd been involved with church music from an early age, so the idea wasn't entirely foreign to her.'

'But the sex thing,' Suzie said, handing him a mug of tea, 'that must have been tough to explain?'

Amused by her directness, he said, 'It was. At the time though,' he added ruefully, 'I was being very restrained. Hoping she'd put it down to religious teaching…'

'Good grief, James, you were walking a fine line, weren't you?'

'Certainly was.' Running fingers through his hair, he said, 'As it turned out, I was accepted for training rather sooner than I expected. Suddenly, it was all very real – I was about to become a student again, at Oxford this time. But I couldn't go away without telling her the truth.'

'And?'

'Well, she was surprised. But she seemed almost relieved. She said she'd suspected I was gay, and in denial!'

Laughing, Suzie said, 'It's not funny, I know, but I can see why. A good-looking bloke with no obvious attachments…' A moment later, her green eyes were sparkling with mischief. 'Go on – tell me she offered to give you lots of practice?'

Suddenly, James was laughing too. 'That about sums it up, yes…'

Eighteen

At least he didn't mind being teased, Suzie thought. They'd
made each other laugh, and he'd started to open up at last.
She was reminded of the boy who'd mystified her all those
years ago – revealing bits of himself, but rarely what he was
thinking. If he'd been like that with Margaret, no wonder it
took so long for their relationship to get going. She must have
been one hell of a strong woman to take James on in those
circumstances. It proved how much she must have loved him;
and how he'd loved her, to be so determined to overcome that
crippling problem. But of course, he'd had not just Margaret,
but God on his side.

Did she believe? He'd asked that a moment ago, and she'd
said yes, even though church-going wasn't part of her agenda.
She could see how faith had wrought huge changes in his life,
but when she said so, he'd looked down, studied his clasped
hands, and said something to the effect that grief had sapped
everything in the last couple of years, including his faith.

Before she could respond, he seemed to shake it off;
suddenly brisk as he joked about the inner man, saying

breakfast was hours ago, and should they go out for something to eat?

She glanced at the clock and shook her head. 'Doubtful – this is Heatherley, not Oxford. Pubs not pizza parlours. How about I make some sandwiches and more tea? That should get you home okay.'

Opening a packet of ham, finding some salad to go with it, she found herself thinking about the past twenty-four hours. After all they'd discussed it was as though time had shrunk; more than that, they'd become more intimate than lovers, sharing secrets no one else was privy to. Sooner or later, she would have to make a decision, but not yet, it was too soon. Aware of his gaze, she heard him sigh.

'What are we going to do, Suzie?'

'You mean, what am *I* going to do,' she said abruptly, and carried on slicing tomatoes.

That killed the conversation.

She set the sandwiches on the table, for a while simply looking at hers. 'You see, James, it dawned on me last night – *you* can't do the search. You weren't registered as the father.'

He stopped eating. 'But I accepted responsibility...'

'Not the same thing. We weren't married, so unless you'd been with me when he was registered...' Pausing, she said, 'I didn't get a copy of the birth certificate, because I was – well, because he was being adopted. But I imagine it would say, *father unknown...*'

It seemed to take a while for that to sink in. Eventually, James said, 'But I thought... You mean, in effect, I could be anybody?'

She nodded. 'I was so shocked when you first mentioned it, it didn't occur to me.'

For a moment, he seemed incapable of speech. Eventually, in a dead voice, he said, 'I shouldn't have asked, should I? I'd say, forget it, but we can't, can we?'

'No, we can't. Not now.'

He looked up, hurt and pleading. 'It all devolves on you.'

'It always did.'

They were back to the nub of the problem. Feeling shaky, Suzie picked up her cigarettes and moved away. 'You remember me mentioning that woman – the social worker who came to the Home just before I left?'

'What about her?'

'She wanted to see my baby. To check him out – make sure he had all his fingers and toes, I expect.' The lump in her throat made it hard to go on. 'Anyway, she told me the adoption society aimed to place each baby with a family like the mother's. On the principle of similar expectations in life. And as you know,' she went on, 'my parents were working class – which could have limited our son's options. But *you* accepted responsibility…'

James looked mystified.

'Don't you see? Your background – public school, university – added to the fact that I was in further education at the time, prompted them to think again. In their wisdom,' she added sardonically, 'the adoption society decided *this* child could be bright enough to fit into a higher social class…'

Even as he muttered an expletive, Suzie said, 'Well, James, you know how it was. Anyway, I was told suitable parents had been found.'

'Go on.'

She took a deep breath. 'A professional couple in their thirties, unable to have children of their own.'

'Good God,' he exclaimed. 'That could have been Maggie and me…'

As he sat with bowed head, Suzie wondered if she should tell him the rest.

It took a while to find her voice. 'I'm not sure if you know this, but in the 1970s the law changed – to allow adopted kids to look for their natural parents...' She paused to clear her throat. 'Ever since, I've thought – hoped – that maybe one day he would come looking for me.

'He could have done,' she added gently, 'once he reached eighteen. But he hasn't, James, and maybe that tells us something. It could be that *he just doesn't want to know...*'

Still bowed, he covered his face, and Suzie realized he was in tears. For a helpless moment, she stared, unsure what to do; until with a muffled sob, he kicked his chair away and turned for the door.

She moved at once, grabbing his arm before he could leave. 'No, not like this – please, James – please calm down...'

Pierced by his glance, she almost let go. For a moment, it seemed he would shake her off; but suddenly the tension was gone. As her arms enfolded him, he bowed his head to hers. The breadth of his shoulders, the touch of his skin against her cheek; most of all the faint, familiar smell of him, caught her by surprise. It could have been yesterday...

It had to stop.

Releasing herself, Suzie sank back into her chair. Squeezing her shoulder, James stood for a moment before heading towards the bathroom.

He was gone for a while.

'Sorry,' he murmured as he came back. His eyes, she noticed, were rimmed with grief.

'No need...'

Another pot of tea, while James attempted to finish his sandwich. Normal, everyday things, pushing back those painful, intimate moments. She asked him to accept that she needed more time to think; and time to speak to both her daughters.

'They're part of me, James. My son – our son – is their half-brother. Whatever happens next is bound to affect them too.'

– o –

The way she said it tore afresh at his self-control. While he was trying to imagine positive things – even attempting to say so – Suzie was clearly reluctant to picture anything at all. Fear, not joyful anticipation was the rule for her. *Expect nothing, and you won't be disappointed*, seemed to be her rule of thumb.

He could understand that. After all, it was much as he'd been in the past, before his faith lifted him out of it. From Suzie's point of view, if she did nothing, she could cling to the hope that one day, her son would come looking for her. And who was to say she was wrong?

A little while later, as they parted, James was aware of unspoken pleas passing between them. She knew what he was asking – no need to repeat it – just as he understood why she couldn't agree. Not yet, at least. He could only hope that her daughters had open minds.

Just as the moment became awkward, she raised her arms for a farewell embrace and he clung to her, briefly, before tearing himself away.

– o –

All the way back to Oxford, that moment was present in his mind. It was enough to say he was in some way forgiven; but the feel of her in his arms bestowed a different gift, one he'd been missing for a long time. The physical warmth of another human being – softness, scent, womanliness – the *otherness* that once had made him whole.

If they'd been at the mercy of desire and emotion all those years ago, now, in maturity, such things were controllable. Except sorrow, perhaps. Sharing it, James felt closer to her; from now on, he hoped they might each begin to mend.

Following the ribbon of the road, he found himself going over lighter moments. Yesterday, in the hall, he'd noticed a framed drawing of Suzie when she was young. Done by her husband, it was a tender, loving sketch that somehow revealed her vulnerability and the man's regard for her. He'd remarked on that, as well as one of the paintings in Suzie's lounge; but apart from saying her husband had been a gifted painter, she'd made it clear that she didn't want to talk about Freddie. Maybe one day, she would. But if Freddie was off the agenda, she had talked about her parents, especially her mother. It was clear they'd had a good relationship, despite some painful mistakes. James was pleased about that.

– o –

Her mother's photo on the dresser had brought back the day they met. He'd been so anxious, fearing the worst, yet Mrs Wallis had been surprisingly kind – and wise. If only he'd had the good sense to act on her advice, had the guts to discuss it with his father, things might have been different.

Leeds station, that muted conversation in the bar; and afterwards, saying goodbye to Suzie – he'd never forgotten that moment. Barely holding himself together, he'd found his train, parked his rucksack on a seat and, as soon as they were moving, locked himself in the lavatory and wept.

Afterwards, drained and numb, he was unable to think beyond the next stage of his journey, although by the time he reached Aldershot and his parents' house, he'd recovered enough to be able to pretend. That he was glad to see them; that he was merely exhausted after a tough couple of months. Whilst there, he read late, slept late, ate and drank whatever was put before him. Christmas TV proved a saviour, excusing him from speech.

He tried to appreciate his mother's efforts; knew she was working hard to make this Christmas – their first in England for several years – a happy occasion. But it felt excessive, over the top. Barely able to cope, he attended a couple of parties given by his parents' friends and tried to socialise with their teenage offspring. He drew the line, however, at going to a dance with the girl they'd selected for him. After managing to put his mother off, James found himself facing his father. Typically, Dad had tried being persuasive and when that didn't work, lost patience.

'What's the matter with you?' he demanded. 'She's a nice girl – why can't you stop being so damn miserable for a change, and take her along? You never know, you might even enjoy yourself!'

Struggling for an answer, James had simply looked down and shaken his head. Should have known it was guaranteed to light the blue touch-paper.

'What is it? Do you find girls repulsive, or what? Don't tell me you're batting for the other side!'

At that, James had lost his temper, not only denying it, but stung into saying he'd met a girl in the summer. It was over, which was why he didn't feel like going out, let alone ruining this girl's evening by refusing to dance...

It was the first time he'd stood up to his father; and it was hard to say who was the most shocked. But the old man was more circumspect after that. Of course, that outburst had led to a string of invasive questions from his mother. She was less easy to deal with, but, unlike Suzie in a similar situation, he'd had no pressing need to confess the truth.

He'd imagined he was doing quite well until his mother began to dig further. 'You fancied yourself in love with her, I suppose?' To his noncommittal reply, she'd said, 'Well, dear, you'll just have to put it down to experience. There are other girls, you know... And if you don't give yourself the chance to know them, how will you ever find Miss Right?'

Miss Right? Even now, the phrase made him cringe.

– o –

First love, he thought; how painful it had been. How much more so for the destruction wrought by a moment's folly.

As last night's confessions sprang to mind, James knew he'd touched raw wounds. Shocking, because he could never have imagined what Suzie had experienced, before the birth or after. As she so rightly said, he'd never been a parent, not in the real sense; never looked upon the face of his child. It hurt, just trying to imagine what it would have been like to see and hold that new-born baby. His son. Given up because he, James Fielding, had been more afraid of what his parents would think, what the future might hold. Fear had killed love and strangled conscience. Above all, he'd wanted to escape. Which he had, at huge cost. One he could never have imagined on the day he denied her, the day he'd said over the phone, *Sorry, but I can't marry you…*

No wonder she'd been angry. She'd said she didn't want him anyway – and why would she, after what he'd done? But without marriage and so-called respectability, James had left her little choice. And now, all these years later, he'd done it again. Left Suzie no choice but to make another heart-breaking decision.

We both took what we thought was the easy way out, he'd said of the past; to which she'd replied, *And only later did we discover the cost…*

What, he wondered, would be the cost this time?

Reflecting on their parting, he knew what Suzie meant: *don't upset the status quo; at the end of the day, it's up to our son.* And that, more than the oath taken forty years before, was why she was afraid to break the silence. Afraid of being rejected in turn by the child she'd given away.

He found himself speaking aloud to his wife, as though she were there in the car. 'Don't you see, Maggie, it's far more complicated than you imagined – than either of us could imagine. I had my doubts even then – even when I promised. You've no idea what we've unleashed…'

It was Maggie who'd picked up on those proposed changes to the law, not long before she died. Even then, she'd been urging him to think about it. He'd fended her off, saying it would be hard enough to make contact with his former girlfriend, never mind persuade her to give him the details.

It was not that he hadn't cared; not that he hadn't prayed for his son over the years; trying hard to imagine a little boy, and later, a teenager growing into a man.

As she was dying, Maggie kept asking for his promise. Never thinking it would be possible, James had finally agreed, while his real intention was to ease her distress. She thought she'd failed him, but she never had, not even in failing to produce a child.

Yes, children would have been wonderful, would have completed them as a family. But the past was past; and anyway, it wasn't so important to him; not as it was for her. He loved *her*, Maggie, for the woman she was. Wise, generous, caring; as loving in bed as her nature had always suggested. She never made him feel as though he had to perform, even though there had been times, according to the baby-making programme, when he should have done.

James shook his head, smiling at remembered inventiveness, her sense of humour. How she'd make some comment about the parishioners – *if they could see the Vicar's wife right now…* That would always make him laugh, dispel the anxiety, enable him to carry on to mutual enjoyment… Mostly, anyway.

His rescuer, his God-given partner in life. How he missed her.

– o –

Skirting Oxford, making his way along familiar country lanes, he came at last to Norton Parva. In the twilight, a group of thatched, black and white cottages by the village green stood out, as did the George and Dragon pub with its flamboyant sign; to one side, barely visible behind trees in the churchyard, stood St George's church. Even in daylight, its pale limestone presence appeared to be standing back as though reluctant to intrude.

It struck him afresh as he slowed to make the turn into his drive. Two days in Yorkshire, and it was as though he'd been away for a year. On the left, further along, the Old Rectory was now a highly desirable residence, sold off in the '70s; his present home, still owned by the church, had been the carriage house and stables. Now, with four bedrooms and a study, it was comfortably modern but far too big for him.

There were letters on the mat, including a note from his curate, about a forthcoming church council meeting at Norton Magna. As a postscript, she'd added, *I hope your trip north went well, and that you won't forget to eat when you get back – I know what you're like!*

That brought a smile. Amy was in her forties, married with a teenage son, and she treated James the same way. But it was nice to be mothered occasionally; it made him feel part of the family. There were even times when both he and the boy exchanged eye-rolling glances over Amy's bossiness.

Following instructions, he went to the kitchen and looked in the fridge. Eggs, bacon – no, not twice in one day. Then he noticed a cooked chicken leg that he'd had the foresight to set aside for this evening. Promising himself that he would have it later, James found a bottle of supermarket red, unscrewed the cap and poured a large glass.

He drank half of it just standing there, looking out at his small garden and thinking of Suzie. Thinking of that moment when suddenly, everything had overwhelmed him. After all that had gone before, why a few bleak words should have crashed their way through his self-control, he couldn't now imagine. All he could recall was a sense of absolution, and the warmth of her embrace.

Nineteen

After James had gone, Suzie collapsed on the sofa, an emotional wreck. Why had she hugged him? Pity, she decided at last. Nothing to do with the shock of holding him the first time, that instant memory flash...

No wonder he'd crumbled, trying to absorb so much in a matter of hours. She'd lived with it for forty years, burying the past over a lifetime of marriage and mothering and work. Finding answers had taken her down avenues she thought she'd forgotten, but at least she'd painted the picture for him, shattering his illusions. In the end, he'd said he understood, and she hoped he did.

His side of the story had certainly been a revelation for her – and nothing illustrated it more clearly than when he'd confessed to the after-effects of that drunken rape. How ironic that her comment, *I hope you're proud of yourself*, had been taken as mockery. Together with her later comment, it was confirmation of his ineptitude, if that was what he was looking for. Not funny when one considered the effects; and yet Suzie had to smile even as she shook her head. Only a self-conscious youth could put those two statements together and make a cross with which to cripple himself.

He'd been young for his years, she could see that now; his tale of a closeted student life was all too believable. A shame, because, as her mother had said all those years ago, James had been a decent lad at heart. A good-looking one, too. No wonder Margaret had been attracted to him. He was, Suzie admitted reluctantly, attractive still, and not just in looks. It was a long time since she'd had the feeling that a man was really listening to her, that he cared about what she was thinking.

A streak of cynicism said he was probably trained to listen, to empathise. Even yesterday, when she was angry, bitter, accusatory, he'd taken it all without protest. Despite everything she'd thrown at him, somehow, James had managed to keep it together. But then, what had she said this afternoon? Something about her own lingering fears – and suddenly, he was broken.

Of course, what she hadn't told him – and she couldn't after that, he was too upset by what she'd said already – was that even if she agreed to search it wouldn't be easy.

She hadn't told him that the people who adopted her son had lived abroad.

– o –

Suzie tried hard to clear her mind, but when deep breathing failed, she gave up. In her office, a light was blinking on the phone. A message from Jo, saying they hadn't spoken for ages, and would she call back?

It must be a couple of weeks at least. At the time she'd said the problem was on the back burner until she had space to think about it. Now, staring at the phone, wondering what to say in the wake of James's visit, finally Suzie picked it up and called Jo's number.

'To be honest,' she admitted when the subject turned to James, 'I asked him to come up so we could talk about everything. He left about an hour ago...'

In answer to the next question, she said, 'No, I haven't made a decision – I want to discuss it with you and Sara first...'

To Suzie's surprise, it didn't take more than a minute or two to arrange a date. Jo said she could come up in a couple of weeks, if that wasn't too late? Checking the calendar, Suzie saw it was the first weekend in June. 'More than fine by me,' Suzie agreed, 'but we'd better check with Sara, first...'

Jo said she'd already spoken to her sister, and Sara was just as keen to know what was going on – in fact, they'd both been waiting for the word from Mum.

When she thought about it, Suzie realized that their missing brother had not been discussed since the day she first told them about him – and that must be almost twenty years ago. How they felt about him now they were older was a mystery – but how they'd react to the idea of the boy's father being back in her life was less so. Resentful, sprang to mind. Ironic, if she ended up defending him.

In something of a daze, Suzie defrosted a sauce and cooked some spaghetti, eating mechanically while her thoughts were elsewhere. On an impulse, after she'd cleared away, Suzie went out for a stroll – not far, only around the village and back – taking note, as she passed the church, of the service times. As she'd guessed, Holy Communion was at ten the next morning.

'Well, it might help...'

– o –

Sunday dawned, thick with mist, the sun beginning to break through as she set off. Wearing heels for once, instead of jeans and walking boots, she felt conspicuous in her good dress and jacket, as though unseen eyes were watching her progress, wondering why Suzie Wallis from the end house was all dressed up and going to church.

The last time was Christmas, and before that, when she came home from Spain. Very much a case of wanting to give thanks to God for being there along the way, and for bringing her home again. Not just safely, but with a calm and settled frame of mind.

Along the Camino, from St Jean Pied de Port at the foot of the Pyrenees, via Burgos, Leon and Santiago, wherever a church was open, she would stop to sit and rest, as much for the cool shade as the peaceful atmosphere. From the simple to the elaborate, each place of worship had its own strange and distinctive beauty; she grew used to the gold and the vividly depicted crucifixions, and even, after a while, started to identify with them. Somehow, by comparison, the restraint of Felton's small parish church seemed, not lacking, but rather like coming home after visiting a palace.

As she'd said to James, she wasn't a churchgoer, but that didn't mean she had no belief; it was more that she did her praying at other times and in other ways.

With the church in sight, she was reminded of Aunt Dolly. For a moment she was back with her, walking up to St Mary's in Richmond, taking part in the service, absorbing the atmosphere of peace. Despite the circumstances, Suzie could see how fortunate she'd been, loved by her parents, cared for by Aunt Dolly, and – for a while at least – living in such a beautiful place.

In many respects, she'd had a lot to be thankful for.

Maybe that was what she should be doing this morning: giving thanks for the good things, rather than begging for what she wanted.

A car passed and pulled behind others in the layby ahead; a middle-aged couple got out and smiled in her direction before heading up the church path. Feeling conspicuous, Suzie followed more slowly, entering the open door to be greeted by Tom Hepworth, the churchwarden who lived across the road. He remembered Freddie well, and always called Suzie by her married name.

His weather-beaten old face creased into a welcoming smile. 'Eh, Mrs Lawrence, how are you? Nice to see you today.'

'You too, Tom,' she said, thanking him as he handed over a hymnal and service book. Looking down the rows of pews where a dozen or so people where already seated, Suzie lowered her voice. 'Is there anywhere you'd prefer me not to sit?'

'Nay, sit where you like – we're hardly likely to be crowded out.'

Moving down the main aisle, she chose an empty pew halfway down, and knelt briefly to calm herself before silently asking God to have patience with this long-lapsed Christian. Seated, she found the first hymn – one she knew from schooldays – and cast her eyes over the first few pages of the modern service booklet, so much easier to follow than the old Prayer Book. And then, as the tower bell began to toll, more people came in – her next-door-but-one neighbours, the lady who used to keep the village shop, a couple more she recognized from her walks.

Inevitably, she found herself thinking of Freddie's funeral, and the girls' idea to hold the service here. The Vicar had been more than happy; although had it been up to Suzie, raging with anguish at the time, she wasn't sure what kind of service she would have chosen. Five years, but she could still see that weeping woman in the back pew, gazing at the coffin as it was carried out of church.

Go away, she thought fiercely; *I don't want you in my mind…*

Drawing breath, she tried to focus on the altar, but it was shadowed now by shifting rays of light. Like an old illustration of angels, she thought at first; but then another image sprang to mind: Gothic tracery half-seen behind a misty blur; and others, depicting fragments of colour amidst angles of grey and white.

Freddie. Freddie had seen it like this, been inspired by it, despite his avowed lack of belief. Freddie the painter had declared his faith in light and colour and creation...

As the first notes of the organ swelled into life, emotion blurred her vision in a surge of thanks for all they'd shared. Despite the ups and downs, the occasional blazing rows and – on her part at least – periods of icy silence, they had made a good team. They understood each other, and she had been happy. What's more, she had Freddie's daughters and they were women to be proud of. With regard to her son, all she could do was pray that life had been kind to him.

Soothed by the light and the music, it would have been enough, she felt, to sit quietly for the next hour; but with a change of melody and a shuffle of movement, people reached for their hymn books and rose to their feet.

The Reverend David Foster walked down the aisle to the chancel steps and turned to welcome his congregation.

Suzie found the format familiar, but things had changed since Aunt Dolly's day and not simply in the language. Addressing God as *you* instead of *thou*, still seemed strange. But then, halfway through the service, after prayers read out by a member of the congregation, the Vicar invited them all to offer one another a sign of peace. At that, the man in the next pew turned and smiled and offered his hand.

'Peace be with you,' he said; whereupon a woman from across the aisle wished the same to him, shaking Suzie's hand too. Getting the message – she'd forgotten this bit – Suzie responded to several others, thinking it was like a family gathering, particularly when Tom Hepworth came to her with a twinkling smile and shook her hand heartily.

And then came the serious part. As prayers were being said, she was watching the Reverend David, but thinking of James, blessing the bread and the wine in his church. It was oddly dislocating, like looking at a familiar picture through a mirror and seeing it differently. For the first time it dawned on Suzie that that she'd never seen James in clerical garb, only in ordinary clothes.

How would she feel if it were James standing before her, while she was waiting, as now, to receive the sacrament?

The idea threw her into such disarray, she was taken by surprise as people in front of her started moving towards the altar.

Tom Hepworth paused by her pew, his gaze asking the question: was she going up, or not? As Suzie hesitated, he bent towards her. 'Take yon book with you, and if you don't want communion, he'll just give a blessing...'

It was the perfect compromise. Clutching her service book, she followed the man in front and knelt beside him. When the Vicar came to her, he placed his hand on her head and gave the promised blessing. Caught by a wave of emotion, Suzie was aware only of thankfulness; no pleas, no prayers, no beseeching words, just gratitude.

Twenty

Monday morning and James was trying to focus on neglected paperwork when his curate, Amy, called. As he invited her into the kitchen for coffee, Amy said she had some sad news. The former blacksmith at Leighton – the smallest of their three parishes – had passed away on Friday. Even though it was not unexpected, James was saddened; he'd liked the old man.

'I think it was the son I was speaking to – he said he'd like you to officiate at the funeral, if that's okay?'

'Of course,' he murmured. He might have to organize cover for a lecture, but he'd known Jack Richardson for almost twenty years and it was only fitting that he should lay the old man to rest. 'I'll give them a call – arrange to see them.'

Spooning instant granules into two mugs, James caught himself thinking that Maggie would have set a tray and taken it through to his study. Amy wasn't one to stand on ceremony, but James had started to wonder if his standards were slipping; he seemed to be acting like a student, leaving everything to the last minute. He'd been mentally absent for weeks; on another planet, as Amy's young son would say.

Hearing his sigh, she said, 'How was your trip away, James? Everything all right?'

'Yes, fine...'

'It's just that you've seemed a bit distracted lately.'

He turned in surprise. 'I'm fine. Tired, that's all. Not sleeping well – you know how it is.'

'No, I don't. What's wrong?'

Looking down, stirring the coffee, he said, 'Personal stuff – getting to me, that's all.'

'Want to talk about it?'

Tempted for a moment, he shook his head. 'Not just now, but thanks. Anyway,' he added with a smile, 'what's new in your neck of the woods? Anything I need to know about?'

'Not particularly, but I'm concerned about the funeral. I'm guessing it'll be a burial.' Amy pulled a face. 'My garden's like concrete, so how they'll get through the clay in Leighton churchyard, I can't imagine.'

'Don't worry,' James assured her, 'it's surprising what those small excavators can get through. Anyway, I understand we're due some rain.'

'Do you think the squire will attend?'

James thought about it. 'Well, Jack Richardson was their oldest living tenant – and his family go back years on the estate. Jeremy ought to be there, but,' he added wryly, 'Mrs Jem will no doubt want to be elsewhere. We'll have to wait and see.'

They passed on to other matters, the children's Sunday School at Norton Magna, various issues concerning use of the Parish Centre over there, and the ongoing problem of Norton Parva's west window. As James was all too aware, the lead was buckling, rain was coming in, and the medieval glass was in need of restoration. The problem, as ever, was raising funds.

'I have made a note of that,' he said, 'to put it to the PCC at the next meeting. We'll see what ideas they can come up with. Meanwhile, I'll have a chat with the Archdeacon, find out what grants we can apply for.'

When Amy had gone, he phoned the number she'd given him for the Richardsons and arranged to visit the son and his wife the following evening. After that, he spent a while thinking about Amy's question as to his state of mind. She was right, he did need to talk. This was not strictly a matter for his spiritual advisor, but James knew from experience that any serious upheaval could disturb the focus. Recalling his piecemeal delivery of yesterday's sermon, James sighed and made a note to phone Father Philip.

– o –

As it transpired, his visit to the Richardsons at Leighton was easier than expected. He'd always enjoyed conversations with the old man, whose simple wisdoms were often thought-provoking. Jack Richardson had followed his father's trade, and for many years had also served as churchwarden of the tiny village church, a 19th Century chapel-of-ease built by the grand family for their estate workers. Nowadays, with modern life and fewer tenants, the congregation was less than a dozen at best, the services restricted to two a month. Despite that, going there was like stepping back in time, to a way of life that had virtually disappeared.

Jack's son, Charlie, was brusque where his father was gentle, but a good man even so. He worked as a farrier, still living on the estate, but with a business that nowadays ranged far beyond it. Amongst the horse-owning community, it seemed he was a popular and busy man.

'Traditional service,' he said, once the civilities were over. 'Or at least as traditional as you can make it, Vicar. Father would appreciate it.'

James, knowing Charlie Richardson's views of old, nodded. 'Of course,' he said, and went on to mention hymns. Making notes as he went, he asked about the old man's early life, and was there anything they would like mentioned in tribute?

'Well, he was an artificer in the Royal Engineers – had quite a time of it after D Day, but never talked about it...' With a sigh, Charlie said, 'It'll be sixty years in a couple of weeks – hard to believe. He went to France, you know, for the half century.'

'Yes, I remember. I was there too...'

'Course you were, Vicar – I'd forgotten.'

'He liked *making* things, Charlie,' Mrs Richardson said. 'Quite an artist, your Dad was. Loved nothing better than his wrought iron work. He made the new gates for the big house,' she said to James. 'The new people – that sculptor chap and the woman who does the screen-printing – they had a lot of respect for Jack...'

In the end, she provided far more detail regarding her father-in-law's life than his son did; but that, James reflected later, was often the case. Women seemed to be the repositories of a family's history, whereas men were more interested in what was coming next.

Was that his problem where Suzie was concerned – too eager to get on with the story, on with the search? He'd never seen himself as impatient, but maybe he was. That could be something else to discuss with Father Philip.

On the way back to Norton Parva, James found himself reciting an old, familiar prayer, not just for its meaning but the beauty of its archaic phrases. Like Charlie Richardson, he found the words of Cranmer's Prayer Book comforting.

'*O merciful Father, that despisest not the sighing of a contrite heart, nor the desires of such as be sorrowful... assist our prayers...*'

In need of comfort, when he reached home he picked up the keys and went across to the church, entering by the vestry door. Going through to the chancel, he paused for a moment as he often did when alone, absorbing the church's space and stillness. And the light, even on a dull day, flooding through the church's mostly undecorated windows. Just a few examples of Victorian stained glass and a tasteful St George over the altar. This saint vanquishing a darker and thankfully less flamboyant creature than the pub's dragon across the road.

Bowing his head, with Amy on his mind James turned his attention to the medieval window at the west end, its mosaic of stained glass consisting largely of fragments from original windows in the nave. Amongst the saints were a few small panels featuring some of the corporeal acts of mercy: feeding the hungry and giving drink to the thirsty; offering hospitality to strangers and visiting the sick. Most of them showing the same man, a local merchant, recorded in local history for his charity to the poor.

Despite medieval aims – charity on earth earning respite in Purgatory – he often thought such work was needed more than ever in the present day, and not just in foreign lands. These illustrations could provide focus for a sermon on how Christ's work was needed here, at home.

A shame so little of the window remained, he thought. Other panels had been broken at various times in the church's history, and past restorers had salvaged what they could, gathering them into this treasury of medieval art. Worthy aims, but they hadn't done a very good job. Today, he could see fresh water marks in the stone ledge below, a reminder that something needed to be done, and soon.

With a sigh, he returned to the chancel steps.

Looking at the cross before him, he focused on the risen Christ, praying for Suzie in her present difficulty, and for himself, that he might have strength to withstand whatever lay ahead. As prayer relaxed into calm, he closed his eyes, emptying his mind, letting the sense of peace wash over him. And then he began to say the evening office.

– o –

James had forgotten it was his birthday until the post arrived at ten. Amongst the circulars and diocesan mail, there were a few cards, one with Amy's writing, another he thought he recognized, and another, with a Leeds postmark – from Suzie?

He opened it at once. Not strictly a birthday card, it showed a street scene in York, the Minster's sunlit towers glowing above the rooftops. Inside, she'd written, *As always, I'll be thinking about you both today – Suzie*

Those few words were both touching and upsetting. *As always…* Yes, he'd thought about her too, but never imagined she would consume his thoughts again; not like this. And his son – what was he doing today? Working, no doubt, and perhaps going home this evening to his wife and family, where cards and a special meal would be waiting…

Refusing to take the fantasy further, James shook his head, wiped his eyes and opened Amy's card – a comic one, thank the lord, which made him smile. Amy didn't know he was sixty years old, but for James it was another decade, with retirement ahead. He didn't relish it, but knew he should begin preparing. The problem was, while this situation – which he had started – was going on, he couldn't plan anything beyond next Sunday's sermon…

– o –

For Jack Richardson's ninety years of faith, of service to the community and, above all, love for his family, the funeral at Leighton that afternoon was more in celebration of a life well spent than anguish at his passing. The congregation filled the tiny church; there were even people outside; familiar hymns were sung with feeling, and a tribute given by Jack's great-grandson brought tears to everyone's eyes.

Despite the number of funerals conducted over the years, James never failed to be moved. Whether for solitary souls with no one but the churchwardens to mark their passing, or for those like Jack, blessed by the love of family and friends, the service was, by its very nature, sad. A stark reminder that death comes to us all; the words, *in the midst of life we are in death*, spelling out that it can come at any time. For the young, it was particularly poignant; those for whom it came gently, at the end of a long and fulfilling life, made the service easier.

The rain held off, the committal to Jack's last resting place in the churchyard went smoothly, and he sensed the family were pleased and comforted by the presence of the squire. That he'd made time to be there said a lot about his regard, and James was thankful.

Introducing his curate as they exchanged a few words afterwards, he could see Amy was impressed. 'Behave yourself,' he said under his breath as the Honourable Jeremy turned away. 'He's not a pop star.'

On the verge of laughter, Amy said, 'He's got all the charm, though, hasn't he?'

'Part of the training,' he whispered, knowing it was more than that. The man cared, and it showed.

Later, as they left the funeral tea, James stood for a moment before getting into the car. From the service to the gathering in the village hall, the afternoon had been uplifted by an atmosphere of love and respect. All funerals, he thought, should be like this.

Looking back at the gateway to the big house, at the wrought-iron gates made by the man he'd so recently laid to rest, James said, 'You know, Amy, today's given us a glimpse of the past, the way things used to be. This place, this way of life, is so rare nowadays...'

'You're not kidding – I'll never forget it, that's for sure. When I think of some poor souls,' she went on, getting into

James's car, 'no connection to the church, looking lost as they sit there – trying to sing hymns they don't know, follow a service they don't know the meaning of – it breaks my heart, it really does.'

Sympathizing, he gave her a wry smile. 'We're supposed to see such occasions as an opportunity for reaching out, Amy. Anyway,' he added, starting the car, 'don't let's depress ourselves after such an uplifting afternoon. Just thank God for today.'

Twenty-One

The promised rain arrived in swathes, backed by winds sweeping down the valley, drumming against the windows in a sharp tattoo. Startled into wakefulness, Suzie rose at once to push back the curtains; the clock showed just after six, but it was barely light. What she could see of the road was a torrent; all else obscured by driving clouds, and the trees, bending and swaying under the force of rain. She'd hoped to go walking, but not in weather like this.

Downstairs, the drain outside the studio was coping; but as she surveyed the garden her heart sank. The shrubs were bowed like umbrellas in a gale, the early summer plants beaten flat. Well, at least James saw it at its best, she thought; and was immediately cross with herself for thinking it mattered.

Making some tea, she went back upstairs to bed, planning to pick up a book and relax for an hour. But the novel, a murder mystery with dozens of characters but not much background, was too confusing in her present state of mind. Anyway, she should get on with some work.

In the studio, surveying a pair of Victorian spoon-back chairs, she could see the seats needed re-upholstering, and chips to the chair legs needed attention. The question was, should she work on restoring them to pristine condition, or take the shorter route and paint them? Suzie would have preferred the former, but the person she should ask was Sara. Making a mental note, she turned to her most recent purchase, a sad-looking pine dresser. No argument there – once painted, it would sell.

With a sigh, she looked around. Her stock of paints on the shelves, and various tools on a workbench before the big, north-facing windows. The usual view – of trees and fields rising to a distant farmhouse – was today a blur of mist and rain.

Freddie's paint-splattered easel stood in a corner; on a nearby shelf were his palettes, multi-coloured abstracts in themselves. Some unfinished canvases were stacked below, while another painting, of a bridge at night, hung on the big wall.

She'd loved it with a passion from the moment she first saw it. With echoes of Van Gogh's *Starry Night over the Rhone*, Freddie's version showed a bridge over the Regent's Canal, not far from where he was living in 1966. Later, he'd said it was derivative, not original enough to please him, although later still, needing money, he'd thrust his principles aside and set about painting in styles that sold.

There'd even been a time, when they were truly struggling, that he'd suggested selling this one. Horrified, Suzie had refused. With its barges and houseboats, and streetlamps rather than stars, this had been painted the week she and Freddie met. For years it had hung in plain sight, in whichever house they'd inhabited, a happy reminder of those early days.

Only after his death had she moved the painting into the studio, to wait until she could face it. For a long time, she couldn't bear to be in Freddie's workplace. Gradually, she'd learned to accept his presence, just as she'd accepted the empty house. It had been easier though, after the Camino. Everything had been easier after that.

Finding his battered metal ashtray, she pulled one of the chairs over to the window and lit a cigarette. Before the children came along, he'd often used her as his model; a few portraits but mostly life studies – usually with a bland title, *Nude 1* or *Nude 6* or whatever. The unsold ones were still stacked away somewhere. She wondered what James would think if he saw them. Would they shock him? All he'd seen was that early sketch in the hall. After remarking on it, he'd said he could tell she'd been loved; adding, before she could answer, that it was important to remember such love, and to let the grief and anger go.

Strange that he should pick up on the difficulties she'd had with Freddie…

Love, how different it was at different stages of life. Had it been love with James, or just a passing teenage fancy? She couldn't help wondering what their lives would have been like if that rape had never happened, if that fateful party had been as relatively innocent as those before it. Maybe they'd have stayed in touch, although given the circumstances, it was unlikely.

She couldn't help wondering what would have happened if she'd ever got so far as to meet his middle-class, military-background parents. What would they have thought of her? It wasn't difficult to imagine preconceived ideas about the type of girl who became an art student: rebellious, subversive, no doubt out to attack the status quo and topple the establishment. But like the man who became her husband, Suzie didn't want revolution, only to open people's eyes to what was there.

– o –

James – and Freddie – were still on her mind as she drove towards York the following Sunday. Turning off the ring road, a few minutes later she reached Sara's home, a modern house behind a pretty village street. As she pulled into the drive, the door opened, and Jo was there with a hug, while Sara ushered them in towards the smell of percolating coffee.

'No children today?'

'No, Rob's taken them out – they'll be back about tea-time.'

The house was quiet without George and Grace, but Suzie understood. Much easier to talk if there were no interruptions.

Suzie found herself studying her daughters. Other people could see the resemblance, but to her they were very different, both in looks and outlook. Jo was dark-haired, with her father's bright blue eyes, but her features favoured Suzie's side of the family. Sara was taller and fairer, her green eyes like Suzie's, with a tendency to flash when she was annoyed. In temperament, she was the fiery one, while Jo was more laid-back. On the other hand, Jo was like a terrier, once she had the scent of a story, she'd pursue it to the end.

As Sara poured the coffee, Suzie wondered about her son. Who did he resemble? Her side of the family, or James's?

Shaking her head, trying to dismiss such thoughts, she focused on Jo's peasant-style blouse, saying it took her back to the 1970s – even to the flared jeans and sandals. The girls both laughed – as ever Sara's look was more tailored – but the atmosphere was taut. She felt it would have been better to have them at the family home for this little chat; but for Jo, travelling by train from London, York was the easier option. As both girls gazed at her expectantly, Suzie apologized for keeping them in the dark for so long.

'As I said to you both over the phone, I've needed time to think about things.'

'That's understandable,' Jo said. 'It must have been one hell of a shock when he turned up.'

'And you say he's a vicar?' Sara said, pulling a face. 'You'd think he'd have more common sense!'

'I know, I know. Cathy and I had the same reaction. I was upset at the time, but I kind of understand it now. And after spending time with him last week, at least I know what was going on when we first knew each other.'

Jo looked sceptical but said nothing, while Sara exclaimed with disgust. 'I bet! Covering his back, more like!'

'Oh, come on, Sara. I didn't get to this stage in life without being able to spot a liar. And don't forget – I knew who and what he was talking about.'

'But it wasn't just a fumble in the dark, Mum, was it?' Jo said. 'Maybe in your day it was called *being taken advantage of*, but today we call it rape.'

Suzie gave her a look. 'You're right, Jo – *date rape*, I believe, is the term?'

'Did you never report it?'

'Who to – the police? It never crossed my mind. Don't forget this was the early sixties – rape didn't get a mention anywhere in those days, except in murder cases.'

'Really?'

'Yes, really. They used to say a woman could run faster with her skirt up, than a man could with his trousers down. And if she did get raped – well then, she had to be asking for it.'

Half-amused by her daughters' appalled reactions, Suzie said, 'So you see why I didn't want anyone to know? And, when I finally told Mum and Dad, why *they* didn't want anyone to know.

'Anyway,' she went on, 'I was lucky in one sense. It wasn't a violent assault – unlike some poor women, I didn't have nightmare flashbacks. At the time, to be honest, I was more shocked than hurt. But as for getting pregnant, well...'

Sara grasped her hand. 'You were *unlucky*, Mum.'

'Yes. That's what your Gran used to say.' On a deep breath, Suzie pulled herself together. 'So no, the incident itself was nothing compared to the consequences. That's where the real damage was done. Psychologically, I mean.'

'That makes it even worse,' Jo said quietly. 'He didn't stand by you, did he?'

'No, he didn't, but I doubt it would have lasted, even if he had.'

'And now he's back, and wants you to search for your son. Our brother. How do you feel about that?'

Feeling a tight constriction in her throat, for a moment, Suzie couldn't reply. 'Other than scared, I don't honestly know. But that's why I'm here. To talk about it – hear what your thoughts are.'

'You should have told him to piss off,' Sara muttered, 'it's nothing to do with him.'

'Sara, I know you're upset – I am, too. That's what I thought at first. Why don't I just tell him to get lost?'

'Why didn't you?'

'Because I wanted the chance to tell him *exactly* what I thought about him – and *exactly* what happened afterwards. What he made me go through. When I was left, literally holding the baby. I wanted to make him suffer.' For a moment, she bowed her head. 'And I did. And he didn't walk away.'

Jo nodded. 'Well, that's something, I suppose.'

'I was curious, too. As I say, I wanted to hear his side of the story – to know why things happened the way they did.'

Both girls were quiet, waiting; even Sara seemed to have calmed down. 'Go on, Mum,' she said, 'what was it all about?'

Suzie found herself explaining James's situation at the time. In the light of past and recent knowledge she hoped she was painting a picture the girls would understand. Student life, James living with his cousin's family for the summer; a series of parties culminating in the fateful evening. And afterwards, the split, when everyone went back to their various colleges and universities.

'James was on a student grant – dependent on his parents, as students were, back then. After the way he'd treated me, I can't say I wanted to marry him – but even if I had, it would have been difficult...' Suzie sighed and shook her head. 'As to why I had the baby adopted, it seemed the only answer. Abortion was illegal then. And girls who had babies outside marriage were regarded as common trollops.'

'How bloody Victorian,' Jo muttered.

'Compared to today, it was. We might have had two world wars between times, but believe me, that kind of prejudice clung on. This was before the Pill, remember – that changed everything...'

Jo, typically, was concerned by these social attitudes, but Sara, as a mother of two who'd also had a termination, wanted to know how Suzie had coped afterwards.

'Because it was a bereavement, Mum – don't forget that. You were a mother who'd lost her child.'

Caught by a wave of emotion, Suzie covered her face. She'd never thought of it like that, but she could see Sara's point. With post-stress illnesses the topic of normal conversation, of course her daughters would see things differently. She thought of her own mother, could almost hear Connie's words: *Baby would be fine; he'd gone to people who longed for a child; they would love him; they'd give him the kind of life he deserved... If she'd brought him back here, how would they have managed?*

It was a while before she could speak, and when she did, it was to use James's words. 'What you have to remember,' she said huskily, 'is that your Gran and Grandad came through the war. With all the shocks and losses and sheer hard grit that went with it. The old wartime saying, urging people to just *carry on*, was their way of dealing with things. Grandad in particular never talked about the past – neither his nor anybody else's.'

'That's terrible,' Jo protested. 'You were grieving, they should have let you talk.'

'Maybe so – but they didn't know any better, and neither did I. After my brief moment of kicking over the traces, I did what I was told. And don't forget, it must have been hard for your Gran too. And Grandad, come to that.'

'But what about *you*,' Sara said. 'How did you cope? You know what I was like, after…' Her words tailed away, but they knew she meant the termination. 'It went on for months, one way or another…'

'I know,' Suzie said, 'and in many respects, it was the same with me. But most of the time I kept it buttoned up. I finally cracked about a year later. Took me a while to get over it, but when I did, I went to London and got a better job.'

'And that's where you met Dad?' Jo said, squeezing her hand.

Smiling, Suzie nodded. 'Yes, I did, and he was exactly the person I needed. He gave me back my self-respect.'

No doubt glad of a break, the girls chatted on about their father. Listening to them, answering questions about those early days in London, enjoying their delight in stories they'd not heard before, for a while Suzie put the angst aside. Thank God, she thought, for her daughters; for moments like this, when talking about the past could be fun. It was good to know they'd been happy, growing up; proud of what their father did, the TV studios they'd visited; the fact that Freddie, with his off-beat view of life, was different from their friends' fathers.

She was thankful too, for the Camino, for those weeks living a life totally removed from the modern world. In the wake of Freddie's death, she'd made that her therapy, and it had worked, enabling her to focus on the good in him – the good her daughters were talking about now – rather than his all-too-human faults. And not just Freddie's faults – her own shortcomings too.

Only as Sara noticed the time did they go into the kitchen. Lunch was almost ready when, with a quick glance at her sister, Jo said, 'But getting back to this James character, Mum – what are you going to do about him?'

'You mean, will I agree to start searching?' As the girls nodded, willing her to go on, Suzie said, 'Well, it's a huge step, isn't it? Your brother isn't a child any more – he's a man. And even if I manage to track him down, what might I find?'

Looking down at her hands, clasped tightly before her, she made an effort to relax. 'Frankly, it scares me...'

'I'm not surprised,' Sara declared. 'Bad enough when you've got care of your own kids – you still worry about their friends, about what they might get up to when you're not around...'

Overcome by that moment of understanding, Suzie had to find a tissue. As both girls came to give her a hug, she said brokenly, 'Guilt – it never goes away.' On a half-laugh, half-sob, she said, 'God knows, I even feel guilty about you two – all the mistakes, all the stuff I did wrong, things I could have handled better...'

'You didn't do anything wrong!' Sara protested, while Jo was saying, 'Mum, I was a nightmare – but you allowed me to be *me*...'

'And you were always *there* for us,' Sara said, crying now.

'Well,' Suzie said shakily, 'let's pray your brother's parents were always there for *him*...'

– o –

Later, when lunch was cleared away, when both girls had said, yes, they would like to meet this long-lost brother of theirs, Suzie nodded. If that was what they wanted...

'But only if it's right for you,' Jo said, with Sara adding, 'You've got to be sure, Mum.'

Suzie swallowed hard. 'The thing is, I never expected to break my oath. To be honest, it's been a bit of a lifeline, thinking one day he'd come looking for me...'

Struggling to get the words out, she tried again. 'He hasn't – but now I know this new law's going through Parliament, I can't ignore it, can I? If I say no, it'll be like living with an elephant in the room...'

Not until it was said did Suzie realize how true it was. Sooner or later, she would have to do something about it.

Jo reached for her mother's hand. 'It's strange, but I've been aware of him ever since you first told us. In fact, I've often wondered if I'd bump into him sometime, never knowing it was him.'

Sara nodded in agreement. 'Me too. How about you, Mum? You must have had moments like that.'

'No,' Suzie admitted with a sigh, 'not really. To be honest, I didn't think he was in this country.' As they both gaped in astonishment, she said, 'The adoption, you see, wasn't quite so straightforward...'

'What do you mean?'

'The couple who adopted him – as I said to James – were from Yorkshire. Or so I was told. What I didn't tell him – and at the time I just couldn't – was that they lived abroad.'

Sara was horrified. '*Abroad?* Did they do that? Let babies be shipped off to God knows where?'

With a helpless shrug, Suzie said, 'I don't know – I'm just telling you what was said to me at the time. *A Yorkshire couple living in an English-speaking country with a temperate climate...* That's a quote, by the way – I remember thinking it must be New Zealand.'

'Vancouver?' Jo suggested. 'It's pretty temperate there.'

'Could be anywhere,' Sara objected. 'Could be a pack of lies designed to stop you looking in prams!'

'True,' Suzie agreed. 'I've thought of that too. But you see the problem? At the end of the day, I know nothing about what happened after I handed him over.'

'Well,' Jo said decisively, 'we'll just have to find out, won't we? I've seen a few reports on adoption in the past few months, and,' she sighed, 'I've thought of you, Mum, every time. It is possible to do a search – so, if you like, I'll start making enquiries?'

Raising her hands, Suzie appealed for calm. 'Please, Jo – don't rush me. Just let me get used to the fact that we've agreed in principle. Okay?'

She needed time alone, a bottle of something fortifying to hand, and an ashtray. *Oh, lord, I could murder a cigarette right now...*

– o –

Inevitably, over the next hour it was like being trapped in a maze. Despite Sara's attempts at humour, and Jo's TV anecdotes, they kept returning to that one point. What could she remember about her first interview in Bradford? And where exactly was the office where she'd parted with her baby? It was in York, she said, but at the time she wasn't familiar with the city and she wasn't exactly paying attention. It could have been anywhere. Her only certainty was the Church of England's involvement.

'Well,' Sara commented with a sardonic smile, 'maybe your Vicar will be able to help?'

That she was set against this man was obvious, and Suzie couldn't blame her. Jo was calmer, more dispassionate, and she was thankful for that.

With the arrival of Rob and the children, further discussion was impossible. Eventually, checking her watch, Jo said it was time she left. She needed to get back that evening for work the next day. Offering to drive her to the station, Suzie gave George and Grace a hug and promised to see them the following week.

'I hope they don't mind too much,' she confessed to Sara, 'but honestly, love, I'm shattered. We'll go out for lunch next Sunday – my treat, how's that?'

In the car, as they waved goodbye, Jo said, 'She feels it more than me – with having kids of her own, I mean.'

'Finds it easier to grasp, I think,' Suzie said, pulling out into the road. With a quick glance at her elder daughter, she said, 'I wouldn't say she feels it *more* – just differently.'

'Perhaps you're right.' Jo was quiet for some time, letting her mother negotiate the traffic through town. Eventually, as they crossed the river, she said, 'It's been quite a day, hasn't it? And quite a week for you – I'm not surprised you're exhausted.' Pausing, she added, 'But do be careful with this James character, Mum – I'd hate to see you get hurt.'

Suzie couldn't restrain a chuckle. 'Oh, Jo, my love, you sound like me!' Reaching out to her daughter, she patted her knee. 'But thank you. I know what you mean, and I will be careful.'

'Is he attractive? I guess he must have been once – how about now?'

Do you fancy him? That's what 35-year-old Jo was asking. 'Well,' Suzie replied with a quirky grin, 'as your Gran would say, *he's worn well*. But don't forget, he's a vicar.'

'He's a man, isn't he? And a widower.' As her mother pulled into the station forecourt, she added, 'Could be vulnerable, Mum – and so could you… Take care,' she added with a swift kiss. Opening the passenger door, she grabbed her bag and was gone.

Ignoring the toot of a car horn, Suzie watched her daughter striding away, catching glances as she disappeared into the crowd.

'You're so like your Dad,' Suzie breathed as she put the car into gear and edged out into the traffic.

Thinking about Freddie as she drove towards home, she wondered – as had Sara, earlier – what his reaction would have been to this situation. Hard to imagine, since if Freddie had been alive, she wouldn't have gone to Spain, wouldn't have written the book, and therefore James was hardly likely to have discovered her whereabouts.

But what if he had? Or what if he'd written to her, first? She would still have found it impossible to ignore him. No doubt she'd have written screeds in reply, before telling him to get lost and never contact her again. But the memories would have been disturbed, and the elephant would still be in the room.

She was weary and over-emotional, but easier in mind now she'd spoken to the girls. Assured of their support, in a way it was like being pregnant the first time, after she'd confessed to Mum and Dad. A feeling of acceptance, resignation. Knowing the ball was rolling, but where it would end, she had no idea.

Twenty-Two

James had struggled with last week's sermon, finding it hard to transmit the joy of Pentecost when he was feeling so dead inside. But for some reason, this week's homily seemed to have hit the mark.

It was Trinity Sunday, and the 60th anniversary of D Day. Hard to recall exactly what he'd said, only that he went off his notes at some point to speak of actions and motives. How sometimes what seems a good move turns out to be not so good for someone else, but how pure motives do have results. Perhaps not always the ones we envisage, but the ones God intends.

He must have sounded convincing, because his congregation looked to be paying attention. A couple of people even remarked on it afterwards. And Mrs Jennings stopped to tell him a story which illustrated it for her – luckily, she was the last one out, but it meant he was still there when everyone else had moved on to coffee in the Parish Hall. Normally he wouldn't have minded – she was a kind old lady who devoted much of her time to the church – but he could feel his smile becoming fixed.

By the time he reached the vestry, the choir had put their robes away and gone. Locking the Communion silver in the safe, he removed his surplice and put it away; a moment of thanks as he bowed before the altar, and he could leave. But not for home – not yet.

Those few minutes of socialising after the service meant he was often cornered on current issues and today was no exception. Two people with family graves took the opportunity to mention grass-cutting in the churchyard. He was saying that Vernon, one of the churchwardens, had it on his list, when he glanced up and saw Ms Eleanor Williams approaching. A divorcee who owned the florists in Norton Magna, she was generous with all she supplied to both churches, but she had a bee in her bonnet about the choir. Keeping his professional cool wasn't easy. Worse, he suspected it was just an excuse to engage him in conversation.

Before she could move in, James escaped to speak to Vernon. Through his contacts on the local council, the churchwarden said he'd managed to organize monthly visits from the Community Service group. He wasn't sure yet about costs, but that could be settled later. Feeling relieved, James thanked him, managing to slip away quietly while Ms Williams was talking to someone else. He sometimes thought that if she commented one more time on the declining quality of the singing in church, he would explode. Their latest choir-mistress, a recent graduate, was doing her best, but the truth was, she didn't have Maggie's experience.

Wondering what Maggie's advice would have been – and not merely about the choir – he found himself thinking about the women in his congregation. In the past couple of years, there had been one who seemed determined to corner him at every opportunity. At the time she'd been new to the area and probably in her fifties. At first, he'd imagined she was genuine, and had tried to help with various problems she was experiencing – some spiritual, but mostly to do with the family who had abandoned her.

He still winced whenever he thought of that embarrassing moment. It was in church too, which made it worse. She'd lingered after Evensong, talking again about the son who'd rejected her, and as he tried – yet again – to suggest ways forward, she'd suddenly embraced him, clasping him to her like a vice. Her strength was a shock, and he'd had to use force to extricate himself – whereupon she burst into tears, said she'd fallen in love with him, and he was the only man who'd ever been kind to her.

Only as she rushed away, and he was shakily trying to gather his wits, did he notice Vernon, equally shocked, standing in the aisle.

'Sorry, Vicar – didn't like to disturb while you were talking, but…'

'Good grief, where did *that* come from?'

'Hard to say, but I've had my eye on her for a while – that's why I hung around…'

Church didn't see her again, but for some time James had done his rounds with care, half-expecting to find her lying in wait for him. But as Vernon said, in most communities there was usually one like that, and priests were always vulnerable. It was a lesson James had never forgotten, and it made him realize how protected he'd been by Maggie's presence.

– o –

Sometimes, he went across to the George for his Sunday lunch, but today, needing solitude, he chose to eat at home with a meal on a tray. With D Day on his mind, he looked to see what was being shown on TV from France.

To mark the 60th Anniversary of the Allied invasion, the Queen and Prince Philip, with several European leaders, were due to be at Arromanches. Switching on, he recognized views of the River Orne between Caen and Ouistreham, where, ten years ago, James had left the cross-Channel ferry with a group of fellow pilgrims.

He paused the TV to look more closely at Pegasus Bridge and Ranville, where his father had landed in 1944. But moments later, watching film-clips of what was happening then, it was hard to believe they were the same places. To think his father had been part of all that was awe-inspiring. Even alarming when he considered that Ted Fielding had been one of the first to land in France, a decorated hero who, unlike many of his friends, had survived.

At the time, James had been just nine days old. What would life have been like, he wondered, if his father had been killed? From a purely financial point of view, it would have been difficult for his mother, and for him, far less privileged. As a boy, the only time it entered his head was when he was reminded of it; usually when he was being browbeaten into some course of action approved of by his father. Play rugby: yes, he had. Not well enough to make the first team, though. He'd preferred cricket, but again failed to make the grade. Singing in the school choir didn't count, although being accepted at Durham did earn a wry, 'Well done.'

'Your father is really proud of you,' his mother had said on more than one occasion. 'You should hear him when anyone asks what you're doing now…'

If that was so, Ted Fielding's praise had turned to disbelief when James finally resigned his lectureship and started training for the Church.

'Do you have no belief?' James had asked at the time. 'Did you not thank God every day for your survival in France?'

There had been a kind of reluctant agreement, dismissed almost at once by his insistence that the *Dear God* prayers before action were just a reflex, something every man said, in the hope God did exist in the god-forsaken world of war. Rather like men calling vainly for their mothers when they knew they were dying.

Sighing, James set his tray aside and closed his eyes. Within minutes, he was asleep.

God the father, Mary the mother... Jesus, son... A broken church, a white-draped steeple, dangling puppets on a wire...

A staccato burst of light and noise woke him. He struggled to know where he was, what was happening; saw images on screen, disconcerting yet familiar. Feeling for the controller, he turned the sound down, sat up and tried to collect his thoughts. He reached for the magazine. Of course, yes, *The Longest Day*. Abruptly, he switched it off.

It had taken years to accept that his father had cared; years to see that what seemed like banishment to boarding school, was in fact the old man's determination to give him a better start. Ted Fielding hadn't been deprived in the way Harry Thornton was, although he'd been sensitive about his less-than-privileged background. The army was his way of making the most of his brains and determination, and he'd seen it as a way forward for his son. But James wasn't like his father – and because of that, he'd always felt the old man's disappointment.

What would he think to my present situation?

Not a lot, was the answer, and with that James went to pour himself a drink. Missing Maggie's comfort and common sense, he picked out one of her favourite CDs, a collection of arias by different artists. For once, not even opera could lift his spirits, and Maria Callas singing, *Oh My Beloved Father*, was too much.

Twenty-Three

Wrung out by the emotional few hours with her daughters, on the way home Suzie turned to Radio 2 for light relief. She didn't often listen in on Sunday evenings, but they were playing a selection of pop classics, ones she remembered from when the girls were young. Cheerful in themselves, but between times the presenter was reading out listeners' letters – mostly pleas to long lost friends to get in touch.

One in particular brought Liz to mind, and she wondered what Liz was doing now. Did she ever look back and think of her old friend Suzie?

Liz had always been a mystery, springing new ideas or changing her mind, often at the last minute. But Suzie had decided long ago that Liz was far from impulsive – she was just what Connie would call *close*. Secretive, playing her cards so close to her chest that not even Suzie knew what was really going on. It hurt more because she'd loved Liz for her loyalty during the dark days. Her letters to the Home, full of amusing gossip about work and parents and what was going on locally, had been a reminder that normal life was still out there. For

Suzie they'd been a lifeline. And not just the letters. If she hadn't had Liz to talk to in the days after her return, she really would have gone mad.

– o –

If Suzie's parents were a little lost when it came to what she should do next, it was Liz who persuaded her to be bold in applying for jobs. And that was where chance turned in Suzie's favour. When she wrote to the store where she'd been waitressing the previous summer – for an assistant's job this time – the woman who interviewed her said she thought Suzie would do better in the display department, where they were looking for a trainee.

Display? Window-dressing? Stammering her thanks, Suzie accepted at once and started work the following week. Liz was delighted and Suzie was so buoyed by this marvellous coincidence, it took a while to realize why the previous trainee had walked out. It was a start, but the pay was minimal, the work tough and the hours frequently unsocial. Luckily, she and Liz managed a night out most weeks, usually to the cinema but occasionally to the Mecca in Leeds. The music was great, but while Liz could always attract a partner, Suzie preferred to stand back and mind the handbags.

In Denshaw, life bumbled along much as it had before. Except as summer gave way to autumn, and winter came knocking at the door, Mum seemed perpetually unwell and even her Dad was sombre, eating his dinner before sliding off to the pub. It was too cold to spend much time in her unheated bedroom, so unless she was busy sewing, most evenings Suzie sat by the fire, watching TV with her mother.

After Christmas, when Liz said she was applying for jobs in London, it was a shock.

'Seriously,' Liz said, 'why don't you think about it? Do you good to get away.'

But Suzie was still finding her feet in Leeds. She was just getting into this window-dressing lark, and there was still a long way to go.

It didn't take long for Liz to land a job as an accounts clerk; and she'd found a flat – well, a bedsit, really – just a short tube journey from the West End. It sounded great, and Suzie tried to feel pleased for her old friend, but in truth she was hurt, shaken by what she saw as Liz's defection.

The milestone of her twentieth birthday in February found Suzie looking at her life with bleak eyes. A few colleagues who were fun to go dancing with, but no close friends; and in the four years since O Levels, what had she achieved? Not much. Art school had proved such a wrong move she no longer wanted to know about painting, and only her sewing machine was in regular use.

Making stylish clothes was one advantage to set against the rest of it, as her mother never failed to point out. Connie also stressed that Suzie had achieved her schoolgirl ambition: she was doing the kind of job she'd wanted from the start, and who could tell where it might lead? That it might lead anywhere at all was doubtful in Suzie's mind. How long she was expected to languish as a trainee, no one ever said. Even though her ability to sketch – anything from kitchenware to clothes – could be used to design displays, no one was interested. As a trainee, all she did was stand at someone's beck and call, holding tack hammer and pins, watching how a paper idea was transformed into reality.

As the weather grew warmer, with music playing in her room, she sketched away at her own designs, finally plucking up courage to approach her boss. If he'd been tactful or encouraging, it wouldn't have been so bad; but he barely glanced at her work before telling her it was far too soon to think about that. She needed to learn the basics first.

Only her Dad's objective comments – *you are a beginner, so learn your stuff and prove him wrong!* – stopped her from handing in her notice. But it was bad timing. The anniversary of going into the Home was succeeded by the low point of her son's first birthday, and that was when she went to pieces. Triggered not by the date, exactly, but a ticking off by the boss. She'd made several blunders in short order; but what cut to the quick was his criticism of her attitude. If she wanted to continue as one of this respected store's display team, he said, she should get to work on time, and show more enthusiasm for the job.

What he did not know was that she was sleeping badly, suffering nightmares, and finding the weight of grief intolerable. She was so depressed, she could barely get out of bed. Mum insisted she went to see the doctor.

Dr Illingworth signed her off work for three weeks and referred her to a psychiatrist. After listening to Suzie, the trick-cyclist said that if she wanted to recover, she should talk about the adoption, most specifically to her parents. After all, he said, they were part of the problem. The pills he prescribed loosened her tongue to an alarming degree. Suzie found herself saying things – hurtful things – that she hadn't been aware of thinking. Well, not for a long time. Her words seemed to shock her parents into silence. At home, anyway. After that they started going out more together, and Connie said she was applying for a house in Heatherley. How she managed to get what she wanted was never fully explained, but that summer they were moving into an older semi-detached on the edge of the market town. The neighbours were friendly, and it was a pleasant walk to the shops.

The downside was the state of the property. The previous tenant had clearly done nothing for years, so Dad started clearing the garden, while Mum got busy with the sugar-soap, scrubbing decades of grime from woodwork and window-frames. Suzie helped with colour schemes, painting with Mum and acting as Dad's assistant with the wallpaper. Yes, there were disagreements and occasional blazing rows, but after working holidays and weekends, by Christmas the house was, as Suzie put it, fit to appear in *House & Garden*.

Working hard on the joint project made a difference to each of them. Connie and Joe were more light-hearted, friendships were developing locally, and Suzie was more or less off the happy pills. She was thankful her parents had been able to get away from Denshaw, to a new place with – in all senses of the word – a different outlook. But as they settled down and the house took on its bright new look, Suzie began to feel unsettled in different ways.

By Christmas she began to feel like going out again, but apart from the staff party her work colleagues had stopped asking, and Liz was in London. Work was another problem. In the spring, the arrival of a new trainee, one who was rapidly gaining favour, made Suzie decide to put her boss to the test.

Tony, a more senior assistant, had always been friendly and sympathetic, passing on tips and tricks, and generally showing her the ropes. Taking him aside, Suzie asked if he would put one of her ideas forward but claim it as his own. Tony got it at once.

'This is because you think it's personal?' As Suzie nodded, he said, 'What if the old misery accepts it?'

'Well, then I'll know for sure it's time to move on...'

'No!' But after a moment's thought, Tony nodded. 'You're right. He does seem to have a down on you, lord knows why...'

With that, he patted her arm, and promised to look at her work. At lunchtime a few days later, huddled by the lockers, they went through Suzie's folio. Within minutes, Tony had chosen three sketches. 'Okay – these look good. A bit different, but I think I can pass them off as my own. I'll have to re-draw them, though.' He turned to look at her. 'You're sure you don't mind? If he accepts any one of them, I know I'll be feeling like a thief...'

'Don't be daft – I want you to do it. I need proof that it's me and not my useless ideas.'

'Suzie, dearest, your ideas are *not* useless – far from it.' Looking determined, he said, 'Let's see what happens – and if you do decide to leave, I'll see what I can glean from my contacts. No point in going from the frying pan into the fire, now is there?'

With that, he placed the sketches in his own locker, and ushered her in the direction of lunch.

Tony, she thought afterwards, was a true friend; attractive, too. A pity he wasn't interested in girls; but on the other hand, if he had been, she wouldn't have asked him. As things turned out, he was faithful to her design while putting his own more professional stamp on it. And yes, as she suspected, it did meet their boss's approval.

Having saved up for a decent camera, Suzie had been taking photographs for a while. The evening her window was installed, she recorded it from several angles, including a crazy one of Tony posing with the mannequins.

She loved that photo; it made her laugh. Contrary to his expectations, Suzie felt vindicated by Tony's success, and, true to his promise, he did phone his friends in the business. One was with a rival store in Leeds, but three more were in London. All, it seemed, were happy to put her name forward. Nothing was guaranteed, but if she was interviewed her folio would at least be looked at. When she related this in a letter to Liz, her old friend replied by return. '*For heaven's sake, get applying and come,*' she wrote. '*There's a room next to mine will be free in a couple of weeks. If I have a word with the landlord, he'll hold it for you…*'

It was one of those deep-breath moments. Dare she do it? Dare she jump from the safety of home into the swirling deep-end of London? If she said yes, would her parents think she was mad – or worse, ungrateful?

Mum was concerned when she put it to them, but Dad, having weighed the pros and cons, told her to go for it. Home would always be here; and if London didn't work out, she would at least have tried.

'And you'll be with Liz,' Mum said; adding, 'But I hope you'll come home more often than *she* does…'

When the day came, Suzie was nervous but excited. She'd never been to London before, but Liz had promised to meet her at King's Cross, and the room she'd talked about was ready and waiting. It was the right time, she told herself, gazing out of the window. Spring was blooming as they sped further south; clumps of daffodils here and there, hawthorn hedges decked out with new leaves. It was a time for fresh beginnings.

Liz was there at the end of the platform, waving as she spotted Suzie, laughing with delight as they embraced. 'I can hardly believe it!' she exclaimed, grabbing the suitcase. 'It's so good to see you – we're going to have a great time, just you wait!'

The tube journey was another first: endless escalators, crowds like ants scurrying everywhere, underground tunnels smelling of dust and smoke. It must be miles, she thought, to where Liz had her place in Kilburn. Changing at Baker Street, she found herself thinking of Sherlock Holmes; caught sight of a sign for Madame Tussauds; felt excitement soaring as she passed walls bright with film posters. Nudging Liz, she said she'd like to see them all. Liz laughed, said she'd have to earn some money first: prices were high in London.

Kilburn station was at street level, and the walk from there was only a few minutes. The High Road, Suzie thought, was like any other city street, lined with shops and businesses. She could not have said what she'd expected, but it was a surprise when they turned into a tree-lined avenue of large semi-detached houses.

'No, the landlord doesn't live here,' Liz said in answer to her question, 'every room is let. We're at the top of the stairs.' She produced her keys and handed one to Suzie. 'Not exactly posh, but it's okay.'

Liz's room was the better of the two, having a window to the front; Suzie's looked out onto a brick wall. But it had a washbasin, cupboards, a wardrobe, miniature oven with hotplate, a chair, an electric fire and a kettle. The single bed looked clean, although the mattress sagged a bit. The bathroom, she discovered, was between her room and Liz's; there was another bedsit next to hers, and a separate lavatory at the head of the stairs.

Compared to the freshly-decorated rooms at home, the whole house was dull, with faded beige wallpaper everywhere. Dumping her folio and art materials on the bed, she planned to pin up a few sketches to brighten the walls. Liz said they'd take a bus into town next day, and walk to Oxford Circus – it would give Suzie an idea of where she needed to be for her interviews. Being Sunday, the shops would be closed, but at least she'd be able to see what the windows were like.

It was certainly a revelation, seeing London from the top of a bus; the slightly tatty Kilburn High Road morphing into smart Edgeware Road, and then suddenly Marble Arch was ahead and they were descending the stairs. Minutes later, with elegant Park Lane on one side, and Hyde Park on the other, between the trees, they could see a crowd of people. 'What's going on over there?' Suzie wanted to know.

Liz laughed. 'Speaker's Corner – do you want to go over?'

It was too tempting. 'Yeah, let's see what they're on about...'

Apart from an eccentric who was all for banning the mini-skirt – to great hilarity from the crowd – Suzie found it mildly disappointing. A few minutes later, dodging traffic, they returned to Oxford Street, the longest shopping street

Suzie had ever seen. So inspiring, she could have spent hours studying window displays from *Selfridges* to *Debenhams*, via dozens of smaller shops between. At last they reached *Peter Robinson*, just where Liz had said, on a prime site by Oxford Circus. Suzie's first interview was there, on Tuesday.

'Oh, Liz, we should have started here,' Suzie wailed. 'There's so much I should be looking at…' Fashion, furniture, fabrics and cosmetics; the displays were fresh, new, exciting. She'd have to work hard to match these. Crossing Oxford Circus, they found another store with grand windows set in white Portland stone; and down a nearby street, *Liberty's*, looking like a Tudor mansion and famous for its wonderful designs…

Suzie thought she'd died and gone to heaven.

– o –

That sense of lightness and freedom never waned. It was the summer of 1966, and London, as Suzie discovered, was the place to be. A blooming of short skirts, rock music and revolution; the love revolution, design revolution, psychedelia to the fore in music as well as the arts.

A few days later, Suzie had three interviews under her belt and two job offers, including a place at *Peter Robinson*. Common sense told her she'd benefit from the broader experience, rather than limiting herself to a small, boutique-style shop; but her main reason for accepting was the man who interviewed her. In his thirties, with an encouraging manner and genuine interest, he could not have been more unlike her boss in Leeds.

Feeling the buzz of success, of busy, cosmopolitan London, she was eager to celebrate with Liz. However, she hadn't envisaged an evening that included Liz's new boyfriend, Chris, plus a boring friend of his. Liz was apologetic afterwards, but it was a signal of what was to come. Apparently, the boring friend was recently divorced, and Chris had hoped he and Suzie would hit it off. That they didn't, seemed to be a mark against her. She wasn't invited out again.

It was not long before Suzie was wondering why her old friend had been so keen for her to come to London. Typically, Liz had said little about this relationship with a man who turned out to be her boss; but after a few casual meetings Suzie wondered what the attraction was. Not only was Chris ten years older, he was the sort who was always right. Liz, it seemed to Suzie, was so firmly under his thumb, she was in danger of losing her spirit along with her sense of humour.

She'd imagined the two of them going out together as in the old days, dancing, or just for a drink and a natter. That never happened, but her unsocial working hours didn't help. When she and Liz did go out together, it was usually to the cinema – always a treat since they didn't have television at the house in Kilburn. Of all the films they saw that summer, *Alfie* was the one Suzie couldn't forget. Both she and Liz thought Michael Caine was brilliant as Alfie, even managing to raise a sneaking sympathy, despite the character being shallow and utterly selfish. The pregnant girlfriends roused throat-catching memories, but somehow it increased her admiration. As for the theme song, it was such a big hit, Suzie heard it everywhere; so haunting, it brought James Fielding to mind every single time.

Yes indeed, Alfie, what *was* it all about?

– o –

Liz's free time was so occupied, that had it not been for Suzie's colleagues, she might have been lonely. Luckily, the atmosphere at work was relaxed and friendly, no doubt thanks to Mark, their boss. Always around, keen-eyed, critical but in a good way; and always with encouraging comments and suggestions. *How different from Leeds*, was a thought that frequently sprang to mind in those early days; but after a while, enjoying life, Leeds was happily forgotten.

Although she didn't have a boyfriend, Suzie had friends who were male, and, thanks to them, she was enjoying the flirting and repartee, even starting to feel attractive again. It was like being back in college in some respects, finding her feet amongst a group of like-minded people who were out of step with the norm. To them, the nine-to-five week meant nothing. In-store displays had to be done out of shop hours and windows were mostly changed on Sundays. Their social life, largely unplanned, consisted of after work gatherings at a pub they favoured, or out for a meal as part of a group. There was the occasional snogging session afterwards – fired more by drink than lust – but nothing serious, and Suzie preferred it that way.

But one evening that summer, life took an extraordinary turn. Mark, their boss, had invitations to the opening of a new boutique on Bond Street. He put them in for a draw and Suzie was one of the winners. Delighted, incredulous, worrying about what to wear and wishing she had access to a sewing machine, she bought a cream mini-dress on staff discount. Adding a string of fat black beads, she polished up her patent shoes and bag, and prayed for a fine evening.

With a girl and two guys she knew only slightly, Suzie went along with the boss for the preview evening. 'Bound to be expensive,' the girl whispered, and Suzie agreed. One of the guys nodded. 'Designer labels everywhere...'

The windows, almost obscured by the trendily dressed crowd outside, were certainly different. The clothes – clearly *haute couture* – stood out against an amazing wall of pattern and colour. Craning her neck, Suzie spotted a stylised design of birds, in blue and yellow and purple – as though someone had captured William Morris and dragged him into the psychedelic age. The effect was stunning. No wonder, she thought, there were crowds outside.

Having gained an entrance, they saw intricate patterns on folding screens, backdrops to mannequins dressed in stunningly simple clothes. Suzie was so taken with the art of it all, she was surprised when Mark handed her a glass of wine. 'That's the designer,' he said, 'over there, in the light blue suit…'

Suzie saw a tall man, about Mark's age, enjoying the crowd's attention.

'Really?' she asked in surprise. 'He looks more like a businessman.'

'That's because he is,' Mark chuckled. 'But he's been featured in everything I've picked up recently, from the Telegraph to the Daily Mirror! Owns a paper business – started designing just for fun. Amazing guy. Anyway, must have a word – see if we can purchase some of his stuff…'

Good-looking too, Suzie decided. But despite the flamboyant tie, she wouldn't have picked him out as responsible for these extraordinary patterns and colours. Smiling, shaking her head, she turned to the items on display. Discreetly examining the clothes, she found invisible zips and hems, interfacing making a smooth and perfect line, price tags to take the breath away…

Suddenly afraid of marking the fabrics, guiltily she stepped back, looking around for the people she'd come in with. In that moment, Suzie saw another face, one she could hardly believe she recognized. Unruly dark hair, an ill-fitting suit, and a most uncertain expression. If he'd worn a label saying he felt out of place amongst this fashionable crowd, it couldn't have been clearer.

She was so astonished, she made her way through to him without hesitation. 'Freddie Lawrence,' she declared, laughing, 'what on earth are you doing here?'

Twenty-Four

For a moment, Freddie gazed in astonishment, his smile broadening as he recognized her. 'I might say the same,' he confessed, blue eyes alight with pleasure. 'Suzie Wallis! I don't believe it – how many years has it been?'

Too many, they decided; and just a little too late did he introduce his companion, a woman whose clothes and jewellery stood out even amongst these well-heeled guests. Exactly who and what she was, Suzie did not quite catch; there was, however, enough in the woman's icy smile to see that Freddie was not free to stand gossiping with some girl he'd known at art school.

Taking the hint, Suzie said she must find her friends from the store. When he asked which store, and Suzie gave the name, the woman's smile became a sneer as she waved a hand at their surroundings. 'I would have thought this was a little out of *Peter Robinson's* range?'

'For the moment, perhaps,' Suzie replied politely, 'but we're here to see how it's done...'

Catching a glance from Freddie, she wondered how he controlled his amusement. Before her own laughter could escape, she gave him part wave, part salute, and backed away into the crowd.

He found her later, while his companion was engaged in conversation with a group that included the designer.

'It really is great to see you. We must get together for a drink – catch up with old times.' Fishing in his pocket, asking for her phone number, he pulled out an invitation card and a pencil.

She hesitated. 'I'm in a bedsit, our phone's in the hall.'

'That's okay,' he grinned, 'I'll keep trying.'

As Suzie gave the number, he jotted it down. 'Sorry, but I've got to go – she's a patron. A bit possessive…'

With that, he bestowed a heart-stopping smile, and slipped away to join the group.

– o –

Still feeling the buzz as she made her way back to Kilburn an hour later, Suzie was longing to share her news with Liz. She expected her to be out with Chris, but as she climbed the stairs and reached the landing Liz was there, beckoning her in. Something was wrong, Suzie could tell from her expression. She was barely through the door when Liz started crying.

While Suzie made them both a cup of tea, Liz poured out her tale of a row with Chris, all because she'd promised her mother she'd go home this weekend. Chris didn't like it; he wanted to take advantage of the good weather to take her down to Brighton.

It took all Suzie's restraint not to curse the man up hill and down dale. Instead, she sat and sympathized, poured more tea and handed out cigarettes until Liz finally came to the conclusion Suzie had reached weeks ago, that Chris wanted Liz entirely under his control and was prepared to go to any lengths to achieve it.

'Well, you've said it yourself, Liz, you can't go on like this. Ditch him.'

'I can't,' she wailed, 'he's my boss!'

'Get another job, for heaven's sake.'

'How can I? He won't give me a reference – he said that tonight, when I said I was going to leave him and hand in my notice.'

'Oh, Liz! What have you got yourself into?'

– o –

Over the following week Suzie tried to put it out of her mind, and, between the challenges of work and the excitement of an upcoming date with Freddie, almost succeeded. He'd sounded keen when they spoke on the phone, but recalling the older woman he'd been with, Suzie wasn't entirely sure where she stood. Best play it down, she told herself; be casual. Even so, she dressed with more care that morning for work, and made sure she had make-up in her bag.

Thursday evening, they were meeting in a pub on the edge of Soho, one he'd described as a favourite with artists and writers. 'Less formal,' he'd added with a chuckle, 'than Bond Street...'

Hesitating as she walked in, Suzie could see what he meant. The bar was smoky and noisy, the clientele mostly male. A few colourful shirts stood out amongst baggy tweeds and sweaters, but she didn't see Freddie until he was by her side, smiling and ushering her towards a quieter table in the corner. As he went to fetch the drinks, Suzie gazed at framed prints on the walls, the vintage cartoons and illustrations making her smile. A moment later, she was raising her eyebrows at an overheard conversation, one man complaining about this so-called psychedelic trend, the other saying all the students would be on LSD now that everyone was talking about it...

'You look surprised,' Freddie said as he set their beers on the table.

She nodded towards the two men. 'They were talking about something called LSD,' she whispered. 'What is it?'

'Mind-bending drugs,' he said dismissively, 'latest thing from the States, apparently. Not my route to fame and fortune – I'd rather keep my sanity!'

'Me too,' she agreed, raising her glass to his. Returning his appraising smile, Suzie felt herself blushing. This evening, in denim shirt and jeans, he was more like the Freddie she remembered.

Just as she began to say how astonished she was to see him last week, he said something similar. 'No, you first,' he insisted. 'Tell me what brought you to London?'

'Well, it's simple really – I was getting nowhere in Leeds, so I applied for jobs here.'

But Freddie wanted more detail – what had she done in Iredale after he'd left? And was it really four years ago? Under his encouragement, she found herself relating the easy, edited version of life since then. Inevitably, having mentioned her failure in the exams, Rod Winter's name came up.

'He was such a snob,' Suzie went on. 'I remember doing some sketches one wet weekend – impossible to get out, the paper would've been soaked. Remember where we lived in those days? Yes, well, one drawing was basically rooftops with mill chimneys in the background – and you know what he said? That it looked like *a particularly nasty sort of council house, seen from the lavatory window…*'

At Freddie's burst of laughter, she saw the funny side of it. 'Anyway,' she added with a giggle, 'he was wrong – it was the landing window.'

At that, he laughed even more. 'And our old house was probably one of them!'

'Must have been. Bloody Rod Winter,' she exclaimed. 'I bet every time he looked in the mirror, he thought he was God Almighty.'

'But you know Winter wasn't his real name?' Freddie said wickedly. 'It was Winterbottom.'

'What? You're making that up!'

Freddie shook his head. 'No, I swear it. Not quite the right *tone*, somehow, for such an arrogant piece of work.'

Suzie spluttered over her drink. 'Rod Winter? *Rodney Winterbottom?*' Laughing about it, she said, 'Thanks, Freddie – you've just cut him down to size!'

With an affectionate grin, Freddie squeezed her hand. 'Believe me, Suzie, he was never worth the grief. Others may have had less clout, but they were far better painters – and pretty good teachers too.' He went on to mention those he'd admired and respected, making her feel that her own summing up had been close to the mark.

Offering her a cigarette, he went on to say he'd been lucky. As a boy with no fixed ideas, he'd simply absorbed the teaching and found he had a talent for exploring different styles, different mediums. 'Yes, praise is great,' he admitted frankly, 'there's nothing like it for boosting the ego and making you think you can conquer the world. But you can't live on praise – or even by selling the odd piece of work.'

Looking, listening, Suzie found she was noticing subtle differences. He was older, for a start; in his mid-twenties now, with four more years of experience under his belt. And in these surroundings, he was able to be himself, as warm and likeable as ever. More than likeable, in fact.

Clearing her throat, she asked, 'What are you doing at the moment?'

'Teaching, mainly – just up the road here, at St Martin's. And painting when I can.'

Eager to have his presence at the boutique explained, she said, 'So what on earth were you doing at that launch party? It didn't look like your sort of place at all.'

For a moment, he was embarrassed. 'Well, it's like this,' he said, lowering his voice, 'not only did Elsa buy a couple of my paintings, she's introduced me to an influential dealer.

And she's trying to fix up an exhibition. At least, that's what she tells me.'

'Really? But that's great...' Except, she thought, he didn't look too thrilled. 'Isn't it?'

'In a way, yes,' he sighed, giving her a rueful glance. 'But there's a price. She seems to get a kick out of showing off her latest acquisition and expects me to escort her everywhere.'

Suzie didn't have the courage to put the real question into words – *and does she expect you to sleep with her as well?* Instead, feeling rather flat, she said, 'And is she horrendously rich?'

'Mm, yes, she is. Her last husband was an Italian count.'

'Oh, that explains the jewellery!' And so much more, she thought.

'Look, I know what you're thinking – but it's not... Well, yes, it is, in a way,' he said awkwardly, 'because I know what she wants. But I'm not as green as she thinks I am.' Breaking off, he leaned closer. 'Last week, seeing your face in that crowd... What can I say? It was like touching ground again. I remembered who I was – where I'd come from.'

Gazing into his earnest blue eyes, she shook her head. 'I don't understand...'

'Work, Suzie – that's how people like us earn our bread. And if we're lucky, a bit of respect along the way. Not by selling our souls to the devil.'

As he dropped his gaze, she struggled to find a reply. To think she'd revealed some kind of truth – albeit unwittingly – was flattering. Even so, she was at a loss. 'Is that how it feels – that you'd be selling your soul?'

With a short, bitter laugh, he said, 'Soul, body, you name it. In return for an easy ride – pardon the pun.'

Her heart sank. 'Oh, Freddie, that doesn't sound good.'

'It's not. Soul, integrity – whatever you like to call it – should not be for sale. The thing is, Suzie – and I'm sure you understand this,' he added seriously, 'true creativity is personal, whether it's painting, music, poetry – you name it. It shouldn't be up for sale to the highest bidder. I know we all need to live – but I don't want to live like that! I'd rather teach – be a carpenter, blacksmith, whatever it takes – and keep my painting to myself.'

Awestruck by that depth of feeling, she found herself wondering what held such importance for her. Only as she recalled her own efforts in the face of contempt – from Rod Winter and her manager in Leeds – did she remember the pain of rejection. As she had discovered since, praise, however small, was vital to happiness – and progress.

'Honestly, Freddie, I know nothing about the art world, but just think – your work must be good to interest a dealer. That says one hell of a lot.'

Glancing up, he gave an unexpectedly bashful smile. 'You're right, Suzie – I should be thankful. Didn't mean to go off like that.'

'No, it's okay,' she said, feeling pleased. 'Maybe you needed to say it?'

As he squeezed her hand in gratitude, she felt a thrill to the core of her being.

'Tell you what – drink up and we'll go and get something to eat. You must be starving – I know I am.'

It was a tiny place with just half a dozen tables, serving mainly pasta with a variety of sauces. Italian food was still relatively new to her, so she said she'd have what he was having. From the first forkful, she was impressed and said so; pleased, he said they must do it again sometime. At that, Suzie felt herself glowing, barely able to believe that Freddie Lawrence wanted to see her again.

He even insisted on seeing her home. Touched by such old-fashioned courtesy, she was suddenly shy as they boarded a rattling old Bakerloo line train. He said he lived in Camden

Town – she wasn't even sure where that was – with a room of his own but sharing a top-floor studio with a friend.

'Is it far?'

He shrugged. 'Probably not, as the crow flies. I could walk if I had a map – but don't worry, I'll get the tube back tonight, it's easier.'

Tonight? It sounded as though he planned to do this again.

Reaching her place, on its tree-lined street, Suzie was tongue-tied, wondering if he expected her to invite him in; she hoped not, as she'd left her miserable room in a mess. But as she turned, Freddie drew her towards him, kissed her lightly on the lips, and thanked her again for an enjoyable evening.

She would have responded, but he was already backing away. 'See you soon, I hope,' he said as he turned to wave. 'I'll be in touch!'

By the door, key in hand, she watched him until he disappeared from view. She felt strange, light, unreal. From barely knowing each other, in just one evening it seemed they'd moved to the intimacy of close friends.

Twenty-Five

Liz's personal drama meant Suzie's news was relegated to a footnote. A few days later, returning from work, she heard raised voices as she climbed the stairs. One of the other tenants – a girl she'd seen just once before – was on the landing, looking scared.

'I've just heard a crash, like someone's throwing things. I don't know what to do – should I call the police?'

'No – give me a second…'

Suzie banged on the door. 'Come on Liz, open up! It's Suzie. What's going on in there?'

With that, the door flew open and Chris barged out, shoving her to one side as he clattered down the stairs. Inside, the place was a mess; a plate, still with dinner on, was smashed on the floor, the table upended, and Liz crouched in a corner, weeping.

Shocked, Suzie ushered their neighbour out, said she'd deal with it; and no, please don't bother the police – or the landlord – all would be fine. Closing the door, picking her way past broken pots, she helped Liz up, wondering what could have caused such violence.

Really, she thought afterwards, she needn't have asked; it was a progression of the story she'd been hearing for the past week or more. Liz wanted out of Chris's life – he was determined she should stay. She'd handed in her notice to Chris's boss, who, stupidly, had told Chris. He'd said nothing at work, but arrived at her place just as she was eating and forced his way in. No, he hadn't hit her, but he'd started throwing things – and she was terrified.

'Look, you've got to report him – to his boss, if nobody else. Write it down. Post it. You can't go back, that's for sure.'

'But he'll come *here*,' Liz wailed, 'what am I going to do?'

Taking a deep breath, Suzie said, 'Pack. We'll pack your case tonight – and you get on a train for home first thing in the morning.'

'But what will my Mum say?'

'Oh, Liz, don't be so daft – she'll be glad to have you back, especially once she knows.'

'How can I tell her? She thought I was going to marry him – I told her we were getting engaged...'

'Well, you'll just have to put her straight, won't you?'

Suzie couldn't believe the change. Liz, the girl who'd been so switched on, who'd seemed to have life sussed and sorted, reduced to this cringing wreck.

'You won't tell him, will you? If he comes here, don't tell him where I've gone?'

'Course not! What do you take me for?'

Liz was so shaken, she was afraid to be alone. They moved her mattress into Suzie's room, but, after all the talking and packing, it was a short night. Suzie, fortunately, was on a late shift next day, able to take Liz to King's Cross and put her on a train for Leeds.

'And Liz,' she reminded her friend before leaving, 'don't forget to write to the big boss and report Chris for what he did.'

234

She said she would, but Suzie was far from convinced. Last night, after talking for hours, few decisions had been made. The trip home, as far as Liz was concerned, was just a breathing space. She'd no desire to spend the rest of her life in Heatherley. Her rent was paid for the rest of the month, by which time she should have a better idea of what to do next.

Waving as the train pulled out, Suzie crossed her fingers and hoped all would be well. Later, at the end of a tiring day, she stayed in town just long enough to grab something to eat before going home. And then she couldn't sleep for thinking about Freddie, the fact that he hadn't been in touch. Six days now, while here she was, wondering if he'd meant it. Wondering, too, about the Italian countess who wanted him, body and soul.

– o –

On Friday evening, the phone on the landing was ringing as she came in. Racing up the stairs, she grabbed the receiver and answered breathlessly; but whoever it was just cleared the line.

'Dammit,' she exclaimed, wondering if it was Freddie. A few minutes later, she heard the phone again. Propping her door open, she went to answer, and yes, it was Freddie; but no, he hadn't tried earlier. They'd barely established that when the front doorbell rang. And rang again, insistently.

She waited, but it seemed the house was deserted apart from herself. 'Sorry,' she said to Freddie, 'I'll have to see who it is – shall I ring you back?'

He said he'd hang on; happy but irritated, she went downstairs.

'Just a minute,' she called out, 'I'm coming ...'

But she'd barely turned the latch when both she and the door were flung back, and Chris was in the hall, confronting her. 'Where is she? Where's Liz?'

Suzie would never have called him big, but in that moment he seemed huge and threatening. 'She's not here. And anyway, what do you mean, bursting in like that?'

'Where is she?'

'No idea. She's left. And so should you – go on...' She waved him towards the doorway but he brushed past, taking the steps two at a time.

'Hey – where do you think you're going?' She ran up after him, but he was already at Liz's door, pounding on it and calling her name.

'She's not *here*, Chris – she's *gone*...'

Grabbing the phone, she heard Freddie's voice. 'Sorry, it's Liz's ex – he's trying to beat her door down...' She heard his exclamation, asking the address, telling her to hang up, get out and stay out – he was calling the police.

But even as he said it, Suzie noticed her door was wide open – bag, money, keys – everything was in there...

Keys, keys, she was thinking; *I can't let him get his hands on the keys...*

As Chris started banging his forehead, she dived into her room, grabbed her bag and slammed the door before haring back down the stairs and out into the street.

Twenty yards away was a footpath leading to a back lane. Hiding behind a spindly hedge, trying to keep her eye on the house, she suddenly realized it was raining, a fine, soaking drizzle.

What was he doing in there?

Several minutes ticked by, but just as she saw him come out, a police car with blue light flashing came hurtling around the corner. Even as Chris saw it and ran, they were there, blocking and grabbing him as he started shouting and waving his arms.

The momentary drama seemed unreal – like an episode of *Z Cars*, she thought, smirking as they pushed this violent stranger into the back seat. The idea gave it distance, just as his

236

confinement gave her courage to move. Shaking and shivering, arms clasped about her body, she hurried back to the house. She was at the door and looking for her keys as another police car drew in by the front gate.

'Excuse me, miss,' one of the coppers called as he got out. 'Do you live here? Did you call us?'

He ushered her out of the rain and into the house; but he'd barely got his notebook out when a taxi pulled up, and Freddie appeared, looking anxious as he strode up the path.

As they both started talking at once, the man in uniform called a halt. 'Would you mind showing me the room in question, miss?'

Suzie took him upstairs, shocked to see Liz's door wide open, the Yale lock broken away. The bed was upturned, chair on its side, wardrobe open with Liz's few remaining clothes in a heap on the floor.

'Has he taken anything?'

For a moment she couldn't speak. 'I don't know,' she said at last, clearing her throat. 'I thought Liz took most of her stuff with her...'

–o–

An hour later, she and Freddie were still at the local police station, telling their stories for what felt like the umpteenth time. At last, having signed their statements and been assured that Liz's ex was in a cell for the night, they were allowed to go.

There was a pub on the corner; but before they could reach it Freddie steered her towards the darkness of a shop doorway. Drawing her into his arms, he held her close.

'God above, I haven't even had chance to ask,' he whispered against her hair. 'Are you all right?'

Shakily, between laughter and tears, she said, 'I am, now...' Clinging to him, burying her face in his shoulder, she drew deep breaths, finding the smell of oil paint and him so intoxicating she didn't want to let go. And then, ridiculously, she started crying.

'I was never so glad to see anybody,' she got out between sobs.

'Thank God I phoned when I did,' he murmured, stroking her hair, smoothing it back from her wet cheek. Between gulps and sniffles, just as she was thinking she must stop this, find a handkerchief, Freddie raised her face to his and kissed her; and as tenderness flared into passion, for a dizzying moment it seemed the night was on fire.

She was gasping as she broke for breath, could feel his chest heaving against hers as he buried his face in her hair and whispered, 'Such salty tears...'

Barely able to stand, Suzie felt herself sinking as he released her; and then they were both in a heap on the doorstep, laughing weakly, clinging together like castaways. Passers-by glanced their way and quickly walked on, making them laugh even more.

'Come on,' Freddie said at last, pulling her to her feet, 'you're frozen. Let's get that brandy I promised you...'

Before, she'd barely noticed what he was wearing, but under the pub's bright lights his paint-stained khaki shirt stood out like a coat of many colours. Even the thighs of his jeans were streaked where he'd wiped his pallet knife. No wonder, she thought, he stank of linseed oil and turpentine.

'Were you painting?' she asked, laughing.

Looking down at his clothes, he grinned. 'Been at it all week – that's why I didn't call you. I'd just finished – thought I'd ask you round to see it. But then,' he added ruefully, 'somebody started shouting...'

His reminder killed the amusement. She glanced at her watch; it was almost ten o'clock. 'I suppose I should get back, see if the locksmith's been.'

'We'll go together,' Freddie said. 'I don't want you there on your own.'

– o –

There was a light showing in the bay window. As Suzie opened the door, a man she'd seen before but never met came out into the hall.

'Are you Miss Wallis from upstairs? My name's Kevin. I understand you had a bit of trouble earlier?' As Suzie nodded, he said, 'The door's fixed now, but the landlord's just gone. Anyway, he's addressed the new keys to you and left them on the hallstand – thought I'd better let you know.'

As Suzie thanked him, he looked Freddie up and down. With an uncertain smile he backed into his room and said goodnight.

Taking the envelope, she turned to Freddie. 'We'd better go up – see what's what.'

Leading the way, noticing the beige wallpaper for the first time in weeks, she felt embarrassed. 'The last time this place was decorated,' she said, 'must've been before the war.'

'I've seen worse,' Freddie commented as they reached Liz's door. A moment later, he was exclaiming at the mess before their eyes, while Suzie was cursing the landlord for leaving the clearing up to her. Between them they set the divan back on its feet and straightened the bedding. Only as she began picking clothes from the tangle of hangers and shoes, did Suzie see that a dress had been ripped from neck to hem. Just one item, but it showed the man's fury. What else might he have done, had Liz been in?

Suddenly weak, Suzie sat down on the bed. 'She won't want to come back here, that's for sure.'

Lighting a cigarette, passing it to her, Freddie said, 'I know he's locked up for the night, but I don't want to leave you here on your own.' Slipping an arm around her waist, he said, 'Do you want me to stay? I could bunk in here for the night… Or you could come back to mine? It's no palace, but at least you'd be away from all this.'

She barely paused to think. 'Yes, please,' she whispered, 'take me to yours…'

Twenty-Six

Not until Freddie hailed a taxi on the main road did Suzie examine her decision. Yes, there was warmth and gratitude – excitement too – but it was more than that. It was just as he'd described on seeing her amongst all those strangers: as though with Freddie she'd touched ground at last.

And yet for Suzie, saying yes meant facing another leap into the unknown. She might have been tempted a few times, but having been cheated by James, she couldn't forget the price she'd paid for that drunken fumble in the dark. Ever since, she'd longed to know what real sex was like; but no matter what her body was longing for, when it came to it, she couldn't help turning away.

What was it Liz's mother had said? Something about the heat of the moment being all very well, but would you give him breakfast in the morning? In the past three years, Suzie had barely reached tepid, never mind heat; at least, not until this evening, when Freddie had kissed her in that shop doorway. And was there anything less romantic? If she'd ever imagined what falling in love was like, it wouldn't have been as she was snivelling like a two-year-old, tears pouring, nose running, and shivering with cold. And yet he'd kissed her anyway; and in that glowing moment, her world had lit up.

– o –

Freddie was right when he said his home was just minutes away, but if Camden's close proximity was a surprise, more so was crossing an old-fashioned bridge with lights reflecting off the water below.

'Regent's Canal,' he said as she remarked on it. 'It's a great view along there – so inspirational…' Almost bashfully, he added, 'It's what I've been working on every night this week – why I didn't phone you earlier…'

When he promised to show her the painting, she was thrilled, but moments later the taxi was pulling up in a street of tall terraced houses, and Suzie was gathering her bag and feeling nervous.

Dizzy after climbing two long flights of stairs, she was relieved to reach Freddie's landing. Whatever awkwardness there might have been was wiped out by the heightened emotions of the past few hours. His roomy bedsit was a tip, but it didn't matter. He offered to sleep on the sofa; then on second thoughts offered her the sofa, as he hadn't changed his sheets in a while. She didn't care. All she wanted was to sleep, and preferably by his side.

Only as she made her way to the bathroom on the landing, did Suzie think of that other time, suddenly anxious that she'd freeze at the last minute. Stepping out of her clothes, she noticed the stretch marks across her hips and quickly donned her nightie, praying he wouldn't notice. Hurriedly, she gathered her clothes and went back before she could change her mind.

Going in, she hesitated. Freddie, minus the shirt of many colours, was looking down at the sofa.

242

'Will that be okay?' he asked, indicating the pillow and blanket; but she was gazing at him, dry-mouthed, torn between desire and dismay. Did he really want her to sleep on the sofa? When he was standing there, belt unbuckled and stripped to the waist.

As she tried to speak, he gave a teasing smile. 'You don't have to – you could risk the bed...'

Quivering inside, she nodded; and then she was touching naked skin as he embraced her, heat blossoming between them as his mouth found hers. Dizzy with longing, she responded, caressing his back and pressing him closer; her head was spinning as he drew her towards the bed.

It was as though he sensed her innocence, taking time to please her, not rushing things even then; but as desire mounted afresh, there came a pause in which he turned away. Suzie wondered what he was doing, until it dawned on her that a condom was involved. Relieved of one anxiety, she lay back with a sigh, only to tense again with trepidation.

'It's okay,' he whispered, rousing her afresh; and as the moment came, she gasped. *So this is what it feels like*, flashed through her mind as her body welcomed him, thoughts drowning in a rising wave of pleasure.

For her, it was over too soon; she wanted it to go on forever. But as he shuddered and relaxed in her arms she held him close; thankful as she slipped into sleep, that at last she'd discovered what it was all about.

Throughout the night, she was aware of him curled around her, an arm across her waist, his thigh under hers as she drifted between dreams. As dawn light filtered between the curtains, she felt him stir, stroking her hip as he kissed her neck. In mock complaint, he said, 'You fell asleep...'

She wanted more and would have welcomed him at once, but Freddie laughingly begged her to wait. Whispering something about babies, moments later he was keen to satisfy that wanton urge, and this time he stayed with her. She cried out with the climax, so unbearably moved she found herself weeping. Nonplussed, he cradled her like a child, apologizing until she could frame the words, 'No, it's me – just me. You've made me so happy...'

Later, when the tears had turned to laughter, and they were reminiscing about the early days, he said, 'I fancied you from the moment I first saw you.'

'Oh, come on, you're just saying that,' she teased.

'No, I mean it.' He kissed her nose, cradled her breast, shifted his thigh to cover hers. 'It's incredible – we must have lived close by for how long? Four or five years? But I don't think I ever saw you before I came to your house that day.'

'When I was sweet sixteen,' she murmured with a kiss.

'That was just it – too young by far!'

'Well, I had a crush on you, so that makes us even...'

Later still, half-dressed, eating toast and drinking coffee, Suzie started to laugh. She quoted Liz's mother on the subject of hasty couplings and morning-after regrets. 'But here I am, having finally experienced *the heat of the moment*, and here we are, having breakfast together...'

He smiled, but it was a quizzical smile. He must have known it wasn't her first time, and Suzie read the question before he uttered a word. All at once she was scared, knowing her answer could risk everything.

She pushed the toast around her plate, took a sip of coffee. 'My first time – three years ago – was a disaster. Last night, with you, was the second time...'

Watching him, she saw astonishment and disbelief; as though he still didn't get it. 'But surely...' he began, leaving the question hanging.

Looking down, she said, 'In short, it happened at a party – and I got pregnant.' Even though it was years ago and she was over it now, Suzie needed a deep breath before saying, 'I had the baby adopted. It was pretty hellish, so I won't go into all that. But afterwards, well, I couldn't, you know, let myself go...'

Her words hung between them for what felt like forever. When he didn't move, didn't speak, her heart sank. 'Not that I'm begging for sympathy or anything – I just wanted you to know. Last night,' she added quietly, 'was different.'

At once, Freddie was beside her, drawing her into his arms and holding her close. 'Oh, Suzie,' he breathed, 'I'd no idea...'

He took her back to bed, soothing her like a child until the whole sorry tale was told. And even though she managed to keep the grief at bay, she knew he cared from the way he held her. He said he wasn't surprised her parents had wanted everything covered up; otherwise, life in Denshaw would have been unbearable.

His sympathy took on a bitter edge as he talked about growing up there. Old Denshaw looking down its nose at the council estate, while the workers despised the middle classes with their cheque books and posh cars. Neither side accepting anyone who was different; and as an artist, Freddie said, he was about a different as they came. He'd felt crushed by the place; couldn't wait to get out.

'Your parents were like mine,' he said, 'city folk who ended up there because of the war. They could see the place for what it was, but they had to stay – no choice. No wonder they wanted better for you...

'And don't think you're the only one,' he added gently, stroking her hair. 'One of my students almost died last year from a back-street abortion – thank God you didn't go down that route.'

He went on to tell her about another young woman, a model he knew, dumped by her lover as soon as she was pregnant. She'd kept her child, but life for her was hard. 'She looks terrible,' he sighed, 'really thin and haunted – and yet the poor girl's in great demand as a sitter. But saying that,' he reflected sadly, 'makes us painters sound like cannibals, feeding off the tragedies of others...'

'No, you're not,' Suzie protested. 'You're observers, drawing attention to things other folks don't see. Or don't *want* to see...'

He kissed her for that, but Suzie was still mulling over what he'd said about Denshaw. She and Freddie might not have known each other in their formative years, but his sentiments echoed her own. She felt she'd known him all her life.

– o –

It was Saturday and her day off, but later, when they were dressed, he took Suzie upstairs to the studio. Unlocking the door, inviting her in, Freddie laughed as she gasped in surprise. Long sloping windows between the roof-beams gave light to a large space. The room looked chaotic, with two or three easels, chairs, a bench, a dais and a couple of tatty sofas. Frames and paintings were everywhere.

'This reminds me of art school,' she said, and he laughed again.

'Not nearly so tidy, though!'

And then she spotted his painting: the bridge, the barges, and the lights; a night scene of dark blues and bright yellows...

'Reminds me of Van Gogh,' she whispered, glowing in admiration.

'I know,' he said, a trace of regret in his voice, 'but I couldn't resist it...'

'And nor should you! It's fabulous...' She couldn't stop looking, going in close, stepping back, marvelling at the brush-strokes, the way mere suggestion became defined by distance. Even though she'd crossed that bridge just once, catching no more than a glimpse of the boats and the lights, Suzie felt she knew it. Yes, the colours and subject reminded her of Van Gogh, but in many respects this painting was more romantic, the style – she realized later – more akin to Monet.

Viewing some of Freddie's other paintings – strikingly modern works that she didn't entirely understand – Suzie could see why the dreadful countess had wanted an exhibition. One day, Suzie was sure, he would manage it himself.

Talking about his work and teaching commitments, they moved on to Suzie's work and her bedsit in Kilburn. Over coffee downstairs, Freddie's concerns became more immediate.

'I know you've got to go back, but I'm worried about that bloke and what else he might get up to. Why don't you give notice and find a place here in Camden? In the meantime, I'll come over and fix a bolt on your door.'

To Suzie, it was like a declaration of love.

– o –

Liz had phoned from Heatherley earlier in the week, although at the time there'd been nothing to report. Since Friday night, of course, there was much to tell, but with no telephone at her friend's house, it was a question of writing a long and convoluted letter or going there in person.

After a chat with her boss, Suzie came away counting her blessings. Mark had given her extra time off to go to Yorkshire: to see her parents and allay their fears, and to explain to Liz what had happened about the room in Kilburn. Dashing off a quick note to both parties, Suzie wrote that she'd be home on Thursday. In the meantime, whatever spare time she had was spent flat-hunting. Keen to move, she'd have taken almost the first thing on offer, but Freddie shook his head and said she could do better for the money. He'd keep looking, he said, and let her know when he found something suitable.

Arriving home at last, Suzie was fussed over by her parents who'd had a visit from Liz. They'd been worried, but Freddie's part in the second half of the story – somewhat abridged – put more of a shine on things. Less so for Liz, who was looking better but still recovering her balance. As to Chris and the events of Friday night, she was horrified.

'With any luck, he'll get the sack,' Suzie said that evening over a drink in the Old White Rose. 'Breaking and entering, it's like burglary – I don't see how he can get away with it.' She paused. 'You did report what he did to you?'

'Well, I wrote to the managing director, telling him why I'd just walked out. And I told him not to reveal my home address to anyone at work, especially that bastard Chris.'

'Did he reply?'

Liz pulled a face. 'It came the other day.' Taking an envelope from her bag, she handed it over.

Scanning the letter, Suzie shook her head. 'Oh, I see – he'll *bear it in mind*. What a prat.' Disgusted, she handed it back. 'God, what do we have to do, to get through to them?'

'I know. It's like I was some vindictive ex-girlfriend, trying to blacken his name.'

Suzie advised telling the MD what else Chris had done. A moment later, she asked whether the police had been in touch; but so far Liz had heard nothing.

Thinking about that night, its mix of frights and bizarre moments, she related the tale of Chris being cornered by the police and managed to make her friend laugh. 'And at least he got a night in the cells for his pains!'

'Not long enough,' Liz replied darkly. 'Should have been permanent.'

As they both drank to that, Suzie said, 'But seriously, what are you going to do? Are you coming back to London, or what?'

With a shudder, Liz said she'd had enough of London, thanks very much, and she'd no intention of staying in

Heatherley either. 'Actually,' she went on, 'I'm thinking of going to Canada.'

'*Canada?*' Suzie was stunned. 'Why Canada?'

Lifting her chin, Liz said, 'New start – new opportunities. Been thinking about it for ages. I knew Chris wouldn't let me go without creating hell, so I applied about a month ago.'

'What? You never told me! You mean you were just going to go through all the formalities without saying a word? Liz – how could you? I thought we were friends!'

'Don't be like that, Suzie – we are!'

It didn't seem so, and Suzie was more hurt than she would have believed possible. Her face must have said it all, because suddenly Liz was eager to placate, laying much of it on Chris and saying she'd had to keep things to herself for safety's sake. Even so, it sounded like an excuse.

'Anyway,' Liz finished with a shrug, 'I didn't get chance, did I? You weren't around much, Suzie – you'd got your own friends.'

'I was working!'

'Okay, but you know what I mean. I had to get on and *do* something, so I did.'

'But what about your Mum and Dad? What do they say?'

She looked shamefaced, Suzie thought, but only for a moment. 'Well, Dad doesn't say much, does he? Mum thinks it's a good idea.'

Somehow, Suzie doubted that.

Needing to calm down, she offered to buy another drink. Coming back from the bar, she said, 'Anyway, I'm moving out, too – but only as far as Camden...' And with that the subject was changed, Liz eager to show some interest in what was happening in Suzie's life.

'And really,' Suzie said with a bright smile as she finished telling her about Freddie, 'when you think about it, Liz, I've got you and Chris to thank for that, haven't I?'

Looking back to the conclusion of the crisis, Suzie could see that in a way, it was inevitable. Liz had always seemed impulsive, but the sudden announcement that she was leaving – not just her job but the country – topped everything.

It was a shock, although as Suzie's mother said, Liz had always been like that. Here today, gone tomorrow. Gone forever, as it turned out. They'd written to each other for a year or so, but after various house moves on both sides of the Atlantic, it was from Liz's mother that she heard the news, and then only occasionally. Marriage, babies, husband with a good job; according to Mrs Bradley, who'd been to visit, it was a great life over there.

Maybe it was. Accepting it at the time – after all, she was struggling with similar commitments herself – Suzie wondered as the years went by. She'd only seen her old friend once, and that was at Mrs Bradley's funeral, sometime back in the '80s. A brief and awkward conversation, which given the circumstances was entirely understandable. Less so, was the broken promise to meet up before she went back to Canada. Suzie had given Liz her address and phone number, but it hadn't been followed up, not even with a letter.

She felt sad, just thinking about it. Liz, her old friend from schooldays – they'd been through so much together, crises which had changed their lives.

What would she have said, Suzie wondered, to this current situation? Would she still be sneering at James Fielding, calling him a selfish little rich boy, and telling Suzie to put a flea in his ear?

Twenty-Seven

While out walking a few days later, Suzie received a text from Jo, saying she'd left a message on the house phone. Slightly mystified, as soon as she came in she played it back.

I'm not trying to jump the gun, Jo's voice said, *just giving you a place to start...* And with that she related the name and address of a national organization dedicated to putting birth families in touch.

Feverishly, Suzie reached for pen and paper and re-played the message. Her daughter was saying something about counselling being part of the process, and Suzie paused, seeing the sense of that. Only as she pondered the wider aspects, did it occur to her that this group must know the names of adoption societies and how they worked. They should be able to advise her, give her an idea what to do next.

She called Jo's number but had to leave a message. Should she call James? Suzie thought for a moment, and then decided not; it might be better to write to these people first and see what came back. Even so, she hesitated. Speaking to Jo that evening, she found herself being encouraged to go for it; after all, her daughter said, she wouldn't lose anything, and could stand to gain a lot. It might even be that he was trying to find her, and this would shorten the process.

Suzie decided to sleep on it, but once she was in bed, the knowledge nagged at her. In the end, she had to go down and rough out an enquiry to these people.

Next morning, she re-wrote it, finally satisfied that she'd covered everything. As an afterthought, once her letter was ready to post, she found a postcard of the cathedral at Santiago and wrote a few lines to James: *Girls in agreement, now preparing myself for the challenge. Say a prayer for me. Regards, Suzie.*

Bland enough for whoever came in to do the housework, but he'd know what she meant. With that she found some stamps and walked down to the post box by the church.

Felton was a small place, consisting mainly of outlying farms. Other than the row of cottages by her own house, there were maybe a dozen stone-roofed houses facing the village green, and a former vicarage, hidden by trees, that now belonged to a local TV presenter. There was only one small new development, and that was behind the village hall. A desirable place to live, according to estate agents, but nowadays, since the closure of both shop and school, the village often seemed deserted.

Before relinquishing her letter to its fate, she stood for a moment, raising her eyes to Heatherside Ridge, thinking of the times Freddie had painted this view in different moods, different styles. Appreciating its quiet beauty, her eyes focused afresh on the church, quietly dominating the village from its rise above the road.

Freddie was fascinated by old churches, and by this one in particular. He liked the way it wasn't hidden by trees, that he could use it as a feature of the landscape. Religion had nothing to do with it, he said while making donations; he was simply helping maintain these architectural features. Suzie generally pointed out that without religion, England's churches would have disappeared centuries ago. Her comments were usually met with a grunt of acknowledgement, but Freddie had little time for those in charge. *Professional God-botherers*, he called them, even though he'd liked their local vicar. Quite how he would have reacted to James, she didn't dare to think.

Glancing up at the church, and then down at the card and envelope in her hand, she sighed, wondering if she was doing the right thing. Gazing at the picture of Santiago, she recalled her journey across northern Spain, the churches she'd entered for shelter; and the sense she'd had on occasion, of someone walking beside her.

Murmuring a prayer, Suzie hoped that God – and James – knew how hard this was.

Apart from the wind in the trees, nothing stirred as she slipped her missives into the box, but she felt calmer walking back towards home.

– o –

Quite how long she'd expected it to take, Suzie couldn't have said, but a few days later, the postman delivered a thick A4 envelope – an answer to her enquiry. Astonished by the speed – even alarmed by what it signified – she took a deep breath before examining the contents.

With the single sheet reply was a form for her to fill in. A copy of the society's journal was enclosed, outlining its aims, with lists of advisors in most areas of the country and also the location of records and regional services. For a modest subscription charge, it seemed Suzie could receive the newsletter every month, and have access to help in her search.

Reading those pages proved a mixed experience. There were letters from members, telling their adoption stories from different aspects. All grateful for the assistance they'd been given, but few of these accounts had happy endings. Like ancient maps bearing the words, *Here be Dragons*, it was as though the society needed to place a warning.

With a lurch of apprehension, Suzie turned to the registration form.

Most of the information required was easy to answer: her name, her son's name, date and place of birth. Okay, fine; but as to which adoption society was involved, Suzie couldn't be sure. Church connections – her original interview, and then the Home itself – suggested the Children's Society, but with West Yorkshire, North Yorkshire, and the City of York involved, she could be wrong. For the first time, she realized that anyone searching for her would have a difficult time of it.

The form also asked for details of the adoptive parents, if known; and had she registered with the Government's Contact Register? Answer, no, but clearly it was something she should do.

'No time like the present,' she muttered grimly. Armed with coffee and cigarettes, she went to her office and photocopied the form. After a practice run in which she stated the church connection and included a couple of sentences to explain her confusion regarding adoption societies, she filled out the original in neat block capitals.

Having signed it with the date, she set it aside.

Applying to the Government's Contact Register was much more challenging. The advice was to enclose a letter to her son, giving some information about herself, her current circumstances, and the reasons for his adoption. A letter to be kept on file, in case he was looking for her. In the end, it took all day to draft on the computer, plus an hour next morning to refine into two pages of basic information, about herself and James, their meeting, parting, and recent re-connection. It was interspersed with what Suzie hoped would come across as warmth.

A couple of sentences had been written and re-written twice until they satisfied her: '*More than anything else, I imagine that as an adopted child you must wonder about your past. Not just about your father and I, but who our families were, what talents, failings and backgrounds we all had. In short, what made us what we are – and what circumstances made you…*'

Before she could waver, she folded the letter, stuck stamps on both envelopes and went to the post. She'd already dropped them into the box when she looked up at the church. 'Now then, God, if you're listening, how about a bit of divine intervention here?'

With that, she walked home again and rang James's number. He wasn't in. She left a message to phone her on her mobile, before going into the studio to tackle those spoon-backed chairs.

– o –

Returning from the training college that afternoon, James went straight to his study. Surprised to find a message from Suzie, she phoned her back at once, so overcome by what she had to say, he could barely frame a reply. Despite her card, he hadn't allowed himself to believe she would go ahead; at least, not with such speed. But even as he found the words, her reply was repressive, telling him not to get his hopes up, it could take forever.

'But you've *started*,' he interjected. 'I hardly dared think you would.'

Enigmatically, she said something about an elephant in the room, and not being able to ignore it.

'Oh. Is there anything I can do?'

There was nothing; and no, she said in answer to his next question, there was no point in them meeting, she just had to wait. If and when she had a reply, she'd let him know.

255

Cut by her brusqueness, he said he'd like to see her anyway; but it seemed she was busy.

Like a teenager who'd just been told to grow up, he found himself staring at the phone.

– o –

Thoughts of Suzie were so dominant, he almost called off the appointment with Father Philip, the Anglican priest who was his spiritual adviser. Except Philip would want to know why, which led back to Suzie and the logical answer: he did need to talk and he did need advice. It was time to bite the bullet and get on with it.

The last bastion of the Roman church in England, a friend had called it, not entirely tongue-in-cheek. In some ways, Pusey House was indeed a kind of relic, a memorial to Oxford's Anglo-Catholic movement, with all the trappings that suggested. But it was also a thriving environment, with scholars, priests and librarians, all dedicated to the word of God.

He'd visited first as a researcher, but over the years he'd come to love the place, not least for its choir. The music – from medieval plainsong to the best of modern composers – was a celebration in itself, and once in a while he liked to take communion there. As a priest, James regarded himself as one of the Church's liberals, as fond of the liturgy as he was keen on the ordination of women; but even so, when he needed counselling, this was where he came.

In Oxford, as he parked the car and crossed St Giles, James found himself thinking of his old mentor, Father Allen, a man whose holiness shone. He'd possessed the God-given ability to discern the true heart of a problem, and in his own gentle way would turn the speaker's viewpoint until he could see it for himself. *God helps us if we allow it*, was one of his beliefs; the whole point being, as James had discovered, that the source of pain must first be identified.

Father Allen had had passed away not long after James's ordination. In the years since, rather than take his problems elsewhere, he'd sought help from Father Philip, one of the old man's successors. Ringing the bell, James gave his name to the porter and went in. Nowadays, the house shared its grounds with a new graduate college, St Cross, and Father Philip had rooms upstairs, overlooking the quad.

'James, come in – good to see you. The kettle's on – what will you have?'

He opted for tea, and for a few minutes the two men chatted about their respective days. By the time they sat down in comfortable chairs, James was ready to explain his current situation.

Father Phil was a chunky ex-rugby player, a man of long experience and infinite patience, with a mind as sharp as a surgeon's scalpel. With long practice at cutting through waffle to find the seat of a problem, over the years he'd learned much of James's background.

After a short prayer, he said, 'So, what brings you here this evening, James? General malaise, or something more specific?'

'Specific, to begin with,' James replied. 'I've been meaning to see you for some time.' He thought for a moment, dismayed by how long he'd been putting it off, by how easily he'd fooled himself into thinking he was coping.

'But recent events have taken over...'

Taking a deep breath, he explained about Suzie and the part she'd played in his life. Giving a brief summary of what had led to this present situation, he said, 'On reflection, perhaps I should have discussed it with you before approaching her like that...'

'You wish you'd gone about it more tactfully?'

James agreed. 'It was thoughtless – shocking for her – and, in retrospect, something I would have advised anyone else against. On the other hand, it did have its rewards.'

At his adviser's quizzical glance, James said, 'I discovered two things – first, that she was as much a virgin as I was, and second that she hadn't been mocking me, the night I forced myself on her. She was simply disgusted by my actions.'

'Rightly so.'

'Indeed.' Thinking for a moment, James said, 'But she'd cared enough to seek me out, later, to talk things over. I keep thinking that if only I'd had the wit to listen – if I hadn't been so self-obsessed – maybe things could have turned out differently.'

'Well, you were a teenager,' Father Phil observed mildly. 'Do you regret it?'

'Very much so.'

After a moment, he said, 'Would it have worked, do you think? I mean, if you'd followed your heart, been bold enough to tell your parents – *married* the girl?'

James shook his head. 'I doubt it. I was too green by half – and too concerned with my own ambitions.'

'Meaning?'

'I'd have resented it.'

'Quite. Not a good recipe for a happy marriage.'

'No, but at least the boy would have had his natural parents.'

With raised brows, the other man said, 'James, if you'd seen as many messed-up kids as I've seen – ones raised by their natural parents – you wouldn't think this was the answer. We all make mistakes – we're human, it's what we do. In the circumstances, it may not have been such a mistake to have the boy adopted.'

Giving him time to think about that, his adviser changed tack, going back to the difficulties James had experienced in the wake of that brief relationship. 'Ask yourself this – would you be the priest you are, without the suffering you went through?'

'Perhaps not.'

'You've had a lot to deal with since Maggie's death. Has that anything to do with how you're feeling right now? Regret, opportunities missed – a desire to make things right?'

The mention of his wife struck home. A difficult couple of years, there was no denying it; and, apart from the grief and the regrets, living alone wasn't easy. 'Perhaps so,' he said. 'But to be honest, if it hadn't been for Maggie, I wouldn't even have thought about searching for my son.'

'You don't know that. Grief can send us down some strange avenues.' He paused for a moment. 'Try leaving Maggie out of this. Just accept that you made the decision, acted impulsively, and now, it seems, you're experiencing something of a backlash.'

Accepting that, James nodded. 'That's about the size of it, yes.'

'Does it surprise you?'

James shook his head. Looked at it like that, it was not surprising at all. 'I've forced her into it, haven't I? And naturally, she's upset.'

'But she's begun the search – surely you should be pleased? After all, she's giving you what you asked for.'

It was the way he said it, the questioning look, that set alarm bells ringing in James's head. What did he mean? Yes, he should be pleased, but he wasn't, he felt guilty. He'd forced her into it, just as he'd forced her into having sex…

He covered his face, shamed by his own selfish desires. 'I haven't changed at all…'

But Father Phil had scant patience with guilt, especially the self-indulgent variety. 'We're all self-centred, James, following our own agendas – you know how easy it is to carry on blindly without seeing the effect on others.'

Pulling himself together, James nodded. 'And when they react in ways we don't expect…'

'Yes, it's a shock, and sometimes a necessary one. So don't flagellate yourself – instead, use it for reflection. Examine why you acted this way – be honest about your expectations, and how realistic they are. And try to see things from her point of view. The road she's on won't be easy.'

As James considered that, the other man said, 'Emotionally, she'll be all over the place, so give her time to come to terms with it. It might help,' he added, 'to take a step back, let her contact you. And in the meantime, focus your mind on Christ and his infinite patience.'

He moved on to ask how this situation was affecting James's ministry, and James admitted it was the reason he'd made the appointment. He was aware that his mind was distracted, that he was not giving his best either to his parish or his students.

Father Philip suggested ways of dealing with that, setting him some spiritual exercises to be done each day; and then, when James had made a few notes, he said, 'How are you feeling? Are you up to making your confession now?'

– o –

Afterwards, as always, he felt better, lighter, as though the page had been wiped clean and he could begin again with the help of Christ to show him the way.

Step back, give her some space… That's what Phil had said, and he was right, of course, while no doubt understanding how hard it was to sit tight and do nothing. What he hadn't asked – and in retrospect, James was surprised – was what he felt towards Suzie. It was probably just as well, because if Suzie's emotions were all over the place, surely the same could be said of his. They'd shared so much, short-circuiting years in terms of experience and emotion, he was no longer certain of anything. But he hoped Suzie could see that he cared, that he felt responsible for what she was going through.

The last thing he wanted to do was pester her with phone calls, but a card might be acceptable. Just a line to say he was there for her, if she needed him.

Twenty-Eight

Suzie was surprised to receive a postcard of a pretty, black and white village street. The main feature was a public house, its sign – what looked like a red dragon curled around the figure of a Red Cross Knight – dominating the picture. Turning it over, she saw that James had written, *'If you need a break from fighting dragons, just let me know. The food is good at the George and I'm told the beds are comfortable.'*

Smiling, she was touched by his humour and brevity – even by what he was suggesting. 'Okay,' she murmured, 'I'll remember that…'

Clearly, a written line or two was better than a terse few words over the phone.

On her next trip into Heatherley, she made a point of looking for cards. Scenes of the town were too bland by far, but in a gift shop she found one of Freddie's paintings reproduced as a greetings card. The surprise gave her a warm glow, and she bought all three, intending to send one each to the girls.

'I didn't know these were still around,' she said to the assistant.

'Oh, we usually have others from the same series, but we've sold out. They're very popular.'

'Are they?' Caught by emotion, Suzie swallowed hard. She'd forgotten they were still in production. Fumbling with her purse, she said, 'My husband painted the originals.'

'Did he?' the young woman was impressed. 'Is he planning on doing more?'

Suzie looked down and shook her head. 'Sadly, no.'

Before any more questions could be asked, she tucked the cards in her bag and beat a hasty retreat. Silly or not, it felt as though Freddie was saying he was still around, still looking out for her.

– o –

The first response to her enquiries came quickly. The Church of England's Children's Society wrote to say that they had no record of an adoption in the name she'd given.

That shook her. Thanks to that first interview in Bradford – and the Mother & Baby Home she'd been sent to – Suzie had been convinced the Church was involved. The letter suggested she try the local authority. She stared at the address they'd given. Not Bradford, not Richmond, not York or even Middlesbrough, but Northallerton, of all places. Apparently, it was the seat of North Yorkshire County Council.

Only when she thought about it, did a reason present itself. When her son was born, Yorkshire's historic boundaries were different. The three areas of North, West, and East Ridings, had been changed sometime in the 1970s. Now it was North Yorkshire, West Yorkshire, *South* Yorkshire, for heaven's sake, and something called Humberside carved out of the old East Riding. Only the City of York had retained its ancient status.

She would never have thought of Northallerton. Now, imagining all those shifts of paperwork over the intervening years, she started to panic. What if there were no records? What if they were lost?

Briefly, she thought of phoning James, and then calmed herself. No. No point until she'd followed the instruction to write to North Yorkshire's Social Services Department. It took a day or so to steel herself. As she explained in her letter, she needed to know which court had handled the adoption order, and whether her son had indeed been taken abroad as was suggested at the time.

Expecting a reply beginning, *We regret to inform you*, Suzie was startled, a couple of weeks later, to receive a highly informative letter from the Northallerton office. As the facts sank in, her head swam with shock.

By lunchtime, after a brief call to James, she was on her way to Norton Parva.

– o –

'Singapore!' Suzie exclaimed, waving the letter in his face. 'How the hell does that equate with *an English-speaking country with a temperate climate*? The lying shits!'

As she paced the room, James scanned the single page, sinking into a chair as he tried to absorb the facts. Not just Singapore, but Suzie's neglect in telling him the whole story. She'd never mentioned that the baby was to be taken abroad.

'Why didn't you tell me?'

She shook her head. 'I couldn't.'

Gritting his teeth, he read on. North Yorkshire held the record of Dominic's adoption, and they could confirm that his adoptive parents were British citizens working abroad. The father was a civil engineer, and the family had maintained a property in the UK, returning for an extended period each summer. Sadly, there was nothing on file to suggest Dominic had tried to make contact with his birth mother. The letter went on to name the Leeds-based agency with which they had an agreement, offering support and intermediary services should they be required.

'I'm so sorry,' James murmured, looking up. He'd said that over the phone, but she'd been almost incoherent. Singapore, yes, he'd got that, but this – this letter – was the reality.

Clearing his throat, James said, 'At least they have the records.'

'But imagine taking a baby – *a fair-skinned baby* – out to a climate like that! Tropical sun – mosquitoes – God knows what the sanitation was like in those days. Were they completely *insane?* I don't know who's more culpable – the so-called parents or the people who allowed it!'

Feeling inadequate in the face of Suzie's furious distress, all he could do was shrug helplessly, even though he was thinking much the same. Would he take a new baby to a climate like that? He didn't think so, but then he didn't know much about babies, other than their tendency to yell when he held them over the font. He told himself infants had to be able to survive, otherwise such places would be wastelands. But yes, he knew what she meant, this was an English baby transplanted to an extreme environment; he would have needed care.

'You can't torture yourself like this, Suzie,' he said at last. 'Think of all the colonialists, people who settled these places, had children out there – and without modern medicine…'

Turning to James, she stopped her pacing. 'But how many *died* in those conditions?'

Right. And the letter said there'd been no contact from their son…

'He could be dead,' she said brokenly. 'God,' she sobbed, collapsing onto the sofa, 'I feel so guilty – why did I ever agree? How could I think it was a good idea? How could I *do* that!'

Going to her, James pulled her into his arms, refusing to let go, holding hard as she shuddered with grief; he held on until she stopped fighting and let him comfort her. As she quietened, he'd think it was over, but the gulping sobs came in seemingly endless waves. He was unaware of his own tears until he smoothed her hair and realized it was wet. Foolishly, all he could think was how fragile she was, and how good it felt to be holding her like this, close against his heart.

'We were young,' he said when she was more composed. 'Brought up to respect those in authority. When they said this was right, and that was wrong, we believed them...'

'Don't tell me,' Suzie muttered, drawing away from him. 'That's how six million Jews were sent to the gas chambers.'

Shocked, James stared at her. 'Oh, come on – don't put us in that bracket.'

'No, I mean it. There was a letter in that magazine they sent me. One poor woman had read something about death camps and why the guards did what they did. All this stuff about obedience to authority, and,' Suzie's voice broke, 'she really believed she was as guilty as them!'

Chilled by her words, he reached out, holding her face between his hands. 'Suzie, you *mustn't* think like that. It's wrong – absolutely wrong. You weren't sending him to his death, but to a better life.'

Suddenly reminded of funerals, he could have bitten his tongue.

'A better life?' she retorted, twisting free. 'They said that about the kids they sent to Australia, after the war – we're only just finding out what happened to them!'

Breathing hard, he bit his lip. 'Okay, I know it sounds bad – and yes, you were lied to – but for the moment, that's *all* we know.'

'The whole thing could be a pack of lies...'

Shaking his head, trying to dismiss similar thoughts, he drew her back into his arms. As she hid her face against

his chest, he tried to find his voice. 'I know, Suzie, I know...
Remember, I'm responsible too...'

– o –

Neither of them could have faced eating out. Suzie wasn't
even hungry, but James said they both needed food. Seated at
the kitchen table with a glass of white wine, she watched him
prepare a simple risotto. He was still in his black shirt and
dog-collar, something she'd barely registered earlier; it seemed
strange to watch a priest, cooking.

Catching her smile, he glanced down and chuckled. 'You're
right – I should have changed before starting this.'

'No, it's just that I haven't seen you wearing the collar
before.'

'Ah – my working clothes. The uniform, Amy calls it.'

An advertisement, Suzie thought, saying who and what James
was. Supposed to make him approachable, while really, it set him
apart. How had she not noticed it when he embraced her? But
maybe she had – maybe that was why she kept pulling away...

The meal was good, and he was right, she did feel better;
fortified by the wine, it seemed the world hadn't quite ended
after all. A little after eight, when he suggested a walk, Suzie
needed no persuading. After a long and emotional day, it was
good to be out, good to see the place where James had spent
the past twenty years.

The sky was clearing after a cloudy day, and in the glow of
evening the village street looked like a film-set. Faced by the
George and Dragon across the road, she remembered James's
card. 'By the way, that card you sent was absolutely right. I *did*
feel I was facing dragons.' A moment later, she said, 'And now,
even more so...'

'Well, don't forget you've got a squire at your back, will
you?'

267

His comment made her smile. She would have squeezed his hand in thanks, but this, she reminded herself, was a small village, no doubt with eyes everywhere. His wife, the remarkable Margaret, would be well remembered.

Earlier, she'd noticed James's wedding photo on a side table. She'd been surprised by his wife's height and statuesque blonde looks. At once she'd pictured a Valkyrie in some Wagnerian opera, and then felt ashamed for such judgements. Now, she found herself wondering how this striking woman – the Vicar's wife – had been viewed by the locals.

'What was she like? Your wife, I mean.'

'Beautiful,' he said, giving Suzie a swift glance, 'in all senses of the word. A good woman with a sense of humour. And she was a musician, of course, as well as a teacher, so we ended up with the best choir around. I used to wonder what I'd done to deserve her.'

As Suzie was wondering what she was really like, James said, 'On the downside, she had what people call an artistic temperament. Fortunately, once she'd let fly, it was soon over. But I must say,' he went on sadly, 'the inability to conceive was a heavy burden. Mostly she just carried on, but there were times when – well, when it all became too much.'

He started to say something, then stopped. Eventually, he said, 'You'll no doubt understand when I say the – *the Change*, I suppose people call it – was the worst time.'

'Yes, indeed,' Suzie murmured, remembering her own upheavals.

'She left me, you know.'

Astonished, Suzie halted. 'Why?'

James shrugged. 'After all the tests, Maggie knew her chances of motherhood were slim – but her age made it final and she really couldn't handle it. Unfortunately, by the time she left, she was in despair. Said if she didn't leave – get right away from her work and all the responsibilities – she'd kill herself.'

'No! What about her faith? She was religious, wasn't she?'

He sighed. 'I think she'd lost her faith in most things – including our marriage...'

Aware of his pain, Suzie scarcely knew what to say. 'I hope you persuaded her to see a doctor?'

'She said she'd had enough of doctors, thanks very much, and besides, she was taking pills already, and didn't want more. Her remedy was to pack a bag and take off for northern Italy – to enjoy the opera season, she said. She had a nest-egg left by her mother, and she couldn't think of anything better to spend it on...

'She went in November,' he added. 'Didn't come back until February.'

His tone was matter-of-fact, but Suzie could imagine the shock – the heartbreak – and the local gossip. At once she felt ashamed. She'd ranted and raged from the moment she arrived, and all the while James had withstood it, holding her close until she calmed down. She'd never imagined years of practice, but now she was picturing beautiful, talented Margaret putting him through hell on a regular basis.

'How on earth did you manage?' she said at last. 'And how was she, when she returned?'

'Better – certainly much calmer. But she was different. The spark had gone.'

'Didn't she talk about it?' Suzie asked, thinking of Freddie's creative tensions, the spark that fired his painting. The periods of gloom that would send him off in search of fresh inspiration – sometimes in unfortunate directions.

'Not much, except to say Italy released something she'd kept locked inside for a long time. Sitting in darkened theatres, overwhelmed by all that operatic emotion, she was able to grieve. Over and over, she said, until it was finally done...'

As they reached the end of the street, with shadowy fields and hedgerows ahead, he stood for a moment, deep in thought. 'I was so relieved to have her back – to have a calmer and happier wife – it took me a while to realize she didn't want to sing anymore – professionally, I mean. All that energy and emotion she'd put into a performance – it just wasn't there. As though in Italy, she'd wept it all away.'

'Perhaps she had,' Suzie said gently.

Pondering that unhappy situation, comparing it to what she'd figured out over the years, Suzie would have liked to ask if his wife's sexual desire had died too. Instead, she said, 'Creativity – it's like the urge to create new life, isn't it? Maybe it sounds like cod psychology, but it strikes me that maybe – just maybe – Margaret's passion was linked to her desire for children? And once that was dashed, her desire to sing died with it...'

James turned in surprise. 'You think so? I've never considered that...'

She thought he was about to say more, but he shook his head. A moment later, he took her arm and they began to walk back.

Above the village, the sky was glowing like fire, making a stark silhouette of the church tower, rising behind the trees. Considering James's work, Suzie tried to imagine what life had been like for him here, carrying on through winter's dark days. Not easy with no wife and little help; living alone, working alone, and no doubt the subject of tattling tongues.

She would have liked to ask, but instead, she said, 'Do clergymen retire?'

His face creased into a smile. 'Of course. Don't you think they deserve it?'

'What do they do afterwards?'

'Help out, usually, when an incumbent's away. Holidays, sickness, that sort of thing. I've got another five years, but I could continue for a while. What about you?'

'Me? Well, now Sara's managing things, I've almost retired already. But I'm trying to pick up the threads again – buying, restoring, that sort of thing. Quite apart from the money aspect, I've never been good at doing nothing.'

'Well, you can certainly write. How about a novel, have you thought of that?'

Pulling a face, she said, 'Thought about it, yes, but fiction's not as easy as it looks.'

'Could you do another travel book?'

'Well, the publishers have asked, but I kind of fudged it.'

'Why not? Another challenge might be good for you at the moment – take your mind off things.'

'It would,' she agreed, 'although I can't plan anything while all this is going on.' Hearing him sigh, Suzie glanced up. 'What is it?'

With a rueful smile, he said, 'If only you weren't three hours' drive away. I'd happily join you for the odd day's walking, wherever it was.'

'Well,' she acknowledged, 'it's an idea.'

He guided her down a side lane, towards a broad stream bisecting the gardens on either side. Along the footpath, with sunset peeping through the trees and water murmuring close by, to Suzie it was like walking through a dream. As the George and Dragon came in sight, she could see people outside in the beer-garden, others enjoying their meals in a softly-lit dining room. It looked attractive, although she couldn't have faced it this evening.

Following her gaze, he said, 'Another time, perhaps? By the way,' he added, 'how are you feeling now – more relaxed?'

'I am – quite tired, in fact.'

'I thought so. How about I carry your bag across, then you can go straight to your room. I'd have suggested bringing your car as well, but it looks as though the car park's full.'

'Is it okay in your drive?' she asked mischievously. 'Sure your neighbours won't gossip?'

James chuckled as they crossed the road. 'If they've nothing else to talk about, we should be thankful.'

Half an hour later, Suzie was smiling as she looked around her room. Oak beams, white plasterwork, a Jacobean four-poster, and a modern bathroom. Bliss. She tried the bed, felt the pillows, and decided not even the ghost of Jacob Marley would disturb her tonight.

– o –

After breakfast at the pub, Suzie paid her bill and walked across to the Vicarage. Knowing James would be busy, she didn't plan to linger, but as she walked down the drive he was coming out of church. For a moment, seeing him in a long black cassock, she was taken aback. He looked imposing, not the James she knew; at least, not until he turned and raised his hand in greeting.

'Don't rush away,' he called out as she opened the boot of the car, 'come and have a look at the church.'

It was bigger than she'd imagined, with a side aisle and Lady Chapel. 'Much of what you see is nineteenth-century, although it dates back to Norman times…'

Only as they moved into the choir – the chancel, James called it – did Suzie notice the St George window.

'Those colours are beautiful.' Smiling, she found herself telling him about Freddie's passion for Gothic architecture, particularly windows like this with light streaming through. He'd painted several, she said, of their local church.

James said he'd love to see them, but Suzie shook her head. 'The best ones sold, but I could email you some photos…'

Walking back down the nave, he pointed to the west window, sharing what he imagined to be its history. To Suzie, it looked like a haze of fragments, most of it grey, although once he'd pointed out the coloured figures in the lower section, she could see how curious they were, not just in what they were doing, but their clothes and expressions.

'Medieval art,' she said softly.

'Yes, it'll be good to see what the restorers can do with it...'

Still talking, they went back to the house for coffee. In the hall, she paused by a familiar picture, overlooked the day before. 'Holman Hunt,' she murmured. 'That takes me back...'

'Does it?' he asked. 'Why?'

'My grandfather was an amateur painter – I never knew him, but he had some wonderful art books. This one – *The Light of the World* – always fascinated me.'

James smiled. 'What is it that strikes you?'

'Well, it's the face, isn't it? So sad – and the way the lamp in his hand reflects upwards to highlight the features...'

'And his other hand,' James said, 'knocking at the door...'

'Which you can barely see for all the dead weeds and brambles,' Suzie added with a wry smile. 'Inspired imagery – and yes, I do know what it's saying...'

The discussion might have gone on, but at that moment, the doorbell rang, and they turned to see a woman's figure outlined through the patterned glass.

Glancing at his watch, James frowned. 'Oh, I'm sorry – that'll be Amy. I'd forgotten she was coming over...'

He didn't seem unduly concerned, but as he opened the door Suzie had a moment's panic. *Amy? His curate?* Introduced, Suzie saw a pleasant-faced woman in dog-collar, blue shirt and jeans, her smile distinctly quizzical.

'Sorry to disturb,' Amy said, 'I can come back later, James, if you'd prefer?'

'No, please don't,' Suzie said, 'I have to get home, and I know James is busy...'

They chatted for a minute or two, until Suzie judged it was time to let them get on with the business of the day.

As Amy went through to his study, he murmured an apology. 'You didn't have your coffee.'

'It's okay, I had enough with breakfast. Anyway,' she added, glancing at her watch, 'it's time I went.'

His eyes, warm and dark, were full of concern for her. 'You'll ring me?'

'I will. And I'll contact that agency they recommended in Leeds. In fact, I wish I'd thought of it beforehand – it might have been less of a shock.'

'True, but I'm glad you came here first.'

She gazed at him, trying to convey more than mere words could say. She would have hugged him, but somehow, the clerical clothes were a barrier. Awkwardly, she said, 'It seems inadequate, James, but thank you.'

It was as though he felt it too. Capturing her hand, he held it for a moment between his own. 'Remember I'm here for you, whenever you need me…'

Only as she reached the car, did the irony of it strike her. She drove off in burst of gravel.

Twenty-Nine

Once she reached home, Suzie re-read the letter she'd received with the quarterly magazine. She hadn't really taken in the part about counselling, but yes, the agency in Leeds was listed, and also recommended in the letter from Northallerton. James was right, she should contact them, make an appointment to see an intermediary. After what she'd been through in the last twenty-four hours, Suzie didn't need a repeat; and, as James said, receiving news through a third person would ensure she had some sort of preparation for the not-so-good stuff.

Sound advice, but first she must text the girls to let them know she needed a chat. Jo rang first, just after six, sounding mortified that the search she'd set in motion had resulted in such an appalling shock.

'Well,' Suzie said, 'I knew he was being taken abroad – what I can't get over is the lie.' Taking a deep breath, she tried to control herself. 'Anyway, I went to see James…'

When she'd finished telling the tale, Jo agreed she'd done the right thing by letting him know just what he'd set in motion. But later, Sara reacted badly. Why, she wanted to know, couldn't her mother have come to *her?* Surely this was a family matter, and after the way that man had behaved in the past, Sara couldn't see why he had to be involved at all.

Not quite prepared for that, Suzie found it hard to answer. In the end, she said, 'Look, love, James started this – and to be honest, I was so furious, I needed to vent it on *him.* Not you – not Jo. You didn't push me into this – *he* did. And to give James his due, he took it – and now, thankfully, I feel a bit better...'

– o –

'She's only being protective,' Cathy said over coffee the following day. 'You're her Mum, she doesn't want you getting hurt.'

'I know, but it worries me. This is just the beginning – who knows what'll be coming up next?'

By then, however, Suzie had been in touch with the agency, and had made an appointment with a counsellor who gave her name as Laura.

Two afternoons later, driving into Leeds, she tried to concentrate on the route. At the last minute she saw the sign. Nerves twitching, she carried on, negotiating two roundabouts before finally making her way back to the entrance. Pulling up in a gravelled forecourt, she glanced at her watch, relieved to see she still had a few minutes to spare. Stepping out of the car, she cast her eyes over what must once have been a gentleman's residence, its Georgian façade stating reliability and permanence. Sadly, the plaques beside the doorway told another story, that times change and nothing is forever.

She gave her name to the receptionist and Laura came down to meet her. About Suzie's age, she seemed a kindly woman with a soothing manner. Reaching her office on the first floor, Suzie was all set to talk about the shock of Singapore, but Laura said that as they hadn't met before, it would help if Suzie could say something about herself first.

With present details covered, they moved into the past, and the reasons behind the adoption. Had Suzie felt pressured at the time?

'Not directly – it was subtler than that. Well, you know how it was back then. Shame, essentially, and it went deep.' Suzie wondered why she felt so emotional suddenly, when she'd managed to talk to her daughters without tears. 'I knew my parents couldn't cope, and I certainly couldn't have managed alone.'

Her voice broke as she forced the next words out, 'After what was done to me, I thought I didn't want this baby. But it was different once he was born...'

... when I held him, and looked into his seal-grey eyes...

Pushing a box of tissues across the desk, Laura waited until she was more composed. 'And what about now?' she asked gently. 'What prompted you to start searching?'

Wiping her eyes, Suzie fudged the truth, saying that recent publicity had made her aware of an upcoming change in the law. 'One way and another, it's been on my mind for years – but then I was contacted by my baby's father...'

Laura studied her for a moment. 'I see. Do you think you'd have reached this decision without such a prompt?' As Suzie nodded, there came another question. 'Are you certain?'

'Not really, but now I know it's possible, I can't ignore it, can I?'

Another lingering look, and then, 'Tell me about the father. Why is it so important for him to make contact with his child?'

Suzie stumbled over her reply. Even as she was explaining James, his life and work, she realized she'd never asked him directly. 'Like me,' she said at last, 'he wants the chance to explain, to say sorry for what he did.'

It was hard to tell what the other woman was thinking. 'You've said you're receiving the society's magazines, so you'll know that not every search ends in a successful reunion. Have you explained this to James?'

As Suzie nodded, Laura asked, 'Do you know if he's receiving counselling?'

Again, she had to think, but then she remembered what James had said about having a spiritual adviser. 'Well, he sees someone fairly regularly, so I imagine he is.'

Before Laura could pursue the subject of James, Suzie went back to her reason for being there. 'But I have to say that finding my son feels even more important now I know he was taken to – to *Singapore*, of all places...'

'Yes, I'm sorry you received that information direct – it must have been a terrible shock for you. I gather it's not what you were told at the time?'

'No, it isn't – I was conned, and it doesn't exactly fill me with confidence for whatever's coming next! What else did they lie about, that's what I'd like to know?' Emotional again, she reached for another tissue. 'Sorry – not your fault – but I'm so angry. Lied to like that. How on earth could a tropical climate be described as *temperate?* That's what I was told. And there I was, imagining New Zealand...'

'Yes,' Laura agreed, 'it's most unfortunate – and distressing. I'm so sorry. But try not to anticipate things. The time in Singapore – one can only assume it was necessary because of the adoptive father's work.' She looked at her notes. 'Ah, yes, he was a civil engineer. People like that tend to move about a lot, so your son may have been there for only a short time.' When Suzie did not reply, she said persuasively, 'Try to see it as part of his life, not the whole. Things may not be as bad as you imagine.'

As Suzie tried to accept that, Laura said, 'I gather James is being supportive in whatever way he can – and that, surely, is a good thing? These shocks will take time to settle, but don't lose hope because of this one piece of information. Remember, this is just a stage in the search for Dominic...'

Just a stage, which could go on for ever. Months, at least, according to Laura.

– o –

Suzie had told him that she'd be meeting the counsellor, so when James received her call that evening, he was keen to know what had transpired. It was good to hear that this woman had been reassuring about their son's early circumstances, but after relating the main points of her interview, Suzie asked what seemed to him a strange question. She asked if he'd discussed the adoption with his spiritual adviser.

'Not in any great depth, I admit, but yes, he does know.'

Before he could ask why, Suzie said that it was important, and he should discuss it. And then she hurried on, claiming that so far, it had all been about her, what *she* wanted. She knew his wife had urged him to find Dominic, but until this afternoon's interview, Suzie had never thought to ask James what he wanted, how *he* felt about it.

Slightly nonplussed, James said he thought he'd explained. 'Like you, I still feel the pain of what happened between us – more so now that I know what you went through...' Before he could go on, Suzie said she thought he'd been cured of guilt when he found God and confessed his sins.

James sighed, wishing they were not having this conversation over the phone. 'It's not like that, Suzie – God can forgive, but he doesn't wipe out the consequences. Whatever we've done, we have to pay the price, whatever it happens to be. If a man committed murder in the old days, he could be forgiven by God, but still hang for the crime. Do you understand? In my case it's the memories I have to live with, the knowledge of what I did to you.' In a softer

279

voice, he said, 'It's worse now that I know how deeply you've suffered…'

She didn't dismiss that, but she did protest, saying that again, James was talking about *her*. She wanted to know what *he* felt about their son – what did James hope to gain by finding him?

The question threw him for a moment. 'But it's not about *gain*, Suzie – it's more a desire to see Dominic, meet him, even if only briefly.' Pressed further, he said, 'Like you, all I really want is a chance to explain…' But he wasn't sure if that was entirely true.

He would have liked to discuss it further – just not on the phone. When he suggested meeting, she said she couldn't at the moment, she was trying to catch up with work.

It was probably true, but again, he felt hurt. There were things he wanted to say, aspects he would have liked to share, especially in the wake of Suzie's sudden concern for his feelings. It was all very well for her, she'd carried his child, given birth to him, held him in her arms – for her, Dominic was as real as her daughters. She could *imagine* him.

James couldn't – not really. Bizarre though it might seem to Suzie, he could picture Christ – as a child, a young man, a man suffering on the cross – but he couldn't summon an image of his own son. And he didn't know why.

He had no right to expect anything. It was just something he had to do.

– o –

Roughly once a week she and James were in touch, if only for Suzie to say there was no news. Although he was keen for them to meet, she kept saying she was busy. It wasn't a lie, but none of her projects had a deadline and she wondered what prompted it, especially when her thoughts drifted often in his direction. She'd be thinking about her son and that shocking news, and, like a wave, the fear and distress would overwhelm her again. *Was he still alive?* Even though she tried to banish it, that question, at night, insisted on creeping out of the darkness.

The last time they met, James had said they couldn't know, that such questions were destructive, that it was wrong to torture herself that way. He'd been emphatic about that, which rather surprised her. Rather more gently, he told her to pray for their son; and if she wasn't comfortable with that, to simply hold him in her heart and mind. Above all things, he said, it was important not to give in to negative thoughts.

Logically, she knew he was right. In the old days, thinking positive, planning positive actions, had hauled her marriage out of many a crisis, and not just financial ones. In her better moments, she recognized this black hole of unknowing as twin to that which had possessed her in the wake of her husband's death.

Not wanting to experience that again, she tried to hold onto James's words, to remember the comfort and support she'd gained from him. She wanted to believe, as he did, that something good would happen, if only she could have faith and keep on praying. Easier said than done. For Suzie, it was like words into emptiness. All very well for James to say he shared the responsibility, that he wanted to be there for her – he was not there in the beginning, when she'd really needed him. And despite his recent kindness, she still blamed him for shattering her fantasies, for jerking her out of her complacent belief that one day, her son would come looking for her.

Let's face it, Suzie thought, looking at her early morning image in the bathroom mirror, it's why you registered the business in your single name. It's why you put that name on the cover of your book…

– o –

Ever since the heatwave in June, the weather had been unpredictable. Suzie had managed a day's walking here and there, and she'd caught up with business affairs, but clearly, interest in her travel book had now died down. For the first time in months she had time on her hands, too much time to worry about things over which she had no control.

With school holidays almost upon them, she knew Sara would need a hand in the shop, if only to give her more time at home with the children. She was about to phone her when Sara called to say she had an afternoon appointment the following week. Millie, their assistant, couldn't come in that day, so could Mum cover for her?

Saying she would, Suzie marked it on the calendar. When the day arrived, she set off to York in the morning. Despite the weight of apprehension, she had a personal task to do first. With the address of the adoption society to hand, she'd consulted a city map and discovered the street where she'd handed over her baby forty years ago. On the other side of town, and surprisingly close to the city walls.

The area was unfamiliar, but the street was found easily enough. Quiet at this hour, so quiet she was able to drive along at snail's pace, ticking off numbers until she spotted the right one. Pulling into the kerb, Suzie spent a minute or two staring at those steps, that innocuous front door, the place where she'd last held her baby son.

There was a lump of grief in her chest, too deep for tears. Passing this place, no one would guess at the pain it had witnessed.

Dear God, let there be an answer soon – let me know he's alive and well...

– o –

Driving on through town, to a car park close by the river, Suzie walked along until she could see the Minster's towers, standing tall above the traffic.

With a sense that she'd done the right thing in braving that ordinary little street, Suzie kept walking towards the Minster. When she'd worked every day, she rarely had time, but in recent years she'd taken to dropping in occasionally. Not so much to pray but to absorb its peace, its sense of calmly going on, despite the heaving world outside. Here, for a while at least, anxiety would subside.

Entering the nave, absorbing the light and the space, her awareness was heightened by a faint echo of voices in the upper reaches. So vast, so simple, the pale gold stone lifting the gaze. And ahead, in their niches, medieval kings were guarding the entrance to the choir. Along a side aisle was an ancient doorway, the steps leading down to a small, stone-vaulted chapel, a place she'd entered first from curiosity and later, after Freddie's death, for refuge.

She rarely had company, and today she had the place to herself. As ever, she was charmed by the medieval cartoons of birds and animals in the windows' leaded glass. There was even a Roman well tucked into a corner, and somewhere beneath her feet, the remains of their ancient fortress.

The distant past was all around, her own life not even a speck on the face of time. She thought of the men who'd worked to make this great cathedral what it was; and the women who had worshipped here. As Freddie had said all those years ago, Suzie was not alone in her experience; many had suffered worse – and for less.

As her unfocused gaze cleared, Suzie realized she was staring at the cross on the altar – and thinking of Christ and his mother…

– o –

A little while later, after a stroll through the sunny Minster grounds, her sadness was gone. Not banished, exactly, but back in its place with the door shut.

When she arrived at the shop, Sara was serving a customer, wrapping a small wooden box, a tiny treasure-chest with brass bands and miniature locks. No doubt designed for some Victorian lady as a repository for letters, Suzie thought, wondering what this modern woman would do with it.

As the door closed, Sara kissed her mother's cheek. 'Cutting it a bit fine, Mum – I've got to go!' She dashed into the back to fetch her bag. 'See you in a couple of hours...' And then she was gone, long hair flying as she hurried past the window and down the street.

Smiling, Suzie glanced around, recognising items she'd collected on buying trips, furniture she'd renovated and chairs re-upholstered. It was an eclectic mix of desirables; *dust-collectors*, her own mother would have called them, and she'd be right; but they sold well.

In a way, she thought, it was a mixed blessing that Sara had wanted to take on the business. Her own enthusiasm had been fading for a while before Freddie's death; she'd wanted more time to travel, time to spend in warmer climes, browsing French country markets while Freddie painted sunlight and shadows. They'd even talked about selling up and re-locating to southern France. But in the midst of debating what to do, Sara had thrown bitter disappointment into the mix. Although she'd trained as a teacher, holiday times she'd worked in the shop since she was a teenager. She knew it inside out, felt it had potential but needed a more modern slant, one that she could provide. The fact that Sara had a husband and two young children didn't seem to bother her. Suzie had agreed to wait another year, while performing a gradual handover of responsibility. But then, with no warning at all, Freddie was gone.

Suzie pulled herself together as the door opened and an older couple came in. Keeping a discreet eye on them as they browsed and chatted, she imagined they were more tourists than buyers; but then they surprised her by asking her advice about a wedding present for a young niece. She, it seemed, was into all things vintage but short on space. They'd spotted a storage chest partly hidden under a drape of linens, and wondered if it was for sale?

'Yes, of course,' Suzie assured them, moving the linens aside to reveal a pine storage chest big enough to be used as a coffee table. 'And your niece could store anything inside, depending on where and how she wants to use it...'

Their pleasure in the find was infectious; and Suzie found she was smiling happily as she assured them that it could be delivered in the next few days, or collected by car after six o'clock that evening. A couple of smaller sales maintained her mood, so that by Sara's return, she was cheerfully admiring her daughter's refreshed highlights, and eager to accept her invitation to come home, see the children, and share their evening meal.

'Good, because we haven't seen you for ages. And that reminds me,' Sara said, her expression changing, 'have you heard anything? You know, about...?'

'Your brother? No, nothing more.'

They talked about it, on and off, between customers, and although Sara's viewpoint was different, she echoed what James had to say, that Suzie shouldn't dwell on the dark side. In her experience, it was important to keep busy; and on that topic, asked if Suzie would be willing to help out during the school holidays.

'I was just about to volunteer...'

– o –

In the midst of the tourist season, the city was busy, even on wet Wednesdays. Saturdays often saw her in the shop during the day and babysitting in the evening while Sara and Rob went out. For Suzie, that was the best part, spending time with her grandchildren. Putting them to bed, telling them stories, Suzie would look at them and think of Freddie, wishing he could be here to enjoy being a grandfather. Inevitably, such thoughts led to her son. Was he a father – and what did he do for a living? Was he arty and creative like her, or academic like James? Or had he inherited completely different genes? She longed to find out, even while she tried to banish such thoughts – it was the not knowing that hurt.

– o –

News came at the end of August. Laura rang to say she'd received documents pertaining to the adoption – no, not her son's whereabouts, they hadn't reached that point yet – but she suggested Suzie might like to come along to see them. Heart pounding, wondering what they could be, Suzie arranged to go in the following day.

This time, she reached the office with ease. When they were settled, Laura said, 'What I have here, are documents relating to both you and James. It includes your agreement to the adoption, and also details recorded from interviews given at the time. You may find,' she added gently, handing them over, 'that you prefer to read them in private.'

Suzie took the folder, staring at her name on the front.

'If you'd like me to leave you for a few minutes?'

Nodding, Suzie took a deep breath. Her own handwriting – neater but unmistakable – was on the first slip, together with the date. A doctor's report, with Baby's name and place of birth, came next.

Lump in throat, she glanced at the series of forms before starting to read. Her details first: address, parents' occupations, schooling, further education, hobbies. But it was the physical descriptions of herself and James that caught her with a

286

dislocating jolt. Reading the interviewers' impressions was like looking through someone else's eyes. From James's, *attractive, very pleasant manner*, to her own *slim, pretty, reserved, good teeth...*

Good teeth? What did that signify? That she went to the dentist? What did that have to do with anything?

Appalled by such trivia, she turned the page. Next, a social worker's typed report caught her attention: *Baby very alert and attractive, looks as bright as a button...*

Grief-stricken, she slapped the file shut.

A few minutes later, Laura returned, bearing a tray of tea. Setting it on the desk, she pushed a box of tissues in Suzie's direction.

'How are you feeling?'

'Weird.' She wiped her nose. 'Like I stepped into a time warp.' Only as the words escaped did she realize how true they were.

–o–

Fazed by the traffic as she left Leeds, she drove under the speed limit, enduring irritated drivers until a near collision at a junction startled her into life. Gasping, sweating, she pulled into a nearby car park to recover.

Home at last, she dumped her bag and collapsed onto the sofa. Weak and shivery, she wanted James, wanted his arms around her, his warmth. But he was miles away and she didn't have the energy to phone him.

When she made the call, a couple of hours later, she found it impossible to describe that sense of dislocation. 'And I wouldn't care,' she said, 'they were just bits of paper – forms – why should a few scribbled words do that to me?'

His attempts to comfort her sounded frustrated. He wanted to be with her, wished he could get to Felton; this week was impossible, but maybe next Friday?

'Look, don't ask me that – I can't even think straight. I was supposed to be working tomorrow, but I'll have to cancel… No, I'll be fine – just need time to myself…'

There was a lengthy pause before he spoke again, asking carefully if there were any clues as to where the family were now.

'No, like I said – it's just what the adoption society had on file. Stuff about you and me. Laura said they can start searching now, but it could be months before anything else turns up.'

She wasn't being fair, she knew she wasn't, but he was the only person she could vent her feelings on. If he didn't like it, he'd only got himself to blame.

– o –

Next morning, the postman popped an A4 envelope through the door. It's thickness and the Leeds postmark made her heart pound. Even before she opened it, Suzie knew what it was: copies of the forms she'd been reading yesterday. She'd left Laura's office without them.

She saw *Diocesan Moral Welfare Board* at the head of one of the sheets – and experienced such a wave of revulsion she could have been sick. 'How *dare* they?' she hissed between gritted teeth.

At once, without reading further, she strode into her office, switched on the photo-copier, and copied each of the half-dozen sheets. Scrawling a comment across the first, she pushed them into an envelope, found a stamp and marched down to the post box. Glancing at the church, she muttered, 'My God, you've got a lot to answer for!' and strode back home.

Thirty

If only you could have been there, she'd said over the phone. *You'd have known what it was like...*

Well, now he did know. Two brief, handwritten histories – two lives condensed into a few lines.

James had buried the memory of his interview in Durham, but as it surfaced he felt an echo of panic. Having to admit to a stranger that he'd fathered this unborn child. The shame – the fear of judgement – returned to attack him now. Like being torn in two: the boy and the man, past and present, separate and together. Shaken to the core, he tore off his glasses to rub at his eyes. Feeling sick, he went to find the whisky. Not trusting himself with a glass, for the first time in his life he took a slug from the bottle. He glanced at the time and swore.

No more. No more papers. He was supposed to be taking communion to the retirement home – and lecturing this afternoon.

Across at the church, trying to pray, that interview from his youth was flashing like a message from another planet. All he'd been required to do was pay for Suzie's upkeep until the baby was adopted. Evenings and weekends, he'd taken a job in a bar; but hard work and late nights were nothing compared to the burden of marriage and fatherhood.

Feeling totally unfit for what lay ahead, he took his stole and surplice from the vestry, the wafers and the wine, placed them in his case and went out to the car.

– o –

That evening, having somehow survived the day, James pushed a ready-meal into the microwave and forced himself to eat. A second glass of red wine helped. After that, taking the bottle with him, he braved his study and the rest of those forms.

Suzie's note was scrawled with such force he could feel the indent of the pen. And yet in all their conversations he couldn't recall a mention of judgemental comments – it seemed most people had tried to be kind. He could only assume it was the letterhead which had upset her. *Diocesan Moral Welfare Board* certainly brought fallen women and patronising Victorian attitudes to mind, but the bitterness of her feelings was expressed in a single, forceful statement: *These are the people you work for!*

'No, Suzie,' he whispered, 'absolutely not.'

Picking up his pen, he began to rough out his letter to her.

I serve Jesus Christ – as do all Christian ministers, no matter the denomination. Jesus wasn't judgemental – except of those who stood by the letter of the law at the expense of humanity. Yes, the Church as a whole has a lot to answer for – it's run by human beings, and as we both know, human beings are experts at getting things wrong.

As for the letterhead – the culprit, I suspect – it is an unfortunate title, and yes, it looks Victorian and judgemental, but with regard to paperwork, the Anglican Church moves slowly – and don't I know it! Which doesn't mean to say that its people are stuck in the past. The key word here is 'Welfare' – and in this case, your welfare and mine. Were you condemned, preached at, made to feel sinful? You've never said so – and I wasn't, even though I was the sinner here.

From all you've told me, these people did their best for you, even though some of them – and I can only think of that dreadful Matron – were hidebound by outdated rules. And in a sense, that was the problem as a whole – society at that time was stuck in the past, unwilling to move on. Enjoying pointing the finger, gossiping, taking the moral high ground. Just as it still does with anyone who doesn't fit the norm.

So please don't say that I work for a moralistic organisation – I don't. Yes, I'm in a privileged position here, I get to exercise my skills as an academic, but have less contact with ordinary people in my three parishes than I would like. I thank God for Amy on a daily basis, and I try to remember that God calls us to use our particular skills in His service.

The Church did its best to care for society's unfortunates – and still does. So please, I beg you, Suzie, remember the kindness of individuals, not the blanket condemnation we both felt was our due at the time.

Reading it through, James sighed and shook his head. It sounded like a lecture. Screwing it up he tossed it aside. This wasn't about him; and it wasn't about the Church. For a few minutes he closed his eyes and focused on Suzie, on what she was going through, on what this bundle of forms had done to him too.

And then he picked up his pen and started again, gently this time.

– o –

Unfolding the pages of James's letter, Suzie saw, *Dearest Suzie,* and began to read.

I understand now how you felt – those forms had a similar effect on me. I had completely forgotten my interview in Durham – yet seeing what was written about me brought everything back with a vengeance. As you said on the phone, it was like being in a time-warp – dreadful. And the sense of shame – still there...

Reading on, turning the page, she found herself nodding in agreement. His words made sense. The shame was in himself – and in her – not imposed by other people. As he said, most people had been kind, doing what they could to turn personal disaster into happiness for some childless couple. Looked at like that – as she knew from experience – made it easier to live with.

A little further on, she found herself smiling when she came to his comment on the letterhead and ongoing problems with paperwork. Thankfully, James seemed to understand her angry words – just a reaction against the whole terrible experience. But if she'd been transported back in time, so, it seemed, had James.

After that sense of dislocation, I'm glad to say that later, when I was able to read the other pages, I found the more detailed description of you, as you were when we first met. It was so exactly you, my dear, not only did it take me back into the past, it was unbearably moving...

He'd signed it with love.

– o –

292

'Why don't you ring James and make a date?' her friend Cathy said over lunch the following day. 'He made you feel much better last time you were together...'

That was the trouble, Suzie thought. He did make her feel better – even his words on a page prompted a glow of warmth. But part of her – the nasty, grudge-bearing part – wasn't yet ready to forgive him for putting her through all this.

'Well, I can't see him just yet,' she said airily, 'because I'm off to London next weekend. Jo's asked me down for a few days, and we're going to do a show and that new exhibition at the Tate...'

As it transpired, the weekend away proved an enjoyable change, and even Marianne – who could be difficult at times – put herself out to be kind. Jo asked about the search, but, like her sister, seemed more concerned for Suzie's welfare than how it was likely to affect her personally. Or was that a mask? Suzie wasn't sure. Equally determined not to worry her daughters, she gave them the facts and kept the rest to herself.

Accepting that this search would take time, Jo wanted to know what she would be doing next. Now the school holidays were over, did Sara still need her in the shop, or were other plans afoot?

The other plans involved Suzie doing some travelling – a part of her job she'd always enjoyed. Visiting auctions and salerooms, searching for something special, while preserving enough of a poker face not to rouse anyone else's interest. And then – on sale day – being tough enough not to go over her limit. On the way home, she found herself thinking of James. Yes, she did want to see him, but didn't want him to think it was special. A casual visit to his area, a sale somewhere close by, and perhaps they could meet for lunch?

She rang him to ask about auction sales in his area. Sara, she explained, wanted her to do some more scouting for the shop. Keen to help, James said he'd see what he could find out and let her know, and next day he rang with some details. He asked if she'd like to stay at the George when she did come down, but Suzie found herself backing off. She suggested lunch instead. He said he'd love to, but midweek was difficult; most venues too far for him to get there and back in the middle of the day.

Disappointed, Suzie said she'd give it some thought. Eventually, the desire to see him won out. Checking the various auction schedules, she came across one at Cirencester, two weeks' hence. The list of items looked interesting, and if she made an early start, she could view in the morning, attend the sale, and drive on to Norton Parva afterwards. James was clearly delighted when she phoned; more so when she asked him to book her a room at the George and Dragon, and a table in the restaurant. The meal, she said, was on her.

James laughed, said they could discuss it later. But if she was free the day after, perhaps they could go walking? It wasn't part of her plan, but she agreed anyway.

As the day approached, Suzie rooted through her wardrobe looking for suitable clothes. She didn't want to seem too prosperous for the auction; on the other hand, she did want to look good later. In the end, she decided jeans and a sweatshirt would do for the day – with boots and a waterproof they'd be suitable for walking – and her good black dress with some discreet jewellery for evening. As she remarked to Cathy, it felt like she was going on a date, which was ridiculous at her age. Cathy laughed, telling her to make the most of it.

After a mixed day at the auction, she phoned James to say she was running late, and could they meet in the bar? In truth, she needed more time to get ready; but later, as she surveyed her image in the mirror, pleasure at the transformation turned to worry. Trying to see herself through James's eyes, she hoped he wouldn't think she was trying to seduce him. And what about the locals – would they think their Vicar was having an affair with this sophisticated woman in black? Maybe she should have stuck to jeans and a tee-shirt – they wouldn't have noticed her then. Or maybe they would – after all, this place wasn't exactly down-market.

Oh, well, she thought, if James was in his uniform this evening, at least they'd be colour co-ordinated.

She glanced at her watch; five minutes early. Hang about worrying, or go down for a fortifying drink? Keys in hand, Suzie picked up her evening bag and made her way downstairs.

– o –

James was talking to the barman. As the man's eyes lit up in a smile, he turned to see Suzie coming towards him. She looked so different – so beautiful – for a moment he could do nothing but gaze. Stammering a greeting, he asked what she'd like to drink, which prompted a knowing smile from the barman as he prepared a gin and tonic.

James felt his face grow warm, but luckily, moments later, a waitress came to say their table in the restaurant was ready. It was early yet, only two other couples, and not people he recognized. Once they were seated, he felt able to relax.

'You look lovely,' he said.

'Thank you, James.' With a mischievous glance, she raised her glass. 'This feels good, doesn't it? To be smiling at each other, I mean…'

'Makes a change,' he agreed, and with a happy smile touched his glass to hers. 'I'll drink to that.'

With the menus before them, he said, 'I can't vouch for everything, but I must say Sunday lunch here is always good…'

'You eat here regularly?'

'Not every week, but often…' And he began to tell Suzie a story which still had the power to move him; about the Sunday after Maggie's funeral, when he'd come back from church to find a note from the landlady.

'I was mystified – but before I could come across, Rosie arrived at my door, carrying a tray. She said, "I hope you're not offended, Vicar, but I've brought you some lunch."'

'What a lovely thing to do…'

'Wasn't it? She was concerned that I wouldn't be eating properly, so she'd brought me a roast dinner. Wouldn't take payment, either. If I'd like the same next week, she said, we could discuss it. But she wouldn't let me pay until I felt up to coming across here in person.'

Smiling, he said, 'So I do – not every week, but it's a change of scene, something to look forward to. And it's not just the food – I've got to know the staff, and quite a few of the regulars. Some of them,' he added with a chuckle, 'even come to church now!'

Suzie raised her glass. 'Sounds like a good thing all round?'

'Well, as I say to my students in college, Christ didn't spend his time in the temple – he met people on the streets and where they went after work…'

James feared he might have gone on at length; but luckily, the arrival of the waitress stopped him. When they'd chosen from the menu, he collected himself and asked about Suzie's day in Cirencester.

'Not bad. The sale was a bit on the pricey side, but I expected that. Anyway, I found some vintage glass and china that'll look good in the shop. It's a balancing act, really – judging the price our customers might be tempted to pay, against the cost of purchase and any restoration needed.'

'You must be good at maths?' he said, but Suzie shook her head, claiming it was years of experience.

'And what about the history of these things? Does that grab you?'

Amusement sparkled in her eyes; he was so distracted by the way she looked this evening, he almost lost track of what she was saying. Something about hating to part with things, her house being like a charity sale...

'... stuff everywhere. Half of it needing some sort of work. I had to force myself to de-clutter, otherwise the girls would have left home, never mind Freddie!'

He heard about the house in Felton, bought cheap but needing lots of work, most of which they'd done themselves over several years. Her husband, she said, had worked originally in the old glass lean-to behind the kitchen.

'Talk about painting in a garret – it was so cold out there, he used to wear an overcoat and mittens. For a workshop, I used the spare bedroom. Still do, for the small stuff, even though I use the studio more now. You know, that building at the side – used to be the garage.'

'Ah, I wondered about that.'

She looked away for a moment. 'Maybe it sounds silly, but it used to feel like Freddie was still there.'

James nodded in sympathy. 'I have that feeling about Maggie, sometimes. I think it's fairly common.' He might have pursued the idea, but their meal arrived – salmon for Suzie and a steak for himself. As ever, it was perfectly cooked, and the dishes of vegetables just right.

Conversation lapsed for a while, but as the food on their plates grew less, he returned to the subject of Freddie. Suzie had said so little about him in the past, he wanted to know more.

'Did you ever feel angry – that he'd gone, I mean?'

'Oh, yes. I was so furious, I couldn't even bear to look at his pictures. Had to put them away.'

James stopped eating. 'Furious? Why?'

With a sigh, she said quietly, 'Freddie had a tendency to stray – quite a few times over the years. The times I knew about, that is. I thought – well, I thought he'd settled down...'

'But?'

'The night he died – he'd been in Manchester, at the TV studios, working on sets for some programme or other. He'd phoned me earlier, saying it was all taking longer than expected, and he was staying over. I didn't think anything of it – until the police turned up.' Pausing, she sighed and shook her head. 'An accident on the M62, heading towards Leeds. Dark, freezing fog – he went into the back of a lorry...'

'Maybe he was coming home?'

'No.' Vehemently, Suzie shook her head.

On an indrawn breath, James tried to speak and failed. He longed to comfort her – hold her hand at least – but as Suzie had observed already, in small communities, tongues tended to wag. Fingering his collar, he told himself they would wag anyway, but still...

'Must've been about nine o'clock. If he'd been coming home, he would have phoned – so where was he going? Not knowing,' she added, 'nearly drove me insane.'

Finding his voice, he said gently, 'Did you ever find out?'

She reached for her glass. 'Not for sure. At least, nothing I could prove. I remember seeing this woman at the funeral. Young, attractive, looking really upset. She was with someone – I didn't know either of them, but something just told me. Instinct, I suppose. Anyway, I asked around, found out who she was. One of the production team – lived in the Leeds area.

'It all added up,' Suzie went on, studying her empty plate. 'I didn't get in touch, there was no point. Besides, I was so mad, God alone knows what I would have done.'

She looked up and he could see the pain in her eyes.

'It wasn't just him, or that woman – I was angry with myself for being too busy to notice. You know, that something was wrong – for not doing something about it. More than that – I was angry because I'd put up with it for years, because

I was scared to strike out on my own. The anger was in the house – locked in with me. I felt trapped – had to get away...'

'Was that why you took to the pilgrim route, to find your peace?'

Agreeing, Suzie blinked hard. 'To be honest,' she added with a little laugh, 'I chose Spain because of the name, *Finisterra*, at the end of the route. *The Ends of the Earth* – that was exactly how far I needed to go!'

'Symbolic – yes, I remember.' Now he could see why.

'As it turned out, running away turned out to be a walking cure. But you're right,' she admitted a moment later. 'I did find my peace along the way. People talk about finding themselves, don't they? In a way, so did I. Being a woman alone, having to face weather and danger and dodgy situations – having to plan the next day, find food and drink and somewhere to sleep – I did it. And it gave me confidence.'

'You found things were different when you got back?'

'Oh yes, very different. I was me, I could cope alone, I'd proved it to myself. And not only that, in the last few years I've discovered I quite like my own company.'

Perhaps it wasn't meant to be challenging, but her statement brought him down to earth. Aware of the empty Vicarage, James shook his head and reached for his glass of wine.

'One does grow used to it,' he admitted at last. 'But surely, none of us is entirely free? I have my commitment to God and my church family. And you have your daughters and the business to consider.'

'True,' she said, raising an eyebrow, 'but it's learning to be alone when you're *not* busy. That's the trick.'

'You're right,' he sighed. 'Not easy...'

Once they'd ordered dessert, James changed the subject, suggesting to Suzie that he join her for breakfast here at the pub – it would give them both a good start to the day. When she asked where they were going, he suggested starting north of Oxford and following the Thames Path into town.

'We can have a look around, then make our way back again. How does that sound?'

'Great idea – I'm looking forward to it.'

Thirty-One

Next morning, before James arrived, Suzie found herself in conversation with the landlady. Just a few minutes, but long enough to confirm her impression that James was liked and respected. Of course, the landlady was also angling for information, but when Suzie said she and James had known each other for years, that seemed to satisfy.

Although it was sunny outside, the day's forecast was for intermittent showers. 'But never mind,' James said when he joined her, 'we can always return by bus.'

After breakfast, they set off separately, Suzie in her red VW following James's blue Fiesta. The first part of the plan was to park near Godstow Bridge, and walk south along the Thames from there.

'Remember Inspector Morse?' James said, drawing her attention to a riverside inn. 'That's the Trout – one of his old watering holes. If you like, we could eat there on the way back?'

'Are you a fan, too?' she asked, so delighted by the idea, she barely noticed the ruin of an old chapel as they crossed the river.

'And over there's the remains of Godstow Abbey. A famous nunnery until the Reformation – but then it was sold off and converted into a grand house...'

'Really?' She turned and looked. 'There's not much left.'

'No, sadly. It was destroyed during the Civil War.' Musing as he looked back towards the old inn, James said, 'Of course, the Trout could have been part of the Abbey at one time – where visitors were housed and fed. Equally, it could have been built from the abbey's fallen stones...'

Comparing the sad little chapel with the clearly prosperous pub, Suzie nodded. 'I like that idea – continuing the tradition of hospitality...'

'So do I,' he chuckled, 'and long may it continue!'

It was peaceful along the Thames, a new landscape for Suzie and all the more enjoyable for James's comments and snippets of history. Passing locks and boatyards as they approached the town, they met walkers going in the opposite direction, exchanging rueful comments about the weather. Sunny one minute, grey and drizzly the next, they reached town in a shower so drenching, for a while it was hard to see anything at all. As they sheltered in a shop doorway, James asked if she'd like to see some paintings – the Ashmolean had an interesting collection, and it was just around the corner. Suzie agreed at once.

'Ah, the Ashmolean,' she exclaimed as they climbed the steps and went inside. Faced with an array of ancient artefacts, she said, 'Didn't Morse have an episode here?'

'That's right – *The Wolvercote Tongue*. Although I don't think there's been one involving stolen pictures...'

'A shame,' Suzie laughed, 'I'd have liked that!'

On the next floor, they entered a gallery of 19th century paintings, including several by the French father and son, Camille and Lucien Pissaro.

Suzie gazed intently, exclaiming as she read the plaque describing the collection's history. 'How wonderful – I'd no idea there were so many. Freddie would have loved to see these… Oh, and especially this one,' she murmured, captivated by the *Village at Eragny*. 'Just look at those colours – and the perspective…'

Smiling, taking her arm, James said, 'And did you see the Van Gogh?'

The pastel-coloured painting was a sunny delight – and there were others by Sickert and Manet, poignant portraits and romantic landscapes. Commenting, admiring, she was still talking as they moved into the next room.

She stopped mid-sentence. Pre-Raphaelite works – paintings and artefacts – she recognized the style at once. Glancing up at James, she shook her head, unable to speak. Turning to her, for a long moment, he held her gaze; it seemed he too was taken back in time. As he clasped her hand, a shock ran through her. That night at the farm; his room; the book he'd been keen to show her…

'Aunt Isabel's book,' he said softly, 'yes, I remember.'

For a moment she was overwhelmed by memory, by regret for an innocence that was lost. It seemed James felt it too. At the sound of voices behind them, he slipped an arm around her shoulders and drew her aside. Suzie found herself staring at a portrayal of grief. A young woman and a boy in a churchyard. As the figures registered, she blinked, drew breath, and looked away.

She turned, and across the room was a massive piece of furniture. Gothic in design, it was covered with what appeared to be medieval illustrations. She was about to ask a question, when James said, 'These are the kind of images that intrigued me all those years ago – and still do, if I'm honest…'

Studying the saints on one side, and what appeared to be Roman figures on the other, Suzie was confused. 'It's strange though – the Romans seem to be in the wrong era, and yet it's surrounded by Gothic detail – even down to the animals. Most odd!'

'Not really, it's very much of its time. Images going back the Roman era – telling us where Christianity began, particularly in this country. You see, these artists were connected with the Oxford Movement – they were trying to get back to the beginning. To what they perceived as the true message of Christ.'

'A reaction to all those mid-Victorian values, you mean?'

He nodded. 'The Industrial Revolution and the scientific age...'

As James moved, drawing her attention to a large but unfamiliar work, Suzie looked more closely. 'Ah,' she exclaimed, 'it's by Holman Hunt.'

'This takes us back to the early days – the persecution of Roman missionaries in this country...'

Suzie read the description beside the painting. 'By druids?'

'Well, pagans.'

'Hmm.' She studied the vivid scene, its lifelike figures, awed by the fine detail. She'd not seen this work before, but recalled *The Hireling Shepherd*, which had so impressed her as a girl. No wonder, she thought, she'd been unable to appreciate abstract art as a student, when she'd been brought up with pictures like these.

Recalling the book James had shown her that night at the farm, she gave him a playful nudge, pretending to be cross. 'You knew, didn't you? That these were here?'

'Honestly,' he swore, hand on heart, 'I'd forgotten...'

She laughed as they moved on. There was another room, but as James glanced at his watch, Suzie realized she was ready for something to eat.

'Come on,' he said, reclaiming her hand, 'let's walk, find some food and drink...'

– o –

Outside, the sky had cleared, the sun was out, the atmosphere sparkling as Suzie's gaze travelled upwards from doorways to windows to roof lines and towers. Taken by the golden, Gothic detail of grand colleges along the Broad, she would have walked on, but James guided her into Catte Street, and at once she had to pause. Seeing the Bridge of Sighs ahead – so like the one in Venice – she took out her camera for a photo.

As she turned, James seemed to have disappeared. And then, to her astonishment, he suddenly reappeared, smiling, from a gap between the buildings.

'This way,' he said, leading her down a narrow alley with soot-blackened walls.

'Where on earth are we going?'

'You'll see...' Taking a right-angled turn along a rough path, he turned again into a small courtyard with tables. Ahead of them was a low doorway, the entrance to a pub. The board outside announced its name – the Turf Tavern.

'Is this another of Morse's haunts, by any chance?'

'Certainly is,' he laughed, ducking his head as he stepped down into the bar. 'What's it to be, Suzie?'

'Lager, I think – a half. And if you're thinking of food, just a snack for me.'

'Okay.' Handing her a menu, James caught the eye of the barmaid and ordered the drinks. Moments later, they were tucked into a corner of the small, low-ceilinged room and studying the list of sandwiches.

'It's becoming a tourist stop,' he commented once they'd ordered, 'but it hasn't changed much. Still as basic as ever,' he chuckled, glancing at the nicotine-coloured walls. 'And if you need the loos, they're outside!'

Suzie laughed. 'Never mind, I love it – I can just imagine Morse and Lewis in here, having a lunchtime pint.'

Over lunch, she discovered James was not only a Morse fan, he liked the psychology of Ruth Rendell's crime novels, appreciating the way the author refused to make judgements. That led to favourite books, and to Evelyn Waugh's depiction of Oxford in *Brideshead Revisited*. Suzie was recommending his *Sword of Honour* trilogy when they both realized it was time to move on. Before they left, she took some photos of the bar; and later, outside, asked James to pose by the doorway to show how low it was. By the nameboard, he took one of her, looking, she said on viewing it, like the cat who'd got the cream.

'Apt,' she said, as they came out, still laughing, into Catte Street. But then she was pausing again, having spotted the great dome of the Radcliffe Camera.

'Is that...?'

'Yes, it is – thought you'd like to see it.'

Moments later, with the great circular library before them, once more Suzie was delighted. Staring at a familiar yet entirely unfamiliar building, with the Bodleian on one side and Brasenose College on the other, she couldn't help laughing. 'I don't know where to look first,' she exclaimed, turning to James. 'I feel like I'm in an episode of Morse!'

Delighted for her, answering questions, minutes later, James was leading them on again. 'How about this?'

There was an archway with barriers, but all it took was a discreet word with the porter, and they were going through to see a typical Oxford quad. Suzie was speechless, gazing at the architecture, the windows, the closely-mown lawn. 'Magnificent,' she murmured, awed by the atmosphere, the sense of history contained.

Turning to look at James, she was suddenly aware of how at ease he was here, while she was still pinching herself, struggling to accept that it was real. 'And to think people actually *live* here,' she said wonderingly. 'Do they have any idea of how the outside world operates?'

He shook his head. 'Not really. The ones I meet – theologians, mostly – are often surprised when I tell them

I'm a working priest. Places like this do tend to narrow the view…'

As they emerged into the street, Suzie said, 'I know you lecture on the history of Christianity, James, but it must be a huge subject? How do you deal with all the wars and persecutions? You know what people say whenever religion comes up – *oh, it's caused more wars than anything else…*'

'They do indeed.'

'So how do you answer that?'

'Well, they're not entirely wrong,' he replied. 'The problem is that over the centuries, particular forms of Christianity were adopted by those in power – it became linked with politics and the power grew. The true message of Christ was quickly distorted. Unfortunately,' he added, 'with every attempt to get back to basics, as soon as man begins again, he starts dishing out a set of interpreted rules. And almost invariably, those who fail to conform are persecuted all over again.'

'It's not a good advertisement, is it?'

'No, it's not,' he said grimly. A moment later, to Suzie's surprise, he chuckled. 'The Pilgrim Fathers – remember them? – are just a small example. As soon as they'd established their ideal way of life in America, they started punishing those who wouldn't toe the line!'

Amused by the irony – relieved that he didn't take her words as criticism – she asked how he coped with it.

'Man is a contrary animal,' he replied, 'and besides, God gave us free will. In the end, how we conduct our lives and faith, is up to us. In the midst of wars and uncertainty, we just have to hold on and pray for the best.'

Thinking about that, she said, 'Do you think it's a case of bad news makes more impact – unlike the good stuff, which hardly ever makes the headlines?'

'Absolutely. And it's not just Christianity – it's true of other religions too.'

Crossing roads, their attention switched to the traffic; but later, as they reached the quieter realm of the Thames, James said, 'Stop me if you think I'm lecturing, but to answer your question – how do I deal with it? – I go back to basics. Above all, Christ bids us to honour God and love our neighbour. And yes, I know some people are difficult to love, but we have to try to understand them.'

They were back, Suzie thought, to psychology.

'The sad thing is, honouring God can become so formalised, it loses its relevance to people in the everyday world.'

'Hardly surprising,' Suzie commented. 'When you think of modern life – everybody working, struggling to keep a roof over their heads and the family fed. No wonder they don't have time to go to church.'

Looking sad, James agreed. 'Which explains our ageing congregations – and the difficulty of addressing it.'

After a while, she asked, 'Do you ever feel cut off from the real world?'

With a sudden bark of laughter, he said, 'Frequently! I often think of Amy, and wish I had half her empathy and sense of humour. Thank God I have my students, full of fire and idealism – they give me a boost, make me feel I'm doing something right at least.'

Thirty-Two

Downloading her photos next day in Felton, Suzie found herself smiling. A few sunny views, but most showed grey skies. Amongst those she'd taken of James, there was one of him frowning as rain dripped off hair and nose. 'Whose idea was this?' he'd demanded as she laughed and pressed the shutter. But he was joking and smiling most of the day. He'd taken snaps of her too, good ones he'd asked her to send on. There was a photo of the two of them on their way into Oxford, taken by a fellow walker met just minutes before. And another at the close of their walk, at the Trout Inn, taken by one of the staff.

Sharing a meal in such an historic setting had closed the day perfectly – so much so, she'd been sorry to leave. And James had been equally sad to see her go, insisting they meet again soon. When he kissed her cheek and held her close for a moment, she'd found it hard to say goodbye.

Only now, as she looked at the photos more dispassionately, did Suzie feel the first qualms. Such a happy-looking couple, she thought; the man head and shoulders taller, the woman leaning into him; they looked like young lovers, despite the silvery hair. Clearly, the attraction was mutual; and he enjoyed her company as much as she did his. Under the circumstances though, where was it going, and was it right?

If it hadn't been for his calling as a priest, she might not have thought twice. Not that she'd ever been promiscuous, but years ago, there had been a brief fling in response to one of her husband's infidelities, a mistake she'd regretted afterwards. And then, after Freddie's death, she'd been disturbed enough to seek out one of their oldest friends in London, an artist who seemed to understand what it was all about. They were still in touch, but those few days of consolation hadn't been repeated. As for other men, most of those she met had wives, and she'd always worn blinkers where married men were concerned.

Later, however, on the Camino – and this memory made her smile – she'd spent the night with a man half her age, enjoying every moment. The sense of freedom, no questions asked, no commitment, and a cheerful goodbye in the morning. That night had made her feel like a woman again.

Since then – and it was more than three years ago – she'd remained both single and celibate, too busy to even think of getting involved with another man. Now, she would have liked nothing more than to let this relationship with James follow its natural course – except for the massive stumbling block of who and what he was. If she went on seeing him, Suzie could see them both getting hurt. And that didn't take into account what they'd set in motion with regard to their son.

– o –

Cathy said she was crazy. If people refused present happiness for fear of what might happen in the future, the whole human race would be suicidal. Or in therapy.

'This is different,' Suzie said. 'This isn't just *us*, James and me. And it's not just about the past, it's about who he is, and where we go from here. If it weren't for what's hanging over us...' She broke off in weary confusion. 'Oh, I don't know, Cathy. Yes, I fell in love with Freddie, but that was different, we didn't have all this baggage between us.'

'Yes, but you had *your* baggage, didn't you? And Freddie had his weaknesses, you've said so yourself. But you forgave him and started again.' She shrugged. 'The same could be said for most relationships. Long-term ones, anyway. Times you want to throttle the other party, but you don't, you have an almighty bust-up and then work through it.

'I know you're not religious,' Cathy went on, 'but cutting aside what he does, it strikes me you've loads in common. So what's the problem? Don't you think you're entitled to a bit of light relief in the midst of all this heavy stuff? As far as I can see, it's still got some way to run. You don't know what answers you'll get, or even how you'll feel when you get them.'

'That's just what I mean...' Suzie broke off, struggling for words. 'It's when I think of it – what might be coming up. I can see us both getting hurt, and it scares me.'

'But you're not alone – James is in this too. Can't you simply share it with him and take each day as it comes?'

Refreshing Suzie's computer screen, Cathy studied the photo in question. 'He looks kind – I'd love to meet him. And you look so *happy* together.' A moment later, giving her friend a searching glance, she said, 'Has he said anything?'

'No, of course not. But I just *know*...'

'That he's in love with you?'

Suzie shook her head. 'No, not that. I mean he *cares* about me.'

'After all you've been through, I should damn well think he does. But you're splitting hairs. How do you feel about *him*? That's what you should be asking.'

'Torn, that's what!' She buried her face in her hands. As Cathy hugged her, Suzie could tell she was trying not to laugh.

'I'm sorry, love, but it's like when we were teenagers. Don't you remember? Heartsick and lovelorn, not knowing which way's up.'

Sniffling, trying to find a tissue, Suzie found herself laughing. 'Do I really sound like that? Lord, it must be bad!'

Later, over a second glass of wine, Cathy said, 'I can't forget what you told me – you know, when you first knew James. That time you were together, in his bedroom. You were smitten then, so it's hardly surprising now.'

'Oh God, don't remind me. I had a moment like that in the art gallery – all those Pre-Raphaelites – took me straight back. Anyway, things are more complicated now.'

Cathy sighed. 'Of course they are. And he's a priest, which means he's not going to leap into bed with you at the first opportunity – always assuming he'd like to.'

'So for me to suggest a roll in the hay, just isn't on, is it?'

Laughing, Cathy shook her head. 'Probably not!'

'For him, it'd be the full commitment job. And I'm sorry, but I just can't see myself as a vicar's wife...' Weighing the conundrum, Suzie shook her head in despair. 'Honest, Cathy, I never thought I'd feel like a mixed-up kid at sixty.'

'You're not sixty, you're only fifty-nine! Seriously, though,' her old friend said a moment later, 'if you're feeling like this, why don't you leave it a while before seeing him again? It might make things clearer.'

'Yes, but in the meantime, do I send him the photos, or not?'

In the end, Suzie emailed most of them, leaving out the best one, of herself and James on the Thames Path. He responded almost at once, saying the photos were great – especially of her. But wasn't there another of the two of them, taken by the bridge?

Feeling like traitor, she emailed back that it was out of focus. But she didn't delete it.

– o –

Keeping busy took her mind off things, although with the change of mood everything began to feel like hard work, including her days in York. And even though she forced herself to get out walking, too often she was mooching along, head down, watching stones underfoot instead of her surroundings.

No word from Laura in Leeds, and knowing James was longing to see her, made everything worse. She re-read his cards and emails, at first warm and descriptive of daily life, becoming shorter as she ran out of reasons for not being able to see him. Consumed by both guilt and longing, she felt compelled to explain. Not in a phone call, but a letter in which she confessed her confusion as well as her anxieties. She wanted to spend time with him, of course she did, but with so much yet to be resolved, she was feeling torn. What she didn't say, was that she was afraid of her own longings, and the price she might have to pay.

She posted the letter from Heatherley on Friday afternoon. Early next morning, on her way to York, she wondered if he'd received it yet, and, if he had, what he would be thinking.

'Cathy's right,' she muttered, 'I'm like a love-sick teenager.'

Switching the radio on, she heard DJ Brian Matthew presenting his *Sounds of the Sixties* and turned it up. But if Mick Jagger could get no satisfaction – ironic, that – a few tracks later, McCartney's haunting voice was plucking at her heartstrings with *Yesterday*.

Thirty-Three

'Oh, dear God,' James exclaimed, reading her letter, 'Suzie – you idiot!' Flinging himself out of the chair, he reached for the phone – and stopped. *No good – she'll be in York by now…*

Guessing her movements, that she was probably with the family until Sunday evening, he cursed with frustration. He didn't want to call her mobile – this was too important. Pacing the house, making a coffee he barely touched, James eventually donned his waterproof and went out. Rain – it echoed his feelings exactly. He'd been busy, yes, but when was he not? Telling himself she needed space to think and work, he hadn't recognized what was happening, hadn't insisted on seeing her when maybe he should have…

An hour later, not far from the Thames, he found himself gazing at the skyline of old Abingdon in the distance. Timeless as a Dutch landscape, with boats and trees and meadows before it. The rain had stopped, and so had his churning thoughts. He'd been intending to bring her here, next time she visited. And so he would; because this time, whatever happened, he was not going to let go.

Turning, heading at a brisk pace for home, he felt better. Recognizing Suzie's wisdom in choosing the Camino over inertia and anti-depressants, he knew he should walk more. And he thought of Amy, with her woman's instinct, offering insights of her own into Suzie's state of mind. Amy had known, of course, from the moment she set eyes on the two of them, just how important Suzie was to him. Naturally, she was curious, so James had given her what Suzie would have called, *the edited version*, saying she'd been a girlfriend from his student days, one he'd lost touch with until her book was published a few months ago.

'I wondered about that,' she'd said then, indicating the paperback on his desk. 'She seems nice, James – I hope it works out.'

'You don't think I'm being impulsive?'

'No, why would I? It's almost two years since Margaret died. Two months, okay, I'd have been worried – but not now… Anyway,' she added, patting his arm affectionately, 'you need someone in your life.'

Another time, when he was clearly worried about Suzie, Amy had said, 'It's a big commitment, James – not just to you, but the Church. I mean, say for instance you asked her to marry you – and I guess that's what you're thinking – she's got to say yes or no to what you *do*… It's not a question of does she love you enough to change her life and come *here*, she's got to consider the job as well. Can she live with it? Not everybody can…'

With more immediate concerns on his mind, James hadn't thought of that; but Amy's comments – stated so plainly – summed up Father Phil's more subtle probing. Racked by uncertainty, James had been unwilling to give voice to his hopes and desires; but now, having read her letter, hope was resurgent. Love had to be acknowledged first. Love and commitment to see each other through whatever was coming next. Please God, may it be soon and may it be good news; he refused to contemplate the alternative.

– o –

Next morning, James felt the words of the Eucharist more powerfully than usual. *'Who, in the same night that he was betrayed, took bread and gave you thanks... this is my blood of the new covenant, which is shed for you and for many for the forgiveness of sins...'*

That evening, he called the landline in Felton.

When she answered, he said, 'Suzie, it's me. I need to see you – please don't put me off this time.'

She said something about her letter, and did he understand?

'Of course I do. You don't want to make a mistake that might hurt us both – but life is about taking risks... Okay,' he responded, 'but you're not exactly risk-averse, are you? What about going to Spain – the Camino? If that wasn't risky, I don't know what is.'

As she laughed, coming back with a dry comment, he said, 'Look, we don't always know the difference between good and bad. Sometimes, what looks like the right thing, turns out to be a wrong move – same with the opposite.'

She said she didn't want either of them to get hurt. 'Fair enough,' he replied, 'I understand... But if we can be happy together,' he insisted, countering another outpouring of doubt, 'even if only occasionally – don't you think we should allow ourselves that? After all, we're not getting any younger...' Hearing a reluctant agreement, he pressed on. 'In the past, you had to handle things alone. This is something we can face together...'

With the words of her letter fresh in his mind, he sensed there was still much left unsaid. Eager to reassure, he said, 'Whatever happens next, I'm stating no limits and asking

316

no commitment from you, except your honesty. If you have doubts, Suzie, *tell me*, for heaven's sake – don't keep them to yourself... Above all, whatever time I have, and whenever possible, I'd like to share it with you...'

As his voice gave out, he swallowed hard. He thought she said something, but it was muffled. A moment later, her words came clear. She said she'd missed him, and of course she wanted to see him. When could they meet?

For a moment James couldn't speak. 'My next day off is Friday...'

For a few minutes, they laughingly tossed ideas around. He suggested York; he hadn't been there for years. Suzie said she'd come to Oxford, her time was less constrained. Finally, they agreed to meet halfway, somewhere they could each do in the day. A recent trip to Derbyshire inspired her suggestion of Chatsworth House – not far from the M1, she said, and easy to reach. With its treasures and gardens, he agreed it would be ideal.

– o –

James had the longer journey, but arrived ahead of time; Suzie, however, was late. Only by fifteen minutes, but she was apologizing as she stepped out of the car to greet him. 'Traffic round Leeds was a nightmare...'

Delighted to see her, he dismissed all that. 'Never mind,' he said, reaching out for her. 'You're here, that's what matters...'

After the briefest hesitation, she embraced him, kissing his cheek, seeming a little breathless as they parted. 'So,' she said brightly, 'which way shall we go?'

The magnificent house, basking in late morning sunshine, was just a short walk away. Even though he knew the answer, James asked if she'd like to do the tour.

'Oh, let's leave the Old Masters for another day. This sun is too good to waste...'

They followed a path towards the lake. October now, and the formal gardens were looking bare, but birds were singing and glimpses of red and gold lured them on, along woodland paths, through rocky glades where maples gleamed in shafts of sun. Like some enchanted forest, its ways were numerous and winding and hard to escape. He took hold of her hand, sharing her smile as she looked up in surprise, enjoying the warmth of her palm next to his. As the leafy path wound its way downhill, they came upon a waterfall, tumbling over rocks and surrounded by ferns, sunlight glinting off drops like diamonds. Pausing, exchanging glances, it seemed to James the gold lights in her eyes reflected the magic of this place. Brushing back an imaginary strand of hair, suddenly he was back to their beginning, to a first tender kiss so long ago.

He couldn't help but repeat it, tentatively at first, but as she responded, passion flared; the warmth of her mouth, the swell of her breasts, set his mind spinning. Shaken by its intensity, as weeks of anxiety broke free, he could think only of naked desire, neither fear nor false constraints between them. Breathless, dragging air into his lungs, he held her against him. She clung silently, until with rueful laughter she pressed a finger to his lips. 'Enough,' she whispered, 'or we'll be had up for indecency.'

Laughing with her, he begged her not to put ideas into his head; except the ideas were there already. It took an effort of will to tear his gaze away, to move; and when he did, he found he was trembling.

With his arm around her shoulders and hers at his waist, James could feel the warmth of her hand beneath his jacket; so intimate, it roused desire afresh. Drawing her close he kissed her again, briefly this time. 'Let me hold your hand,' he smiled, 'because just there, at my waist, it's giving me wicked thoughts...'

Chuckling at that, she said, 'I thought clergymen weren't supposed to have wicked thoughts?'

'Maybe not, but we are human...' As they moved on, he said, 'This place is like the Garden of Eden – let's find a way out, before I succumb to temptation...'

'Perhaps we should've viewed the house instead?'

'Funnily enough, I was just thinking that...'

Kicking at leaves as they followed another path, she said haltingly, 'But seriously, James, now you've mentioned it, I – well, I have to ask, how do you feel about that?'

He paused, studying her frown, the way she held her head, bit her lip. He couldn't insult her by pretending he didn't know what she meant. 'You mean sex,' he said. 'What do I think about sex outside marriage?'

His frankness surprised her into laughter. 'Yes, that's exactly what I mean.'

'Well,' James began, trying to be serious, 'I have to say that in my position, I shouldn't countenance such behaviour.' He paused, giving her a sidelong glance. 'But as for you and me – well, there is no simple answer.'

'Rules?'

'Yes, rules. Against adultery, against fornication – such an ugly word.' He shook his head, aware that he'd thought of little else for weeks. He took a deep breath. 'But to be honest, Suzie, in this abnormal situation, as I see it, there are no rules...'

She gazed at him then, wide-eyed. For all her age and experience, in that moment she looked like a girl again, the honest, trusting girl he remembered, the girl he'd betrayed. With all the pain of regret, he knew he had nothing to give but himself.

'I mean it. I'm not asking for commitment, because we both know the time isn't right.' Reaching for her hand, he warmed her chilled fingers between his own. 'But if you want me, Suzie – if being with me makes you happy – maybe we can be happy together. For a while, at least.'

'Are you sure? Whatever happens?'

'I'm sure.'

'What about your work?'

Smothering a whisper of doubt, he shook his head. 'I'll deal with it.'

After all, this wasn't just about him, it was about the two of them. He wanted to hold her close, seal his promise with a kiss, but something held him back. Taking her hand, he led her into the open, away from this enchanted place.

– o –

It seemed the world had somehow tilted on its axis. Feeling light but bemused, Suzie followed blindly, having to trust to James for direction. Surprised to find the rustling woods behind them, as they came into sunlight she paused to take breath, to feel the earth beneath her feet and the wind against her face.

James turned and smiled, his dark eyes warm and reassuring as he drew her on. A few more paces and they were on the crest of a hill, and over there, beneath an old oak with russet leaves, was a seat perfectly placed to enjoy the view. As the valley revealed itself, she saw patches of autumn woodland on a distant hill, stone walls dividing a patchwork of fields below.

'We can't call them gardeners, can we?' Suzie murmured at last. 'The people who designed all this – they were artists, creating a setting.' A seductive setting, she thought, thinking of woods and winding paths, that moment by the waterfall.

'Using God's materials,' James agreed, squeezing her hand. 'And look – there's even some sheep over there...'

Suddenly, a huge flock of starlings appeared, swooping and wheeling across the vale. The sound as they surged through the air; the shapes they formed, wheeling, clustering, spreading;

breath-taking as they massed and hovered; then the speed as they turned and curved and swept away.

'What a display,' he exclaimed, 'I've never seen so many. Why do they do that?'

Although she'd seen it many times, Suzie found it disturbing. 'It's the time of year – they're looking for a roost.'

Drawing her closer, James kissed her cheek. 'Sounds like a good idea. Maybe they're telling us something? Should we look for a roost, do you think?'

His smile, the light in his eyes, dispelled the shiver of a moment ago. 'Tonight, you mean?'

– o –

With its imposing buildings, the spa town of Buxton reminded Suzie of Iredale. With a wry grin, James said, 'Well, maybe we can lay a few ghosts to rest...'

In M&S, she bought an overnight bag and a silky nightie. As she held it against her, James raised an eyebrow and said he was looking forward to seeing her in it. In Boots, nearby, she shopped for toiletries, James adding a razor and shaving cream.

'Don't you feel sinful?' she teased, determined to test his nerve.

'Not in the least...'

But he took a deep breath, she noticed, as they went into the hotel. It was part of a chain, which at least promised a certain standard. Quelling a sudden flutter of nerves as they approached the desk, Suzie tried to look bored as James booked a double room.

'Are you sure about this?' she murmured on the way to the lift. 'I don't know about you, but I feel like a Victorian virgin on her wedding night...'

He seemed to think she was joking. In the lift, his eyes were sparkling and she was trying not to laugh. What the porter was thinking, she didn't like to guess. By the time they reached the room James was grinning like a schoolboy. As the door closed, his laughter broke free.

'Come here,' he ordered, pulling her into his arms. 'You're a wonderful woman, do you know that?'

'I was being serious,' she protested, laughing.

'Serious is forbidden...'

They were on the bed, still dressed, when Suzie, breathlessly, called a halt. 'Darling James, I'm sorry to be a spoilsport, but before we go any further, I have to take my clothes off...'

With a swift kiss, she fled with her bag to the bathroom. There was no way, she thought, he was seeing her undressed. Brushing her teeth, folding her clothes, pushing undies into her bag, she donned the nightie and surveyed her reflection in the glass. Not too bad, but her heart was racing like a Grand National winner, and she was praying there wouldn't be a fall before the last fence...

Whether it was right she no longer cared, she just wanted him to succeed this time.

Success? Was this what it was all about? Why he'd dismissed the rules so easily?

It brought her down to earth with a bump. For a second, she considered calling a halt and walking out, but she couldn't do it. In the cool light of the bathroom mirror, she knew she cared about this man, liked him, loved him, despite all that crap in the past. She wasn't going to suffer agonies of conscience about it. So, if it was important to him, she'd make damn sure it worked this time.

– o –

Praying his arousal wouldn't let him down, James rose and half-drew the curtains before undressing and climbing into bed. Supressing negative thoughts as he waited, he told himself that making love was not a competitive sport, that the past was irrelevant, and all that mattered was here and now. Suzie and himself...

With the light behind her she emerged from the bathroom; he could see her form through the thin material, and at once his fears fled.

'You look beautiful,' he murmured as she joined him. With skin against skin, the warm scent of her intoxicating, he was lost, heat flaring as they kissed and caressed. Afraid of coming too soon, he tried to hold back, but succeeded only in losing it. Pressing close, she murmured in his ear, saying it was a penalty of abstinence, all he needed was to relax, focus on pleasing her instead...

Caressing her, aware of mounting pleasure, his confidence returned and with it a surge of heat and strength. This time he didn't hold back; entering her afresh, he came at last with soul-shaking intensity.

As light and sense and calm returned, he raised his head to see a tender, slightly tearful smile. As emotion welled, he kissed her tenderly. 'Dearest Suzie, I love you so much...'

Thirty-Four

Twenty-four hours of bliss. It was on the surface of her mind for days. She'd smile to herself, thinking of that beautiful day, and how pleasurable the night had been. Yes, there had been some anxious moments, but all was well in the end.

How decadent they'd felt, ordering food and wine to the room. Not exactly restaurant standard but it was worth it to stay where they were. Chatting about their lives, about Suzie's family, favourite places, likes and dislikes, they laughed a lot. And, as James said, with 'serious' put in a box, they were discovering so much more about each other. Perhaps it was strange way to go about a relationship, but she wasn't objecting. And if that night had been spurred on by James's need to prove himself, well, she thought, it hardly mattered now.

The softly-lit room had felt like a place out of time, never more so than when they settled down to sleep. Emotional warmth, intimacy, the sense of protection as his arms enfolded her; and the sensuality on waking. Relaxed and peaceful in his arms, she wondered afterwards why she'd been so apprehensive. They were no longer teenage virgins, they'd both learned a thing or two about life and loving along the way. Maybe age had something to be said for it, after all.

Recalling that moment each morning, she'd smile before rising, stretching out in bed, enjoying the touch of the covers against her skin. Showering, dressing, going about the day's tasks proved a light-hearted pleasure.

A couple of weeks after Buxton, James came to her in Felton. His name was on her lips so often, both Cathy and the girls were asking when they were going to meet him. Sara, it had to be said, was more than a little tight-lipped, as though she were the mother in this situation, not the other way around. Jo, thankfully, seemed happy to wait on judgement; but that was over the phone. Face to face, it could be different. All Suzie could do was repeat a version of the agreement she and James had reached, to take one day at a time, with no commitments; situation to be revised when they knew what they were facing. Oddly enough, that shocked Sara the most. She was, she said, suspicious of a Church of England clergyman who was taking advantage of her mother's willingness to forgive. What would her father have said?

'Your father has nothing to do with this,' Suzie had snapped back. 'Besides, with his record, he'd be in no position to judge!'

Sara had apologized, but it left an awkwardness between them. Cathy reckoned it was only natural – a strange man Sara hadn't met, perhaps liable to take her mother away. No wonder she was suspicious, and possibly jealous too.

Suzie was thankful for a wise friend like Cathy, one with whom she could share some of the difficulties of this new relationship. Not just Sara's disapproval, but concerns to do with the investigation. She'd made it clear to James she didn't want to talk about the future, but every now and then he'd start to speculate and she'd have to remind him. Maybe, she said to Cathy, she was being superstitious, but to talk about future possibilities felt like tempting fate.

'What worries me, he seems to be weaving some kind of fantasy – thinking we'll be one big happy family and live happily ever after.'

'Surely not?'

'I don't know, Cathy, and I don't want to go there. The thing is, James wasn't what you'd call close to his own parents, and he hasn't had kids of his own. I don't think he appreciates what normal family life is like. Apart from that, we don't know where our son is, or even,' Suzie went on, voicing her deepest fear, 'if he's still alive. And if he is, please God, we mustn't forget that he's had a family for the past forty years – parents and maybe brothers and sisters too.'

'He could be married with a family of his own by now...'

'Yes – so why would he want us?'

'Curiosity,' Cathy declared. 'Did you never think, when you were a kid, that maybe you didn't belong, and you were adopted?'

Astonished, Suzie shook her head.

'Well, I did. Mind you,' she laughed, 'I had brothers, of course – totally alien at times. I was convinced I'd been a foundling, and my real parents were rich and titled, or some such nonsense.'

'You always did have too much imagination!'

'I know, I know – too romantic by half. But I'm sure your son will know he was adopted – it's been advised for decades. And he's bound to have wondered – especially as a teenager – who his birth parents were, and why they didn't keep him.'

Suzie sighed. 'But why, in that case, wouldn't he initiate a search himself?'

'Loyalty? A sense of responsibility? Fear?'

– o –

Remember, remember, the fifth of November, gunpowder, treason and plot...

Guy Fawkes' Night, and Suzie was driving into town to do her Friday shop. The air was heavy, the Ridge looking black against a louring sky. Not good weather for fireworks. All at once she was reminded of childhood, of local kids with a straw-filled figure, trundling it round in an old pushchair, shouting, 'A penny for the Guy!'

She wondered if children today did that; or even knew what it was about. No doubt in the modern world, someone had deemed it politically incorrect to burn effigies of long-dead traitors. Anyway, she'd always thought the figures macabre, sympathizing with Fawkes, a York man who'd taken the rap for a ring of Catholic plotters in 1605. Religion again, she reflected with a sigh. Anyway, she had fireworks and sparklers on her shopping list; Sara was giving a little party tomorrow evening for the children.

Back home that afternoon, Suzie was in the studio, working on a chest of drawers, when suddenly it was so dark she could barely see. With a sigh of frustration, she stood up as a huge flash zig-zagged across the sky. Storms no longer bothered her, not since the ones she'd experienced along the Camino, but this was annoying. She flicked the light switch but nothing happened. Dead. As she dashed to the house, the first drops of rain hit with the force of pennies. Indoors, it was drumming on the extension roof.

No lights. Fetching a chair, she went to the box in the hall – the mains switch was down. Pushing it back up, nothing happened. The landline was dead too. But at least her mobile was working. Not for long, though – it needed charging.

Matches, lighter – where were the candles? She'd better find those before real darkness descended. One of the drawbacks to living out in the sticks, they still had overhead lines. Sometimes it was hours before they were reconnected; and the kitchen, of course, was all electric. Looked like she'd be having sandwiches for dinner. Suddenly concerned about her elderly neighbour, Suzie donned her waterproof and dashed next door to check she was all right. But Elsie was organised already – she had the fire lit in the lounge and candles at the ready. It would be hot buttered toast for tea, she said, with a bottle of Mackeson. 'And if you want to join me, you're welcome!'

Suzie laughed and said she was going back to light her own fire now she knew her neighbour was okay.

Back home, she made a quick call to James. 'Can't chat tonight,' she said, 'we've got a storm and the electric's out…'

Telling her not to worry, he said he would call her next morning, when things should be back to normal. With the fire lit and an oil lamp she kept primed for such occasions, Suzie read for a while; but as the rain finally stopped, flashes and bangs from nearby took her outside. No bonfire that she could see, but plenty of fireworks going off. Looking forward to seeing her grandchildren's faces tomorrow, she thought of her son. Did he have children – and would they be celebrating Guy Fawkes Night? Maybe – but not if they were living abroad. Inevitably, that led to Laura and the investigation, but she'd promised herself she wouldn't pester the woman. When Laura had news, she would let Suzie know.

She was dozing when the lights came on and startled her into life. With a sigh of relief, she made herself a hot drink and phoned James to let him know all was well.

'Not sure if I said, but I'm in York tomorrow, and I'll be off on a buying trip midweek… No, not your neck of the woods,' she added, laughing, 'that's the week after. I'll see you then…'

– o –

After a happy weekend with her grandchildren, by Monday morning Suzie was back in the studio. Working away, planning the next few days, the morning was gone before the job was done. Surprised by the time, Suzie realized she was hungry.

Sandwich in hand, she was reading a magazine when the phone rang. Her heart leapt as Laura from the adoptions agency gave her name. Some news had arrived, and she hoped Suzie could come into the office for a chat.

'I can,' she said, 'what's it about?'

Laura was cagey, saying something had come up, and she'd prefer, if possible, to convey the news in person. Sinking into a chair, Suzie had a feeling it wasn't good. Clearing her throat, she said, 'How about this afternoon? I can be there in an hour, if that's okay with you?'

After a scramble to get ready, just over an hour later, Suzie was parking outside the office in Leeds. Heart pounding, she locked the car, went in and gave her name to the receptionist. Minutes later, she was making her way upstairs to see Laura.

The welcoming smile was sympathetic, not happy. Trying to steel herself against what was coming, Suzie asked what Laura had discovered.

'Surprisingly,' she began, 'tracing Dominic was fairly straightforward. Not living abroad, as you'd feared, but in this country.' As Suzie looked up in astonishment, she said, 'The records say he's married, with a family, which I'm sure you'll agree is good news...'

As her voice tailed away, Suzie said, 'But what?'

'Well, we don't know why,' she added gently, 'but I'm afraid he's said no, he'd prefer not to be in touch with his birth parents...'

An instant of disbelief.

'No!' And then she felt it, like a physical kick to the gut. Head buzzing, tears streaming, she could barely breathe. She jerked in alarm when Laura touched her.

'Come on, Suzie, take a deep breath... That's it, and another...'

'But *why?*' she wailed.

'We don't know,' Laura said gently. 'There could be many reasons...'

I gave him away...

She hadn't smoked for months, but once she could breathe again it was the first thing she asked for. With no sign of surprise, Laura produced a packet of Marlborough Lights and an ashtray. She left the room and a few minutes later returned with a cup of tea. It was horribly sweet, but Suzie drank it. After a while, Laura wanted to know how Suzie felt. Was she feeling better? Was there anyone at home, did she have someone she could call on?

No, no and no. Suzie was reeling. Too soon, couldn't think. Couldn't wait to get out.

Laura suggested another meeting, perhaps next week, when Suzie would no doubt feel the need to talk. 'Meanwhile,' she added, 'there's a room downstairs where you can sit and collect yourself. What you mustn't do just yet,' she said firmly, 'is drive. So come along with me. Take as long as you need, but just be sure you're in control before you leave...'

Thirty-Five

Somehow, Suzie made it back to Felton, glad to be home, glad to close the door on the world. Shivering, she turned up the heating and went into the front room to light a fire. Right now, she needed to see warmth as well as feel it.

She sat back on her heels, willing the fire to take hold. How was she going to tell James?

Trying to make sense of whirling thoughts, flashes of memory, she shook her head. But she kept hearing Laura's voice, saying, *living in this country… prefers not to be in touch with his birth parents*. Offering straws of hope, telling her not to despair, this was first contact. Bound to be a shock, and when he's had chance to think about it…

Only later, with cigarettes and a tot of brandy to hand, did she consider James. She should call him. But to transmit such devastating news over a phone line – no, she couldn't do it. If he were here to share it, that would be different. Maybe she should get in the car and go to him; but she couldn't face such a journey, not alone, not tonight. Tomorrow would be better.

Should she call the girls? No, she needed to be more in control.

Cathy – not involved – probably best. But for the moment, she didn't even want to speak to her oldest friend.

Mulling things over, she took the three extensions and put them in the studio. The main phone, in her office, could bleep to its heart's content – she wouldn't hear it. Her mobile, she switched off.

– o –

She slept for an hour or so, waking before four and already planning what she was going to do next. Walk. That would set her right. Just a few days, nothing massive. If she didn't get away she'd go mad. The gear from her Spanish walk was in the spare room. Everything lightweight, even down to the socks and knickers. Layers, that was trick. Thermal vests and long-johns, cashmere sweater, a warm fleece jacket and Gore-Tex waterproof.

She stuffed the essentials into her backpack, together with a thin plastic poncho. Handy when she'd done the Coast to Coast walk – from the Cumbrian coast to the bracing North Sea, the weather had been atrocious. There had been travel to organize at both ends – all good practice for Spain. But the Pennine Way was accessible from home.

She didn't need to travel to the start, or even go on to the Scottish borders. Once she was ready with food and a flask, she could simply walk out the door. Last time, she'd started at Skipton before heading south towards the Derbyshire Peak district; today, the northern route was calling. She looked at her local map. West along the valley, and some twenty miles to Skipton. From there she could walk north-west to Malham, and on towards Hawes. Four days, maybe five at most. She'd get back easily enough, even if it was via Richmond.

But what about James? And the girls…?

Emails, that was the way. She didn't want to talk, just let them know she was off walking and not to worry.

– o –

Grimly determined, once the emails were sent and most things packed, Suzie made herself a good breakfast – two eggs with baked beans on toast. Reminding herself that walking used up an awful lot of energy, she forced it down. Adding sandwiches, water, and a small flask to the backpack, plus her favourite snack bars, she was ready to go.

She pulled her woolly hat down over her ears and donned her waterproof coat with its reflective bands. The wind would be stronger over the tops, and most likely raining too. Patting her pockets, she checked the day's map in one and her mobile in the other. Glancing at her watch while pulling on her gloves, she saw it was 7:30. Soon be light, and even with a lunch break, she should make it to Skipton well before dark.

Familiar footpaths took her westwards from Felton and along the north side of the valley, past patches of half-naked woodland and fields of grazing sheep. Invigorated by an edge of winter in the wind, she walked on without looking back; and as the sun rose, the sky cleared, promising a bright few hours. Suzie pressed on through hilly country, not steep until she was approaching the moors. Battling the wind, she climbed to a high point, pausing to admire the golden rise of moorland on one side, and the dark, frowning line of a sheer escarpment across the valley.

She ate her lunch while sheltering in the lee of a drystone wall, idly wondering what James would make of this rugged landscape. At once her mind clamped shut. She refused to think of him, refused to contemplate what had brought her to this point. Swallowing the coffee, stuffing the remains of her sandwich into the bag, she pulled herself together and moved on. Downhill now, and a couple of miles to the junction below. The day was too short to linger, and certainly too short for a detour. A path avoided the busy main road, except it only went so far. The last two miles were on a grass verge with traffic whizzing past.

Head down, she ploughed on into Skipton, reaching the town as the sun disappeared. Weary and footsore, she was relieved to be almost there. The B&B she'd booked earlier was one she'd used before, on the far side, going out towards Gargrave, her first destination in the morning.

The landlady, Mrs Weston, said she remembered Suzie and gave her a warm welcome. Walkers were frequent guests and she understood about muddy boots and the need for a hot bath. Evening meals were not usually provided, but to Suzie's surprise, Mrs Weston said that she could offer one this evening. 'We don't have any other guests,' she added, 'but there's plenty and it would save you going out again. Of course, if you're vegetarian, I understand…'

Suzie could have kissed her. 'No, I'm not vegetarian, and that would be wonderful – thank you.'

Restored after a hot bath, she washed out her socks and undies and draped them over the radiator. Checking her mobile – switched off during the day – she ignored the messages but made a call to the YHA hostel at Malham to book herself a bed for the following night. After that, she switched off and plugged it in to recharge. In clean essentials she went down to the breakfast room to eat, enjoying the meat and potato pie so much she barely glanced at her paperback. Even so, she found herself pondering those responses to her morning's emails. A little later, back in her room, she studied James's words. *You didn't say you were planning a trip. Where are you going & are you ok? Love James x*

Sara's message was on similar lines, except she wanted to know if Suzie would be back in time to work in the shop on

Saturday. That was easy to answer – no, in short, but she did apologize and say she needed a break. All this hanging around for news, she added, was too much.

A lie, but what else could she say? As for James, she couldn't speak to him. If it hadn't been for James, she wouldn't be in this mind-shattering mess. And if she hadn't fallen for him – *not once, but twice, for God's sake!* – would she be in this state right now?

A state she hadn't been in, until his text brought everything back. Thinking about yesterday, misery swept over her in waves – *I gave my son away, and now he doesn't want to know.* She hadn't wept before, but now she sobbed until there were no tears left. Finally, she roused herself, collapsing into bed to sleep the sleep of sheer exhaustion.

– o –

Suzie woke before dawn with what felt like a hangover. Thumping pain behind puffy eyes, a body aching from yesterday's twenty miles. It was almost seven and time to get up, get the breakfast she'd ordered, and get on the road. Not a good day for it. The wind had dropped, but in the street outside, cars were swishing past in the darkness.

Not far to Gargrave, though, and there was access to the Leeds-Liverpool Canal just up the road. Following the towpath would make for easy walking, a blessed relief for her knees and ankles. A few yoga exercises helped both limbs and mood, but even so, going down to face a full English breakfast, she felt sick. Essential calories, she told herself as a plate of bacon, eggs, tomatoes and mushrooms was set before her. She managed half of it, apologizing as she asked for a second coffee to be added to her flask.

'I don't envy you all this rain,' Mrs Weston remarked, 'and it's not a good forecast, either.'

'Well,' Suzie said, forcing a smile, 'it is as it is…'

A short while later, she was booted and jacketed and had paid her bill. The extra charge for dinner last night was minimal, and she thanked Mrs Weston again. To a friendly wave from the door, she set off in the direction of the canal.

Rain pattered on the hood of her waterproof, but even so it was good to be walking. Trees almost bare now, flotillas of leaves floating on the water; not much movement from the brightly-painted narrow boats, although the ducks and waterfowl were enjoying themselves. Leaving Skipton behind, the tarred towpath gave way to gravel and mud, but apart from puddle-hopping every few yards, it was an easy four miles to Gargrave. Taking a detour in search of coffee and a break, she noticed three missed calls on her mobile, and another message from James which she deleted.

By the time she left the café, the rain was easing off; just as well, she thought, considering the journey ahead. Back at the canal, by the bridge over the locks, the signpost to the Pennine Way pointed directly north, across the fields and towards Eshton Moor. Six miles to Malham, and steeply uphill.

Thirty-Six

Two days since Suzie's email, and despite his messages no answer. What was going on? Was the mobile not working, or what? He tried not to think in terms of accidents, but between imagining the worst and praying for the best, he'd hardly slept. He'd even been tempted to call the police, but what could he say? *My friend's gone walkabout and isn't telling me where she is...*

Did you have an argument, sir? James had watched enough crime dramas to know it was the first thing they asked. 'Absolutely not,' he muttered to himself, almost tearing his hair in desperation. Where could she be? What direction did she go in? By car or on foot?

Why?

He was convinced it was something to do with the search, that she'd had news she didn't want to share. Which meant bad news – although why she wouldn't share it, was beyond him. At this stage of their relationship it made no sense at all. Which brought him back to some kind of accident – or even that she'd forgotten to pack her phone charger.

He was supposed to be at the training college this afternoon but couldn't think about that until he'd had some kind of answer. Directory enquiries had given him the number of Suzie's shop in York, and he'd phoned first thing this morning. The assistant said Mrs Charlton – Sara – would be in later; if he left his number, she'd call him back.

Well, it was half-past ten now. James was just wondering if he should try again when his phone rang. A voice that sounded remarkably like Suzie's, greeted him.

'Suzie? It's James...' But before he could ask what was going on, the voice – rather less welcoming now – said she was Sara, Suzie's daughter.

'Ah – I'm sorry – you sound just like her...' Stumbling, he tried to sound rational, less like some bumbling old fool. 'Hello Sara, what I meant to say was, have you heard from your mother? Do you know where she is?'

Clearly, Sara was surprised he didn't know; and yes, she'd had an email to say her mother had gone walking for a few days. And a text, last night, to say she was fine, but wouldn't be back this week. No, she didn't know where her mother had gone.

'But did she say *why* she'd decided to go?'

At that, the cool voice dropped by several degrees. The stress of waiting for news, apparently, had finally become too much. Mr Fielding really shouldn't worry, her mother was careful, organized and capable – and no doubt when she got back she would give him a call.

With that, Sara Charlton said goodbye, leaving James staring at the phone. He felt as though he'd been slapped. Astonished by the total lack of warmth or sympathy, he couldn't believe this woman was Suzie's daughter. And yet knowing Suzie, could he have predicted such behaviour – that she would literally walk away without saying where or why?

What to do? Try to track down Jo Wallis through the TV company? That could take forever, and would she know any more than Sara? Maybe Suzie really was okay, just angry with him – but *why*? Last time they'd been together, all was well – and they'd spoken on the phone several times since. All she'd been concerned about was the storm they'd had on Friday, and something about a chest of drawers – and that she'd be away on a buying trip this week. She'd even said she was looking forward to seeing him the week after...

It had to be Monday. Something had happened on Monday. The only thing that made any sense was the search for their son. That had to be it. She'd had some news and simply couldn't cope. Couldn't even speak about it – that much was clear from his conversation with Sara.

The only alternative was to tackle that woman in Leeds...

But what about her friend Cathy? They went back a long way – maybe she'd confide in her, if not the girls? But James didn't know the surname, only that her husband was a doctor. In the end, he knew he had to try Laura first. Aware of time passing, he glanced at his watch – almost eleven, and he was lecturing at half past two. Enough time to find the number and make a call.

With clasped hands over his desk, James closed his eyes and tried to focus, murmuring a heartfelt prayer for Suzie's safety. Only as he tried to pray for himself, did he feel, quite suddenly, like the biblical traveller, lost and bleeding on life's road, desperately in need of help and assistance from a stranger.

Thank God, the number was easy to find. *Please, please*, he thought, waiting to be connected to the faceless Laura, *don't fob me off. Don't give me some guff about confidentiality and walk by on the other side...*

He gave his name and formal title, taking a deep breath as he was put through to Laura. She sounded sympathetic; he tried to sound in control. Not like some panic-stricken idiot, burbling a load of useless detail.

339

'This is about one of your clients,' he said. 'Her name's Suzie Wallis. I'm concerned, because she seems to have disappeared...'

Asked to explain, James did so, as clearly and concisely as he could. 'Her daughter Sara has heard from her – but only by text message, last night – so I'm assuming Suzie is presently okay. The worrying part is that she's said she's gone walking, but no one knows where...'

Laura interjected, asking what he meant by walking? It seemed Suzie had never mentioned her passion for long-distance treks, or that she'd written a book about the Camino.

Having explained Suzie's thinking, James said, 'You see, Laura, the weather is pretty bad at the moment, and at this time of year likely to get worse – but she's not actually speaking to anyone, least of all me. Which leads me to think this sudden decision is connected with the research you've been doing into the whereabouts of our son...'

Into the following silence, he said Suzie had been sharing information with him, so he understood about confidentiality. 'Particularly,' he added, 'since I'm a clergyman...'

It seemed Laura already knew that. Sounding concerned, she said she couldn't reveal or confirm any details, but given the circumstances she could see why Suzie might have felt a need to be alone.

'Look, Laura, I appreciate your position, but just tell me this – is our son alive or dead?'

Until he uttered the words, he hadn't been conscious of thinking them. When Laura said he was alive, the relief was so profound James could barely speak. 'Thank you,' he managed at last. Another silence followed. 'So that means he's turned us down...'

The words, *I'm sorry*, reached him as though from a different universe. He was aware of her voice but couldn't take in the rest of it.

'Forgive me, but I have to go now…'

Time ceased to have meaning. Too shocked to think, he stared unseeing at the window, at rivers of tears running down the glass.

Thirty-Seven

After Eshton Moor, the downhill stretch to the River Aire was a relief, less windy and less of a battle once the rain had eased. On reaching the old Quaker settlement of Airton, Suzie found the village teashop was closed. Glad of her flask and the sandwich bought in Gargrave, she ate lunch sheltering in a barn doorway. A couple of walkers going the other way grinned and waved as they passed, but they were the first she'd seen.

Another mile along the Aire – more a broad stream than a river – and she was approaching an 18th century mansion looking south along the valley. A watery sun had broken through the cloud, lighting nearby woodland with tints of purple and gold. Like a painting by Stubbs, she thought, there were even horses grazing in the lush green paddocks nearby.

The peace it suggested caught her with unexpected force. Suddenly grief stricken, she leaned against a nearby wall and sobbed. *Why, why, why had this happened?* Did she really need to be punished like this?

She knew why. She had given away her child. To strangers. No wonder he didn't want to know.

After a while, cursing her own weakness, she forced herself to move, crossing a stile by the road through the village. Wearied by a steep climb, she plodded up to the signpost at the top. There, the path led on through fields towards a point marked on her map as Windy Pike. Reaching the heights, caught by the spectacular view under a clearing sky, she had to rest and take a drink. Below, the infant river with its weir and waterfall; and just a mile or so beyond, Malham, backed by the great limestone cove.

Along the path, in the distance, she spotted a pair of walkers, heading towards the village, and two more, climbing the hill towards her. Buffeted by the wind, she carried on, summoning a greeting as they passed by.

Less than an hour later, crossing the bridge over Malham Beck, the buzz of her phone intruded again. Annoyed, tempted once more to ignore it, she sighed and fished it out. Several messages waiting. Surprisingly, one from Cathy: *How are you? Gone walking I gather. Hope you ok? Let us know and stop me worrying xx*

She'd not told Cathy what she was doing, for the simple reason her friend wouldn't have been satisfied with the kind of brief message she'd sent to the girls. Cathy would have ended up worming the whole story out of her. So, who'd phoned Cathy – and why? It was a mystery, but not one she wanted to solve right now. She sent a bland reply, assuring Cathy she was fine, and she'd be in touch when she got back.

Now Jo. From her text it seemed she was taking time off over the weekend and wanted to visit. Groaning, wondering what that was about, Suzie opened the next message, from Sara: *HE phoned the shop just now wanting to know where you are. Good question. Getting worried so call me xxx*

'Oh, hell…'

To Sara, she tapped out: *In Malham but keep to yourself. Feeling better for walking. Should be home Sat or Sun will explain then. Whats up with Jo? Maybe coming this weekend. Can you deal with it? Love mum x*

And a message from James. Only the fact of Sara's message stopped her from deleting it unread.

Darling Suzie I understand. Spoke to Laura. Know how you feel. Struggling here. Need to speak to you. Please phone x

'Bloody hell,' she muttered. 'I don't bloody need this...'

Cursing Laura for telling him, she texted back: *I am fine.* Hesitating, trying to think what to say to put him off, she added: *Signal poor. No wish to speak right now.*

With that, she pushed the mobile into her pocket and glanced up the road, looking for signs to the YHA.

The hostel, just a few paces from the upmarket Lister Arms Hotel, had no pretensions but looked well-kept, and the Warden's welcome was warm. The place was quiet at the moment, so he could offer Suzie a single room with bathroom nearby. A cooked breakfast in the morning was all part of the service.

'By the way,' he said as he led the way to her room, 'you'll find our mobile reception's a bit hit and miss – indoors, I mean. Outside's better, but it depends where you are...'

Thanking the warden as he left her to settle in, she glanced around. The room was small, the bed narrow but welcoming. She'd only walked about twelve miles but she was exhausted. Dumping her things and peeling off some outer layers, she collapsed on the bed and opened her paperback. Within minutes, she was asleep.

Waking suddenly, she didn't know what was real, the dream or these strange walls. Dragged back by phantoms, her heart was racing as she forced herself to sit up, take hold of reality.

– o –

James was trying to understand why Suzie hadn't told him. Did she hate him or was she trying to protect him? Was it really so vital to drop everything and leave with barely a word? His rational mind pointed out that he knew she was walking – for the moment, it would have to suffice. Beyond sending messages, all he could do for Suzie was pray. But this morning, after half an hour on his knees, half an hour in which it seemed all lines of communication were down, he'd given up and driven to the college.

The afternoon's lecture had been delivered so badly, someone had asked if he was okay. Saying only that he'd had some bad news, James finally escaped. In the car, he checked his mobile, heart leaping at a message from Suzie. She was fine – thank God! – but had no wish to speak...

Driving home in the dusk, the traffic was a blur. In church a short while later, he lit two candles in the Lady Chapel and made another attempt at prayer. Somehow, amidst the chaos of his thoughts, he found a recognisable thread. Christ healing the sick; not directly, not always, but *hearing* the call for help, healing at a distance. Focusing on Suzie, knowing she was vulnerable, he prayed for her safety and wellbeing; for himself, that he might have the strength to withstand this. For his son, James prayed that a door might open somewhere, giving light for a way forward...

Exhausted as he left the church, he checked his mobile again. Nothing from Suzie, but to his astonishment there was a message from her friend Cathy, giving him her landline number and asking him to call.

'Oh, thank God,' he breathed, hurrying into the house. With shaking hands, he sloshed whisky into a glass and went through to his study.

Keying in the numbers, James waited while the ringtone buzzed in his ear. Just as he was thinking no one was home, a breathless female voice answered. As he introduced himself,

Cathy thanked him for calling back. She didn't really have any news, but she'd spoken to Sara that afternoon, and gathered that James was also concerned about this sudden jaunt of Suzie's. It wasn't like her to go off for more than a day without leaving details.

'You're right, and that's why I'm worried. I've no idea where she is, and the weather's not good...'

There was a slight pause before Cathy said she understood Suzie wasn't too far from home, although she gathered Sara had been sworn to silence as to her exact location.

Recalling his conversation with Laura, James took a chance on Cathy's discretion. 'Well, I can't tell you exactly what I know, either, Cathy, but I can say Suzie's had some upsetting news, and that's no doubt why she's taken off like this.'

At Cathy's exclamation, he said, 'Part of me wants to rush off and find her – which I'm sure you'll understand. But – like Sara says – we have to remember that Suzie is an experienced walker...'

For a second or two there was silence, and then Cathy was telling him she knew all about the search and Suzie's anxieties – and whatever this news was, she was afraid Suzie wasn't thinking properly. After all, she'd been so up and down in recent months, anything might happen. James understood her concerns entirely, but it didn't help his state of mind. Eventually, uttering calming phrases, he drew the conversation to a close. Thanking Cathy for calling him, he promised to let her know if he heard anything more.

Putting the phone down, he tried to marshal his thoughts. If Suzie wasn't too far from home, then in which direction was she likely to have gone? He knew she was fond of well-marked trails leading through challenging parts of the country.

South, would only take her through urban sprawl. North, towards the Yorkshire Dales, was a distinct possibility, while to the east lay the comparatively flat Vale of York.

Only as he fetched a large-scale road map from the car did he see Felton's position with regard to moors and rivers. The Yorkshire Dales were to the north-west, but – under the light his eye picked it out at once – a dotted line indicated the route of the Pennine Way, coming up via the Lancashire/Yorkshire border and heading on towards Hawes in Wensleydale. At once he felt a surge of excitement. He knew Suzie had walked the southern section, joining the route on foot from home. Would she have done something similar this time, but opted to go north instead?

If that were the case – and instinct said it was – there were two obvious routes from Felton. But whichever one she chose, he could see that Malham, on the Pennine Way, would be reasonably accessible. Judging time, measuring the distance, his certainty deepened. She could even be there already, perhaps heading out tomorrow...

As he checked again, he saw Malham was the last township before Horton-in-Ribblesdale. Between the two, lay the mountain of Pen-y-Ghent...

His heart sank. Once, with a group of rugby-playing students, he'd climbed it. May, and they could barely see the man in front for mist and rain. Would she go that way? God, he hoped not. Hoped she hadn't had time to get that far. She wasn't one for wild camping, so she'd overnight at a pub or B&B, somewhere she could get a bed and a decent meal. Distracted or not, Suzie wasn't stupid. She wouldn't ignore the need for food and rest.

At least he hoped that was the case. Thinking of the day he'd had, James told himself it was ridiculous to think of setting off now. Better to go first thing in the morning – it could be a long day tomorrow.

Checking his diary, he saw several notes. A meeting with the Archdeacon, to discuss plans and costs for restoring the West Window. *Dammit!* And he was also due to see Amy for a working lunch at her place. Maybe he could get her to stand in for him with the boss. Glancing at his watch, he knew it would be best to make the calls now.

Before he did that, he tapped out another message to Suzie: *Remember I love you x*

– o –

Faced by the Buck Inn as she crossed the packhorse bridge, Suzie recalled drinking in there with a crowd of students. A coach trip from college, the aim being to capture some dramatic features of the local landscape; and Freddie was there, so it must have been her first year. He and a couple of friends went on towards Gordale Scar with one of the tutors – complete with paints and big sheets of hardboard. Following on, her group with their little sketchbooks were torn between awe and laughter – it seemed such a crazy thing to do. But while Suzie and friends were trying to grasp the enormity of those cliffs and the narrowing gap ahead, Freddie and friends were climbing the waterfall, passing things up, hand to hand, to the top. She hadn't thought of that in years; but tomorrow, yes, she would go that way tomorrow. And meanwhile, for old times' sake, she'd have a drink in the Buck.

Thanks to a quartet of walkers sitting in a corner of the bar, one glass of lager turned into several – she even had a meal with them. Two men and their wives, well past retirement age, fit as fleas and as hooked on walking as she was. They were doing the Pennine Way in stages, having started from Edale in Derbyshire; this time, Malham was as far north as they were going. When Suzie mentioned her plans for tomorrow, up to Gordale Scar and past the Tarn, they said they'd been exploring up there earlier in the day.

'Wouldn't advise it,' one of the men said. 'There's a lot of water coming down…'

'And you're on your own,' his wife said, shaking her head at Suzie. 'Best not risk it...'

Suzie said she just wanted to have a look for old times' sake, and the talk passed on to the state of the paths, the challenges they'd faced on other walks. Recalling her own experiences, Suzie was able to keep up, enjoying the banter, impressing them later when she said she'd done the Camino in one go, and had even written a book about it.

The bar grew busier as they talked, mainly locals but a few more walkers keen to have a drink and a meal. It was almost nine when Suzie left, amidst laughter and good wishes and promises to look out for her book. Staggering a little as she crossed the bridge, she was almost at the hostel door before she thought to check her mobile.

Remember I love you x

'I can't,' she whispered, sinking onto a wooden bench, staring down at the brightly lit message. 'I can't do this anymore – it's all wrong. Don't you see we're being punished?'

She didn't have the energy to type out a reply on those fiddling little keys. Anyway, she could barely see. Resisting the urge to throw the annoying thing into the nearest bush, she closed it down and shoved it into her pocket.

– o –

That evening, James found his thoughts descending down dark alleys. For a long time after Maggie, it was the happiness he mourned. Only in recent times, talking to Suzie, did he find himself speaking of the misery he'd endured latterly. But if the agony of Maggie's suffering had shaken his faith at times, losing her had rocked his foundations, and he could see why he'd leapt at the chance to contact Suzie. It was a way to move forward, away from the misery and into something more positive.

He supposed it was a common feature of age.

Looking at himself with detachment, he could see this search as an old man's quest to find the young man he'd fathered, in whom something of himself might live on. But in chasing the dream, he'd been compelled to revisit the past, to re-live it through Suzie. He'd borne the pain because he deserved it, but what he hadn't bargained for was falling in love.

Not that it was anything like the first time, nor was it the kind of attraction that had first drawn him to Maggie; what he felt for Suzie was different, marked by shared history, by pain as much as joy. Only now, recalling the passion of recent weeks, did he wonder what had possessed him to say that for him and her there were no rules.

'No rules?' he muttered, pouring another whisky. There were always rules for men in his position. He was ordained to serve others, not himself. All very well to say he was in love with Suzie, that he was comforting her as well as himself, but that would count for nothing if the affair came to light. Personal feelings were irrelevant – he was supposed to be above reproach. Public gossip didn't just cast stones at him, it was what he represented. As a minister of the Church, he was supposed to be above that kind of self-indulgence, supposed to keep a rein on lustful thoughts and deeds.

'Not to mention excessive consumption of alcohol…' he added wearily. Dragging himself to his feet, James replaced the cap on the bottle, switched off the opera CD, and went to make himself a hot drink. Waiting for the kettle to boil, he checked his mobile again. No messages, nothing from Suzie.

Thirty-Eight

She didn't sleep much. Tossing and turning, dogged by grief and doubt and a desperate need for comfort, several times she tried her mobile; but, like the man said, there was no signal inside these walls. She even thought of dressing and going outside, but it was far too late for phone calls, even to James. Anyway, what could she say? Short of *all is forgiven and I'm coming home*, or even giving him her location – which would surely bring him running – there was nothing to be said. Anyway, she hadn't forgiven him – or herself – so she'd best think of tomorrow and get some sleep.

Next morning, surveying low cloud and misty drizzle, it seemed ironic that she'd planned to pay homage to happy, innocent, sunlit memories. That first student trip at seventeen, and a couple of times when the girls were young. But today, following the path to Gordale Scar was nothing like those summer visits. With the sky closing in and water rushing just inches away, entering the gorge was like entering a giant's lair. As ragged limestone cliffs loomed closer at every turn, she felt under siege; battered by boulders, no way out.

For the sake of those distant days she pressed on. For Freddie who'd rescued her, put her back on her feet, given her children, supported her ambitions. So what if he sometimes strayed, felt the need to rescue other bruised and broken women, at least he'd stayed with her. He wouldn't have abandoned her, not really; he always came back.

But he isn't here – can't ever be – he's gone now…

Reaching the head of the gorge, as the cliffs opened out she felt the threat subside. It was okay, she could picture him now, picture that day. Breathing more easily, surveying the climb, it seemed less high than she remembered, but with more water coming down. There was a route from here, involving a scramble up the side of the waterfall, and via the Tarn to the Pennine Way. The other route – safer, less challenging – meant going back almost to the village.

Gazing at the water, she couldn't recall much of what lay beyond it – other than rocks and sky and another climb. Once, with the girls, she'd climbed the first section, posing on a big dry rock, mid-stream; and Freddie telling them about a painting he'd done as a student. Suzie didn't even have a sketch from that day, only a memory of it, hazy and obscure.

Like the face of her son as she handed him over to strangers. The thought came out of nowhere, startling, unwelcome. *I could have drawn him – why didn't I?*

You didn't want the reminder…

Suddenly, she had to sit down. It wasn't her son she wanted to forget, it was the Home, the desperation of those final weeks. All she'd wanted was to care for her baby – that was the agony she'd tried to forget…

Guilt. That was what they'd talked about, she and James. Maybe he'd come to terms with his; she'd claimed she had too, drowning it in the flow of life, rushing on like the stream at her feet. If James had given his life to Christ, she'd had her daughters, giving to them what she couldn't bestow on the little lost soul in her heart.

And now she never would.

All very well for James to say that God was love, that love didn't work in vengeful ways, but Suzie wasn't convinced. What about Karma? In her experience, what goes round comes round, and now they'd got their comeuppance. James had rejected her, she'd rejected his child, and now their child was rejecting them. *Get out of that one, James!*

Fortified by anger, she found a tissue, blew her nose and stood up. The rain wasn't passing, it was getting heavier. If she was planning to reach her next stop before dark, she'd better get a move on. Briefly, she considered going back the way she'd come. Easier, no doubt, but another hour on the journey at least. Getting closer to the fall, she could see a kind of path to the left, avoiding the central, water-splashed rocks. Risky, no doubt, but at least it was more direct.

Despite the footholds, the path was even harder than it looked from below; and she was hampered now by age and the weight of her pack. Scrambling, gasping for breath, bent almost double, she stopped halfway, knowing this was a stupid mistake. A quick glance down and she felt sick. Could she safely retrace her steps? No – the only way was up. Sweating inside her clothes, face wet and frozen, hands chilled in their gloves, Suzie tried again. It seemed to take an age, but slowly, one slippery foothold at a time, she reached the top of the first waterfall and collapsed on the rocks.

Cursing when she could find her breath, slowly she gathered strength to move. To sit up, slip off her pack and find her bottle of water. A few gulps, a chunk of chocolate, and she was almost ready to face the next section. Between massive rocks, Gordale's rushing waters were barely visible here, but she could see the second fall now, and beyond that, the sky.

Luckily, the way forward was less steep than before. Almost blinded by the rain, she climbed slowly between wet and gleaming boulders, and stopped again to catch her breath. Waterfall to the right, some patches of green, and then, between looming limestone cliffs, she was onto something resembling a rubble-strewn path.

At last the ravine opened out, and as she stopped to rest, Suzie looked back, more scared than thankful at what she'd overcome. 'You're a bloody fool,' she murmured, taking another bite at the chocolate bar. She glanced at her watch, shocked to see it was already way past noon, and no progress made at all. She'd be crazy to think she could reach Horton today, especially with Fountains Fell and Pen-y-Ghent between. Better to make her way back to Malham and the hostel; she could try the safer route tomorrow.

A wide, grassy path beckoned, with a view of cairns through the drizzle. The heavy rain was easing off, the sky lighter in the distance. The path led to a wall, and further on, a stile into the lane leading back down to Malham. Should she go back now, Suzie wondered, or plod on to the Tarn? Cheered by a brightening sky, she chose the Tarn. It was, after all, the highest lake in England, and not much more than a mile away. She could eat her lunch with a pleasant view and gather herself for an easier return to the village.

She walked on to a boathouse at the head of the lake, eating her sandwich in its shelter. A couple stopped to pass the time of day – they were just here for a day's walking, they said, and heading back to Malham and their car.

'Quiet, today,' the man remarked. 'When we've been before, it's been crawling with people. Mind you, that was in summer! Better to see it like this, despite the weather...'

Wishing her a safe journey, they walked on. A little while later, feeling better and stronger for her rest, Suzie set off back to Malham.

– o –

She passed shake holes and outcrops, the grassland looking brighter under a watery sun. The limestone Cove was hidden from here, but as she trekked along the footpath, suddenly the great pavement at the top – what looked like acres of it – was spread out before her. Level at first glance, close up it looked like a giant's attempt at crazy-paving, a vast mosaic of blocks and crevices. It brought forth a joyful smile. She felt like a child again, on top of the world, uplifted, free. She'd read that once, in some far distant age, water greater than Niagara Falls had poured over its lip to the valley below. Now, all that remained was this water-scored pavement, and all that could be seen was the silvery glint of a stream, way below, winding its way through the valley...

Crossing to the far side, enjoying the view, Suzie heard a muffled ringing. Fishing in her pocket, cold fingers grasping at cold plastic, she dropped her phone. As it bounced and disappeared into a crevice, she lunged after it, caught her foot and fell.

Stunned by the impact, for a while she just lay there, gasping, wondering why she was flat on her face. With grit under her fingers she realized she'd fallen. All she could do was groan at the folly. Trying to move, pain registered. Foot, ankle? *What a bugger*. Shock made it hard to think. Remembering where she was, she tried to raise herself, cried out and collapsed again. Her right elbow hurt, but that was probably just a bruise; the real problem was her left foot. It didn't seem part of her, not like her elbow and sore knees. Not good. Suspecting it was stuck in a crevice – possibly broken – she had a moment of panic.

Breathing slowly, telling herself to be calm, Suzie raised her head and tried to get her bearings, but all she could see was a mosaic of grey, a strip of green, and the sky. She'd been pleased to be alone before, but now she needed help. Where the hell was everyone? The only ones she'd seen today were back at the Tarn. At this time of day, logic said people were more likely to be coming down from the moors, rather than up from the village. What she needed to do was attract attention. If she could only get up and get the backpack off, her high-viz poncho would make her visible.

Of course, the best way of calling for help, was via her mobile. But where was it? Not far, it couldn't be. But on every side were deep fissures in the stone, like cart tracks through mud. God alone knew how deep they were; although peering down the nearest one, all she could see was moss and miniature ferns. On another deep breath she looked to the left: more greenery but no phone.

She tried raising herself to get the backpack off, but between a tender right knee and the drag on her left ankle, it was agony. Gasping, crying out with pain, she managed it eventually, pulling the poncho around her neck and using the backpack as a pillow. Trying to formulate a plan as the pain subsided, Suzie figured that if she was going to move at all, her energies needed to be directed towards getting her left foot out of the crack. She backed up, tried to turn; but even that hurt. An attempt to grasp the heel of her boot was so agonising she almost passed out.

Afraid that twisting would damage the ankle beyond repair – always supposing she could bear it – Suzie stopped and tried to consider her options. It was barely three o'clock, there had to be people around, walkers heading down to Malham...

Thirty-Nine

James's mobile rang a couple of times while he was on the motorway. He stopped just short of Leeds to check the messages. Both the same number, but not one he recognized. To his surprise, the caller was Suzie's daughter, Jo. She was worried about her mother, and wondered if James had heard anything since his call to Sara yesterday? Either way, she hoped he would call her back.

He did so at once, relieved to be speaking to her. It seemed that the women – Sara, Cathy and Jo – had been conferring. Their instincts were the same as his: Suzie wasn't thinking straight, and something could be wrong.

It took a moment for James to collect himself. 'I'm just south of Leeds,' he said. 'I haven't heard from your mother, except a brief text yesterday to say she didn't want to speak to me. Fair enough, but like you, I'd rather see her face to face and be sure she's okay...'

Jo was surprised. Had Cathy told him where she'd gone? 'No,' he said, 'but I'm guessing the Pennine Way. Malham – or close to it. I'll start from there...' He heard an indrawn breath, then a low chuckle. Jo said it was a good guess, and to let her know when he got there.

So, he was right. Suzie had been in Malham; his decision to pack a bag and head north was not a crazy impulse after all. Boosted by what felt like a vote of confidence from Jo, James finished his coffee, tucked the flask away, and got back on the road.

She could be halfway to her next destination by now. He couldn't hope to overtake her on foot, but with the car – and the aid of a walkers' map – he hoped to be able to intercept her. Or, failing that, be at Horton when she arrived. But first of all, he needed to be certain she was heading in that direction.

By the time he reached Malham, it was almost two o'clock. He parked outside the Buck Inn and went in. While the barman was pouring his half-pint of lager, James asked about Suzie, whether she'd stayed the night there.

'No, but I remember the lady you describe – she ate with some folk who were staying here.' He set the glass on the bar. 'There's a few B&Bs around, but not all of them are open this time of year. If I were you, I'd start at the Youth Hostel, just over the bridge.'

Thanking him, and ordering a sandwich to take away, once James had slaked his thirst he went on to the hostel. The man on the desk checked the names in the book, and said yes, a single lady, Suzanne Wallis, had signed in last night, and out this morning.

'Did she say where she was going?'

'Not to me, I wasn't on duty.'

James sighed, trying not to show his irritation. 'Look, I'm sorry to bother you with this, but I'm worried about her. I've been trying her mobile all day, but getting no reply...' At the man's look of concern, he pressed a little harder. 'Do you know who was on duty this morning – someone Suzie may have spoken to?'

He said he'd have to ask the warden, returning a few minutes later with an older man who first of all asked James who he was, and why he was concerned.

Giving his name, James handed over his card and said he was a friend. Thankfully, his position was accepted without need to go into further detail. After he'd explained that Suzie's family were anxious, and that she'd had some bad news before suddenly leaving home, the warden seemed to grasp that it could be serious.

'She probably walked from Skipton yesterday,' James said. 'So where would she be heading next?'

'If she was set on the Pennine Way, Horton would be the obvious place, but...' He shrugged, as if to say the people who passed through here had their own plans, not always shared with the people on duty. 'If you give me a moment, I'll see who was on this morning...'

Another wait while the warden returned to his office. James sat down, trying to curb his impatience. Eventually, the man returned, holding out his mobile to James. 'Barbara spoke to her – it'll be better if you have a word...'

Taking the call, James said he would appreciate anything that had a bearing on Suzie's plans. There was a pause before Barbara said she'd mentioned Gordale Scar, and that she was planning to go on to Horton that day. Thanking her, James handed the phone back.

Ending the call, the warden turned to him and said, 'Not good, if she's tried to take the route by the Scar – it's pretty wet up there at the moment...'

Reaching for a local map, he indicated the different routes out of Malham, giving a rough idea of the time it would take to reach Horton. Pursing his lips, he said, 'Could be six hours depending on pace – more, allowing for stops. But if she avoided Pen-y-Ghent, she'd be quicker – there's a path to the road, you see...'

As James studied the route, familiar names caught his attention, reminding him of the trek he'd done, almost forty years ago. His heart sank as he considered the weather.

'Barbara says she left just after nine this morning, so she could be in Horton already,' the warden said, glancing at the clock.

'Is there a youth hostel?'

The warden shook his head. 'B&B, or one of the pubs. We've got phone numbers, so you could give it a try – but I'd wait a while, if I were you, give her chance to get there...'

Weighing the options, James asked for the information now. 'I'll phone them all, ask them to let me know when she arrives.' Glancing at his watch, he calculated another hour or so to sunset. After that, he stood little chance of finding her. Unless, please God, she'd reached Horton safely.

The man on the desk was looking at his list of bookings for the night. 'We've got six so far, but I'm pretty sure they all came up from Gargrave. A couple more booked – probably from Horton, but they haven't arrived yet. When they do, I'll ask if they've seen your friend...'

Even though he made the calls from the hostel's phone, James was starting worry about the battery level on his mobile. Memories of Gordale Scar were also pressing. In Suzie's present frame of mind, it was hard to predict what she'd do, but he decided to go up there while he was waiting for someone in Horton to get back to him.

Studying the local Ordnance Survey map, he realized he could take the car part of the way. Jotting down a few more tips, James thanked the warden for his help and set off.

– o –

Driving up to Gordale Bridge, he parked in a layby, and changed his shoes for boots. Setting off at a brisk pace, he followed the path to the Scar. The sunny spell had passed, and he was aware of a deeper chill as he entered the gorge, the only sound that of his footsteps crunching on gravel, and water rushing beside him. Concentrating on the path, sorting shadows from rocks and pools from holes, he tried not to think of what he might find.

He heard the waterfall before he saw it. Although he'd been walking hard, James shivered as he gazed up at a gap between the cliffs. Wild, lonely, and cold, the place was deserted. Crossing the stream, getting close to the waterfall, he could make out a vestige of steps up the central outcrop, and a path of sorts to the left. No cave that he could see, no sign of a living soul. He shouted Suzie's name, shivering again as the echo came back. He waited, called again, but heard no answering cry.

Surely, she wouldn't have attempted to climb up there?

Checking the shadows for a good fifty paces to either side, shining his torch here and there, a battered white trainer caused his heart to leap; but he found little else. Why Suzie had felt the need to come this way he could not imagine, but it was a huge relief to leave it behind. Spurred on by a bruised and yellowing haze in the west, he almost ran the last few hundred yards to the bridge. Please God, he prayed as he started the car, she'd be in Horton by now, no doubt infuriated by all the fuss.

Even so, something told him to keep on looking. He drove along to the next turning, taking the right fork which should bring him out on the tops. Following the steep and narrow road, he paused by a signpost indicating the Cove to the left. Strongly tempted, James carried on, looking for the signpost to Gordale Scar. From there he'd walk back in search of Suzie – he had to check she'd not been stranded beyond his sight.

Another mile and he spotted it. Pulling off onto a narrow grass verge and crossing the stile, he set off at a brisk pace, glancing keenly at rocky outcrops along the way. No sign of movement, no glimpse of high-viz fabric, only the sheep looking indignant as he hurried past. Finding himself in a dry ravine, he was glad of his torch as the dark closed in. Slowing his pace, stepping carefully as the path descended, he kept calling Suzie's name. Every so often he paused to listen, but apart from rushing water nearby, he heard nothing. Above the falls he stopped to look down, suspecting it was the place he'd been standing half an hour earlier.

Caught between relief and frustration, James turned to climb back. Struggling for breath, desperation kept him going until he reached a smooth outcrop where he could sit and let his heart and lungs rest for a while. The last few hundred yards were an effort but he made it to the stile. His mobile hadn't rung, but he checked it anyway. Nothing.

The road was so narrow, it was difficult to turn the car, but at last he was facing the right way. By the path for the Cove, he parked to walk downhill this time, thankful to find it was lighter here, despite the early evening clouds. Scanning to either side, peering at shadows, he began to hurry as the distant pavement came in sight. Apart from a pair of crows, flapping away, he saw not a living thing as he approached – just dark grey blocks and endless lines. A vast, empty expanse, making its own horizon as it met the darkening sky.

Despairing, James slowed as he crossed the last few yards of grass, expecting nothing as his feet touched solid stone. But with his change of perspective, sunlight appeared beneath the cloud. He scanned the pavement again and saw what looked like a black rock some distance in from the edge. Except it wasn't a rock, and light was glinting off something – a speck of orange...

Oh, dear God – could it be Suzie?

Biting back the urge to run, he forced himself to walk.

When he reached her, she was prostrate, the poncho around her head and neck. For a second, James couldn't breathe. He thought she was dead. Only as he touched her did she moan.

Thanking God, he stroked her icy cheek. 'Suzie, it's me, James – can you hear me?'

Another moan, and then, faintly, 'James?' A long pause, then, 'Why...?'

As relief surged, he felt his heart beating again. He unzipped his jacket, peeling it off to cover her legs and back. Gently, he squeezed her hand. 'You're hurt, darling, but I don't want to move you. I'm calling for help...'

His hands were shaking. Finding his phone, gripping it firmly, he pressed the digits. Within seconds, a female voice answered.

He asked for Mountain Rescue, and in answer to her question, said he was on top of Malham Cove. 'I'm with a lady whose foot is stuck in a crevice. I'd say it happened some time ago. She's conscious but very cold...'

He was asked to hold while she transferred his call to the Cave and Mountain Rescue service. Having gone through the details, James had a promise that a fully qualified team would be with him soon – probably within half an hour. In the meantime, he was to keep the lady as warm as possible, and try to keep her talking.

Getting little in the way of replies, James abandoned his kneeling position for something colder but less painful. Lying down with her, trying not to touch her leg, he held her close. Talking face to face, he was rewarded by a faint smile. He looked at his watch. Five minutes since his call, and it felt like an hour. He felt frozen to the unforgiving stone. *How long had Suzie been here?*

Between bouts of shivering, he talked about the walks they'd done together. Every now and then, he'd ask, 'Do you remember when...?' And sometimes she smiled or murmured a response. Encouraged, he kept telling her how much he loved her, how she had to stay awake because he needed her love to keep him warm.

She didn't seem in pain, but she was icy to the touch. Uttering another fervent prayer, moments later he heard a noise – a car, climbing the hill. With difficulty he raised himself and saw a flash of light. And then several lights, red jackets, figures striding purposefully towards them. Dear God, he was never so thankful in his life.

Blankets, a stretcher; discussions on how to release her foot. Above the boot top, her leg was swollen; someone said she was hypothermic. Another said he was giving Suzie a pain-killing injection. Minutes later they were easing her foot from the hole, and soon after that they had her on the stretcher. As she was borne away towards a big, bright Land Rover, James was being helped up. Despite the warm blanket, his jaw was trembling, his body jerking in cramp-like spasms. To his dismay, a second stretcher was produced for him.

Once they'd reached the Land Rover, James insisted he was fine, he didn't need the stretcher. As he was helped into a seat, the man asked if the blue Fiesta by the road was his. He said it was.

'Well, sir, if you'll give me the keys, I'll take it back down for you…'

Someone said an ambulance was on its way, and Suzie would be taken to hospital in Skipton, and with that the Land Rover was bumping its way across the field and onto the road. The man with the keys got out, the Land Rover set off again, and minutes later they were in the village, crossing the bridge and pulling up outside the pub.

From the window, James saw his car being driven into the car park; shortly after that, an ambulance, its lights flashing, turned the corner and pulled up behind them.

As Suzie was transferred, he longed to go with her, stay with her, get the facts first-hand. But he wasn't Suzie's next of kin, and he knew only too well what hospitals were like. Asked for his details, he found his mobile and gave Sara's number as well. He said he was fine, he hadn't been up there long, and no thanks, he didn't need treatment beyond that promised hot drink; he'd make his own way to the hospital as soon as he could.

A female paramedic introduced herself as Jenny and after praising James for what he'd done, insisted on checking him over. She smiled kindly but refused to leave him to his own devices, insisting he went with Suzie in the ambulance. Someone else said his car keys would be with the landlord at the Buck. James barely had chance to thank the man before they were on their way.

Suzie wasn't stirring – she seemed to him to be barely breathing – but Jenny assured him she was okay. James found himself answering her questions, explaining something of the circumstances.

When she asked how he knew she was in Malham, James shook his head. 'I prayed – kept on praying. I knew I had to find her, and God led me here…'

Sensing the truth of it, James felt strange, suddenly, as though his body no longer belonged to him. 'Do you mind if I lie down?' he whispered, and with that he passed out.

– o –

Wondering where on earth he was, James came to himself with a tight band around his arm. The young woman, Jenny, was leaning over him. 'It's all right, James – you're okay…'

Releasing the blood-pressure band, she said, 'Tell me, when did you last eat?'

'Don't know.' He recalled buying a sandwich, but not eating it.

'Well, then, it's hardly surprising you fainted – your blood sugar is probably way down.' She smiled. 'But we're nearly at the hospital – they'll give you a thorough check, just to be sure.'

He felt empty, hollow, desperately in need of something – hot coffee, soup, the sandwich he'd left in his car.

'How's Suzie?' he asked, turning to see her tremulous smile as she gazed at him.

'Hi James,' she whispered; and then, before he could express his relief, 'I'm so sorry...'

Too choked to reply, all he could do was reach for her, squeeze her hand.

Startled by the sound of a siren and a sudden burst of speed, he let go. Jenny smiled. 'Traffic,' she said calmly.

Minutes later, the ambulance was slowing, turning, pulling up. Jenny opened the doors. It was dark outside. As Suzie's stretcher was eased out, James looked at his watch. Just after five and it felt like midnight. How could so much have happened in so short a time?

He was about to get up, but Jenny stayed him. 'No, stay on the stretcher, James – we don't want you collapsing on the way in.'

Losing sight of Suzie, he was wheeled into a curtained cubical and assured that someone would be with him soon. To his surprise the promise was fulfilled a short while later. A young doctor checked heart, lungs and blood pressure. A nurse took his temperature.

Consulting his notes, the doctor said, 'Nothing to worry about, but you need to rest. We'll get you some tea and biscuits, but I want you to wait at least couple of hours before driving anywhere.'

'What about Suzie – Suzie Wallis – the woman I came in with? Malham Cove – I think she has a broken ankle,' James added by way of explanation.

'Ah, yes. She's being attended to at the moment – we'll know more later.'

With that the doctor was gone. The nurse smiled and followed him.

He couldn't fault the service. A few minutes later, she brought him tea and biscuits – nothing had ever been more welcome. She stayed long enough to explain that Suzie had been admitted to a ward, and that he'd be able to see her once he was rested.

She glanced at her watch. 'Give it another hour,' she said kindly, 'and if you feel light headed, don't hesitate to call. But before you set off home, have something more to eat. Nothing heavy, mind you – we don't want you falling asleep at the wheel...'

– o –

Lying there on the hard bed, anxiety set in. Mainly about Suzie, but also about his car. He'd have to get a taxi back to Malham, but as for driving home, it would be better to stay overnight at the Buck – that is, if they had a room...

The minutes seemed to drag past. He was just wondering what to do – should he go and find someone, or what? – when the curtain was swished back and the smiling nurse appeared.

'Okay, Mr Fielding, let me check your blood pressure again, just to be sure.'

A few minutes later she was giving him the number of Suzie's ward, and telling him he could see her. At once he got up and bent to retrieve his muddy boots. Still slightly dizzy but he'd be okay. To cover the hesitation, he apologized for the state of them, but she said not to worry, they got all sorts in A&E.

Carrying his jacket, James found the nearby exit and stamped a few times to get rid of the loose mud. After that he followed a maze of corridors to Suzie's ward, gave his name at the desk and was directed to her bed.

She looked to be asleep; her lower leg and foot encased in pot, her face as white as the pillows. He moved quietly, but she heard him anyway. Opening her eyes, she smiled, raising a hand in welcome.

'Thank God you're safe,' he whispered, embracing her, not wanting to let go.

'Oh, James, I'm such an idiot…'

In those few moments, they were both beyond words. Handing him a tissue from the box beside her, she gave a watery smile and asked if he was okay.

'Yes, of course – but what about you?'

'Fine, now…' She stroked his face. 'I still can't believe it. How did you find me?'

Reluctantly, he released her and pulled up a chair. Holding her hand between his own, he said, 'I knew something was wrong, so I phoned Laura…'

'She told you?'

'Not in so many words. But I got the message. He said no, didn't he?'

At her gasp of anguish, James could have bitten his tongue. In that moment, grief, sorrow, the bitterness of guilt, overwhelmed him. As he bowed his head, suddenly she was comforting him, stroking his hair, telling him it was okay, she shouldn't have taken off like that…

'I was praying for you,' he said brokenly. 'Praying I'd find you and we'd be able to talk. But when I found you…' He couldn't say that he'd thought she was dead. Aware of how close he'd been to losing her, he longed to enfold her in his arms and never let go. 'Promise me,' he begged, 'you'll never do anything like that again?'

There was so much more he wanted to say, but not here, not now. With difficulty, he pulled himself together, cleared his throat, and asked how long she would be in hospital.

'They say,' Suzie began, wiping her eyes, 'the bones need pinning. Otherwise it's not too bad. They'll do the op in the morning…' Her words tailed away as she glanced up in surprise.

James turned to see a young woman standing behind him, so like Suzie he knew at once that this was Sara. He stood at once, offering her the chair, backing away as she brushed past to embrace her mother. Expecting a difficult moment, he wondered if he should leave; but then Sara turned to him, holding out her hand and thanking him.

'Jo said you were already on your way when this happened?'

As he nodded, she looked down; then, with a catch in her voice, said, 'I don't know how you worked it out, but thank you – thank you for finding her and getting help.'

Overcome, he could only say the rescue team were brilliant, there so quickly…

'But if you hadn't found her, how would they have known where to look?'

Reflecting on that, on the search he'd done, on the speed with which he'd found her, James could only smile and shake his head. All he could recall was the feeling – so strong – that Suzie was somewhere in Malham, that he would find her if only he tried hard enough.

Lost for a moment, he came back to the present as Suzie said to her daughter, 'The thing is, love, I'm not sure when I'll be out of here.'

'But you'll need looking after,' Sara said, 'for a while at least. You'd better come to me – the kids will love having you to stay. And Jo wants to see you, she's coming up tonight.'

Looking tearful, Suzie shook her head. 'I'm so sorry to mess everybody about like this – especially you, James, dropping everything to find me.'

'Not a problem,' he said quickly, forcing a smile. 'Amy was happy to hold the fort today…'

Before he could say more, one of the nurses appeared. It was time for them to leave. As they began to say their farewells, Sara hugged her mother. 'I'll keep in touch with the hospital,' she promised. 'And with James – so everyone knows what's going on.'

Unable to trust his self-control, James brushed Suzie's cheek with his lips and turned away.

– o –

Endless corridors until he and Sara reached the main entrance. He noticed the café just as she asked if he'd like a coffee. It sounded the best idea ever. As they sat down, he thought she seemed tense. He was about to ask after her children, when she said quietly, 'About the other day, on the phone – I'm sorry if I sounded curt.'

'Not at all – you were worried.' A moment later, weighing his words, he said, 'Do you know why your mother took off like that?'

She glanced up. 'Yes, Jo said…'

'About the rejection?' In some corner of his mind, James was surprised he could sound so detached. 'I was shattered when I found out. I knew at once why she'd gone. If only she'd told me…'

Sara gave an exasperated sigh. 'I don't know, Mum gets an idea in her head and just forgets everyone else. Dad was the same. And what a day I've had – Grace at home with tonsillitis, Rob's supposed to be in London tomorrow, and here I am, worried sick about Mum…'

'I'm sorry,' he murmured, but clearly it wasn't enough.

'Why,' she asked suddenly, 'did you have to put this idea in her head? This needn't have happened.'

James bowed his head. 'I know, Sara, I know. I've been telling myself the same thing.'

'No, I'm sorry – shouldn't have said that after all you've done today…' She took a deep breath, clearly trying to control some raging thoughts. 'Look, I can see you've become important to Mum, and it's not my place to interfere, but – but – I just hate to see her *hurt*.'

'Of course.' He sipped at his coffee, wishing it were something stronger. Trying to ignore the exhaustion dragging him down, he said quietly, 'I love your mother very much. I wouldn't hurt her for the world – and yet, unwittingly, I have. I can't tell you how much I regret it.'

As she gave an abrupt little nod, he said haltingly, 'It's hard for me – not knowing you all – to appreciate how this – this

370

issue – affects you. But perhaps I understand a little,' he added, recalling arbitrary decisions taken by his own parents. 'I know it's hard, but perhaps we should leave your mother to decide where we go from here.'

It was the best he could say.

– o –

After Sara had left to return to York, James found the public phone and rang the Buck Inn. Yes, they could offer him a room and a meal. Next, he phoned for a taxi, and just over half an hour later he was back in Malham.

He felt weird, detached, so dogged by fatigue he could barely summon a smile as he was praised for what he'd done that afternoon. Just hours ago, yet it felt like years; and although he'd eaten little all day, the meal set before him was too much. He managed half of it, apologising to the landlady as he staggered like a drunk to his room.

Falling into bed, he slept at once, stirring hours later to a dream of Suzie in happier times. Clinging to the memory, seeking her warmth, he turned, only to find empty space.

The digital clock said it was 06:07. He sat up, switched on the bedside light. She would be having her operation today. He should call the hospital, find out what time, ask if he could see her on his way south.

What day was it? Thursday – lecture at two-thirty. No – call in sick, cancel. Need to call Amy. What was Sunday? He looked at his mobile for the date. Oh, lord, no. Remembrance Sunday – he'd forgotten.

Missed calls from Jo and Cathy – but no doubt Sara had been in touch with them since – and one from Amy asking if everything was okay. Too early to call her – better after breakfast.

Out of bed, to the bathroom. A full glass of water was followed by a more welcome cup of tea and a couple of biscuits. Reminded of yesterday, he shook his head, no longer wondering why he felt so stressed.

Aware that his heart was racing, James made a conscious effort to relax, to push such thoughts aside. Closing his eyes, he focused on calm, emptying his mind of all these worldly anxieties. There was no need to rush. He would take a shower, say his prayers, and then go down for breakfast. After the trials of yesterday, his body, as well as his mind, needed care.

– o –

He made his first call to the hospital, only to be told that visiting this morning was out of the question. Suzie was being prepared for the operation on her ankle, and she would be asleep for some time after that. His informant couldn't say when she'd be well enough to be discharged.

Briefly, he thought of writing a few lines and dropping the note off as he passed the hospital, but all things considered, she might not receive it. Better to write from home, to Sara's address.

Amy, when he gave her a quick summary of yesterday's events, was relieved to find things had turned out well, but concerned for him. *Take it easy*, were her final words. She'd skated over yesterday's meeting with the Archdeacon, but James knew he would have some explaining to do when he got back.

Forty

Solving several logistical problems in one, Cathy volunteered to collect Suzie from the hospital. On the way to York, they stopped off in Felton to pack some essentials and let Suzie's neighbour know she was going to be absent for a while.

By the time they reached Sara's, it had been a long and tiring day, but on the plus side, it had given them chance to talk. Since the accident, Suzie had been distracted by three days of hospital routine, an operation on her ankle, and anxiety over her immediate future. Being with Cathy was her first opportunity to discuss the accident – and James – and most of all, the shocking news that had sparked the whole thing off.

Wisely, her old friend didn't ask questions but simply listened and sympathized. By the time they parted, Suzie was feeling drained.

'Thanks for everything, Cathy. You must be shattered – I know I am. But I think I might sleep tonight.'

'I'm fine. But call me if you need a chat.'

'I will,' Suzie promised.

– o –

If Sara was anxious about her mother, the children seemed confused, even shocked by the sight of their grandmother on crutches, her foot encased in an enormous boot. Collapsing on the sofa, she gave them both a hug, forcing herself to sound bright and cheerful as she joked about falling down and breaking her ankle. Luckily George knew about broken bones, his friend at school had broken his arm a few months ago. Focusing on that, Suzie managed to distract them, saying she was a poor old lady now and would have to rest and be looked after until she got better.

'We'll look after you, Grandma,' Grace said, patting Suzie's face and giving her a kiss. Not to be outdone, George snuggled in on her other side. 'And you can read us stories…'

Suzie laughed, saying she could certainly do that. Their love and concern brought a lump to her throat, so much so, she had to blink hard to dispel the tears. Luckily, Sara rescued her, saying tea was ready in the kitchen, and after that they could watch their favourite TV programme.

To her mother, she said, 'A cup of tea, or something stronger?'

'A drop of brandy, if you have it?'

'Oh, by the way…' She indicated the beautiful display of flowers on the window ledge. 'These came for you yesterday. And a letter…'

– o –

The flowers and James's tender note touched a well of emotion, of love and guilt and sorrow. Longing for his presence, Suzie knew she needed to talk this nightmare through with him; but when they spoke next day, he sounded tired and depressed, even distant. She'd hoped he would suggest a visit, but it seemed he was busy. A crumbling church, sick parishioners, a homeless family Amy was trying to help – a whole army of problems he'd rarely mentioned before.

After that, as the days passed, she was at the mercy of every doubt in Christendom. Glad to be alive, yes, but even that paled in the wake of sadness and fresh anxiety about James. It was as though what she'd done in shutting him out had killed something, and she grieved for that as much as she regretted her actions.

Sara was still upset by what had happened, that much was clear. Upset by the whole situation, if truth be known. On one level she was more amenable towards James, but it seemed she still blamed him for kicking the whole thing off. Without him, she said, none of this would have happened.

'You don't know that,' Suzie retorted. 'It could have happened anytime, anywhere…'

'Yes,' Sara fired back, 'it could have happened last time you took off into the blue – after Dad died!'

Good grief, Suzie thought, did everyone's kids assume the mantle of parents beyond a certain age? Was she not allowed to have a life of her own? Even Jo was getting over-protective. Like Sara, she insisted on being informed in future. And like Sara, with regard to their brother's rejection, Jo's feelings could be summed up in just a few words: *It's his loss…*

Suzie could understand that, especially given the underlying message: *Are we not enough?* She'd tried to reassure them, but it was hard to explain. At heart, all she really wanted was the chance to say sorry to her son – she wasn't sure her daughters grasped its importance.

For James it was different, and, with time to think, Suzie was beginning to understand the drive behind his need to search. He had no one, whereas she had children and grandchildren. He'd never said so, and it wasn't something she often paused to consider – in the midst of a busy life it was easy to take her own family for granted. But being with George and Grace in the past few days had shown her how fortunate she was. She loved them and they loved her, but it was more than that. Like her daughters, they were the future and she felt privileged to be part of it. And to think she'd so nearly cut it short...

It was rare for her to spend more than a night in York, but now the children were part of each day, and she looked forward to them coming home from school. Little Grace was over her tonsillitis but still looking pale, preferring to sit with Grandma on the sofa and watch Teletubbies, while George was keen to have help with his Lego castle and innumerable tiny knights. Battles, that's what George wanted, while his poor father seemed to be involved in real-life ones at the office. Not to mention Sara, managing the shop and all the minutiae Suzie knew only too well.

Meanwhile, her own battles were internal. The only thing she could say about this enforced rest was that she was learning to accept what couldn't be changed. Nothing could be done, either about the broken ankle – which would heal in its own good time – or the fact that her son had said no, he didn't need her in his life. She was wounded to the core, but somehow, she'd have to learn to live with it.

Since leaving hospital, she'd done little but lie on the sofa with her leg in its boot propped up before her. With books or the TV for company, she was also trying to solve the mysteries of a new mobile phone – a challenge in itself – while between times, she'd been learning how to get about on crutches with a cannonball weight attached to her foot. Hard work, but after the second week, the desire to be back on home ground – whether she could manage alone or not – was growing with each passing day.

Although Sara protested when the subject was broached, Suzie knew her daughter would be glad to get back to normal. Clearly, help was needed, but with professional care set in motion, and her immediate neighbours in Felton notified, Suzie looked forward to getting back home.

— o —

Cathy was waiting when Suzie arrived with her son-in-law, ready to help a hobbling Suzie into the house. Pleased to leave her in safe hands, after a quick cup of coffee, Rob said he'd better be getting back to York.

For the two old friends, it was an emotional couple of hours, Cathy giving voice to her concerns, particularly about James. 'You say you haven't seen him since the accident – when is he coming up?'

'I don't know. I mean, we've spoken on the phone, but it's been strange – not exactly heart-to-heart. A bit stilted, to be honest. And he seems to be really busy at the moment...'

'Well, of course, you've been at Sara's.'

'Yes, but...' After a moment, she said, 'Oh, I don't know, Cathy, it's like there's a blanket of fog between us.'

'Neither of you talking about the elephants in the corner?'

With a half-hearted laugh, Suzie agreed.

Cathy's expression assumed that of a not-very-pleased mother with a recalcitrant child. 'And which elephant is it you're not talking about? The one where you dashed off without telling him, the fact that he saved your life, or the really big one? Your son's rejection?'

Amusement died. This was serious stuff, and suddenly, she wanted to cry. 'All three...'

Later, when Cathy had gone home and Suzie had crawled up the stairs, she thought about what her friend had been saying. In going to find her, James had no doubt saved her life, but in Cathy's view, the emergency had denied him so much else. If Suzie needed to be comforted, so did he. His hopes for the future had been blighted, but he hadn't been able to share it with the one person who mattered. He was grieving, and he was alone – probably with no one to confide in. More significantly, she said, he was a man, and probably not thinking straight anyway.

In suggesting they needed to meet as soon as possible, Cathy was right.

Next day, she phoned James to let him know she was back in Felton. Now she was feeling better, she said, she could see how crazy she'd been in just going off like that. 'Most of all, I want to see you, to be with you, talk to you,' she added. 'We haven't had much chance while I've been in York...'

He sounded very low, sighing as he mentioned Christmas coming up, admitting that he was dreading it already. Inwardly cursing the weight on her ankle, Suzie said, 'I'd come to you, but it'll be ages before I'm driving again. Are you sure you can't manage a night away before your Advent services get going?'

In the end James said he could probably manage Friday, if that was okay. But as ever he'd have to be back by Saturday evening.

'More than okay – I can't wait to see you...'

– o –

It had been a stressful few weeks since his return from Malham, and driving up from Oxford, the traffic had been horrendous. Reaching Felton, James pulled into the layby and sat for a moment before going on to Suzie's.

Behind the trees, the sun was setting in a blood-red sky. Needing a breath of air, he stepped out of the car and took a few minutes to walk around the churchyard, gazing at weathered memorial stones as he passed. For some reason, Uncle Harry sprang to mind, and James could almost hear his voice: *Never mind, lad, it'll all be the same in a hundred years. All we can do is our best for now...*

Surprised by the memory, comforted by it, he returned to the car and drove on to Suzie's.

The back door was unlocked. Going in, he met her in the hall, his pleasure on seeing her almost outweighed by the shock of this new Suzie, balancing on crutches, the injured ankle encased in a heavy-looking boot. Hugging her close, James hid his face as weeks of anxiety were washed away. It seemed like months since they'd been here together – the catastrophe between times a nightmare of grief and unknowing.

Between kisses, Suzie was saying how glad she was to see him, how sorry she was for putting him through such hell, and the words kept flowing even as they made it into the sitting room. It was as though Suzie had to tell him everything at once – how being with her grandchildren had made her count her blessings; how being stranded up there on Malham Cove had shown her how worthwhile life was. And how she'd thought she was dreaming when James appeared, not believing he was real until she was told who'd saved her...

'And there you were at the hospital,' she said at last, 'and we barely got chance to speak before Sara arrived and visiting was over...'

'I'm here,' he whispered, 'and we're together – that's all that matters.'

'Do you forgive me?' she asked. 'For just taking off like that – for being so horrible to you?'

Even though it still hurt, he smiled. 'Of course – how many times do you need me to tell you? You weren't in your right mind that day – no more than I was, dropping everything in Amy's lap and just tearing off in pursuit...'

Eventually, he got his mug of tea and began to relax. Despite the shocks and the sadness, it was good to be with her again, away from the awful emptiness of home. He would have liked to talk about it, but couldn't find the words. They were quiet for a while, but as Suzie turned to look at him, her smile turned to a frown. 'You look so down, love. Is it just the rejection or something more?'

James shook his head. 'Blighted hopes, I suppose. Hard to come to terms with.' As she nodded, he said, 'Mostly, I feel guilty. For starting this, for putting you through it. The thing is, can you forgive *me*?'

He could tell it was a difficult question. 'I don't know,' she admitted, and his heart sank. 'I want to, but the trouble is I still can't forgive myself. Do you understand? It hurts like hell.'

He drew her close and kissed her hair, feeling desperately sad for them both. Searching for the right words, he said, 'You did what you thought was right at the time. We both did. Only now, with hindsight, does it seem so wrong.

'I think I told you this before, but it's worth saying again. Years ago, when I was crippled by guilt, Father Allen asked if I believed in God. And when I said I did, he said, *Do you believe God can forgive you?* I had to think about it, but I said yes. And do you know what he said next? *Did I think I was greater than God that I couldn't forgive myself?*'

For a while he was silent, holding her while she absorbed his meaning. 'It lifted the weight – helped me to see the light...'

When she didn't respond, he said, 'You may find praying alone helps, asking God sincerely for forgiveness... But I think if you spoke to your local priest it would be better. I'm not the one, obviously – I'm much too involved.'

And I'm struggling too...

'But how do I do that when I can't get out?'

'Phone him – he'll come to you.'

Far from sure that she would, he was reluctant to press her.

– o –

Later, after they'd eaten, James returned to the subject of guilt and grief. 'The thing is, Suzie, we don't know why Dominic said no. I'm sure it has nothing to do with retribution, so stop thinking that. It could simply be that he's finding life complicated enough, without the additional stress of coping with you and me.'

'You think so?'

'I'm certain. In my work, I come across all kinds of problems, particularly sickness in the family, people struggling to cope. Marriages going wrong – kids going wrong. Sometimes, as Amy says, it seems people don't have time to breathe, much less find time for God.'

'Or the birth parents who gave them away...'

He sighed. 'Please, Suzie, try not to go down that road. Speak to your local priest – I'm sure it will help.'

'Who do you speak to?'

'Father Philip – I think I mentioned him before.'

'And what does he say about all this?'

James took a moment to reply. 'Not a lot, at the moment – I haven't seen him recently.' He couldn't bring himself to say that he too was in the wilderness just now, and with so much else on his mind he felt like a fraud every time he tried to pray.

'You should...'

Agreeing, not wanting to tell her that if he did, he was afraid he'd have to confess so much more, James changed the subject. 'Anyway, how's the ankle progressing? How long before this boot thing comes off?'

'Not sure. But I'll still need crutches for a while after that. They tell me it'll be three months before I'm walking properly again.'

'Three months?'

'Yep. As for driving – don't know. Makes life difficult, doesn't it? For you and me.'

'Certainly does – and with Christmas coming up, it's my busiest time...'

All at once, the thought of lonely weeks ahead was too much; he wanted to celebrate their reunion, not mourn its passing. Telling her to drink up, James gathered their glasses and took them through to the kitchen. Just for a moment, glancing at the family photos on the dresser, he felt the pangs of envy. Before misery could grip him again, he squared his shoulders and returned to the sitting room.

Suzie, fighting the sofa, was trying to get to her feet. Summoning a smile, he bowed and offered her his arm. 'May I assist, madame?'

Hopping, trying to keep her booted foot off the ground, she made it to the stairs. Amidst laughter, she refused help, insisting on crawling up while he carried the crutches.

'It takes me an age to get undressed,' she confessed breathlessly as they reached the bedroom. 'If you can give me a hand, it'll make it quicker…'

With tender amusement James set about helping her. She sighed with relief as he unbuckled the straps holding the boot's casing together, but he was shocked by the sight of her injured ankle. Stroking the line of her foot and calf, he kissed it gently before helping to remove her clothes.

Kneeling before her, he kissed the soft warmth of her thighs. She held him closer, until with a little gasp of pain and laughter, she stopped him, saying it was too much; she needed to lie down.

In bed, deep inside her with passion spent, he cradled her in his arms. As satisfaction sighed away, he couldn't help thinking of the last time he held her, trying to warm her, trying to keep her awake on that hard, cold stone. 'I thought I was going to lose you,' he whispered.

She stirred, pressing his hand against her breast. 'Don't…'

Holding her tight, loving her so much it hurt, James wanted to take her away, keep her always with him. The only way it could happen was if they were married, yet when he'd broached it some weeks ago, Suzie had stopped him, saying they couldn't talk about permanence when so much was in limbo. That was no longer true – they both knew it, and it hurt beyond bearing. Even being with her like this – so intense, so brief – had its own sharp edge, because he knew it couldn't go on. For a while, maybe, but not indefinitely.

– o –

Despite his fatigue, James didn't sleep well. He was aware of Suzie getting up in the night, returning to bed at some point, cold and shivering and trying not to wake him. He didn't mind, it was good to be close, to drift into dreams where they were safe at home and she was bringing an early morning cup of tea to bed... But then the door burst open, a man in clerical garb strode in, and suddenly it was a nightmare...

He woke, sweating, breathing hard, a shaft of sunlight in his eyes. For a second, he didn't know where he was, why all was quiet; but then he saw the room and Suzie, beginning to stir, beside him. Sighing with relief, he turned to her, breathing in the scent of her skin, pressing against her, finding comfort in every soft swell and curve of her body.

A while later, when they were both awake, he volunteered to make some tea. Reaching for his dressing gown, James swung his legs out of bed and padded across the room. By the door, he remembered his dream. 'Oddly enough,' he said, 'I dreamt you were bringing tea to me...'

Suzie laughed and raised her leg. 'No can do, sir – it'll have to be another time.'

Downstairs, waiting for the kettle to boil, he thought about the figure in his dream. He'd had a few nightmares since Suzie's misadventure, most of them graphic, but this was the first time the Archdeacon had invaded his sleep. Anxiety, he supposed, and impossible to mistake the message – it had been on his mind for weeks.

All down to the appointment he'd missed the day he headed for Malham. It wasn't Amy's fault that she'd had to stand in for him at that meeting, and thinking about the Archdeacon's summons a few days later, James shook his head. It was, in his superior's words, 'a little chat', but James – too shaken by events to dissimulate – had found himself confessing not just the reason for his absence that day, but the story behind it. He hadn't confessed to an affair, but the man wasn't born yesterday. To give the Archdeacon his due, he'd listened, and his reprimand had been a gentle one. All the same, he said, James must endeavour to put his life in order, particularly with regard to his relationships. Clergymen having affairs – even in this day and age – could not be looked upon lightly.

Banishing the Archdeacon, James made the tea, added biscuits to the tray and returned to Suzie. 'How are you feeling this morning?'

'A whole lot better,' she smiled. 'How about you?'

'Me too,' he said, setting the tray down and giving her a kiss. 'Did you sleep okay? I thought you were up during the night?'

'For a while, yes.' She patted her leg. 'Makes it difficult to get comfortable. Thought I'd get up – didn't want to disturb you.'

'Where were you? You were frozen when you came back to bed.'

'Oh, I was reading in the spare room,' she said, as he handed her a mug. 'Anyway,' she went on, 'how about a walk today? You'll need to push me round in the wheelchair, of course, but the sun's shining and it'll do us both good...'

'You're not thinking of mountain climbing, I hope?'

Suzie laughed. 'No, just a stroll around town. We could have a proper lunch out, and then you won't have to bother when you get home, and nor will I.'

Happy with that idea, he helped Suzie to dress and replace the boot, asking how she managed when she was alone.

'Well, I do manage, but it takes time – and when my carer comes in, she helps me shower and wash my hair. I've resigned myself to a strip wash on alternate days – it's easier...'

Saturday lunch in a local restaurant was good, and Heatherley – which he'd passed through but never explored – was an attractive market town. Although shoppers and some uneven pavements slowed their progress, it gave him time to notice not just the fine old church, but a huge Christmas tree sparkling with lights in the market place.

Christmas, he thought, feeling his mood slip; how would he get through it?

He was still feeling anxious as they made their way back to the car. Suzie suggested a detour to enjoy the view along the river, and as they reached it, James began to feel lighter. The wind had dropped, the trees were still, and further up the valley the sun was sinking into a colourful sky; reflections along the water made a perfect picture.

'I've always loved it here,' Suzie sighed. 'And today's been wonderful.' She turned to glance up at him. 'Thank you, James – you've made such a difference…'

Feeling blessed by her happiness, he bent to kiss her. 'No thanks needed – except from me to you.'

– o –

On the long drive home, James contemplated his spiritual state. A couple of weeks since his interview with the Archdeacon, and, apart from the reprimand, he'd advised James to see Father Philip. And for *advised*, James thought, read *instructed*…

He should make an appointment, but he knew what Phil would say. The thing was, he didn't want to hear it.

Forty-One

Suzie found herself thinking about James's suggestion to contact her local vicar, but from what he'd said about his own commitments, she hesitated, thinking the Reverend Foster would be too busy, what with three parishes to cover and Christmas on the horizon.

A few days later, her spirits were lifted by a call from James. With college closed and no lectures for the next couple of weeks, he said he could get away early on Tuesday next, and would like to spend them with Suzie. Always providing, he added lightly, she happened to be free…

'For you,' she laughed, 'I'll cancel the trip to Tangier,' and blew him a kiss down the line.

Cheered by the prospect of a happier few days in which James could relax without keeping his eye on the clock, she started planning at once. Months ago, he'd mentioned York, but at the time she'd been reluctant, and since then there hadn't been time. Now there was, and she was looking forward to showing him around and visiting the shop.

Although James was smiling when he arrived, she could

tell he was weary. She'd noticed last week that his face was thinner, the lines deeper; today, when he took off his glasses, the shadows around his eyes were darker than ever. He looked like she felt when alone, Suzie thought, weighed down by sadness and regret. She longed to bring him coffee and cake, make lunch for him – anything to make him feel cared for; but the difficulty of getting about, of handling kitchen things as well as crutches, made it almost impossible.

Hoping the prospect of a day out would cheer him, over a simple dinner that evening, she outlined her plans for York. 'And I thought we could end the day with Evensong in the Minster. Does that appeal?'

He brightened visibly. 'It certainly does. Although I hope for both our sakes it's a better day tomorrow.'

'We'll have a look at the forecast, later – see what's in store for tomorrow.'

As they finished eating, James glanced at his watch. 'I'll go and switch on.'

Following him, Suzie hobbled through to the sitting room. The TV summary wasn't brilliant, but as she said, York mostly enjoyed drier weather. 'Anyway, we'll give it a go.'

Before Suzie could switch off, he suggested watching one of the Inspector Morse episodes, showing on another channel. A repeat but he hoped she didn't mind; he'd been working hard to get away today, and just wanted to unwind.

'Not a problem, you know I love Morse…'

Reminded of their day in Oxford, they settled down together on the sofa. Like an old married couple, Suzie thought, smiling to herself as James identified various colleges shown on screen. Between spotting the murderer – they'd both seen it before – and trying to recall the motives, she noticed that James was drinking rather more than usual. And once the wine was finished, he moved to whisky.

She didn't comment, but she did wonder. And for the first time, when they went to bed, he didn't make love to her. He held her close and caressed her lovingly, but that was as far as it went. She didn't mind, but she did wonder why. Yes, he was tired, he'd said so, but drink was the most likely suspect. Not knowing what was going on down there in Norton Parva, kept her awake for some time.

– o –

The weather, next morning, was not encouraging. Beneath a bank of drizzling rain, the Ridge was invisible, Felton itself sunk in gloom. Rather like James himself, Suzie decided; saying little but clearly hungover. Refusing to let it spoil her plans, she insisted on toast and coffee, telling him to eat up and the day would get better.

Finally, with the wheelchair packed into the boot of Suzie's VW, and James at the wheel, they set off. Both kinds of gloom were soon left behind, and, as she'd predicted, across the Vale of York the sun was peeping through cloud, promising a better afternoon.

The city with its narrow paths was not entirely wheelchair friendly, but apart from the climb from the riverside car park, at least it was flat. For Suzie, tucked in with a travel rug and swathed in scarves, it was a whole new experience to be wheeled through streets she normally strode along – especially at child's height. To be disabled, she realized with annoyance, was to be almost invisible to the average passer-by.

She was no historian, but over the years she'd picked up enough to show James around – starting with the ruins of St Mary's Abbey and the King's Manor. Thanks to the wheelchair, the city walls were out, but as they passed through the medieval gate of Bootham Bar, suddenly the great west front of the Minster was ahead.

James was drawn to it, as she'd known he would be, but with lunch in mind she directed him into Stonegate and down a narrow alley to an ancient pub she knew he would like. Ordering coffee for her and a beer for himself, James came back with the bar menu. Steak and ale pie sounded just the thing, and an hour later, fortified for the afternoon, they turned again towards the Minster. Before they could reach it, she made another diversion down yet another alleyway; and as he laughingly protested, she said, 'Later, later – this is Coffee Yard. It leads to a medieval hall...' and went on to describe its discovery amongst a mish-mash of much later alterations. To Suzie the new building looked out of place with its light oak timbers and lime-washed walls, but James was impressed, saying he'd love to see what it was like inside.

'We can,' Suzie said, pointing to the next narrow opening. Hidden by shadows beneath the building's upper storeys, a plate-glass window revealed the hall's interior restored to its 14th century glory. James was delighted, saying the bright hangings reminded him of medieval illustrations. 'All it needs is the King and his courtiers, and piles of exotic food...'

He was still remarking on it as they emerged into a narrow, cobbled street of restaurants and dress shops. Turning her head, Suzie smiled up at him. 'And this is Grape Lane,' she said, 're-named by the Victorians.'

'From?'

'Grope Lane...'

'*Grope* Lane? So what was it,' he laughed, 'the medieval red light district?'

'Apparently so!'

They were both laughing as they carried on up the street. 'But I think you'll appreciate our next stop...'

By a row of jettied cottages, Suzie called a halt. 'Here we are – Lady Row, the oldest houses in York... And if we go down here,' she said, indicating yet another opening, 'we'll find a church I want you to see...'

The tiny, peaceful churchyard could have been mistaken for the Row's back gardens, a haven of quiet in the heart of the city. The church – no electricity, she informed him, and still using candles – was generally open to visitors, but as they arrived the attendant was just about to lock up.

'Not that you'll be able to see much,' the woman said, opening the inner door, 'you've left it a bit late...'

She was right, Suzie thought, wishing she'd brought James earlier; but in the fading light the east window stood out. The stone-flagged floor was uneven, so she elected to stay with the attendant while James looked around. As he made his way between the old box pews, she waited with bated breath, watching as he bowed before the altar and stood for a while, looking up at the saints depicted in the medieval glass.

Suddenly, he turned and smiled, and there was a spring in his step as he came back down the aisle. 'Have you seen it? There's a St George, up there, in full armour, vanquishing a red dragon.'

Suzie chuckled. 'Yes, isn't it wonderful? I was waiting for you to spot that!'

'What we've got at my church, is the Victorian version – but this is your genuine, fifteenth-century image...'

As James remarked on its survival, the attendant said York had been lucky, particularly during the Civil War. 'After the Siege, thanks to Lord Fairfax, Cromwell and his men didn't get chance to sack the city and destroy the churches.'

'Ah, Lord Fairfax – of course. Wasn't he a Yorkshireman?'

'Yes, indeed – too fond of the city to see it destroyed...'

As James and Suzie gave thanks for that, their companion held up the great iron key to the outer door, and smiling, guided them out.

– o –

James was still remarking on the ancient church as they emerged into the street. Shop windows were glowing in the dusk, Lady Row looking like an illustration from Dickens. A little further along, *The Wallis Collection* advertised Suzie's shop.

As she pointed to it, James chuckled in approval. 'I'm intrigued already...'

Taking a deep breath before they went in, Suzie hoped that yesterday's phone call to Sara had prompted her to be civil. As it transpired, she needn't have worried. Hugging Suzie and giving James a warm welcome, she introduced him to her assistant, and invited him to take a look around.

They were all chatting for a while, but as Millie led the way to the upstairs showroom, Sara asked about Christmas. 'Is Jo really thinking of bringing Marianne this year? If so, I don't know where I'm going to put them...' Lowering her voice, she said, 'And what about James? Will he be joining us too?'

Surprised, Suzie shook her head. 'I doubt it – he'll be far too busy...'

The bell rang and two women came in, Suzie moving her wheelchair to give them some space. As they went upstairs, James came down. 'Thought I'd better let Millie carry on...' Complimenting Suzie and her daughter on the collection, a moment later, he said, 'You'd do well with a branch in Oxford. It's the kind of shop visitors enjoy.'

'Well, you never know,' Sara replied, giving her mother an arch little smile. 'It could be something to think about...'

Frowning, Suzie looked at her watch and said it was time to go.

Outside, she was about to tackle James about that, but she was distracted by Sara's window display. Lamps and fabrics, baubles spilling like jewels from brass-bound boxes; and even a model galleon, together with an old book, resting on a tattered map.

At once, Suzie's jangled feelings were dispelled. 'Oh, look – it's *Treasure Island!*'

'Very clever,' James chuckled. 'And I know who she takes after!'

Above the street, Christmas lights were sparkling, but rounding a corner, they were faced by an open space. As James stopped, Suzie didn't need to ask why. Before them, illuminated against a darkening sky, the Minster's east end stood out like a Gothic jewel.

'Now that,' he said softly, 'is a sight to behold...'

Minutes later, they were being directed past the medieval kings and into the choir. Suzie's wheelchair had to be left by the steps, but the effort of stepping up and into one of the front choir stalls was worth it. As James knelt for a moment, she bowed her head, giving thanks for this day together.

Rising, he glanced at her, eyes shining, pressing her hand. 'This is special,' he whispered.

All was quiet, barely a rustle as the congregation waited. Suzie found herself gazing at intricate arches, at gilded carvings glowing in the candlelight. And then came the first whisper of sound, angel voices in the upper reaches, swelling in plainsong, growing closer as unseen choristers moved in procession towards the choir. Closer, clearer, until the youngest singers appeared before them, the purity of their voices sending a shiver down Suzie's spine.

They took their places, the air vibrating with sound as the first notes of the organ swelled forth, taking up the melody of a familiar hymn. It took Suzie most of the first verse to find her voice, but James, with his rich baritone, was note perfect. Thinking he must get lots of practice, finally she joined in, trying not to think of his wife as she flunked the high notes.

The service, sung by the priest and the choir, required little participation from the gathered congregation. Here were vestments, colour, soft lights and transcendent music, so moving, it clouded her vision. This is what James does, she thought, leading services in his church. Admittedly, with less stage management, but even so, it was a kind of revelation. With secret glances she noticed his lips moving through traditional phrases she recalled from her youth. She'd thought to please him today, show off a little; but this, the first service they'd attended together, was unexpectedly humbling.

Forty-Two

As it ended, James's glowing smile gave truth to his words, that it had been the perfect end to a perfect day. Reflecting on that as they drove towards home, Suzie was pleased it had been such a success. They were both in good spirits, James looking happier than he'd been for some time. Apart from the joy of the Minster service, he said he'd been impressed by Suzie's shop; by the time they reached Felton, he was talking as though opening a branch in Oxford was a real possibility.

As she struggled to get into the house, Suzie wondered where he was going with this. Had he forgotten her age, did he not understand the extent of the work involved? Trying not to sound irritated, once she was inside and seated, she told him she'd handed over to Sara because after ten years she'd had enough.

'Running a business is hard work. Not only have you to identify your customers and find the right stock, there's paying rent and rates and wages, and balancing the books. I don't know, it's like...' Struggling for comparisons, she said, 'Like if you were personally responsible for the upkeep of your church, and you had to pay for it through what the congregation hand over each week. You'd be out there, all the time, trying to get more people in.'

To her annoyance, he started to laugh. 'Well, the truth of it is, it's not so very different…'

'Yes, but your diocese isn't going to turf you out for not paying the rent!'

'No, but if it goes on too long, they'll either close the church completely or put it under a group ministry – like Leighton and the two Nortons. Like you, I'm responsible for income, as much as everything else.'

'But it's not the same as a commercial business, is it? Anyway, you know what I'm talking about. Just accept that I've been there, done that, and have no desire to start again.'

'Glass of wine?' James asked, extracting a bottle from the rack. As she nodded, he said evenly, 'In many respects, I've been lucky, assigned to a parish with a curate, and continuing to do what I do best. But things are changing. When I retire, the next incumbent will probably be running the three parishes single-handed. He or she won't be lecturing at the college, of course – they'll probably use someone from the university.'

'So where will you live?'

Handing her a glass of ruby-red merlot, he shrugged. 'When I sold up in Bristol, I bought a property to let in Oxford. With that and what Maggie left, there should be enough to buy a modest place somewhere.'

'But you haven't decided where?'

'Not yet, no.' Raising his glass to her, he said, 'I'm hoping – when the time comes – you'll help me choose…'

Heart racing, she didn't know what to say. *Was this a proposal?* Even as it flew through her mind, he gave a tentative smile and reached for her hand.

'I'm asking you to marry me, Suzie – will you?'

Releasing a breath, trying to keep calm, she said, 'I love you, James, you know that, but I thought we'd agreed...'

'I don't mean immediately – you'll need time to recover, of course you will, and get to know more about my part of the world. But it would answer so many problems – won't you at least think about it?'

Answer so many problems? For him, maybe – but what about *her* problems? And why this sudden urgency, when they'd edged around this issue before, and he knew how she felt?

'Why now?' At his blank look, she said, 'What's prompted this?'

He shook his head, trying to pretend he didn't know what she was talking about; but as he reached for his glass, Suzie placed her hand over the top. 'Come on, James, just tell me what's going on...'

Using words like *under the circumstances*, and *I didn't want to put pressure on you*, eventually he got to the heart of it. It began, he said, the day he'd abandoned everything to drive to Malham. That morning, he'd missed a meeting with the Archdeacon – afterwards, he'd been asked to explain why.

'Who exactly is the Archdeacon?'

'My immediate boss – under the Bishop.'

'You told him about us?'

'Not the entire truth, no. Just about our son. He probably guessed the rest.'

'I see.' She frowned. 'What did he say?'

'He reminded me of my commitment to God, and advised me to put my life in order.'

'Meaning?'

'Our relationship is – well, it's against the rules.' With a weary smile, he added, 'You know, the rules I said didn't apply to us...'

'Oh, for heaven's sake,' she exclaimed, 'that's ridiculous. We're not harming anybody – what's it got to do with him?'

James sighed. 'Nothing, at the moment. But if it comes to light, I could be accused of bringing the Church into disrepute. Preaching one thing, doing another.'

'Aren't you entitled to a personal life?'

'Sadly, no. Not like this, anyway.'

She stared at him. Even as he started to speak, she said, 'I don't believe this. I'm still recovering from a mammoth crisis, and you're doing it again – pushing me where I don't want to go!'

Denying that, he said sharply, 'I'm not pushing you anywhere – you asked what was on my mind, and I'm trying to tell you…'

'James, you've just asked me to marry you – in effect, to get yourself out of a hole!'

She heard muffled swearing as James nipped the bridge of his nose.

'Suzie, please. You know it's been on my mind – the words have been on my lips so many times. And you've deflected them. Not wanting to discuss it, telling me – and you weren't wrong – that we couldn't make decisions like that until we knew where we stood. Sadly, now we do know…'

'Maybe we do, but we're hardly in calm waters, are we?'

'No, and I'm deeply, heart-wrenchingly, sorry.' He looked up, holding her gaze. 'Ever since that day, you've kept asking me what was wrong. And for all the aforesaid reasons, I didn't tell you. I couldn't. But today,' he added, 'today, you were happy. And so was I. I thought, I hoped…'

She shook her head, looked away from the appeal in his eyes. 'I'm sorry,' she said tersely, 'but it's too soon. And anyway, you're asking me to choose between the life I've made for myself here – and the life of a vicar's wife in Norton Parva. I'm not that woman, James. And if you count the times I go to church, I can barely call myself a Christian…'

'There's more to Christianity than attending church every week.'

'Maybe you're right – but would your parishioners see it that way? And what about your Archdeacon?'

'You wouldn't be marrying him,' James said heatedly, 'you'd be marrying *me*. And if I don't have a problem with the fine detail of your beliefs, then why not?'

'You should be asking, do I have a problem with *your* beliefs?'

Shocked, he said, 'Well, do you?'

'Not your beliefs as such. Your work, I'm not so sure. I've barely glimpsed it. Yes, the village is beautiful, but I haven't a clue what goes on there. You're asking me to make a blind decision, James, but I'm too old for that. And what's more, this really *isn't* the right time!'

She stood up, fumbling with her crutches. 'I don't want to discuss it any more. I'm sorry, but I don't.'

– o –

Angry, hurt and disappointed, Suzie made her way to the sitting room. Switching on the TV, she told herself she didn't give a damn if he walked out now and went home. It was a while before he joined her, but when he did, he said gruffly that he was sorry, he hadn't meant to insult her.

Somewhat ungraciously, she accepted the apology. In silence, they continued to watch TV, James made some supper, and she began to unwind a little. By the time they went to bed, Suzie was trying to imagine where the relationship could go from here. She didn't want to lose him, but nor was she prepared to lie down beneath the steamroller of someone else's beliefs.

In bed, almost with the first contact, passion flared; but it was a desperate coupling, more like foes than lovers. Afterwards, James fell asleep almost at once, his arm still holding her close. As his weight became more painful than comforting, she pushed him away, hearing him murmur as he turned over. Lying on her back, she closed her eyes, trying to banish the question: *where do we go from here?*

There was a kind of weary familiarity to it; she'd asked similar questions while struggling with her marriage to Freddie. Once again, she was left with a sense of frustration, except that between her and James, it seemed nothing had gone right – ever. From start to finish, their relationship was a mess-up of misunderstandings, a history of two people whose language might have been Finnish on one side and Serbo-Croat on the other.

And now God was involved – a male God, obviously, or at least according to the Bible – and having grabbed James in a weak moment, wasn't about to let go.

Where was the earth-mother in all this? The female half of the equation, without whom nothing would get done, nothing would multiply, no one get fed? Without Mary, there'd have been no Jesus, and as for Eve – well, let's blame it all on the woman, why not? She tempted Adam and he was weak enough to fall for it. *Not my fault, sir...*

Religion, she thought, had a lot to answer for. Not least in this situation, which as far as Suzie could see, effectively transported her and James back to where they began. Back to the '60s, when she'd been the sinner, while James had literally zipped up his flies and walked away. Okay, to be fair, he'd paid for it in other ways – if he hadn't, he wouldn't be here in her bed. But religion was making a sinner of him now, and all because she, Suzie, wasn't ready to marry him. At least, not on his terms.

Would she ever be?

She didn't know. She honestly didn't know. The way she felt at the moment, she could have kicked him; and if it hadn't been for Malham, she might have done.

He did love her, no doubt about that. And yes, she loved him too, but it didn't excuse this situation. Every instinct said it was wrong to marry someone as a matter of convenience. Once the heady drug of passion waned, mismatched couples ended up in the divorce court. There had to be a willingness to accommodate the other half, be it the job, the kids or the way of life. Margaret might have been the perfect partner for James, but Suzie wasn't. She couldn't even *sing*, for heaven's sake – or play the bloody piano.

And could she live in the home James had shared with Margaret? It was clearly still hers, from the photos to the furniture, never mind the baby grand taking up a room to itself. Okay, the Church owned the building, but James couldn't move from there, not until he retired.

Why did this Archdeacon, whoever he was, have to stick his nose in? In the wake of everything else – their son's rejection, her instinctive reaction – this marriage question was all too much. And as for his suggestion that she open a shop in Oxford – that was the craziest thing ever. Did he not know her at all? Apart from anything else, she was still gasping like a fish at the end of a line, out of her element and stranded by injury. Couldn't he see that? Why couldn't he understand?

Tense beyond enduring, longing to toss and turn and pound the pillows, it seemed the ache in her leg amplified that in her mind. And then it was a real headache, pounding behind her eyes. She had to move, find the painkillers. Fumbling in the darkness, Suzie reached for her crutches. Trying to be quiet, she closed the bedroom door, switched on the landing light, and made her way downstairs on her bottom, step by step, until she reached the hall.

– o –

Disturbed by something, James woke, and after a moment or two realized Suzie was no longer there. He switched on the bedside light and waited for a while. When she didn't return he pulled on his dressing gown and went downstairs. He found her in the kitchen, making tea and smoking a cigarette.

'Oh, hi – would you like some tea?'

'I thought you'd given up?'

She waved the cigarette. 'Still had a few stashed away.' She reached for another mug, and when the tea was made, pushed it towards him. 'Couldn't sleep – sorry if I disturbed you.'

'It's okay. Want to tell me about it?'

'I don't know. I'm still confused – trying to sort things out in my head.'

'Try me.'

If she was confused, so was he – wondering how on earth all this had started. Maybe he wasn't fully awake, but he was trying to grasp her meaning – something about loving him, against his sense of what was right and wrong. Desire overcame scruples in Buxton, Suzie said – well yes, he could see that – but then she was talking about when she was a teenager, going with him to his room, giving him the wrong idea...

'What's that got to do with it?'

'No, don't interrupt, I'm trying to tell you something. About me being older now, and more cautious. I know how you feel, James, but don't you think we've both been guilty of using each other? As a kind of – I don't know – *pain-killer*, against all the stress we've been under?'

There was, James thought, something horribly familiar about that.

'The thing is,' Suzie went on, 'we're in an impossible situation – can't you see? You're eager for me to marry you, so we can go on being together – basically, so we can go on having sex without it affecting your job. And *because* of what you do, I can't spend time with you at your place, because it's unacceptable...

'Which leaves you, asking me, to make a blind decision on a lifelong commitment. I can't do that. Not at the moment,' she said, tapping the crutches, 'and yet you can't see it!'

'I can – I do,' he said distractedly. 'You're right – I'm sorry – I shouldn't have asked. I saw that amazing shop of yours, and got carried away. Grasping at straws...'

With a frustrated sigh, Suzie shook her head. For a while, they sat in silence. He drank his tea, wishing it were something stronger, despairing at the mess he'd made of everything. Dear God, he was so tired.

He was staring blankly at the table top when Suzie took his hand and said gently, 'I'm still grieving, love, and so are you – it's no time to be making decisions like this. If you were in your right mind, you'd understand.' When he didn't answer, Suzie sighed again. 'You know, James, it's all very well you saying I should talk to someone, but what about you? Isn't there someone you can talk to? That chap you mentioned – what was his name?'

'Father Philip,' he said dully.

'Yes, him. Haven't you been to see him yet? You were going to.' As James shook his head, she pursed her lips. 'I really think you should.'

Before they went back upstairs, Suzie rooted around in her medicine cupboard. 'Here, take one of these. They're only herbal things – pretty mild – but it might help you sleep.'

He didn't have the heart to tell her that a large whisky would have better effect.

Watching him as he swallowed the pill, she said, 'If you're on your own, you'll stand a better chance. I'll go in the guest room so I don't disturb you...'

– o –

It felt like a final rejection. Alone, staring into the darkness, his mind refused to let him sleep. Attacked by past and present, only when he turned did James feel the pillow wet beneath his cheek. Muffling his grief, he wept in earnest for the lost dreams, for the fantasy he'd woven from straws of hope. He might have found it hard to picture his son, but being with Suzie, falling in love, he'd clung to the idea that one day, they would be together. Not just the two of them, but with a son somewhere in their lives, sealing the bond between them.

For that, he'd abandoned his beliefs, drawn Suzie into a damaging relationship, and never considered the fallout. And yet she'd warned him – not just once but several times. Why hadn't he listened? What on earth had possessed him?

Sleep claimed him for a while, but it was no more than a light doze, punctuated with a repetitive dream of Suzie saying, *I told you so...*

Waking alone in Suzie's bed, reality flooded in with misery in its wake. She'd said they should take a break for a while. She'd said she hoped they could remain friends, but he couldn't see that working. The thing was, while ever he was telling himself he intended to marry her, he hadn't even felt guilty; at least not until the Archdeacon found the chink in his armour.

Suzie was right. He did need to see someone. And that someone was Phil.

Forty-Three

Suzie's mind was still chewing like a dog with a bone. It wasn't just her sense of outrage at such an untimely proposal, but concern for James's state of mind. If she was the one visibly injured by this situation, it seemed he'd been knocked senseless in other ways.

He thought she was being unreasonable, but she knew she couldn't marry him under these circumstances. And besides, over the last few years, she'd grown used to living alone. James might be lonely, longing for another wife to support him, but she liked her own space, the freedom to do as she pleased. How on earth would she cope in a Vicarage, with people calling all the time? When it was all boiled down, if the physical side was forbidden, it was folly to go on.

Even so, over the past few months he'd become part of her life – even to picture being without him was like another bereavement, one she wasn't sure she could bear. But no matter how she looked at it, Suzie couldn't find an answer. Except the one she'd already suggested – take a break, get back to more stable ground.

By the time James was moving about, she was dressed and downstairs, steeling herself for whatever was coming next.

When he appeared, he looked grey and haunted. Apologising for last night, he said she was right. It was indeed time he got himself sorted out. 'I've already spoken to Father Phil – he can see me later today, so I'd better be getting back.'

'What, now?' That was a blow. Despite everything, she didn't want him to leave. Not when they were still in the midst of things. That all this could have blown up out of a simple desire to show him the business in York, seemed crazy, monstrous.

James bowed his head, doing that thing he did whenever he was stressed, taking off his glasses and pinching the bridge of his nose. She wanted to knock his hand away.

'So when will I see you again?'

'I'm sorry, Suzie – at the moment, I've no idea.'

'Right.' Swallowing hard, she managed to say, 'Won't you have a coffee or something?'

He shook his head. 'Thanks, no. I'll stop somewhere.'

'Well then…' Her voice was a croak. 'Let me know when you get home – a text – just to stop me worrying.'

With a reproachful look, he said, 'Of course.'

He took his overnight bag to the car and came back to say goodbye.

Suzie struggled to her feet. A brief embrace and then he was pulling away like someone she barely knew.

As the door closed, it was as much as she could do to stumble into a chair and wonder what she'd done.

– o –

That afternoon, a message came through. *Reached oxford but will be out of touch for a while – James x*

No explanation. Suzie felt as though she'd been kicked.

Hours later, bursts of sobbing were still catching her unawares. Her mind was all over the place, going from James to her son, from her broken ankle to her broken heart; from the sheer inability to get about to the fact that she couldn't even take a shower without help. From time to time she forced herself to eat, but by Friday evening, even the snacks had run out. Anyway, she was sick of soup, sick of feeling sorry for herself, sick of weeping and sick of the empty house. What's more, the state she was in, she couldn't even go out for a walk, never mind run to James for consolation.

In the freezer she found a single portion of chicken curry. Defrosting that, heating it, boiling some rice, was the most she'd done for three days. Despite the effort, she felt stronger, and, with a glimmer of common sense, phoned her carer to ask if she could come in the following day. By the time she arrived, it was easier for Suzie to pretend she was okay. Not that Paula was fooled.

Giving Suzie a long, hard look, she said, 'Would you like breakfast first, or a shower?'

With a wry grin, Suzie opted for the shower. Having her hair washed and body sluiced was almost like washing the misery away. Dressed, with her hair dried and a touch of make-up on her face, she felt able to face the day.

That afternoon, when Cathy called to see how her friend was faring, she shook her head at the news. As ever, she was sympathetic, understanding the reasons why, even when she didn't agree with Suzie's decision.

'He's a good man, Suzie, and like I said before, he's been through the mill, same as you. It must be breaking his heart, having to choose between you and what he feels is his duty...'

But that didn't help.

Having talked things over, Cathy's advice was to make an appointment at the surgery, to ask if she could see a counsellor. Suzie almost laughed. 'Well, it'll be different from seeing a priest,' she said dryly, 'although I suppose they'll be singing from the same hymn sheet...'

– o –

On his arrival in Oxford, James had half-expected Father Phil to berate him for not seeking help earlier. But the priest seemed to grasp that James was on the point of collapse, insisting he spend the next few days at Pusey House.

At the time, James's head had been ringing with confusion. All he'd wanted to do was pour it out, make his confession and get back to work. It was Advent – almost Christmas with all those services. How would poor Amy manage?

'Not your problem, James. I'll phone the Archdeacon's office to let him know. He won't abandon Amy – or you. Trust him – he will have his resources. If you need to talk, I'll be available for a short period each evening. Apart from that, all you need to do is rest.'

As he took James's mobile phone away, the last thing Father Philip said before leaving, was, 'Focus on the silence...'

Easier said than done. But in chapel that first evening, the beauty of Evensong washed over him like balm. Attending again for morning prayers, he avoided the Mass. As Father Phil said, he needed to be sure of his sins before he confessed them. Only then would he be fit to receive Communion. Slowly, over the next few days, he began to feel an improvement. With simple meals provided and a simple room in which to sleep, he followed instruction like a child. He read the psalms, passages from the Bible and collects from the Prayer Book, the aim being to help him focus. Beyond that, his mentor said, James should simply listen to the silence...

As his thoughts ceased rampaging, James was able to see how skewed they'd been. If he hadn't followed his own inclinations – not just recently, but from the beginning – Suzie's injury might never have happened. Worst of all, in the guise of comfort, he'd persuaded her into a sexual relationship – which was not only against the rules of his job, it flew in the face of common sense. Love was one thing and lust another, but there was no such thing as free sex. It always came with a price for someone.

'And it's not as if I didn't know that,' James admitted one evening. 'From personal experience too – so how I could have let myself go so far awry...'

Father Phil stopped him. 'Don't castigate yourself, James. Try to be detached...'

'Of course.' Taking a deep breath, he tried again. 'It was comforting at the time, but I can see how our bonding took the emotional stakes so much higher – for both of us...' After a moment, he said, 'Given the age I am, I should have foreseen that when the crash came, it would be so much more damaging.'

Nodding in approval, Father Phil said James was getting there. 'And I'd like you to look at how you've been dealing with the pressure of those mistakes – drinking too much seems to be a factor...'

James shook his head at an image of himself, sitting in isolation like a priestly Morse, listening to opera and drinking himself into a stupor.

As he put it into words, the other man raised an eyebrow. 'Well, as you've discovered, alcohol doesn't just mask the problem, it compounds it.'

Before closing their discussion with a prayer, Father Phil said, 'Rather than dwelling on the wrong you've done, James, put it out of your mind for the moment. Tomorrow, try considering how you might put things right...'

That was the biggest challenge. No matter how he looked at it – and no matter how much it hurt – it seemed the best thing he could do was to leave Suzie alone. Suzie had said she hoped they could remain friends – but James was far from sure he could handle that.

When he mentioned it the following evening, Father Phil agreed. 'Friendship can be difficult in such circumstances – particularly in the beginning. It might be best to leave things as they stand for now. See this as an opportunity, rather than a punishment. Let your passion – and hers – subside. It will give her the chance to recover too. In the meantime, James, make your confession to Almighty God, and focus on the work you were called to do...'

Forty-Four

Suzie's GP saw the need for action. Writing a prescription, he also advised counselling; and if she could afford to pay privately, he said, it could be arranged to her convenience. But with a hospital appointment coming up, and Christmas almost upon them, Suzie decided to leave it until January.

She was going to Sara's for a few days over the festive season. Although she'd done little in the way of shopping for presents, she was looking forward to being with the children on Christmas morning. And Jo would be joining them on Boxing Day, for the first time with her partner, Marianne. Fortunately, they'd booked themselves into a hotel.

When they arrived, just before lunch, Jo & Marianne were eager to share their good news. An upcoming change in the law – another one, Suzie thought – was about to allow civil partnerships between same-sex couples. By this time next year, Jo announced with stars in her eyes, she and Marianne would be able to get hitched.

'It's not *marriage*,' she stressed, 'but it will come, I'm sure of it. The thing is, we'll be a legally recognized couple – and apart from all else, whichever one of us dies first, will be able to inherit the other's estate...'

Suzie was pleased for them, but somehow, thinking in terms of money and wills seemed to take the shine off romance. She told herself they'd been together for five years now, and they were both delighted, which was all that mattered.

'So, as from now, we're engaged. Come on, Marianne, show them...'

The ring – an amethyst surrounded by diamonds – was unusual and very pretty, and Suzie said so, hugging them both and offering her congratulations. She wished them a world of happiness – but if the huskiness in her voice was mostly due to Freddie's absence, moments later she was also thinking of James, wondering what her family's reaction would have been if she'd accepted his proposal.

That she hadn't was perhaps fortunate; apart from anything else, it would have stolen Jo's happy moment. Amidst the laughter and the champagne bubbles, Suzie sat back with a drink and a smile, playing the part of the old dear, content to let the youngsters celebrate.

Just before bedtime, the children were watching a film. Suzie barely noticed when it finished and changed to the news, but as Sara was ushering the little ones off to bed, Rob turned up the sound and drew their attention to the screen. Stunned by what was being announced, they gazed in silent horror. Far away in the Indian Ocean, a violent earthquake had occurred, wreaking devastation in the surrounding region. Worst affected seemed to be southern Thailand, where huge tsunami waves had brought death to thousands of holiday-makers.

The tragedy was shocking, emphasising the transience of life. To Jo and Marianne, who'd been in Thailand a couple of years before, it was particularly upsetting; as for Suzie, faced by all that death and destruction, she was thinking of her son and his family, and praying they were safe.

Two days later, on returning home, she picked up James's card. At first, the image of a Madonna and Child seemed purely seasonal, but as she read the attribution on the back, she gave a quirky smile. The painting was by a Renaissance monk, one who'd had his own difficulties with the rules of the cloister – *Fra Lippo Lippi*. Recalling Browning's poem, studied at school, Suzie shook her head. 'Well,' she murmured, 'at least you've kept your sense of humour, James…'

By contrast, the words written inside were so few, it was hard to tell if they were fact or fiction. He thanked her for her good wishes, said he was much improved and hoped she was too. All very formal, she thought with a sigh; but anything more, and she might have been tempted to phone him.

– o –

Released from the boot's imprisonment at the end of January, for the first few days Suzie was unbalanced. She still needed crutches for a day or so, and after that it was another couple of weeks before she could get about the house unaided. The aches and pains – in different places now – were exhausting, and yet she had to keep up the daily exercises in order to keep going. Although the walking stick was still needed outdoors, she hated the thing, felt like an old lady limping about, but there was no option.

Once she could drive, her weekly appointments with a female counsellor were easier to manage. Encouraged to be honest, at first it was good just to let the anger out, not just about James, but the whole situation. As Gail took Suzie back and forth, through old events as well as recent ones, there were many unexpected questions, most linking back to the events of 1964.

'After you'd given up your son for adoption, how did you feel?'

What a question! To Suzie's astonishment, tears sprang at once. Sobbing and gulping, her words were broken, making no sense, and yet her counsellor seemed to understand.

When she'd calmed down, Suzie found herself talking about her mother.

'Mum kept saying, *It's just one of those things.* Like I'd broken a cup or something. Making it sound so trivial. As for Dad – he said to put it behind me, look to the future...'

'And did you?' As Suzie nodded, Gail said, 'A heavy burden to carry around.'

'Managed it for a year,' Suzie said, 'before I cracked.'

'Hardly surprising,' came the comment. 'You'd lost your baby...'

Which made Suzie sob again.

– o –

Thinking about it later, Suzie could see Gail was right. Like Sara had said months ago, it was a bereavement – her baby had gone, as irrevocably as if he had died. No wonder she'd needed to grieve. And again, last autumn, his denial – his rejection – had brought another death. The death of hope.

Under Gail's questioning, Suzie could see she'd never been good at letting things out. Her parents had both died suddenly, albeit some years apart. She'd kept going because her daughters were devastated. She'd needed to comfort them.

Gail said, 'And who comforted you?'

It was a shocking question. In trying to answer, only then did Suzie realize that Freddie had tried; but beyond the initial shock, Suzie had simply squared her shoulders and carried on. Busy with work, Freddie had assumed she was okay; although after a month or so, in each case, Suzie had been physically ill, floored by whichever virus was going around at the time. After Freddie's death, instead of taking time to weep, she'd started planning her trip to Spain. And then literally walked away from it all.

She could see the pattern. This time, however, there had been a difference. Again, she'd tried to run away, but in being laid low at once, she was the one needing care and attention.

She couldn't deny that, Gail said; and yet she'd rejected James, the one person who shared her grief. Suzie protested at that, saying it wasn't the love she'd turned down, but the terms on which it was offered. Her counsellor asked why the terms were so bad. Why was she so reluctant to commit herself?

'Because it felt like I was being forced – again!'

The questions felt like scalpels, exposing old, unhealed wounds. As past and present connected, one rejection linking with another, she sobbed like a repentant sinner.

But she didn't change her mind.

Forty-Five

Life cooped up in Felton in mid-winter, was depressing. As an antidote, Suzie tried to keep busy, but her heart wasn't in the restoration work, and de-cluttering had its limits. She played music to cheer herself up, singing along with all her old favourites. Simon & Garfunkle were great, until the lonely defiance of *I am a Rock*, brought a lump to her throat. After that, the wisdom of McCartney's words in *Let It Be*, really did make her weep.

Even the early Beatles had their moments, although it wasn't until she was playing the Sgt Pepper CD that she was transported back to that time – London, 1967 – when she and Freddie were living together and planning to marry. Inspired to search, a few minutes later, she dug out some of some of Freddie's old drawings, and suddenly wanted to try something herself. Just for the challenge, just to see if she still could.

She arranged some objects – a jug, a plate, a dish – on her table. Trying to see how they related to each other, shifting them slightly for better effect, at first it didn't occur to her that she was obeying instruction from decades ago. Or that years of watching Freddie had developed her eye for what worked and what didn't.

Her first attempt was an outline, and the thrill she felt at being able to describe a curve was like a shot of cocaine – she could still do it! Hand and eye were still working together – she wanted to shout for joy. After that, she was hooked. Hours flew by as she drew different things in different styles. With pop songs from the past urging her along, she went from pencil to charcoal, pastel to paint; and having raided Freddie's materials, didn't want to stop. Practising with paint – once she'd produced something that pleased her – was like raising two fingers to the ghost of Rod Winter.

'No, Rod *Winterbottom*,' she said and started to laugh. That moment in the pub with Freddie kept her chuckling for quite a while. With only herself to please, she felt free, no longer imprisoned by the house, the weather, or impossible goals.

One day, she persuaded Cathy to sit for an hour while she drew her. The first attempt wasn't brilliant, so she discarded it, but on the second try she managed something passable. Anyway, Cathy liked it and insisted on taking it away with her. After that, Suzie started drawing herself. With the long mirror from her bedroom propped up near the window, she looked at herself – really looked – for the first time in years. Not only had her body become flabby with lack of exercise, her face showed lines of suffering. She drew portraits expressing that; portraits with all the anger, sadness, and longing she felt inside.

– o –

Even so, it wasn't enough. Suddenly, much as she had when returning from the Camino, she had a desire to record the events of last year with a view to making sense of them. When she mentioned it to her counsellor, Gail said she'd noticed a more positive attitude developing over the past few weeks. This creative spirit was a sign of healing. If she wanted to write, then she should do it.

Where to start, though?

In the end it seemed best to start at the very beginning, since Freddie was a part of her story as much as James. *Just get it down*, Jo the journalist had said after the Camino; *you can sort it out later…*

Writing, Suzie found, was less upsetting than talking about it. Writing put events at a distance. Like drawing and painting, she was the observer, the recorder, going in close to look at details, stepping back to see the whole picture. It was personal, so it didn't matter how or what she wrote; and maybe some kind of sense would emerge by the end. She wrote something most days, but not obsessively. With the first signs of spring, she began to go out walking. Still using her stick, but, having regained her confidence, she felt able to venture a little further each day.

At Easter, instead of a card to James, Suzie sent one of her sketches, a small one of a gnarled hawthorn trunk she'd done whilst out walking. As she said in her note, it was just to let him know she was making progress.

He responded a few days later with one showing Oxford's dreaming spires. His enclosed note said he treasured her drawing: *particularly as it illustrates how I've been feeling of late. Much better now it's joyous Easter Day – the sun is shining and the daffodils are in bloom beyond my window. Best of all, it's been good to hear from you. I'm pleased you're making progress and walking in the light – as I aim to do each day.*

Walking in the light – Suzie liked that phrase, it reminded her of spring and rebirth, the surge of hope after the bleak months of winter. Any weather was welcome now, because she was out there, experiencing it. Reminded of the Camino – the occasional wild storms, morning light in the mountains, the peace she'd found in the unfamiliar landscape of northern Spain – she pulled out her book to read some of the descriptive passages. It was good to remember how healing those weeks had been.

James had signed his note with love; and she felt the familiar tug of longing and regret. But no, she would keep in touch as she'd promised, no more than that. Maybe when she'd finished writing – when she'd recorded the anguish and quite literally put it in a box in the attic – maybe then she would feel able to see him again.

– o –

In May, she bought two birthday cards, one for James and one she would have liked to send to her son. They stood on her workroom table for several days, a deliberate reminder of what once had been, what couldn't be, and what James had offered.

She needed to be able to look at what they represented, until she could accept that the measure of her love for her son had been her desire to do her best for him. It was reflected in the anguish she'd suffered throughout his first weeks of life. She had survived, and evidently, so had he. And perhaps, as her counsellor suggested, Dominic's rejection of Suzie was simply because he'd been happy with his adoptive parents and had no desire to hurt them. Like a lifebelt in a rocky sea, she'd been clinging to that for months.

In all of winter's storms, she'd proved, if proof were needed, that she could survive. She had good friends and a loving family; she had her health, and her strength was returning.

Signing the card to James, she addressed the envelope and walked down to the post box. There, she was faced with the church and what it represented – James's life, her inability to accept it, and the wedge it had driven between them. She'd been living with a sense of antagonism, but now even that was slipping away.

– o –

In Norton Parva, there was a card from Amy and several from his parishioners. Proof, if it were needed, that he was held in some affection, and – James hoped – doing a reasonable job in caring for his church family. But in recognizing Suzie's handwriting, he was overwhelmed. Thinking of her, remembering their son, James prayed for all of them.

The pain was bearable now. A sign that he was recovering, that last autumn's traumatic events were slipping into the past. James glanced at Suzie's drawing, framed now on his desk, and recalled his first reaction to it – that he was as bent and twisted as the poor old hawthorn. But at last, thanks to Father Philip, he'd begun to straighten out.

James had been seeing him throughout the winter, taking a silent retreat when he could, and keeping up – mostly – with the spiritual exercises. If Christmas had been difficult, the weeks of Lent had been a long, hard path. Times when he'd asked himself what it was all about, times he'd been tempted to give up, retire, and attempt to claim Suzie back; but then he'd think of Maggie, and others he still ministered to, suffering from terminal illness. Thanking God for his health and strength, he'd managed to push the self-centred complaints aside.

He must have spent hours in church contemplating the crucifix; not just the physical pain of such a death, but the temptation Christ must have gone through beforehand, knowing he could have escaped it. Even, as James had once explained to Suzie, simply by walking away. Jesus didn't have to cause trouble in Jerusalem at such a time – the fact that he did, was deliberate. Jesus had something to prove: that each man and woman was important in the eyes of God; that a life lived according to a set of rigid and outdated rules was wrong…

And that was where the doubts would creep in; when he had to remind himself that Christ did not reject the Ten Commandments, just the pettifogging rituals that enabled the wealthy to lord it over the poor. James had to remind himself that Christ's message of love said that sometimes you had to sacrifice what you wanted, what you longed for, in favour of the greater good.

Right. But there had been times when he questioned everything, from Christianity in general to his minor part in spreading its message. He'd even wondered if he should have chosen to be a monk, cutting himself off from the love of women entirely. Father Phil had smiled at that. In another low moment, when James said he'd had enough of struggling with right and wrong and perhaps he should retire, the priest had firmly rejected it.

'You are what you are,' Father Phil had said. 'The man Christ called to follow him. The sum of your experience – good and bad, both now and in the past – is what makes you the priest and teacher that you are. Believe in yourself the way God believes in you – the path will straighten, become smoother…'

And he was right. The path was becoming easier, he'd stopped fighting loneliness, and was starting to accept that with Christ by his side, he could carry on.

– o –

It was some weeks later that Amy commented on how well James was looking. They were at Norton Magna's church fête, an annual fund-raising event that fought hard to compete with the little town's Saturday market. It was Amy's second year of supervising the team of organisers, and her success was as clear as the sun on this beautiful day.

Surveying the stalls with their bright awnings, the marquee serving teas to the accompaniment of a local jazz band, James beamed with approval. Noting the people still coming in with children of all ages, he said, 'I can barely imagine the work that's gone into all this, Amy – you've done really well…'

'Oh, not just me, James – it's these amazing women! The talents they have – and the way they get the men organized – you wouldn't believe it!' Laughing, she shook her head.

'Yes, but you've given them back their enthusiasm – that's the important bit.' Glancing around, he spotted Amy's husband and son, one on the book stall, the other serving teas. 'And I see you've persuaded Nick and Josh to get involved as well.'

'That wasn't easy – not in the midst of the F1 season – you know what Nick's like, has to watch every single race and the qualifying too!'

'Ah well, I suppose cars are his business, after all.'

Smiling, agreeing, Amy patted his arm. 'Can I just say – in the midst of all these compliments – that it's really good to see you looking so well. You know, I was quite worried about you in the winter.'

'Were you?' Deeply touched, James felt his face grow warm.

'I know you don't want to talk about it – it's just that it's good to have you back.'

'Thank you, Amy – it means a lot...'

– o –

Her words proved a much-needed boost to his morale. Appointments with Father Phil had decreased to one a month, more in the nature of a check on James's progress, with the occasional piece of advice where needed. It seemed the Archdeacon was also cheered by James's dedication, particularly the efforts made with regard to the West Window.

Throughout the year, Norton Parva's PCC had been organizing their own fund-raising, and by the autumn, aided by some national grants, the window had been removed by a firm of church glass restorers. How long it would take, James was not sure – six months at least was the estimate – but it should be back by next spring. In the meantime, the west end of the church was dark, the empty space blocked by substantial woodwork. James was leaving church after saying Morning Prayer, when he paused to look up at the wood. For some reason it seemed significant, but he could not have said why. Like a blank canvas, Suzie might have said, waiting to be filled with colour.

– o –

Needing a break from the heavy stuff, Suzie left her computer to go for a short walk. Air and exercise, that's what she needed. Over the past few months she'd discovered it worked well – whenever she got stuck, a walk allowed something in her subconscious to work out what should come next. When she returned, it was not to her office but her workroom. Something about the self-portraits reminded her of… What was it? Suddenly she remembered those paintings of Freddie's. What had she done with them?

In the early days, in London, they'd hung in his studio, but once the girls started bringing their friends home, Suzie had insisted on putting them away. In this house, they'd lived in the attic for years. Returning from the Camino, ready at last to sort out Freddie's things, she'd found them, only to hide them away again. And there they were – at the back of the old built-in cupboard.

Dragging them out, blowing off dust and cobwebs, she propped them up against the wall. One, painted just a few months into her relationship with Freddie, showed her with long dark hair, reclining on a couch like some modern odalisque. Her expression, Suzie thought now, was slightly ironic, with a lift to one eyebrow which seemed to ask why she was sitting there, completely starkers, when she had better things to do. In this painting, the slight sag of her breasts was clear; not so in the later one, done when she was six months pregnant with Jo. There, her breasts were full and round, as was her belly – it was a celebration of expectant motherhood, a woman more than pleased with her lot.

Dear God, the joy of being pregnant again! How wonderful it was, how special – and the birth, so easy. The joy as this beautiful baby was placed in her arms – Freddie, awestruck, and herself a confident mother, knowing, just knowing, all that she needed to do… She played music to her baby, picked her up often, fed her when she was hungry, cuddled her when she was not. And Mum and Dad were over the moon…

The only regret she had with darling Jo, was in not breast-feeding her – she should have done. But by the time sweet little Sara was born, breast-feeding was back in fashion again. And that was why Freddie had painted this third picture, showing Suzie with Sara at her breast.

Overcome, she marvelled again at his talent. This was in the style of a Madonna and Child, even to the draped blue shawl, partly hiding her face. Softer, less a portrait than an expression of love – between mother and child, between the painter and his subject…

Suzie sank into a chair, wanting to weep for all that was lost. Not just Freddie but James, and her first-born son.

Thank God for creativity, she thought as she pulled herself together. She was getting better, seeing the light as well as the shadows. Unlike fiction, life had no happy endings, but looking back, setting it down on a page, was a bit like drawing and painting. To do it, you had to put everything in perspective.

Forty-Six

The first day of November and the Feast of All Saints. The trees in the churchyard were shedding their leaves in earnest now, and somewhere close by a garden fire was burning. Soon it would be Bonfire Night, that herald of winter. Assailed by memories of a year ago, James shook his head and went inside. At least it was a fine morning. Once he was through the paperwork, he'd get his boots on and go for a walk.

He was yawning, stretching, thinking it was time for a coffee when the doorbell rang. In the moment before he reached the door, he seemed to recognize the silhouette beyond the glass. *Suzie?* Disbelieving, heart pounding, he grasped the handle and wrenched the door open.

He stood there for several seconds, bereft of words, unable to move.

'Hi, James.' With an uncertain smile, she said, 'Sorry to startle you like this...'

Jerked into action, he stood back. 'No, no – come in, come in.'

Closing the door, he couldn't stop looking at her; as though if he did, she would simply disappear. 'Why?' The word was more of a whisper.

She shrugged. Again, the smile, but brighter now, almost teasing. 'It's been a while, hasn't it? Thought I'd surprise you.'

A short, involuntary laugh released him. 'Well, you've certainly done that.'

Not quite touching her arm, he ushered her through the hall and into the sitting room. He found he was stammering as he tried to formulate some opening words.

'How are you? Are you here for long – another auction, perhaps?'

'Not today, no. But I tell you what, James, I'd love some coffee?'

'Yes – of course!'

In the kitchen, for a long moment he leaned against the sink, breathing hard, eyes shut, trying to control the racing of his heart. His hands were shaking as he filled the kettle and plugged it in. *Why was she here?*

Spooning instant granules, adding the water, somehow, he managed not to spill it as he took the coffee mugs through on a tray. 'I can't quite believe this, Suzie – its so good to see you.'

'Good to see you too,' she admitted, bestowing a happy smile. 'I was praying you'd be in – not off lecturing somewhere.'

He shook his head. 'No, that's tomorrow. You're looking well – walking again – last time I saw you, you were…'

'On crutches, yes – don't remind me. Thank God that's over.' With a little shudder she reached for her bag. When she looked up, her eyes were shining. 'It really is over, James. Yesterday, I was in Leeds…'

Dumbstruck, he could only watch as she withdrew an A4 envelope from her bag and passed it across to him. He took it as though it were alive. 'What is it?'

'A letter. Two letters, in fact. Read them – just read them.'

He stared at her, mind reeling, his voice a whisper. 'From our *son?*'

As she nodded, James took off his glasses and rubbed at his eyes. The emotion was too much. With an effort he managed to say, 'Read them to me – I can't.'

She came and knelt beside his chair. Taking the envelope, she set it down and put her arms around him. 'It's all right, James – it really is…'

When he was calmer, she took out several sheets of paper and began to read from the first typewritten note. '*Dear Suzie, I am your son Matthew – my friends call me Matt. I have to say I'm good with computers but not much good at writing. My daughter Karen is the writer in our family, so I've asked her to tell you why it was impossible to get back to you last year. I'm so sorry. Maybe we can meet up some time? I hope so – Matt…*'

Moved by those few words, taking the page to read for himself, James said huskily, 'Matthew – it's a good name.'

'Isn't it?' Suzie chuckled. 'The surname's Armitage – a good old Yorkshire name, if ever there was one! Here – this is Karen's letter…'

James gasped as the address caught his eye. '*Chipping Norton?* But it's less than an hour from here!'

'I know, I looked it up – isn't it incredible? Do you want to read it yourself?'

His fingers were trembling as he took the pages from her. The girl – his granddaughter, James realized with a shock – began her story with a brief introduction.

Hi, I'm Karen. I guess you must be my sort of grandparents, which is a bit weird because we already had four when we were growing up. Anyway, Dad wants me to explain what was happening when he heard you were looking for him, so here goes.

My Dad's great, he really is, but it's been a crap couple of years. Probably longer than that, but the point is, it was a really bad time when you got in touch. He didn't even tell us about it until a few weeks ago.

Dad's CV says he's an automotive engineer, which could mean anything, so I'll just say he works in Formula 1. He designs and modifies computer programmes that make the cars go faster. He used to work at the factory and that was okay because he used to be home every night. Crazy hours sometimes but Mum could cope with that. But then Dad got promotion to trackside engineer. He had to travel all over the world in the F1 season, to all these different countries, and sometimes we didn't see him for weeks. When he did come home, he hardly had any time off and then he was away again – to the next race.

It was really tough on us, Mum especially, and my brother Nicky – he's 15 now – was having a hard time at school. What made everything worse was that Granny and Grandpa – Dad's parents – were both quite ill. Grandpa's always been a bit strange, but he got worse with his dementia, and Granny's diabetes was making her ill too, and she couldn't handle him on her own. Mum was helping out as well as working – she's a nurse, by the way – and Dad was hardly ever there.

Overcome, unable to read further, James removed his glasses and wiped his eyes. He felt Suzie's hand on his shoulder, gently stroking his back. After a while, swallowing hard, he picked up the pages and resumed.

Mum wanted him to give up the travelling, but his team had a really brilliant car, and it looked like they might win the championship this year so he couldn't let them down. Then Mum said he wasn't thinking of his family, who really needed him – so they split up and Dad went to stay with Granny and Grandpa. It was a tough time for all of us.

Then at the end of last season Dad heard someone was looking for him – his birth mother. He didn't tell us because he says he couldn't even think about it, there was too much going on.

We've always known Dad was adopted, so that part wasn't a shock to anyone, it was just a really terrible time. He says he's always wondered about who you were and why you had to give him up. As you can probably imagine, that made it even harder for him to say no.

Anyway, what happened was he got Grandpa into a care home, to make life easier for Granny, but then just after Christmas, just as she was starting to feel better, she got a really bad dose of flu. She died in hospital two days later. We were all so shocked and it was an awful time for Dad. Poor Granny didn't deserve that, and Dad was really upset.

In February, he was back travelling with the team again, and he says he was glad he had to work, because at least it took his mind off it. They didn't win the championship this year after all, so that was a great shame. But at least he can give up travelling now, and he's going back to proper hours at the factory. Best of all, he and Mum have got back together, and we're a family again.

Grandpa is still in the care home, but at least he doesn't know what's going on, so Dad doesn't have to tell him. It won't upset him like it might have done. It's not like my Dad needs another set of parents or

anything, but he would like to know where he came
from and if he has brothers and sisters.
    Like Dad says, I hope we get to meet you soon.
    Best wishes, Karen

With his arm around Suzie, James was too moved to speak. He re-read Karen's words, trying to absorb the life they suggested. All these years, knowing nothing, and suddenly there was so much to take in – and all through the pen of his granddaughter.

'Our granddaughter,' he said wonderingly, 'and imagine, we have a grandson too...'

Suzie turned to him, burying her face in the crook of his shoulder. 'But oh, that poor family!'

'I know – but look, things are improving, she says so...' After a moment, he started to laugh. 'A Formula One engineer – it's incredible!' Thinking of Amy, and her husband's passion for the sport, he shook his head. 'She'll never believe it.'

'Who won't?'

'Amy – when I tell her.' Laughing, he explained about her husband. 'Don't worry, I'm not about to tell all and sundry – it's between you and me for now. But I can just see Amy's face!'

And then Suzie laughed too, telling him that Sara had been equally stunned. 'Rob's the same. It's the noise – and the frantic commentators. Why is it men love that sort of thing, and women hate it?'

'Fast cars,' he chuckled. 'Boys' toys.' A moment later, he said, 'So you have told the girls?'

'Oh yes – I went straight to York from Leeds. We had to tell Jo over the phone, of course... But they were so pleased for me,' she said huskily, 'and quite understood when I said I had to come and tell you in person...'

Moved by their generosity, James hugged her; he didn't have words to express how thankful he was for her presence.

'But you know,' Suzie remarked a little while later, 'our son must be awfully bright to be able to do that kind of work.'

Picking up Matthew's note, studying the brevity, he said, 'I wonder if he's dyslexic? Struggling with words, but having compensating talents? They say it often happens.'

'You could be right,' she agreed. 'But if he is, he'd have needed guts and determination to get where he is today.'

Thinking about this stranger, his son, James shook his head. 'He must have an extraordinary mind – where does that come from, I wonder?'

Smiling, Suzie patted his hand. 'Come on – what were you expecting? Another historian in the family? I thought he might be artistic, creative – but Karen doesn't say so. In fact, if we're talking inherited talent, the closest I can think of, is my father. Dad wasn't a genius, but he was an engineer, and he certainly had a mathematical mind...'

Reflecting on that, James nodded. 'Oddly enough, my father was like that too. Statistics, strategies – chess. And a phenomenal memory.'

'Well, then – there we are, it's jumped a generation.' After a moment, she said, 'And after all my anxieties, Matthew was lucky, wasn't he? Getting an adoptive father who was also an engineer...'

Overcome by emotion, she clung to him. James knew why – it could have been so very different.

'I wonder what he looks like,' he murmured, 'who he takes after?'

'Ah, well,' Suzie chuckled, pulling away and reaching for the envelope. 'I can answer that...'

As two photographs fell into his hands, James laughed in astonishment. The uppermost looked like a school photo, a teenage girl with a beautiful smile and rippling red hair. 'Pre-Raphaelite hair!'

'I know, isn't it lovely?'

'I can't see the colour of her eyes,' he said, peering closely, 'but I bet you anything, they're like yours...'

'Maybe. But here, just look at Matt...'

In a shirt emblazoned with logos, he was leaning over a computer desk, turning to smile at the camera. Short-cropped hair, and a strong face that seemed somehow familiar.

'He's got dark eyes, like you – but he reminds me of my father,' she said. 'A much younger version, of course.'

'Mine too,' James said a moment later. 'Isn't that odd?'

Laughing, Suzie shook her head. 'Not at all. My parents – and Freddie's – used to look at their granddaughters and tell us they were just like various members of *their* families.'

'Heredity,' James mused, 'strange how it works...'

Only when he pictured Matt and this forthcoming meeting, did he find it slightly daunting. In his experience, scientific minds tended to be set in opposition to people like himself. James could understand why, but sometimes their attitudes were offensive. At best, he was often viewed as a kind of relic from a distant age.

'Oh, don't worry,' Suzie said. 'When we do get to meet him, there'll be masses to talk about. He'll want to know all about us, and we'll be asking about his wife and family. He's not going to go out of his way to be rude, now is he?'

James hoped not.

– o –

For the moment, Suzie had different concerns. In her letter, Karen hadn't mentioned the one Suzie had written to be lodged with the National Contact Register, so she was unsure how much they knew about herself and James.

Having fetched her computer from the car, she copied Matt's email address into the server and paused. 'What do I say?'

James had already jotted down a few words, so she used them to rough out an email to their son.

Dear Matt, thank you for contacting me – words can't express my happiness. As you guessed, last year's message was something of a blow, but having read Karen's lovely letter, I fully understand. This year can't have been easy, either – a sad and difficult time, I imagine, for both you and your family. So I really appreciate hearing from you now...

Suzie went on to say where she lived. Explaining James, she added that he was now the vicar in Norton Parva, as well as lecturing at the nearby Anglican training college. They had remained in touch since starting the search, and for the moment, she, Suzie, was staying locally...

'Seems a bit basic – do I need to say anything else?'

'Only that we're looking forward to meeting them in person, and hope it can be soon...'

Adding her mobile number and James's words to the draft, Suzie rounded it off by saying she hoped Matt would call them soon to arrange a get-together.

At the last minute, as she was copying the final draft into an email, something else occurred to her. 'Should I attach a photo, do you think? So they'll recognize us when we do meet?'

'Good idea.'

Searching her files, Suzie found the best one. A picture of the two of them, taken last summer near Oxford. When James saw it, he frowned. 'Why don't I recall seeing that one before?'

'Because I didn't send it to you...'

Until that moment, there had been no hesitation; but now Suzie felt scared, about to be judged by people she and James had never met, people who were immensely important to them both. Would it be a good meeting? There was so much to learn about this new family – especially what life had been like for her son as a child.

And now he's Matt, not Dominic...

The change of name, she thought, emphasized the years of not knowing. The distance between her baby and this man, this stranger...

James was standing at her shoulder as the cursor hovered over the send button. As though he read her mind, he said, 'I think we can assume he had a happy childhood, otherwise the two families wouldn't have stayed so close.'

Glancing up at him, she could see he was tense, as anxious as herself. She gestured at the computer. 'Are you sure this is okay?' As he nodded, she took a deep breath. 'Well, then – here we go...'

With the click of the button, all the excitement that had kept her going since she'd had that phone call from Laura, was gone. She felt deflated, weak, and horribly vulnerable. She looked around and it was like waking from a dream, as though until now she hadn't noticed where she was. Somewhere she'd said she would never be again.

As she covered her face, wondering what James must be thinking, Suzie felt his hand gently touching her head. A surge of confidence flowed through her, and something was saying all would be well. So profound, it brought a well of gratitude in its wake.

Silently, James moved away. When she looked up, he was seated nearby, his dark eyes warm with love and tenderness. Smiling through tears, for the first time Suzie noticed how much younger he looked. Since their last meeting a year ago, he seemed to have shed a decade.

'All we need now,' he said softly, 'is a little faith...'

No longer fearful, she nodded. With love and respect, things would work out. A little give and take on both sides, and with the help of her daughters – and, please God, Matt and his family too – she and James would find a balance.

He seemed to read her thoughts. 'You probably don't want to discuss it,' he began, 'but about last year. Can I just say, you were right and I was wrong? I shouldn't have pressured you like that, and I'm sorry. I promise it won't happen again.'

'I'll hold you to that,' she said, 'because it is important, James. And we should discuss what happened last year, because yet again we're facing huge changes. Changes that affect us both...'

An hour later, they were still talking things over, when Suzie's mobile interrupted with its jingling tune. There was no name and she didn't recognize the number, but with a leap of the heart, she knew. 'Hello?'

Hesitantly, a male voice, slightly husky, said that he was Matt. He'd received her message, and was very much looking forward to meeting her and James. Wanting to laugh and cry and shout for joy, Suzie stammered a reply.

Hearing him say, *I hope it can be soon*, she turned to James. 'Our son,' she whispered. 'When can we meet?'

Serious a moment ago, joy and amazement transformed him. 'Whenever it suits him...'

Once they'd both spoken to Matt – exchanges full of warmth and emotion – it was arranged for the following evening. They'd meet halfway, in Woodstock.

As she ended the call, Suzie hugged James and held him close. 'He sounds kind,' she said at last, drying her eyes. 'Oh, I do hope it goes well.'

'We'll get there,' James murmured, kissing her forehead, 'and I don't just mean to Woodstock.'

With a shaky little laugh, she nodded. 'We will,' she said, laying her finger across his lips, 'as long as you don't talk to me about marriage. Remember, James, I'm me, Suzie Wallis - unmarried mother of Matthew Dominic Armitage...'

Acknowledgements

As ever, my thanks go to members of the Blue Room Writers' Group, for keeping me writing, providing ideas, and asking the right questions: Jenni Jacombs, Tessa Warburg, Mike Hayward, Adrian and Evelyn Harris, Meraid Griffin, Deanna Dewey, Donna Mcghie, and the late, much missed, Mike Plumbley.

Revd Paul Roberts answered some important questions, and Fr Graham Whiting suggested books helpful to my research. Charyl Whiting read one of the early drafts, as did my dear friends, Françoise du Sorbier, Patricia Byrne and Maureen Morgan. I thank them all for their assistance and positive comments. My husband Peter deserves a special mention for his love and understanding, not simply in the last couple of years, but over a lifetime of being married to a writer.

Last but not least, I couldn't have written Suzie's story without contributions from friends who prefer to remain anonymous. My thanks to you all.

CPSIA information can be obtained
at www.ICGtesting.com
Printed in the USA
LVHW080517110620
657839LV00010B/639